PENGUIN CLASSICS

AROUND THE WORLD IN EIGHTY DAYS

JULES VERNE was born in 1828 in Nantes, then as now one of France's most important ports. He developed from childhood a romantic fascination for the sea and ships. After a childhood and adolescence spent in his home town, Verne moved to Paris in 1848, ostensibly to complete his studies and become a lawyer like his father, but his real ambition was to be a writer. With this aim he frequented the Parisian literary *salons* of the period. Verne's early works were written for the stage, but during the 1850s he also wrote short stories that were published in one of the most successful illustrated magazines of the time.

Verne's career as a novelist began in 1863, when the publisher Pierre-Jules Hetzel accepted for publication the manuscript of what was to become an instant popular success, *Five Weeks in a Balloon*. All Verne's best-known and most successful works were published under his contract with Hetzel, who gave them the collective title of 'Extraordinary Journeys into the Known and Unknown Worlds'. These works include *Journey to the Centre of the Earth* (1864), *Twenty Thousand Leagues under the Sea* (1869) and *Michael Strogoff* (1876), as well as *Around the World in Eighty Days* (1872). Several of Verne's novels were also successfully adapted for the stage, including again *Around the World in Eighty Days* (1874).

From 1869 until his death Verne lived in the town of Amiens in Picardy, where he became increasingly active in local politics and administration as a moderate Republican. After Hetzel's death in 1886 Verne continued to publish prolifically, working for Hetzel's son. Novels from this period include *The Carpathian Castle* (1892) and *Propeller Island* (1895). After Verne's death in 1905 his son Michel edited and published a number of posthumous works, though recent scholarship has re-established the original versions of these texts. Verne continues to be one of the most popular and frequently translated of nineteenth-century French writers.

MICHAEL GLENCROSS was born in South Wales and educated there and at Pembroke College, Oxford, where he read modern languages. He is the author of a book (*Reconstructing Camelot,*

1995) and various articles in academic journals on nineteenth-century French literature and culture. He now lives in France, where he works as a translator.

BRIAN ALDISS has been writing for half a century. He is best known for his science fiction novels and stories, but has also written several novels on contemporary subjects, poetry and non-fiction. Aldiss was born in Norfolk in 1925. He soldiered in the Far East, chiefly Burma, Sumatra and Hong Kong, during and after the Second World War. In 2000 he was made Grand Master of Science Fiction by the Science Fiction Writers of America and given an Honorary D.Litt. by the University of Reading. His history of science fiction, *Billion Year Spree* (1973), is generally considered to be the best and wittiest survey of the field.

JULES VERNE

Around the World
in Eighty Days

Translated with Notes by MICHAEL GLENCROSS,
with an Introduction by BRIAN ALDISS

PENGUIN BOOKS

PENGUIN BOOKS

Published by the Penguin Group
Penguin Books Ltd, 80 Strand, London WC2R ORL, England
Penguin Putnam Inc., 375 Hudson Street, New York, New York 10014, USA
Penguin Books Australia Ltd, 250 Camberwell Road, Camberwell, Victoria 3124, Australia
Penguin Books Canada Ltd, 10 Alcorn Avenue, Toronto, Ontario, Canada M4V 3B2
Penguin Books India (P) Ltd, 11, Community Centre, Panchsheel Park, New Delhi – 110 017, India
Penguin Books (NZ) Ltd, Cnr Rosedale and Airborne Roads, Albany, Auckland, New Zealand
Penguin Books (South Africa) (Pty) Ltd, 24 Sturdee Avenue, Rosebank 2196, South Africa

Penguin Books Ltd, Registered Offices: 80 Strand, London WC2R ORL, England

www.penguin.com

Le Tour du monde en quatre-vingts jours first published in book form in 1873
This translation first published 2004

2

Translation, Notes and Chronology copyright © Michael Glencross, 2004
Introduction copyright © Brian Aldiss, 2004
All rights reserved

The moral rights of the translator and the author of
the Introduction have been asserted

Set in 10.25/12.25 pt PostScript Adobe Sabon
Typeset by Rowland Phototypesetting Ltd, Bury St Edmunds, Suffolk
Printed in England by Clays Ltd, St Ives plc

Contents

Chronology

1828: Born on 8 February, first of five children, two boys and three girls. Father, Pierre Verne, followed family tradition of law. Mother, Sophie née Allotte de la Fuÿe, came from family of Nantes ship owners and merchants, of distant Scottish descent (Allott).

1829: Birth of brother, Paul, later to become naval officer, then stockbroker.

1833–46: Primary and secondary schooling in Nantes. Develops fascination for sea and ships. Falls in love with cousin Caroline Tronson. Obtains his *baccalauréat*. Begins law studies to please father.

1847: Goes to Paris to sit law exams. Engagement of cousin Caroline to another man.

1848: Settles in Paris. Continues to study law but main ambition to become writer. Introduced to literary salons by maternal uncle, relative of Chateaubriand. Friendship with the Dumases, father and son. Begins to write plays.

1849: Obtains law degree. Father allows him to stay on in Paris. Writes more plays.

1850: Publication and staging of one-act comedy *Les Pailles rompues* ('Broken Straws'). Beginning of friendship with musician Aristide Hignard, also from Nantes.

1851: Becomes secretary of *Théâtre-Lyrique*. Publishes in illustrated family magazine *Le Musée des Familles* first short stories, 'Les Premiers navires de la Marine mexicaine' ('A Drama in Mexico') and 'Un Voyage en ballon' ('Drama in the Air').

1852: Refuses to take over family law practice in succession to father.

1852–5: Publishes further short stories in *Le Musée des familles*, including 'Martin Paz', 'Maître Zacharius' ('Master Zacharius'), 'Un Hivernage dans les glaces' ('Winter in the Ice'). Also continues to write for theatre in collaboration with Hignard.

1857: Marries young widow from Amiens with two children, Honorine de Viane. Becomes stockbroker.

1859: Visits England and Scotland with Hignard.

1861: Birth of only child, Michel.

1862: Meets publisher Pierre-Jules Hetzel and offers him manuscript of *Voyage en l'air*. Hetzel suggests alterations but agrees publication under title of *Cinq semaines en ballon* (*Five Weeks in a Balloon*). Offers Verne first contract and takes him on as contributor to new children's magazine *Le Magasin d'éducation et de récréation*.

1863: Publishes *Cinq semaines en ballon*. Immediate commercial success. Writes *Paris au XXᵉ siècle* (*Paris in the Twentieth Century*). Novel rejected by Hetzel and not published in France until 1994.

1864: Launch of Hetzel's *Magasin d'éducation et de récréation*. First issue contains opening instalment of *Les Voyages et aventures du capitaine Hatteras* (*Adventures of Captain Hatteras*). Publication in book form of *Voyage au centre de la Terre* (*Journey to the Centre of the Earth*). Publishes in *Le Musée des Familles* essay on Edgar Allan Poe. Gives up working as stockbroker.

1865: Serial publication in Hetzel's magazine of *De la Terre à la Lune* (*From the Earth to the Moon*).

1866: Hetzel invents collective title for Verne's novels, *Voyages extraordinaires dans les pays connus et inconnus* (*Extraordinary Journeys into the Known and Unknown Worlds*).

1867: Visits America with brother Paul. Serial publication in *Magasin d'éducation et de récréation* of *Les Enfants du capitaine Grant* (*Captain Grant's Children*).

1868: Visits London.

1869: Rents house in Amiens. Serial publication in Hetzel's magazine of *Vingt mille lieues sous les mers* (*Twenty Thousand Leagues under the Sea*) and of *Autour de la Lune* (*Around the Moon*) in newspaper *Le Journal des débats*.

1871: Father dies.

1872: Settles in Amiens and becomes member of *Académie d'Amiens*. Serial publication in newspaper *Le Temps* of *Le Tour du monde en quatre-vingts jours* (*Around the World in Eighty Days*). Enormous success. Published in book form following year.

1874: Successfully adapts *Le Tour du monde en quatre-vingts jours* for stage with Adolphe d'Ennery. Serial publication in Hetzel's magazine of *L'Île mystérieuse* (*The Mysterious Island*) and in *Le Temps* of *Le Chancellor* (*The Chancellor*).

1876–7: *Michel Strogoff* (*Michael Strogoff, the Courier of the Czar*), *Hector Servadac* and *Les Indes noires* (*The Black Indies*).

1879: Serial publication in *Le Temps* of *Les Tribulations d'un Chinois en Chine* (*Tribulations of a Chinese Gentleman*), and in Hetzel's magazine of *Les Cinq cents millions de la Bégum* (*The Begum's Fortune*).

1881: *La Jangada* (*The Giant Raft*).

1882: Moves to a larger house in Amiens. Publication of *Le Rayon vert* (*The Green Ray*).

1883–4: *Kéraban-le-têtu* (*Keraban the Inflexible*).

1885: *Mathias Sandorf*.

1886: *Robur-le-conquérant* (*The Clipper of the Clouds*).

9 March: Shot and wounded in foot by nephew Gaston (eldest son of brother Paul) after refusing to give him money. Gaston interned in psychiatric hospital. Verne never fully recovers from injury.

17 March: Pierre-Jules Hetzel dies.

1887: Louis-Jules Hetzel takes over father's publishing business and continues collaboration with Verne.

15 February: mother dies.

1888: Elected local councillor in Amiens on moderate Republican platform. Plays active role in local politics and public administration over following years.

1892: *Le Château des Carpathes* (*The Carpathian Castle*). Pays debts of son Michel.

1895: *L'Île à hélice* (*Propeller Island*).

1896–7: *Face au drapeau* (*For the Flag*) and *Le Sphinx des* *glaces* (*The Sphinx of the Ice Fields*). Health deteriorates. Brother dies.

1900: Moves back to smaller house in Amiens where lived previously.

1905: 17 March: Falls seriously ill from diabetes.

24 March: Dies and is buried in Amiens.

Introduction

Around the World in Eighty Days comes to us in the twenty-first century from a time when machinery was bringing a great change – and great optimism – to the world. The story is a celebration not only of the energies of humankind but of machines. It is possibly for this reason that the hero, Phileas Fogg, is so machine-like. Even the chapter headings reflect the fact, as for instance that of chapter 14, 'In which Phileas Fogg travels the whole length of the wonderful valley of the Ganges without thinking it worth a look'. Fogg does not see the opposite of the *Umwelt* in which he lives: the small skinny men, burnt black by the sun, who labour by the mighty river, knowing no means of transport other than a water buffalo.

What a figure – what an embodiment – of the nineteenth century is Jules Verne! Born in 1828, he managed to outlive his century by five years. His amazing industry may be compared with that of Honoré de Balzac, with his *Comédie humaine*, and Émile Zola, with his Rougon-Macquart novels. But Verne's novels, those sixty-four *Voyages extraordinaires*, have never achieved the same critical acclaim as have those of Balzac or Zola. (Authorities disagree about their number. Professor I.F. Clarke, for example, speaks of forty-seven in his *Pattern of Expectation 1644–2001* (1979). Sixty-four is now the accepted number, including as it does posthumously published work.)

Verne was popular, and remains so, but his favourite stories, such as *Journey to the Centre of the Earth*, are relegated to children's bookshelves. He was at first a believer in the progress of humankind through science; his vision grows darker as a materialist technology takes hold and large-scale industry –

the production line – increases human wretchedness. His later novels become darker still in their vision, and problems of social organization intrude. This is true of *The Begum's Fortune*, published in 1879, with its chilly description of Stahlstadt, the steel city of the future, and with *Propeller Island* (1895), in which an island is eventually destroyed by greed and rivalry. Darkness gathers as the age of imperialism strengthens. The viability of human society is called into question. In the post-humously published *The Eternal Adam* (1910), men in the far future excavate the remains of our civilization. Survivors of volcanic eruptions have left a testimony: 'Our thinking life is gone . . . Food, food, that is our perpetual objective. We think about nothing else . . .' The vision is as gloomy as that of H.G. Wells in *The Time Machine*.

In 1872, however, Verne remained optimistic. *Around the World in Eighty Days* is a paean to the speeding up of the human world. Not only was it possible to circle the globe in eighty days; the journey could be done in seventy-nine! For the Suez Canal had been opened, and it had become possible to travel by railroad from one coast of North America to the other. The Franco-Prussian war, during which literary men such as Théophile Gautier, Hippolyte Taine and Edmond de Goncourt had confessed to eating half the animals in the zoo, was over. Paris was returning to normal, and to normal cuisine.

Publishing had come to a virtual standstill during the war. Now publishers were taking down their shutters again, among them Pierre-Jules Hetzel. Verne's relationship with Hetzel, his publisher, went deep; Hetzel was himself a writer (under the name Stahl) and gradually came to play the role of father to Verne, or at least of father-figure. That the father grows richer than the son remains the case still, in most publisher–author relationships. Hetzel was the publisher also of Balzac and George Sand, both of whom sought his advice and submitted to his corrections of their manuscripts. With peace, a natural sense that the world was opening to travel and exploration returned. The steamship and the railway were enlarging vistas. An article published in *Le Magasin pittoresque* suggested that a trip round the globe could now be made in only eighty days. Verne saw

that the International Date Line would alter the case; the traveller would take either seventy-nine or eighty-one days, depending
on whether he went from west to east or east to west. This
phenomenon has a crucial effect in his story. If the same kind of
tale were to be set today on the planet Mars, another difficulty
would arise; for the question remains, how and where does one
set a date line on a planet without an ocean stretching almost
from pole to pole?

Around the World in Eighty Days was published at a buoyant
time. It was serialized in *Le Temps*, which more than tripled its
circulation as a result. Everyone wished to read it; some placed
bets on whether Fogg would succeed or not. Steamship companies offered to pay for the use of one of their vessels to enable
Fogg to complete his journey across the Atlantic; Verne turned
down the offer: it would not be gentlemanly to accept. The story
was popular then and has remained so ever since. An unprecedentedly lavish play was made of it, which increased its popularity
further. An unprecedentedly lavish film was released in 1956, for
which the great showman, Mike Todd, persuaded forty-six stars
to appear in cameo roles. (David Niven at his most urbane
played Phileas Fogg, with the Mexican actor Cantinflas playing
his faithful servant Passepartout.) This is the novel which, more
than any other, made Verne's name known round the world.

That name still remains within the palisades of fame, despite
often irresponsible translations from the French and incursions
from Verne's worrisome son, Michel. Verne survives perhaps
because he has no marked style, no particular elegance of language, no great command of metaphor. His style is tough and
workmanlike, rather like his heroes. One who admired it was the
poet Guillaume Apollinaire, who exclaimed, perhaps imitating
Verne, 'Jules Verne! What a style! Nothing but nouns!' The
metaphysical artist Giorgio de Chirico saw rather more than
nouns, praising Verne for capturing the metaphysical element
of a city like London, with 'its houses, streets, clubs, squares and
open spaces; the ghostliness of a Sunday afternoon in London'.

Verne declared to Hetzel that he wished to be a stylist. It may
be that his choice of subject matter, and the hard facts with
which he preferred to deal, militated against elegance. His kind

of story demanded to be seen through plain glass, without frills, not stained glass. The type of story he practised was virtually an innovation, seeking as it did to marry literature with science.

Many fanciful portraits of the future had already appeared. For instance, Mary Shelley's 'The Last Man' was published in 1826. Richard Adam Locke produced a good hoax in the New York *Sun* in 1835, claiming that Sir William Herschel's telescope had disclosed humanlike citizens on the Moon. The hoax, which ran for several days, was so popular that the *Sun* set a record for the largest circulation of any daily newspaper anywhere. More to the point is Sebastien Mercier's *L'An deux mille quatre cent quarante* (The Year 2440), published in 1787 and translated in various European languages. As Prof Clarke says, 'By the 1830s the idea of the future had become a familiar element in contemporary thinking throughout the industrial nations.'

Let us take one of these hard facts which delight by their oddity, and which it pleased Verne to include in a story: the matter of instant ice. At the start of the Second World War, in the severe winter of 1939–40, the Soviet Union attacked Finland. To the north of Leningrad lies the shallow Lake Ladoga. A detachment of Russian cavalry decided to attack across the lake on to Finnish territory. It was a still winter's day. The temperature was four or five degrees below zero, but the water remained unfrozen. The cavalry began a charge. The waters of the lake, on being disturbed, immediately froze solid. Struggle as they might, both men and horses were held tight, locked in the ice. There they stayed, ghostly statuary, until spring. With the spring melt, the bodies sank into the lake, where they decomposed.

Anyone who has read Verne's *Hector Servadac* (Servadac being an anagram of 'cadavers'), published in 1877, will have recognized this phenomenon at once. The fact is that the temperature of an undisturbed body of water can sink to five degrees below freezing point and the water still remain liquid. Any sudden disruption, and it turns promptly to ice. In Verne's novel, part of the North African coast is carried away into space by a comet. Some of the Mediterranean Sea goes with it. A stone is hurled into the sea, which freezes instantly.

Hector Servadac is a poor and highly unlikely story. I read it in an abridged version, published by Ace Books in New York under the title *Off on a Comet*. (Perhaps it was abridged because of its anti-Semitism.) This is a good example of how many of Verne's novels have been chopped about and mistranslated; sometimes the 'scientific' passages have been removed for a juvenile audience. It is true to say that some at least of Verne's longevity as a writer is owed to mistreatment!

Verne's innovation, the introduction of scientific fact, has not been rewarded by loud applause from critics. Of the few books on my shelves dealing with French literature and the novel in France, none chooses to mention Verne, even in passing, while they cast a benevolent eye on Dumas *père*'s historical adventures. However, the critical situation is slowly improving. In 1990, two books on Verne appeared in England: William Butcher's *Verne's Journey to the Centre of the Self: Space and Time in the 'Voyages extraordinaires'* and Andrew Martin's *The Mask of the Prophet: The Extraordinary Fictions of Jules Verne*. There is also an interesting study of earlier vintage: Jean Chesneaux's *Une lecture politique de Jules Verne* (1971), which was translated and published in English in the following year as *The Political and Social Ideas of Jules Verne*.

Whatever the critical stance on Verne's work may be, there is little doubt that his success in introducing scientific fact has been rivalled only by the worldwide success of H. G. Wells. Understandably, neither Verne nor Wells enjoyed being compared with each other.

Wells said of Verne: 'His work dealt almost always with actual possibilities of invention and discovery, and he made some remarkable forecasts . . . But these stories of mine . . . do not pretend to deal with possible things, they are exercises of the imagination in a quite different field.' It is an interesting distinction he makes, even if not an entirely correct one. Verne responded somewhat grumpily, 'It occurs to me that [Wells's] stories do not repose on very scientific bases. No, there is no rapport between his work and mine. I make use of physics. He invents.'

Continuing in the same vein, he claimed that his visit to the Moon was based on physics, whereas Wells used cavourite. 'I

go to the Moon in a cannonball, discharged from a cannon.'
Whereas Wells goes to the Moon in a machine constructed of a
metal which does away with gravitation. 'Just show me this
metal,' said Verne. 'Let him produce it.' Which ignores the fact
that the acceleration of Verne's cannonball would have sufficed
to spread its passengers over the walls in a thin pink paste.
Whatever the truth in this disagreement, we do see in Wells the
more subtle mind, a mind moreover persuaded by the gloomier
facts of nineteenth-century science, in particular by Darwin's
theory of evolution, of which the religious-minded Verne takes
no cognizance.

Unlike the life of Balzac, which was marked by excess, Verne's
is respectable, *presque* bourgeois. He was born in 1828, the first
of five children, to a family of ship owners and merchants living
in the port of Nantes, on the mouth of the River Loire. There
he acquired a fascination for ships – among the masts of which
funnels were soon to appear. The great city of Nantes remains
proud of its famous son, and annually hosts a conference for his
less distinguished successors, the science fiction writers of today,
in the fine modern Cité des Congrès, close by the Loire. Visitors
to the city can visit the Jules Verne Museum, near the quayside.
  At the age of nineteen, Verne went to Paris to study law, as
his father wished him to do. There he gained a law degree.
Rather more importantly, he made friends with Dumas *père et
fils*, and began to write plays. Alexandre Dumas *père* produced
300 romances in a lifetime which somewhat resembled Balzac's,
in that it was choked with industry and debauchery. It was the
industry rather than the debauchery which proved the abiding
influence on Jules Verne. He stayed on in Paris, writing plays
and soon becoming secretary of the Théâtre-Lyrique. In 1851 –
the year of the Great Exhibition in Britain – he published his
first stories. Refusing to join his father's firm, he made a living
by writing not only stories but songs, theatrical sketches and
operettas, all fashionable Second Empire material. Writers generally read omnivorously; they are, in a sense, products of the
writers who have gone before them. Verne read Sir Walter Scott
and Fenimore Cooper; but an enduring influence was Edgar

Allan Poe. He read Poe in Baudelaire's translation. In 1864, Verne wrote a critique praising Poe's works. In particular, he was attracted by Poe's strange *Narrative of Arthur Gordon Pym of Nantucket*. In 1897, Verne endeavoured to continue Poe's story with *Le Sphinx des glaces* (*The Sphinx of the Ice Fields*), as if returning to a first love.

The raffish life ended and greater respectability set in in 1857, when Verne married Honorine de Viane, a young widow of twenty-six with two children. The wedding took place in Paris with a minimum of display, in January. The wedding breakfast was held in a second-rate restaurant. But Verne now had a wife to keep his nose to the grindstone. With the assistance of his father, he then became a stockbroker for a while. His one and only visit to Britain took place in this period. He admired the Scots (his own family had distant Scottish connections), but was always prejudiced against the English and their pursuit of profit, although he admired their energy, and possibly their empire-building. It cannot be said that Phileas Fogg is exactly a friendly portrait of an upper-crust Englishman.

Verne's meeting with Hetzel in 1862 changed his life. Hetzel put him on contract. Verne agreed to produce three volumes per year, which Hetzel would buy outright. It was in 1863 that *Five Weeks in a Balloon* appeared, to prove an immediate success. At that time, the problem of steering a balloon had yet to be solved. Verne's grandson, Jean Jules-Verne, says that, studying the question, Verne used the principle of a heated coil which would cause the hydrogen to expand inside a sealed envelope. By this means of control, the balloon could rise and descend to take advantage of the winds at different altitudes. Great publicity attended the *Victoria*, Verne's fictitious balloon. The facts in *Five Weeks in a Balloon* proved to be accurate. A new form of novel had been launched; from then on, Verne was always careful, even pedantic, with regard to the accuracy of his facts; not that this prevented him imagining a temperate climate at the centre of the Earth.

In the following year, 1864, *Journey to the Centre of the Earth* was published in book form. Like many other Verne novels, this was filmed, once in 1909 (the print is lost) and again in 1959, in a moderately dreadful version starring James Mason and the singing teenage star Pat Boone. *Journey to the Centre of the Earth* is one of Verne's most enduring stories. I have never forgotten my entranced reading of it while at school. Later, I flew over the extinct volcano Vatna Jokull, in Iceland, by the dead throat of which the intrepid explorers enter the strange intestines of our globe.

In 1866, Hetzel produced a running title for Verne's novels, *Voyages extraordinaires dans les pays connus et inconnus*. Among the *inconnus* was the Moon; *From the Earth to the Moon* had just been serialized in Hetzel's magazine, *Le Magasin d'éducation et de récréation*. The story ventures no landings on the Moon; some feel that here Verne missed a golden opportunity. By then he had given up his work as a stockbroker.

Now Verne's career as a writer was set fair. It was to continue until the early years of the twentieth century. Verne's father, Pierre, died in 1871. 'He was truly a saint,' wrote Verne to Hetzel. But saints are notoriously difficult to live with. When Jules Verne was eleven years old, he had run away from home and signed on as cabin boy on a three-master due to sail for the Indies. Pierre caught Jules and dragged him back home, where he may or may not have been thrashed and put on bread and water. The father remained a pious and orthodox Catholic until the end. When Verne and his wife Honorine settled in Amiens, he became a member of the Académie d'Amiens, and embarked on a life of deadening respectability. He was received by Pope Leo XIII, and we may assume he is the one and only person to be blessed by a pontiff for writing science fiction.

One of the difficulties afflicting Verne was that well-known scourge of the quiet life: relations. After refusing to give his nephew Gaston money, Verne was shot by him in the foot. The nephew was then shunted into a psychiatric hospital, but his uncle never entirely recovered from the wound. Then there was the son, Michel Verne, who became a turbulent teenager. It appears that much of his trouble stemmed from his father's aloof attitude towards him. To punish his unruly behaviour, Verne sent him to prison, and then – in a strange reversal of his own father's behaviour – to sea. Michel seems an attractive character. He voiced no objections to being jailed, as long as he could continue to receive his father's books as they were published. Later, after Jules Verne's death, Michel finished several of his father's unfinished manuscripts, and even produced his own Vernian sagas under his father's name, including possibly *The Barsac Mission*, first published in 1920, and *Paris au XXe siècle*. Verne himself had offered a version of the latter to Hetzel in 1863, at the beginning of his association with the publisher; Hetzel had turned it down, possibly on the grounds that it was too pessimistic. The book was eventually published in 1994 in Paris, and in 1996 in the USA, under the title *Paris in the Twentieth Century*.

Whatever happened, Verne went on writing. He ran a sumptuous yacht, to which he invited titled personages, he held grand fancy-dress balls, and was honoured by the Académie Française. He became a member of the right-wing anti-Dreyfus league, thus opposing Émile Zola, whose pamphlet, *J'accuse*, was instrumental in securing the release of the Jewish officer Alfred Dreyfus from imprisonment.*

Verne remained active in local affairs in Amiens for many years, dying from diabetes in March 1905. His grave in Amiens cemetery is suitably grandiose. It depicts, in solid stone, Verne rising naked from the earth, lifting his gravestone on his broad shoulders. His effigy is in a state of undress which would surely have embarrassed the living author, although fortunately only his torso is revealed. He raises an arm in greeting to the world with a gesture that suggests the word 'Hi!' Only the most stony-hearted Protestant could suppress their amusement, but I noted when I visited the cemetery that a fresh posy of forget-me-nots had been laid on the grave that morning.

The grand rollcall of Verne's titles embraces many parts of the world, often those places where a revolution is taking place. For instance, *Claudius Bombarnac* depicts a Muslim insurrection in

---

* Dreyfus was a French army officer accused of selling military secrets to Germany. He spent two years on Devil's Island until being exonerated, mainly through Zola's intervention. His retrial took place in 1899. But it was only in 1906 that Dreyfus was reinstated in his military rank.

Chinese Turkestan, *Family without a Name* the revolt of French Canadians against the British, *Tribulations of a Chinese Gentleman* the Taiping rebellion, and *Danube Pilot* the Bulgarian nationalist movement. Many novels are set in the more inhospitable parts of the globe, where men have to fight for survival. In this respect, *Around the World in Eighty Days* differs from most of Verne's novels. The hero, Phileas Fogg, an Englishman, forges no new pathways; he travels well-known routes, since his objective is to defeat not space but time. Of course, the path of travel never did run smooth, then or now, and many unforeseen obstacles confront Fogg, despite his statement that there is no such thing as the unexpected.

Fogg employs a servant, Passepartout, and it is Passepartout who suffers emotionally on the journey, while Fogg appears to be impregnable to misfortune. This relationship of master and man occurs fairly frequently in Verne's work; it was, or it had been, a commonplace of the time; one thinks of Mr Pickwick and Sam Weller. Passepartout's function is to get into various scrapes, while Fogg's function seems to be to pay his way out of trouble. Money is the lubrication of the plot.

Fogg departs precipitously, escorted by a somewhat dazed Passepartout, whereupon Verne builds up the case against Fogg's success. An article in the *Proceedings of the Royal Geographical Society* attempts to prove the madness of the undertaking. It emphasizes, in a somewhat nineteenth-century way, that in Europe trains may be expected to run to time; such would not be the case in India. (And indeed, we understand that even today certain timetables on Indian stations bear the legend: BELOW ARE THE TIMES BEFORE WHICH TRAINS WILL NOT LEAVE THE STATION.) During the seven days it took to cross the United States of America, the unexpected might be met with – breakdowns, derailings, herds of bison . . . Steamers were at the mercy of wind and tide. It required only a single hold-up for Fogg's entire plan to be disrupted.

The public is greatly excited by the bet and this article in the *Proceedings* is represented as influential. Fogg is thus rebelling against the common instinct, and in a sense against civilization, as represented by the members of the Reform Club, much as does the individualist Captain Nemo in his submarine, in *Twenty Thousand Leagues under the Sea*. (Another great Vernian success: the first movie version was made in 1916; many of us remember the brilliant Disney film of 1954, where James Mason is splendidly cast as Nemo.)

The present novel celebrates various improvements in travel arrangements, on Indian railways as well as on Lesseps's Suez Canal and the Union Pacific Railroad. (Ferdinand de Lesseps was a friend of Verne's.) The journey, travelled in an easterly direction, can be divided into eight parts: from London to Suez; from Suez to Bombay; from Bombay to Calcutta; from Calcutta to Hong Kong; from Hong Kong to Yokohama; from Yokohama to San Francisco; from San Francisco to New York; and from New York to London. And this journey can be accomplished in eighty days, ten times faster than could be done a hundred years earlier.

My helpful local travel agents, Oxonian Travel Services, worked out how long the circumnavigation would take in the present day, travelling by regular airlines on regular routes and current timetables.

London Heathrow–Sydney, Australia	21.10 hours
On the ground	4.10
Sydney, Australia–Los Angeles	13.30
On the ground	6.25
Los Angeles–London Heathrow	10.25

So today the journey would take 55 hours. If one flew early on Monday (there is a British Airways flight leaving at 07.50 hours), one would return early on Tuesday afternoon, bearing in mind the International Date Line. Of course, this is a much faster time (thirty-five times faster) than in Verne's day, but it would make a less interesting film. Hijacking and terrorism, those modern energizers, would need to be added.

In order to ginger up the plot a little, Verne introduces an Inspector Fix, who plans to arrest Fogg as soon as he receives a warrant, on the mistaken grounds that Fogg has robbed the Bank of England. (The money question is always before us.)

The whist-playing Phileas Fogg, 'one of the oddest and most striking members of the Reform Club', has bet his acquaintances – for he claims to have no friends – at the Club £20,000 that he can complete the journey in the time stated. When he is told that to achieve this end he must change with mathematical precision from railway to steamship and from steamship to railway, he replies that he will do it with mathematical precision.

Fogg achieves his aim by using all possible means of transport: not only trains and steamships, but carriages, a yacht, a tramp steamer, an Indian *ghari*, a sledge and an elephant. On the way, he spends a small fortune but gains the hand of the Indian widow of a rajah, a lady referred to throughout as Mrs Aouda. Fogg rescues her from suttee, her dead husband's funeral pyre. From then on, Mrs Aouda accompanies Fogg wherever he goes – and is forever admired by Passepartout.

The journey permits Verne to drop a number of geographical and cultural facts into his narrative. 'Allahabad is the city of God, one of the holiest cities in India, because it is built where two sacred rivers meet, the Ganges and the Jumna, whose waters attract pilgrims from the whole subcontinent. In addition, it is well known that, according to the legends of the *Ramayana*, the Ganges has its source in the heavens from where, thanks to Brahma, it comes down to this earth.' Only a few paragraphs later, Fogg is arrested in Calcutta and sentenced to eight days in prison – a sentence that would completely wreck his travel plans. He pays £2,000 bail and then departs. By this time he has used up more than £5,000. This is another way in which the clock ticks against him.

Passepartout (this 'dear fellow', as Verne rather irritatingly calls him) is often the most interesting actor in the story. During a break in Singapore, before the steamship *Rangoon*, having coaled up, continues the journey to Hong Kong, Fogg has a stroll with Mrs Aouda. He takes, we are told, 'little notice of what he saw'. It is Passepartout who buys a few dozen mangosteens, and he who presents them to Mrs Aouda. Then, on the China Seas, the *Rangoon* runs into heavy weather. We are told that the ships of the P&O line have a serious defect. 'The ratio between their draught when laden and their depth has been wrongly calculated.' The French mail ships are far superior. The *Rangoon* is forced to heave to for half a day. It arrives in Hong Kong harbour twenty-four hours late: which means that they will miss the ship departing from Yokohama. Passepartout is upset. Fogg is calm as always. Fortune is on his side. For the *Carnatic*, which should have left for Yokohama, has had its departure delayed while a boiler is repaired. It is announced that it will sail on the morrow. Thus Verne teases his readers.

When Passepartout goes to book cabins on the ship, he encounters Inspector Fix, to learn that the time of sailing has been changed: the *Carnatic* will depart that very evening at eight o'clock. Pursuing his own purposes, Fix takes Passepartout to an opium den. Opium smoking is 'one of the most deadly of human vices'. Assisted by brandy, Fix drugs Fogg's faithful servant, who passes out. Fogg and Mrs Aouda, thus not informed of the altered sailing time, miss the boat. So the clock-work of the story unwinds. Every setback has to be overcome, as Fogg progresses with machine-like purpose.

When crossing North America by train, our travellers encoun-ter two novel impediments. First comes a great herd of bison ('which the Americans wrongly call buffalos'). The passing of the herd stops the train. Passepartout is furious, Fogg is calm. The herd takes three hours to cross the line. The passengers have to endure a lecture on Mormonism, and so do we. More exciting is the attack on the train by a band of Sioux warriors. Some of them get aboard the train and attack the passengers. This is a chance for Mrs Aouda to behave with great courage, but it is Passepartout who is the hero of the encounter. As a result of the attack, Fogg falls twenty hours behind schedule. Employing a variety of diversions, Verne maintains the pressure on Fogg, who is continually falling behind time or gaining a few hours. Does he manage to return to the Reform Club within his eighty days? Does he manage to win his bet? What does the hazardous journey bring him? Nothing, except for a charming wife . . .

We seem to find in Verne none of that madness in creation which assailed and propelled Balzac and Zola. Zola, when he was writing, passed into a different state of being, where private terrors, clogged memories, dreams of sensual delight and abominable visions took possession of him. Many lesser writers have confessed to similar 'different states of being', when their fictitious characters, mere curlicues on the computer, seem to speak in their own voices – often saying what the writer in less inflated moments may reject.

It is hard to think of Verne in such fevers of possession; nevertheless, it does appear that he was haunted by the Other Self, to which writers will sometimes confess, a self which speaks up for something buried. Life in Amiens, which was to conclude with that naked torso under that stone slab, was respectable, conformist. Life in the books was different: there were no churches, scant mentions of God, except as an epithet, terrifying conditions of life, mutinies, shipwrecks, rebellions, defiances of tyranny and climate, murder, heroism abounding, and that passion for geography, peeled back like the skin of a ripe orange to reveal itself.

We can only speculate about the effect on the eleven-year-old Verne's psyche of his father dragging him off that ship due to sail for the Indies. But it appears not improbable that this episode was what prompted his fertile mind to dreaming. And that he provided ballast for his dreams with scientific accuracy, while simultaneously lightening them with speculation based on technological prospects. When all is said, Verne's is a romance with geography as much as with science, as *Around the World in Eighty Days* amply demonstrates.

Brian Aldiss

Suggestions for Further Reading

Apart from *Around the World in Eighty Days*, Verne's most popular works remain *Journey to the Centre of the Earth* (1864) and *Twenty Thousand Leagues under the Sea* (1869). However, Verne was one of the most prolific authors of the period and the series of novels to which his publisher Hetzel gave the collective title *Voyages extraordinaires dans les pays connus et inconnus* (*Extraordinary Journeys into the Known and Unknown Worlds*) contains many other interesting works. Another typical novel combining travel and adventure is *Michael Strogoff, a Courier of the Czar* (1876). More unusual but also of interest are *The Begum's Fortune* (1879), the story of a foiled attempt at world domination and a parable – not to say parody – of Franco-German relations, and *The Carpathian Castle* (1892), a Gothic tale with a scientific twist. A considerable number of works by Verne were published posthumously after significant revision by his son Michel, but modern scholarship has increasingly made available (mainly in French) the original versions of these works, often with new titles. Among books by Verne that have only become available relatively recently in English are *Backwards to Britain* (1992), based on his visit to England and Scotland in 1859, and *Paris in the Twentieth Century* (1996), a work rejected by Hetzel because he felt its view of modern industrial society was too critical and negative.

Modern academic studies of Verne have sought to raise his status as a literary figure and to rescue him from his reputation as primarily a writer for children and the (grand)father of science fiction. The two best examples of such scholarship in English are William Butcher's *Verne's Journey to the Centre of the Self*:

Space and Time in the 'Voyages extraordinaires' (Basingstoke: Macmillan, 1990) and Andrew Martin's brilliant and controversial study *The Mask of the Prophet: The Extraordinary Fictions of Jules Verne* (Oxford: Clarendon Press, 1990). For a recent biography of Verne see Herbert. R. Lottman's *Jules Verne: An Exploratory Biography* (New York: St Martin's Press, 1996).

There is an excellent website devoted to Jules Verne, devised by Zvi Har'El. It contains much useful information as well as links to sites of related interest: http://www.jv.gilead.org.il

Note on the Translation

This translation is based on the French text of *Le Tour du monde en quatre-vingts jours* edited by Simone Vierne (Paris: Flammarion, 1978). The translation aims to give a modern, idiomatic rendering of the original. More than most fictional texts of the period but like the majority of Verne's writings, this novel makes frequent reference to the literary, scientific and material culture of the nineteenth century and to real-life events. Occasionally these references have been explained in the translation itself; otherwise they are glossed in the notes. Place-names have, where appropriate, been anglicized and modernized, with the exception of 'Bombay', which has been retained instead of the new official form of 'Mumbai'.

I

*In which Phileas Fogg and Passepartout agree their
relationship, that of master and servant*

In the year 1872, the house at number 7 Savile Row,[1] Burlington
Gardens – the house in which Sheridan[2] died in 1814 – was lived
in by Phileas Fogg, Esq., one of the oddest and most striking
members of the Reform Club,[3] even though he seemed determined to avoid doing anything that might draw attention to
himself.

And so one of the nation's most brilliant parliamentary
speakers had been replaced by the enigmatic figure of Phileas
Fogg, about whom nothing was known except that he was the
most courteous of men and one of the most handsome gentlemen
in English high society.

People compared him to Byron – because of his good looks,
certainly not because of a limp – but a Byron with a moustache
and whiskers, an impassive-looking Byron, who could have
lived for a thousand years without showing the signs of age.

Though he was undoubtedly English, Phileas Fogg was not
necessarily a Londoner. He had never been seen at the Stock
Exchange or the Bank of England, or in any of the financial
institutions of the City. No dock or basin in London had ever
handled a ship whose owner was called Phileas Fogg. The gentleman in question did not figure on any list of board of directors.
His name had never echoed through an Inn of Court,[4] either the
Temple, Lincoln's Inn or Gray's Inn. He had never pleaded in
the Court of Chancery, nor on the Queen's Bench, nor in the
Court of Exchequer, nor in the Ecclesiastical Court.[5] He was
neither a factory owner, nor a businessman, nor a merchant,
nor a landowner. He was not a member of the Royal Institution,
nor of the London Institution, nor of the Artisan Club, nor of

the Russell Institution, nor of the Literary Society of the West of England, nor of the Law Society, nor of the Combined Society for the Arts and Sciences, which enjoys the direct patronage of her Gracious Majesty. He belonged to none of those numerous societies that proliferate in the English capital, from the Harmonic Society down to the Entomological Society,[6] whose main purpose is the destruction of harmful insects.

Phileas Fogg was a member of the Reform Club, and that was it.

Anyone who may be surprised that a gentleman so shrouded in mystery should belong to this honourable association should realize that he had been admitted on the recommendation of Messrs Baring Brothers,[7] with whom he had an account. His financial standing was such that his cheques went through immediately and his current account was always in credit.

Was Phileas Fogg a wealthy man? There could be no doubt about that. But even the best-informed people were unable to say where his wealth came from, and Mr Fogg was the last person they would have dared to ask directly. In any case, he was careful about money without being mean, since whenever a noble, useful or generous cause was short of funds, he made up the amount required without making a fuss, without even giving his name.

In a word, he was the most uncommunicative of gentlemen. He talked as little as possible and this silence served only to increase his aura of mystery. Though he lived his life quite openly, he carried out his activities with such mathematical precision that it fuelled other people's imagination.

Was he well travelled? Quite probably, since he had a better knowledge than anyone else of world geography. There wasn't a single out-of-the way place that he didn't seem to know in detail. Sometimes, by a brief but precise intervention, he corrected idle club speculation about travellers who had disappeared or got lost. He offered the most likely explanation of what had happened to them, and his words often seemed to be inspired by a second sight, since they were always borne out by events. Here was someone who must have travelled a lot – in his head, at any rate.

What was beyond doubt, however, was that Phileas Fogg had not been outside London for many years. Those who had the privilege of knowing him better than most could confirm that the only sightings of him were as he walked each day from his house straight to his club. His only pastimes were reading the newspapers and playing whist. He often won when he played this silent game that was so well suited to his temperament, but his winnings never went into his own pocket. They made up instead a large part of what he gave to charity. It should also be noted that it was obvious that Mr Fogg played for enjoyment and not to win. The game of whist was for him a combat, a struggle against difficulty, but a struggle that did not require him to go anywhere or travel around or tire himself out, and all that suited his temperament.

As far as was known, Phileas Fogg didn't have a wife or children – something that can happen to the most respectable of people – but he had no relatives or friends either, which is less common. Phileas Fogg lived alone in his house in Savile Row, and never let in visitors. The inside of his house was never mentioned. A single manservant was enough for his needs. He took lunch and dinner at the club like clockwork, always in the same dining-room and at the same table. He never entertained his fellow members at table, never invited guests, and went back home only to sleep, at exactly midnight, without ever making use of one of the comfortable bedrooms that the Reform Club makes available to its members. Out of every twenty-four hours he spent ten in his home, either sleeping or getting himself ready. When he went for a walk, it was always at a carefully measured pace and in the club's entrance hall, with its inlaid wooden floor, or in the round gallery, above which rose a blue stained-glass dome supported by twenty Ionian columns in red porphyry. When he had lunch or dinner, it was the club's kitchens, larder and pantry, its fish store and dairy, that supplied his table from their delicious reserves. It was the club's servants, solemn-looking figures dressed in black uniforms and wearing soft-soled shoes, who served the meal in special china and on the finest table linen. It was the club's cut glass, made to a one-off design, that held his sherry, his port or his claret served with cinnamon and herbs. It was also the club's ice, brought at great expense from the lakes of North America, that kept his drinks chilled to just the right temperature.

If this is what it means to be an eccentric, then it must be admitted that eccentricity has something to be said for it!

The house in Savile Row, without being luxurious, could be considered extremely comfortable. In any case, because the habits of its occupant never varied, serving him was a simple matter. However, Phileas Fogg required his only servant to be extremely punctual and reliable. On that particular day, 2 October, Phileas Fogg had dismissed James Forster, as the fellow had committed the crime of bringing him his water for shaving at a temperature of eighty-four degrees Fahrenheit, instead of eighty-six, and he was waiting for his replacement, who was due to arrive between eleven o'clock and half past eleven.

Phileas Fogg, firmly ensconced in his armchair, with his feet close together like those of a soldier on parade, with his hands on his knees, his back straight and his head raised, was watching the hands of the clock move forward. It was a complicated piece of machinery that showed the hour, the minute, the day, the month and the year. On the stroke of half past eleven Mr Fogg was due, according to his daily routine, to leave the house and go to the Reform Club.

Just at that moment there was a knock on the door of the small drawing-room in which Phileas Fogg was sitting. James Forster, the manservant who had just been dismissed, appeared.

'The new servant,' he said.

A man aged about thirty presented himself and bowed.

'You are French and your name is John?' Phileas Fogg asked him.

'Jean, if you please, sir,' replied the new arrival. 'Jean Passepartout, a nickname that has stuck and that I earned by my natural ability to get myself out of tricky situations. I consider myself to be a decent fellow, sir, but, to be quite honest with you, I've had several different jobs. I was a travelling singer, a horse-rider in a circus, a trapeze artist and a tightrope walker. Then I became a gymnastics instructor in order to put my talents to more practical use, and most recently I was a fireman in Paris. I've even been on the scene of some famous fires in my time. But five years ago I left France and, since then, because I wanted to live with a family, I've been a manservant in England. However, when I found myself without a position and when I learnt that Mr Phileas Fogg was the most precise and most stay-at-home person in the United Kingdom, I came to sir's house in the hope of being able to lead a quiet life and put behind me everything associated with Passepartout, even the name.'

'Passepartout suits me,' replied the gentleman. 'You have been recommended to me. I have good reports of you. Do you know my terms?'

'Yes, sir.'

'Good. What time do you make it?'

'Eleven twenty-two,' replied Passepartout, as he took out from the depths of his waistcoat pocket an enormous silver watch.

'Your watch is slow,' said Mr Fogg.

'Forgive me, sir, but that is impossible.'

'Your watch is four minutes slow. It's not important. All that matters is to note the difference in time. So from this moment onwards, eleven twenty-nine[8] on the morning of 2 October 1872, you are working for me.'

With that, Phileas Fogg got to his feet, took his hat in his left hand, put it on his head with the precision of clockwork and disappeared without saying another word.

Passepartout heard the front door close a first time: it was his master going out. Then it closed a second time: it was his predecessor, James Forster, leaving in turn.

Passepartout was now alone in the house in Savile Row.

2

*Where Passepartout is convinced that he has at long
last found his ideal*

'In all honesty,' Passepartout said to himself, somewhat be-
mused to begin with, 'I've encountered wax figures in Madame
Tussaud's with more life about them than my new master!'

During the brief opportunity he had just had of seeing Phileas
Fogg, Passepartout had quickly but carefully observed his future
master. He was a man of perhaps forty, with fine and noble
features, tall of stature if slightly portly, with fair hair and
whiskers, a smooth forehead with no sign of wrinkles around
the temples, a complexion that was pale rather than full of
colour and magnificent teeth. He seemed the very embodiment
of what the physiognomists[1] call 'stillness in the midst of agita-
tion', a quality common to all those who prefer action to words.
Calm, phlegmatic, with clear eyes and a firm gaze, he was
the perfect example of the cool-headed Englishman, a type
commonly encountered in England and one that the paintings
of Angelica Kauffmann[2] have captured perfectly in rather a
formal pose. As he went about his daily business, the gentleman
gave the impression of something perfectly calibrated and finely
balanced, like a chronometer made by a master craftsman.
Phileas Fogg was indeed the paragon of precision, as could be
seen from the expressiveness of his feet and hands since in
human beings as well as in animals the limbs are themselves a
means of expressing feelings.

Phileas Fogg was a person of mathematical preciseness, someone who was never rushed but always ready, always economical
in his movements. He never took an unnecessary stride and
always chose the shortest route. He never allowed himself to be
distracted. He was careful never to make a superfluous gesture.

He had never been known to be upset or disturbed. He was the least hurried person in the world, but he always arrived on time. However, it is easy to understand why he lived alone and without any social relationships: he knew that everyday life involved social contact and because such contact took up time he chose to live without it.

As for Jean, who was known as Passepartout, he was a Parisian through and through. During the five years he had spent in England working as a manservant in London, he had looked in vain for a master who he could devote himself to.

Passepartout was not one of those cheeky or scheming servants who strut about, trying to be clever and cocky. On the contrary he was a good chap with a friendly face and prominent lips that were made for eating, drinking and kissing. He was a kind and helpful soul, with just the type of roundish head that you'd like to see on a friend's shoulders. He had blue eyes, a bright complexion, a plump face and puffy cheeks, a broad chest, a thick waist, powerful muscles and an immense strength, further developed by plenty of exercise during his youth. His brown hair was rather unruly. If the sculptors of antiquity knew eighteen different ways of arranging Minerva's tresses,[3] Passepartout knew only one way of doing his hair: dragging a comb through it three times.

Whether someone of his extrovert nature would get on with a person like Phileas Fogg was too early to say. Would Passepartout be the sort of servant, precise as clockwork, that his master needed? Only time would tell. After having had an adventurous youth, as has been seen, all he wanted was a quiet life. Having heard people sing the praises of the methodical nature[4] of the English and the proverbial coldness of their gentlemen, he had come to England in search of fortune. But so far luck had not been on his side. He had not been able to settle down anywhere. He had worked in ten different households. In every one the people had been temperamental or unpredictable, eager to seek out adventure or explore other countries, something that no longer suited Passepartout. His most recent master, the young Lord Longsferry, a Member of Parliament, regularly needed to be helped back home by policemen after his late nights out on the town. Since what Passepartout wanted most was a master he could look up to, he ventured some polite observations, but they were not appreciated and so he left. He discovered in the meanwhile that Phileas Fogg, Esq., was looking for a servant. He made some enquiries about this gentleman. Someone whose daily life was so well ordered, someone who never spent the night away from home and didn't travel or even go away for a day, was bound to suit him. He went along to his house and was taken on in the circumstances already outlined.

And so, as half past eleven struck, Passepartout found himself alone in the house in Savile Row. He immediately began to look around. He inspected it from top to bottom. The house was clean and tidy, austere and puritanical, and well planned for servants. He liked it. For him it was like being inside the shell of a snail, but a snail that had gas lighting and heating! Coal gas supplied, in fact, all that was needed for heating and lighting. Passepartout had no difficulty in finding the second-floor bedroom that was to be his. It pleased him. Electric bells and speaking tubes made it possible to communicate with the suites of rooms on the ground and first floors. On the mantelpiece an electric clock matched the clock in Phileas Fogg's bedroom, and both instruments showed exactly the same time, down to the last second.

'This really suits me down to the ground,' Passepartout said to himself.

He also noticed in the bedroom a piece of paper above the clock. It set out the daily routine for domestic service. It contained – from eight o'clock in the morning, the set time when Phileas Fogg got up, until half past eleven, the time when he left for lunch in the Reform club – all the details of domestic service: tea and toast at eight twenty-three, water for shaving at nine thirty-seven, doing the master's hair at twenty to ten, etc. Then from half past eleven in the morning until midnight – the time when this methodically minded gentleman went to bed – everything was written down, planned out and taken care of. Passepartout was overjoyed to contemplate this timetable and to commit every detail to memory.

As for the gentleman's wardrobe, it was very extensive and

carefully thought out. Each pair of trousers, each jacket or waistcoat, carried a roll number that was also recorded in a logbook, showing the date when the items of clothing, according to the time of year, were to be worn in rotation. The same system applied to the shoes.

In a word, this house in Savile Row – which must have been a monument to disorder in the time of the famous but dissolute Sheridan – was comfortably furnished, a sure sign of considerable wealth. Mr Fogg didn't have a library or books. They were unnecessary since the Reform Club gave him access to two libraries, one for literature and the other for law and politics. In the bedroom there was a medium-sized safe, built to withstand both fire and theft. There were no firearms in the house, no hunting guns or weapons of war. Everything indicated peaceful pursuits.

After examining the residence in detail, Passepartout rubbed his hands in glee. His broad face was beaming and he repeated joyfully, 'This suits me down to the ground. It's just what I wanted. Mr Fogg and I will get on famously. A home-loving and well-ordered man. Someone who functions like clockwork. Well, I'm not sorry in the least to be working for someone who functions like clockwork!'

3

*In which Phileas Fogg becomes involved in a
conversation that could prove costly to him*

Phileas Fogg had left his home in Savile Row at half past eleven
and, after putting his right foot in front of his left foot 575 times
and his left foot in front of his right foot 576 times, he reached
the Reform Club, a huge building in Pall Mall that had cost no
less than £120,000 to construct.

Phileas Fogg went immediately to the dining-room, with its
nine windows opening on to an attractive garden with trees that
had already turned an autumn brown. There he sat down at his
usual table where his place was already set. His lunch consisted
of a starter, followed by poached fish served with a first-rate
Reading sauce,[1] a blood-red steak accompanied by mushroom
ketchup,[2] a rhubarb and gooseberry pie and a slice of Cheshire
cheese, all of which was washed down by several cups of tea, an
excellent variety that had been specially picked for the pantry
of the Reform Club.

At forty-seven minutes past midday, the gentleman got up
and walked over to the main drawing-room, a magnificent place
decorated with richly framed paintings. There a servant handed
him an uncut copy of *The Times*, which Phileas Fogg proceeded
to carefully unfold with a skilfulness that demonstrated a considerable familiarity with this delicate operation. Phileas Fogg
continued reading this newspaper until three forty-five, following it with the *Standard*, which took him up to dinner. This
meal followed the same pattern as lunch, except for the addition
of 'Royal British sauce'.

At twenty to six the gentleman appeared again in the main
drawing-room and engrossed himself in the *Morning Chronicle*.

Half an hour later, various members of the Reform Club came

in and went up to the fireplace, where a blazing coal fire was burning. They were Mr Phileas Fogg's usual partners, fanatical whist players like him: the engineer Andrew Stuart, the bankers John Sullivan and Samuel Fallentin, the brewer Thomas Flanagan and Gauthier Ralph, one of the directors of the Bank of England – all wealthy and distinguished figures, even for a club whose members included the leading lights in industry and banking.

'So Ralph,' inquired Thomas Flanagan, 'what's the latest on this business of the robbery?'

'Well,' replied Andrew Stuart, 'the Bank isn't going to get its money back.'

'On the contrary,' said Gauthier Ralph, 'I hope that we will be able to get our hands on the criminal. Police detectives, the best in the business, have been sent to America and Europe, to all the main ports of entry and exit, and it will be extremely difficult for this person to escape them.'

'So you have the description of the thief, do you?' asked Andrew Stuart.

'In the first place he's not a thief,' Gauthier Ralph replied in all seriousness.

'What, you don't call someone who's got away with £55,000 in banknotes a thief?'

'No,' replied Gauthier Ralph.

'So he's a businessman, is he?' said John Sullivan.

'The *Morning Chronicle* tells us that he's a gentleman.'

The person who gave this reply was none other than Phileas Fogg, whose head emerged at that point from behind the pile of paper surrounding him. At the same time Phileas Fogg greeted his colleagues, who greeted him in turn.

The incident under discussion, which was a subject of heated debate in the various British newspapers, had occurred three days earlier, on 29 September. A wad of banknotes, amounting to the enormous sum of £55,000, had been taken from the desk of the principal cashier of the Bank of England.

To anyone who expressed surprise that such a theft could have taken place so easily, the deputy governor Gauthier Ralph merely replied that at that moment the cashier was busy recording a taking of three shillings and sixpence and that he couldn't keep an eye on everything.

But it should be pointed out here – and this makes what happened somewhat easier to explain – that this admirable institution called the Bank of England seems to be extremely concerned for the dignity of the public. There are no guards, no former soldiers and no grilles. Gold, silver and banknotes are on open display at the mercy, so to speak, of all-comers. It would be unthinkable to question the honesty of any member of the public. One of the keenest observers of English society even recounts the following anecdote: one day when he happened to be in one of the rooms in the Bank, he was eager to have a close-up view of a gold ingot, weighing between seven and eight pounds, which was lying on the cashier's desk for all to see. He picked up the ingot, examined it, handed it to the person next to him, who in turn passed it on, the result being that the gold bar went down to the end of a dark corridor only to come back to its original place half an hour later, without the cashier even looking up.

But on 29 September things didn't quite turn out the same way. The wad of banknotes did not come back, and when the magnificent clock above the cash desk struck five o'clock, closing time, all the Bank of England could do was to register in its accounts a loss of £55,000.

Once the theft had been duly reported, police detectives, the pick of the profession, were dispatched to the main ports, Liverpool, Glasgow, Le Havre, Suez, Brindisi and New York, with the promise of a reward of £2,000 plus five per cent of the amount recovered if they were successful. While waiting for the results of the investigation that had got under way immediately, the inspectors were given the task of keeping a careful eye on all passengers entering or leaving these ports.

As it happened, just as the *Morning Chronicle* claimed, there was reason to believe that the person responsible for the theft was not a member of the criminal fraternity. During that day of 29 September, a well-dressed, well-mannered and distinguished-looking gentleman had been noticed pacing around in the cash room, the scene of the crime. The investigation had made it possible to put together quite an accurate description of the gentleman and it had then been sent immediately to every detective in the United Kingdom and on the continent. Some wise souls – and Gauthier Ralph was one of them – therefore felt justified in thinking that the thief would not get away.

As can well be imagined, this incident was on everyone's lips in London and the whole country. It was the subject of heated debate, with differing opinions on the chances of success for the Metropolitan Police. It should come as no surprise, then, to hear the members of the Reform Club discussing the same issue, especially as one of the Bank's deputy governors was among their number.

The highly respected Gauthier Ralph had no intention of doubting the success of the police investigation, since he considered that the reward on offer should act as a considerable incentive to the energy and competence of the police. But his colleague Andrew Stuart was far from being so confident. And so the discussion continued between these gentlemen as they sat at the whist table, Stuart partnering Flanagan and Fallentin partnering Phileas Fogg. During the game the players didn't speak, but between the rubbers the conversation resumed, more lively than before.

'I maintain,' said Andrew Stuart, 'that the thief is likely to get away with it, since he's bound to be a smart individual.'

'Come off it,' replied Ralph. 'There isn't a single country where he can hide.'

'What are you talking about?'

'Where do you expect him to go?'

'I've no idea,' replied Andrew Stuart, 'but after all, the world's a big place.'

'That used to be true,' said Phileas Fogg quietly. Then he added, 'It's your turn to cut, sir,' showing the cards to Thomas Flanagan.

The discussion was broken off during the rubber. But soon Andrew Stuart brought the subject up again:

'What do you mean "used to be true"? Has the earth got smaller, by any chance?'

'Certainly,' replied Gauthier Ralph. 'I agree with Mr Fogg. The earth has got smaller because you can now travel around it ten times as quickly as a hundred years ago. And, in relation to this particular case, that's what will speed up the police inquiries.'

'And that's what will make it easier for the thief to escape as well!'

'Your turn to play, Mr Stuart,' said Phileas Fogg.

But the sceptical Stuart was not convinced, and when the game was over he added, 'I must admit, Ralph, that you've got a funny way of saying that the world has become smaller! Just because you can now go around the world in three months –'

'In a mere eighty days,' said Phileas Fogg.

'Quite right, dear sirs,' added John Sullivan, 'eighty days since the opening of the section between Rothal and Allahabad on the Indian Peninsular Railway. This is how the *Morning Chronicle* worked it out:

From London to Suez via the Mont Cenis tunnel[3] and Brindisi, by railway and steamship	7 days
From Suez to Bombay, by steamship	13 days
From Bombay to Calcutta, by railway	3 days
From Calcutta to Hong Kong, by steamship	13 days
From Hong Kong to Yokohama (Japan), by steamship	6 days
From Yokohama to San Francisco, by steamship	22 days
From San Francisco to New York, by railroad[4]	7 days
From New York to London, by steamship and railway	9 days
Total	80 days'

'Yes, eighty days,' exclaimed Andrew Stuart, accidentally trumping a winning card, 'but that doesn't take account of bad weather, adverse winds, shipwrecks, derailments, etc.'

'It does include them,' replied Phileas Fogg while continuing to play because by now the whist was taking second place to the discussion.

'Even if the natives of India or North America take up the rails?' exclaimed Andrew Stuart. 'Even if they stop the trains, ransack the wagons and scalp the travellers?'

'Including all that,' replied Phileas Fogg, laying out his hand and adding, 'Two winning trumps.'

Andrew Stuart, whose turn it was to deal, picked up the cards and said, 'In theory you are right, Mr Fogg, but in practice . . .'

'In practice too, Mr Stuart.'

'I'd like to see you prove it.'

'That depends only on you. Let's do it together.'

'Heaven forbid,' exclaimed Stuart, 'but I'm quite prepared to bet £4,000 that such a journey undertaken in these circumstances is impossible.'

'Quite possible, on the contrary,' replied Mr Fogg.

'Well, try it, then.'

'To go around the world in eighty days?'

'Yes.'

'I'm quite prepared to.'

'When?'

'Straightaway.'

'This is madness,' exclaimed Andrew Stuart, who was beginning to get annoyed at his partner's persistence. 'Come on, let's get back to the game.'

'Deal the cards again, then,' replied Phileas Fogg, 'because there's been a misdeal.'

Andrew Stuart's hands trembled as he took back the cards, and then he suddenly put them down on the table, saying, 'Well, all right, Mr Fogg, all right. I'll bet £4,000.'

'My dear Stuart,' said Fallentin, 'calm down. You must be joking.'

'When I talk about betting,' replied Andrew Stuart, 'I'm never joking.'

'I accept,' said Mr Fogg. Then he turned towards his colleagues:

'I have £20,000 deposited with Baring Brothers. I'm quite prepared to risk them . . .'

'£20,000!' exclaimed John Sullivan. '£20,000 that you could lose as a result of an unexpected delay!'

'There's no such thing as the unexpected,' was all Phileas Fogg said in reply.

'But Mr Fogg, this period of eighty days is calculated only as the minimum time.'

'A minimum put to good use is enough for anything.'

'But in order not to exceed it, you have to change with mathematical precision from railway to steamship and from steamship to railway.'

'I will do it with mathematical precision.'

'You must be joking!'

'A true Englishman never jokes about something as serious as a bet,' replied Phileas Fogg. 'I bet £20,000 against anyone that I will go around the world in eighty days or less, in other words 1,920 hours or 115,200 minutes. Do you accept?'

'We do,' replied Messrs Stuart, Fallentin, Sullivan, Flanagan and Ralph after agreeing among themselves.

'Good,' said Mr Fogg. 'The Dover train leaves at eight forty-five. I shall be on it.'

'On it tonight?' asked Stuart.

'Yes, tonight,' replied Phileas Fogg. 'So,' he added as he consulted a pocket calendar, 'since today is Wednesday 2 October, I must be back in London in this very drawing-room in the Reform Club on Saturday 21 December at eight forty-five in the evening. Otherwise, the £20,000 now in my account with Baring Brothers will legally be yours to share. Here's a cheque for the same amount.'

The terms of the bet were drawn up and signed on the spot by the six parties concerned. Phileas Fogg remained calm and collected. He had certainly not made the bet in order to win money and he had only committed these £20,000 – half of his fortune – because he expected to have to spend the other half on carrying out this difficult, not to say impossible, mission. His opponents, for their part, seemed uncomfortable, not because of the amount of money at stake but because they felt embarrassed about the one-sidedness of the arrangement.

Seven o'clock then struck. They offered Mr Fogg the possibility of stopping the game to enable him to prepare his departure.

'I'm always ready,' replied this impassive gentleman and, handing out the cards, he said, 'Diamonds are trumps. Your turn, Mr Stuart.'

4

*In which Phileas Fogg takes his servant Passepartout
completely by surprise*

At seven twenty-five, after winning about twenty guineas at
whist, Phileas Fogg said goodbye to his distinguished colleagues
and left the Reform Club. At seven fifty he opened the door of
his house and went inside.

Passepartout, who had been conscientiously studying his
work schedule, was quite surprised to see Mr Fogg appear at this
unusual hour, committing such an error of timing. According to
what was written down, the occupant of Savile Row was not
due to return until exactly midnight.

Phileas Fogg first went up to his bedroom, then called out,
'Passepartout.'

Passepartout did not reply. The call couldn't possibly be for
him. It wasn't the right time.

'Passepartout,' Mr Fogg repeated without raising his voice.

Passepartout appeared.

'That's the second time I've called you,' said Mr Fogg.

'But it's not midnight yet,' replied Passepartout, with his
watch in his hand.

'I know,' replied Phileas Fogg, 'and I'm not criticizing you. In
ten minutes we leave for Dover and Calais.'

A puzzled sort of expression appeared on the Frenchman's
roundish face. It was obvious that he had misheard.

'Is sir off somewhere?' he asked.

'Yes,' replied Phileas Fogg. 'We are going around the world.'

With his staring eyes, raised eyelids and eyebrows, limp arms
and slumped body, Passepartout at that moment displayed all
the symptoms of surprise bordering on stupefaction.

'Around the world!' he muttered.

'In eighty days,' replied Mr Fogg. 'So we don't have a moment to spare.'

'But what about the suitcases?' said Passepartout, whose head was rocking involuntarily from right to left.

'No suitcases. Just an overnight bag. In it two woollen shirts and three pairs of socks. The same for you. We can buy things on the journey. Bring down my raincoat and my travel rug. Get some sturdy shoes. In any case, we won't be doing a lot of walking. Off you go.'

Passepartout would have liked to respond. He was unable to do so. He left Mr Fogg's bedroom, went up to his own and collapsed into a chair. Lapsing into a colloquialism, he said to himself, 'Well! That takes the biscuit. Just when I was looking forward to a quiet life . . .'

And so, like an automaton, he got ready to leave. Around the world in eighty days! Was he dealing with a madman? No. It was a joke . . . They were going to Dover. Fair enough. To Calais. Fine. After all, that was nothing for the dear fellow to get upset about when he hadn't set foot in France for five years. Perhaps they would get as far as Paris and, to be honest, he would be pleased to see the great capital city again. But certainly a gentleman who was so careful not to take one step too many would go no further than that. Yes, that was it, quite probably, but it was also a fact that this gentleman, who up to then had been so much of a stay-at-home, was about to set off, to get on the move.

By eight o'clock Passepartout had prepared the smallish bag containing his and his master's clothes. Then, still feeling at a loss, he left his room, carefully closed the door and rejoined Mr Fogg.

Mr Fogg was ready. He was carrying under his arm Bradshaw's *Continental Railway Steam Transit and General Guide*,[1] which was to give him all the information needed for his journey. He took the bag from Passepartout, opened it and slipped into it a thick wad of those splendid banknotes that are legal tender all over the world.

'Have you forgotten anything?' he asked.

'Nothing, sir.'

'My raincoat and my rug?'

'Here they are.'

'Good, take this bag.'

Mr Fogg handed the bag to Passepartout.

'Be careful with it. There are £20,000 inside.'

Passepartout almost let go of the bag as if the £20,000 had been in gold and too heavy to carry. Master and servant then went downstairs and they double-locked the front door behind them.

There was a carriage rank at the far end of Savile Row. Phileas Fogg and his servant got into a cab, which drove quickly to Charing Cross station, the terminus for one of the branch lines of the South-Eastern Railway.

At twenty past eight, the cab stopped in front of the railings of the station. Passepartout jumped down. His master followed and paid the coachman.

At that moment a poor beggar woman with a child in her hands, barefoot in the mud, wearing a tattered shawl over her rags and a battered hat decorated with a pathetic-looking feather, went up to Phileas Fogg, asking for charity.

Mr Fogg took out of his pocket the twenty guineas he had just won at whist and, as he gave them to the beggar woman, said, 'Take this, my poor woman. I'm glad to have met you.'

Then he went on.

Passepartout felt as if tears were coming to his eyes. His master had made an impression on his heart.

Mr Fogg and he immediately went into the main hall of the station. There Phileas Fogg told Passepartout to buy two first-class tickets for Paris. Then, as he turned around, he noticed his five fellow members of the Reform Club.

'Gentlemen, I'm on my way,' he said, 'and the various stamps in the passport I'm taking for this very purpose will enable you to check where I have been when I get back.'

'Oh, Mr Fogg,' replied Gauthier Ralph politely, 'that's not necessary. We will rely on your word as a gentleman.'

'I prefer it this way,' said Mr Fogg.

'You won't forget, will you, that you must be back –' remarked Andrew Stuart.

'In eighty days,' replied Mr Fogg, 'by Saturday 21 December 1872, at eight forty-five in the evening. Goodbye, gentlemen.'

At eight forty Phileas Fogg and his servant took their places in the same compartment. At eight forty-five the whistle blew and the train set off.

It was pitch dark, and it was drizzling with rain. Phileas Fogg, sitting in his corner, didn't say a word. Passepartout, still in a state of shock, was clinging on to the bag of banknotes, like an automaton.

But the train had got no further than Sydenham when Passepartout let out a real cry of despair.

'What's the matter?' asked Mr Fogg.

'What's the matter is . . . in the rush . . . my state of confusion . . . I forgot . . .'

'What?'

'To switch off the gas lamp in my bedroom.'

'Well, my dear fellow,' Phileas Fogg replied coldly, 'you'll be paying the bill!'

5

In which a new type of share appears on the London market

When he left London, Phileas Fogg could have had little idea of the impact that his departure would have. The news of the bet first went around the Reform Club and had a considerable effect on the members of that distinguished institution. Then, from the club, its effect spread to the newspapers via reporters and from the newspapers to the public in London and the whole United Kingdom.

This issue of the 'journey around the world' was discussed, argued about and analysed with as much passion and energy as if it had been a major international dispute like the *Alabama* Claim.[1] Some people sided with Phileas Fogg, others – and they were soon in the majority – came out against him. To go around the world, other than in theory and on paper, in such a short time and with the means of transport currently available, was not only impossible, it was madness.

The Times, the *Standard*, the *Evening Star*, the *Morning Chronicle*, and a dozen other newspapers with a wide circulation came out against Mr Fogg. Only the *Daily Telegraph* supported him up to a point. Phileas Fogg was in general considered an obsessive and a madman and his fellow members of the Reform Club were criticized for having accepted this bet, which was evidence of a decline in the mental capacities of the person who had made it.

Some extremely heated but well-argued articles were published on the subject. It is well known how seriously anything involving geography is taken in England. And so there was not a single reader, regardless of social class, who failed to devour the columns devoted to the case of Phileas Fogg.

In the early days, some independent-minded people – mainly women – were for him, especially when the *Illustrated London News*[2] published his portrait, based on a photograph from the archives of the Reform Club. Some gentlemen went as far as to say, 'Well, why not, after all? Stranger things have happened!' They were mainly readers of the *Daily Telegraph*. But it soon became clear that even the support of this newspaper was beginning to wane.

In the event, a long article appeared on 7 October in the *Proceedings of the Royal Geographical Society*.[3] It examined the question from every perspective and proved conclusively the madness of the undertaking. According to this article, everything was against the traveller, human obstacles and natural ones. For the plan to succeed would require a miraculous coordination of departure and arrival times, a coordination that didn't exist and that couldn't exist. At a pinch and in Europe, where the length of the journey was relatively short, the trains could be expected to arrive on time, but when they take three days to cross India and seven to cross the United States, how could anyone consider them reliable factors in such a calculation? And with mechanical breakdowns, derailments, encounters with the unexpected, bad weather, heavy snow, surely everything was against Phileas Fogg? On steamers, were you not in winter at the mercy of gusts of wind or patches of fog? Was it that unusual for the fastest transatlantic ships to be two or three days late? Yet all it needed was one single hold-up for the whole chain of communication to be irreparably broken. If Phileas Fogg missed a steamer by only a few hours, he would be forced to wait until the next steamer, and that would be fateful for his whole journey.

The article had a considerable impact. It was reprinted in almost all the newspapers and shares in Phileas Fogg fell considerably.

During the early days after the gentleman's departure there had been some heavy betting on the risks involved. It is well known that in England betting is an activity practised by a more intelligent and select group of people than gambling. Betting is part of the English character. So, not only did various members

of the Reform Club place considerable bets for or against Phileas
Fogg, but the public as a whole followed suit. Phileas Fogg was
treated like a racehorse, entered in a sort of form book.[4] He was
also made into a new sort of share that was immediately quoted
on the London market. There were buying and selling prices for
'Phileas Fogg', and large amounts of money changed hands. But
five days after his departure, after the article in the *Proceedings
of the Royal Geographical Society*, people began to sell. Shares
in 'Phileas Fogg' fell. There was a wave of selling. Quoted first
at five to one, then ten, the odds then became twenty, fifty and
a hundred to one!

He had only one supporter left. This was the elderly, paralysed
Lord Albermarle. The noble sir, confined to a wheelchair, would
have given his whole fortune to go around the world even if it
took him ten years! So he was the one who bet £5,000 on Phileas
Fogg. And when people showed him not only how foolish the
plan was but also how pointless, he merely replied, 'If it can be
done at all, then it's only right that an Englishman should be
the first to do it!'

This, then, was the situation: the supporters of Phileas Fogg
were becoming fewer and fewer; everyone, and not without
reason, was turning against him; the odds were now one hundred
and fifty, two hundred to one. Then, seven days after he had
left, something quite unexpected resulted in no odds being given
at all.

What happened was that during that day, at nine o'clock in
the evening, the Commissioner of the Metropolitan Police had
received the following telegraph message:

*To: Rowan, Commissioner, Police Headquarters, Scotland Yard,
London
From: Fix, detective inspector, Suez*

Trailing bank robber, Phileas Fogg. Send arrest warrant without
delay Bombay (British India).

The effect of this telegram was immediate. For 'honourable
gentleman' people now read 'bank robber'. His photograph,

which was kept in the Reform Club along with those of all his fellow members, was carefully examined. It reproduced down to the last detail the features of the man whose description had been provided by the police investigation. People remembered how secretive an existence Phileas Fogg led, how solitary he was, how sudden his departure had been, and it seemed obvious that by inventing this story of a journey around the world and then backing it up with an absurd bet this individual had acted with the sole intention of putting the British police force off his scent.

6

In which the detective Fix shows a quite understandable impatience

The circumstances leading up to the sending of this telegram about that man Phileas Fogg were as follows:

On Wednesday 9 October, the liner *Mongolia* was due to arrive in Suez at eleven o'clock in the morning. The *Mongolia*, which belonged to the Peninsular and Oriental Steam Navigation Company,[1] was an iron-hulled, propeller-driven steamer with a spar-deck.[2] It weighed 2,800 tons and had a nominal 500 horsepower. The *Mongolia* regularly did the run from Brindisi to Bombay via the Suez Canal. It was one of the company's fastest vessels and it had always exceeded its scheduled speed, namely 10 miles per hour, between Brindisi and Suez and 9.53 miles per hour between Suez and Bombay.

While they waited for the *Mongolia* to arrive, two men were walking along the quayside, mingling with the crowd of natives and foreigners that flock to this town, which was until recently only a village, but which can look forward to a successful future thanks to Ferdinand de Lesseps's great feat of engineering.[3]

Of these two men, one was the United Kingdom consul based in Suez, who – despite the pessimistic forecasts of the British government and the bleak predictions of Stephenson,[4] the famous engineer – saw British ships going through the canal every day, thereby reducing by half the journey from England to India compared to the old route via the Cape of Good Hope. The other was a small, skinny man, quite intelligent-looking but nervous, with an almost-permanent frown on his face. His long eyelashes concealed a piercing gaze, but one that he could soften at will. At that particular moment he was showing signs of some impatience, pacing up and down, unable to stay still.

This man was called Fix, and he was one of those English detectives or policemen who had been sent to the various ports after the discovery of the theft at the Bank of England. Fix was supposed to keep a careful watch on passengers travelling via Suez and, if one of them aroused his suspicions, to stay on his track until he received an arrest warrant.

As it happened, two days previously Fix had received the description of the suspected thief from the head of the Metropolitan Police. It was a description of that distinguished, well-dressed gentleman who had been seen in the cash room in the Bank of England.

The detective, obviously spurred on by the prospect of a large reward for a successful arrest, was therefore waiting for the *Mongolia* to arrive with understandable impatience.

'Am I right, sir,' he asked for the umpteenth time, 'that according to you the ship must be in soon?'

'Yes, Mr Fix,' replied the consul. 'It was reported yesterday as being off Port Said and a vessel as fast as this will get through the hundred miles of canal in next to no time. I should remind you again that the *Mongolia* has always earned the £25 bonus that the government gives every time a ship arrives twenty-four hours ahead of schedule.'

'The ship's coming straight from Brindisi, isn't it?' asked Fix.

'Yes, straight from Brindisi, where it picked up the mail for India. It left Brindisi on Saturday at five o'clock in the evening. So be patient. It must be in very soon now. But I really don't understand how, with the description you've got, you'll be able to recognize your man if he really is on board the *Mongolia*.'

'My dear sir,' replied Fix, 'you sniff out this sort of individual rather than recognize them. It's nose that you need and nose is like an extra sense, a combination of hearing, sight and smell. In my lifetime I've arrested more than one of these gentlemen, and as long as my thief really is on board I can guarantee you that he won't slip through my fingers.'

'I hope not, Mr Fix, because it was a substantial theft.'

'A magnificent theft,' the detective replied enthusiastically. '£55,000! We don't often get such big windfalls! Thieves are becoming petty criminals. The great English thief is a dying breed. People get themselves hanged for only a few shillings these days.'

'Mr Fix,' replied the consul, 'the way you talk I wish you every success, but I must repeat that given the circumstances I'm afraid your task will not be an easy one. You must realize that from the description you've received the thief is a perfectly respectable-looking person.'

'My dear consul,' the police inspector replied in a dogmatic tone of voice, 'great thieves always look like respectable people. You must understand that people who look like crooks have only one option, to remain on the right side of the law. Otherwise they would be arrested. It's the honest-looking faces you have to examine closely. A difficult task, I admit, and one that makes this not just a job but an art.'

It is clear that the aforesaid Fix had a strong sense of his own importance.

Meanwhile the quayside was gradually getting busy. Sailors of different nationalities, shopkeepers, brokers, porters and fellahs[5] were flooding in. The liner was obviously about to arrive.

The weather was fairly good, but the air was chilly because of an easterly wind. Some minarets stood out above the town in the pale sunshine. Towards the south a jetty about 2,000 metres long stuck out like an arm into the harbour of Suez. Several fishing boats or coastal vessels moved across the surface of the Red Sea, some of them still having the elegant outline of an ancient galley.

As he made his way through this crowd Fix ran a rapid eye over the passers-by out of sheer professional habit.

By now it was half past ten.

'But this liner doesn't look as if it's ever going to arrive,' he exclaimed as he heard the harbour clock strike.

'It can't be far away,' replied the consul.

'How long will it stop in Suez for?' Fix asked.

'Four hours. The time needed to take on board more coal. From Suez to Aden at the far end of the Red Sea it's 1,310 nautical miles, so it needs to have a fresh supply of fuel.'

'And from Suez, does the boat go straight on to Bombay?' asked Fix.

'Straight on, without unloading.'

'Well, then,' said Fix, 'if the thief is coming this way and on this boat, it must be part of his plan to disembark at Suez in order to find another way of getting to the Dutch or French possessions in Asia. He must be well aware that he wouldn't be safe in India, which is British soil.'

'Unless he's a very clever man,' replied the consul. 'As you know, an English criminal is always better off hiding in London rather than abroad.'

After this remark, which gave the detective food for thought, the consul went back to his office, which was only a short distance away. The police inspector remained alone, an impatient bag of nerves. He had a strange sort of premonition that the thief was bound to be on board the *Mongolia*, and in all truth if the crook had left England with the intention of reaching the New World, it would be logical for him to prefer the route via India because it was less carefully watched or more difficult to watch than the route across the Atlantic.

Fix didn't remain lost in his thoughts for long. Some sharp blasts on the whistle announced the liner's arrival. The whole horde of porters and fellahs rushed towards the quayside, threatening injury and damage to the waiting passengers and their clothes. A dozen or so small boats set off from the bank of the canal and went out to meet the *Mongolia*.

Soon the enormous bulk of the *Mongolia* came into view, moving along between the banks of the canal. Eleven o'clock was striking as the steamer dropped anchor in the harbour, noisily letting steam out of its funnels.

There were quite a large number of passengers on board. Some remained on the spar-deck, gazing at the picturesque panorama of the town, but most of them disembarked in the small boats that had come alongside the *Mongolia*.

Fix examined closely all those who set foot on dry land.

At that moment one of the passengers came up to him after briskly pushing aside all the fellahs who were accosting him and offering their services. He asked Fix very politely if he could point out to him the office of the British consul. At the same time this passenger showed a passport that he presumably wanted to have stamped with a British visa.

Fix instinctively took the passport and rapidly read the description of the bearer.

He had difficulty controlling his reaction. The document trembled in his hand. The description provided on the passport was identical to the one he had received from the head of the Metropolitan Police.

'This passport doesn't belong to you, does it?' he said to the passenger.

'No. It's my master's passport.'

'And where is your master?'

'Still on board.'

'I'm afraid,' continued the detective, 'he has to go in person to the consul's office to prove his identity.'

'What! Is that really necessary?'

'Indispensable.'

'So where is this office?'

'Over there, in the corner of the square,' replied the inspector, pointing to a building about 200 yards away.

'In that case I'll go and fetch my master, who certainly won't be pleased to be disturbed.'

With that, the passenger said goodbye to Fix and went back on board the steamer.

7

*Which proves once again that passports serve no useful
purpose in police matters*

The inspector went back down to the quayside and headed off
quickly towards the British consulate. As soon as he got there,
and at his insistence, he was ushered in to see the consul in
person.

'Sir,' he said, getting straight to the point, 'I have good reason
to believe that our man is a passenger on board the *Mongolia*.'

Fix then recounted what had taken place between the servant
and himself concerning the passport.

'Well, Mr Fix,' replied the consul, 'I'd quite like to see what
this crook looks like. But perhaps he won't come to my office if
he really is your man. A thief never likes to leave any trace of
where he's been, and in any case it's no longer compulsory to
show your passport.'

'Sir,' replied the detective, 'if he's as clever as I think, he will
come.'

'To have his passport stamped?'

'Yes. All that passports do is inconvenience law-abiding
citizens and enable crooks to get away. You can be sure that
his will be in order, but I really do hope that you won't
stamp it.'

'Why on earth not? If this passport is in order,' replied the
consul, 'I'm not in a position to refuse a visa.'

'But, sir, it's essential for me to keep him here until I receive
the arrest warrant from London.'

'Well, Mr Fix,' replied the consul, 'that's your business. It's
not up to me to –'

The consul was unable to finish his sentence. At that moment
there was a knock on his door and the office boy showed in two

strangers, one of whom was none other than the servant who had spoken to the detective earlier.

This time it was the master and his servant. The master showed his passport and asked the consul in the fewest possible words to be so kind as to stamp it.

The latter took the passport and read it carefully, while Fix, standing in a corner of the room, looked or rather stared hard at the stranger.

When the consul had finished reading it, he asked, 'Are you Mr Phileas Fogg?'

'Yes, sir,' replied the gentleman.

'And is this man your servant?'

'Yes. A Frenchman called Passepartout.'

'Have you come from London?'

'Yes.'

'And where are you going?'

'Bombay.'

'Good, sir. Are you aware that visa formalities are unnecessary and that it's no longer compulsory to show your passport?'

'I am aware, sir,' replied Phileas Fogg, 'but I want a visa to prove that I've been through Suez.'

'Very well, sir.'

And so the consul signed and dated the passport and then stamped it. Mr Fogg paid the cost of the visa and, after politely saying goodbye, went out, followed by his servant.

'Well, then?' asked the inspector.

'Well,' replied the consul, 'he seems a perfectly law-abiding citizen.'

'That's as may be, but it's not the point,' replied Fix. 'Don't you think that this phlegmatic gentleman looks exactly like the thief I've received the description of?'

'I agree, but as you know all descriptions –'

'I want to get to the bottom of this,' replied Fix. 'I think the servant will be easier to fathom out than his master. What's more he's French, which means he won't be able to hold his tongue. I'll see you again soon, sir.'

With this the detective went out and began to search for Passepartout.

Meanwhile, Mr Fogg, after leaving the consulate, had headed towards the quayside. There he gave his servant some orders, then got into a small boat that took him to the *Mongolia* and went back down into his cabin. There he took out his notebook, which contained the following entries:

> Left London, Wednesday 2 October, 8.45 p.m.
> Arrived Paris, Thursday 3 October, 7.20 a.m.
> Left Paris, Thursday, 8.40 a.m.
> Arrived Turin via Mont Cenis, Friday 4 October, 6.35 a.m.
> Left Turin, Friday, 7.20 a.m.
> Arrived Brindisi, Saturday 5 October, 4 p.m.
> Boarded the *Mongolia*, Saturday, 5 p.m.
> Arrived Suez, Wednesday 9 October, 11 a.m.
> Total time in hours: 158 ½, making 6 ½ days.

Mr Fogg had written down these dates on a travel plan laid out in columns, showing from 2 October to 21 December the month, the day in the month, the day of the week, the estimated time of arrival and the actual time of arrival for each main staging point, Paris, Brindisi, Suez, Bombay, Calcutta, Singapore, Hong Kong, Yokohama, San Francisco, New York, Liverpool and London. This enabled him to work out the time gained or lost at each point of his journey.

The carefully calculated travel plan thus took account of everything, and Mr Fogg always knew whether he was ahead or behind schedule.

So he wrote in for that day, Wednesday 9 October, his arrival in Suez, which as it coincided with the scheduled time of arrival was neither a loss nor a gain.

Then he had lunch brought to him in his cabin. As for looking around the town, he never even gave it a moment's thought, as he was the sort of Englishman who gets his servant to do the sights for him.

8

In which Passepartout talks perhaps rather more than he should have

It didn't take Fix long to catch up with Passepartout on the quayside, where the latter was strolling around and observing things, showing none of his master's reluctance to take in the sights.

'Well, my friend,' Fix said as he went up to him, 'has your passport been stamped?'

'Oh, it's you, sir,' the Frenchman replied. 'Pleased to meet you. Our papers are all in order.'

'Are you looking around the area?'

'Yes. But we're travelling so fast that everything seems a blur. So now we're in Suez, aren't we?'

'Suez it is.'

'And that's in Egypt, isn't it?'

'In Egypt. Quite right.'

'And that's in Africa, isn't it?'

'In Africa.'

'In Africa,' repeated Passepartout. 'I just can't believe it. I tell you what, sir, I didn't expect us to go further than Paris, but I only got to see that wonderful city again between seven twenty and eight forty in the morning, from the Gare du Nord to the Gare de Lyon, through the window of a cab and with the rain pouring down. What a pity! I really wanted to see the Père-Lachaise Cemetery again and the circus in the Champs-Élysées.'

'So you're in quite a hurry, are you?' asked the inspector.

'Not me but my master. Incidentally, I must go and buy some socks and shirts. We left without any suitcases, just with an overnight bag.'

'I can take you to a bazaar where you'll find everything you need.'

'Sir,' replied Passepartout, 'you really are too kind.'

And so the two of them set off. Passepartout kept chatting.

'Most of all,' he said, 'I must make sure I don't miss the boat.'

'You've got time,' replied Fix. 'It's still only midday.'

Passepartout took out his big watch.

'Midday,' he said. 'Come off it! It's nine fifty-two.'

'Your watch is slow,' replied Fix.

'My watch! A family heirloom, from my great-grandfather. It doesn't lose more than five minutes in a year. It's as accurate as a chronometer.'

'I get it,' replied Fix. 'You've kept London time, which is about two hours behind Suez. You must be careful to set your watch to the right time in each country.'

'Me alter my watch!' exclaimed Passepartout. 'Never.'

'Well, in that case it won't be in time with the sun.'

'That's too bad for the sun, sir. It's the sun that'll be wrong.'

With that the dear fellow proudly put his watch back in his waistcoat pocket.

A few moments later Fix said to him, 'So you left London in a rush, did you?'

'I should say so! Last Wednesday, Mr Fogg came back from his club at eight o'clock in the evening, which was quite unlike him, and three-quarters of an hour later we were on our way.'

'But where exactly is your master going?'

'Straight on. He's going around the world.'

'Around the world!' exclaimed Fix.

'Yes. In eighty days! It's for a bet, he says, but between you and me I don't believe a word of it. It just doesn't make sense. There's something more to it.'

'Oh! This Mr Fogg's a bit of an eccentric, is he?'

'Looks like it.'

'So he's rich, is he?'

'Obviously, and he's carrying a tidy sum with him, in fresh banknotes. And he doesn't mind spending it on the way. That's why he's promised the chief engineer of the *Mongolia* a huge bonus in Bombay if he gets us there with plenty of time to spare.'

'And you've known your master for quite some time, have you?'

'What, me?' replied Passepartout. 'I started working for him the day we left.'

It is easy to imagine the effect these replies were to have on the already overexcited mind of the police inspector.

The sudden departure from London, shortly after the theft took place, the large sum of money being carried, the eagerness to arrive in far-off countries, the excuse of an eccentric bet, all these things helped further to confirm Fix's suspicions, as was to be expected. He got the Frenchman to tell him more and became convinced that this fellow didn't know his master at all, that the latter lived alone in London, that he was thought to be rich but no one knew where his money came from, that he was an unfathomable individual, etc. But at the same time Fix felt sure that Phileas Fogg would not disembark at Suez and that he really was going to Bombay.

'Is Bombay a long way?' asked Passepartout.

'Quite a long way,' replied the detective. 'It'll take you ten days or so by sea.'

'And where exactly is Bombay?'

'In India.'

'That's in Asia, isn't it?'

'Of course.'

'Heavens above! There's something I've got to tell you . . . There's something that's been on my mind . . . It's my lamp!'

'What lamp?'

'My gas lamp, which I forgot to switch off and which I'll have to pay the bill for. Well, I've worked out that it'll cost me two shillings per day, exactly six pence more than I earn, and you can well understand that if the journey goes on . . .'

It is unlikely that Fix understood this business about the gas. He wasn't listening any more but was deciding what to do next. The Frenchman and he had got to the bazaar. Fix let his companion buy what he needed, urged him not to miss the departure of the *Mongolia*, and hurried off back to the consul's office.

Now that his mind was made up, Fix had fully regained his composure.

'Sir,' he said to the consul, 'I no longer have the slightest doubt. I've got my man. He passes himself off as an eccentric who's trying to go around the world in eighty days.'

'So he's cunning,' replied the consul, 'and he's planning to go back to London after throwing all the policemen on two continents off his scent!'

'That remains to be seen,' replied Fix.

'Are you sure you're not making a mistake?' the consul asked once again.

'I'm not making a mistake.'

'In that case, why was the thief so keen on having his passport stamped to show he's been through Suez?'

'Why? I've no idea, sir,' the detective replied, 'but listen to what I have to say.'

And in a few words he summarized the main points of his conversation with the servant of the said Fogg.

'Well indeed,' said the consul, 'everything seems to point to this man. So what are you going to do?'

'Send a telegram to London with an urgent request to send an arrest warrant to Bombay. Then I'll get on board the *Mongolia*, keep track of my thief all the way to India and there, on what is British territory, I'll go up to him politely with my warrant in one hand and I'll put the other on his shoulder to arrest him.'

After coldly speaking these words, the detective took his leave of the consul and went to the telegraph office. From there he sent the head of the Metropolitan Police the telegram already mentioned.

A quarter of an hour later Fix went on board the *Mongolia*, taking with him some light luggage but plenty of cash, and soon the fast-moving steamer was speeding down the Red Sea.

9

Where the Red Sea and the Indian Ocean prove favourable to Phileas Fogg's purposes

The distance between Suez and Aden is exactly 1,310 nautical miles and the company's sailing schedule allowed its steamers a period of 138 hours to cover it. The *Mongolia*, whose engines were at full throttle, was moving fast in order to arrive ahead of schedule.

Most of the passengers who had embarked at Brindisi were travelling to India. Some were going to Bombay, others to Calcutta but via Bombay, because since the opening of the railway that goes right across the subcontinent it was no longer necessary to go around the tip of Ceylon.

Among the passengers were various civil servants and army officers of all ranks. Of the latter, some belonged to the British army proper and the others were in charge of native troops, or sepoys. All of them received handsome salaries even now that the British government has taken over the responsibilities and costs of the former East India Company.[1] Second lieutenants get £280 per annum, brigadiers £2,400 and generals £4,000.*

Life on board the *Mongolia* was therefore one of luxury with a society made up of public servants supplemented by the occasional young English millionaire off to set up a trading post in some far-off part of the empire. The purser, the company's most trusted employee and the equal of the captain on board, did things in style. At breakfast, lunch at two o'clock, dinner at half past five and supper at eight o'clock, the tables groaned

* The salaries of civil servants are even higher. Clerical assistants, at the very bottom of the hierarchy, get £480, magistrates £2,400, high court judges £10,000, governors £12,000 and the Governor-General £24,000. [Author's footnote]

under plates of fresh meat and side dishes served up from the ship's meat store and galley. The female passengers – there were some – changed dresses twice a day. There was music and even dancing on board, when the state of the sea allowed.

But the Red Sea is unpredictable and only too often rough, like all long, narrow gulfs. When the wind was blowing either from the Asiatic or the African side of the coast, the *Mongolia*, shaped like a long propeller-driven rocket, was caught in the beam and rolled horribly. At such times the ladies disappeared, the pianos fell silent and the singing and dancing all stopped. And yet, despite the gale and the swell, the steamer, thanks to its powerful engines, continued on schedule down towards the Strait of Bab-el-Mandeb.

What was Phileas Fogg doing meanwhile? It might have been thought that he would be worried and anxious all the time, concerned that a change in wind direction might affect the ship's progress or that a sudden surge of the waves might damage the engines, in a word that some incident might force the *Mongolia* to put in to port, thereby threatening the success of the journey.

Nothing could be further from the truth, or rather, if the gentleman did think about these possibilities, he didn't let it show. He was still the same impassive person, the imperturbable member of the Reform Club, impervious to any incident or accident. He showed no more sign of emotion than the ship's chronometers. He rarely put in an appearance on deck. He showed little interest in observing the Red Sea, so full of associations, the scene of the earliest episodes in human history. He didn't come out to view the fascinating towns scattered along its shores, their picturesque outlines occasionally standing out against the horizon. He never even dreamt about the dangers of the Red Sea, which the ancient historians, Strabo, Arrian, Artemidorus and Idrisi,[2] always wrote about with awe, waters that the navigators of old never dared to enter without first making ritual sacrifices to their gods.

So what was this eccentric doing, imprisoned as he was on the *Mongolia*? First of all, he took his four daily meals, without the rolling or pitching of the ship ever being able to disturb such a perfectly regulated piece of machinery. Then he played whist.

Yes, he had found partners as keen on the game as he was: a tax inspector on the way to his post in Goa,[3] a church minister, the Rev. Decimus Smith, returning to Bombay, and a brigadier-general in the British army, who was rejoining his regiment in Benares. These three passengers shared Mr Fogg's passion for whist and they played it for hours on end, as noiselessly as he did.

As for Passepartout, he didn't suffer at all from seasickness. He had a cabin at the fore of the ship and he, too, took his food seriously. It has to be said that given these conditions he really enjoyed his trip. He had come to terms with the situation. With good board and lodging, he was seeing the world and, in any case, he kept telling himself that this whole bizarre episode would come to an end in Bombay.

The day after they had left Suez, 10 October, Passepartout was on deck when he had the quite pleasant experience of coming across the helpful person to whom he had spoken on arrival in Egypt.

'If I'm not mistaken,' he said, going up to him with his most engaging smile, 'it's you, sir, who was so kind as to act as my guide in Suez, isn't it?'

'Yes indeed,' replied the detective, 'I do recognize you. You are the servant of that eccentric Englishman –'

'Exactly, Mr . . . ?'

'Fix.'

'Mr Fix,' replied Passepartout. 'Delighted to meet up with you again on board. So where exactly are you going?'

'Well, to Bombay, like you.'

'How fortunate. Have you done this trip before?'

'Several times,' replied Fix. 'I work for P&O.'

'So you must know India, then?'

'Well . . . yes . . .' replied Fix, not wanting to be drawn.

'Is it interesting, India?'

'Very interesting. There are mosques, minarets, temples, fakirs, pagodas, tigers, snakes, dancing girls! But with any luck you'll have time to look around, won't you?'

'I hope so, Mr Fix. As you will well understand, a man in his right senses cannot take it upon himself to spend his life going straight from a steamer on to a train and from a train back on to a steamer again just because he's supposed to be going around the world in eighty days! No. This whole performance will come to an end in Bombay. You can take it from me.'

'Is Mr Fogg keeping well?' Fix asked, sounding quite casual.

'Very well, Mr Fix. And so am I, for that matter. I'm eating like a horse. It's the sea air.'

'But I never see your master on deck.'

'Never. He's not interested in his surroundings.'

'Do you realize, Mr Passepartout, that this so-called journey in eighty days might well be a cover for some secret mission . . . a diplomatic mission, for example?'

'Quite honestly, Mr Fix, I've no idea, I must admit, and when it comes down to it I couldn't care less.'

After this meeting Passepartout and Fix often chatted together. The police inspector wanted to get to know the servant of this man Fogg. He might be of use to him at some point. So in the bar of the *Mongolia* he often offered to buy him a few glasses of whisky or pale ale, and the dear fellow accepted them without protest and even returned the compliment, not to feel indebted to him. He thought that this Fix was after all a decent sort of chap.

Meanwhile the ship was making rapid progress. On 13 October, Mocha[4] was sighted, surrounded by its ruined walls above which stood out green date palms. In the distance, towards the mountains, huge fields of coffee plants stretched out. Passepartout was delighted to contemplate this famous town, and he even thought that with its circular walls and its tumbled-down fort sticking out like a handle it looked like a giant-sized coffee cup.

In the course of the following night the *Mongolia* crossed the Strait of Bab-el-Mandeb, whose name means in Arabic the Gate of Tears, and the next day, 14 October, it put in at Steamer Point, to the north-west of the harbour at Aden. This was where it was due to take on more fuel.

Catering for the fuel needs of steamers when they are so far away from large industrial centres is a serious and important business. Just to take the case of P&O, this represents an annual expenditure of £800,000. It has proved necessary, therefore, to set up depots in several ports, and in these distant parts coal costs over £3 per ton.

The *Mongolia* still had 1,650 miles to do before reaching Bombay and it would take four hours at Steamer Point for it to refill its coal bunkers.

But this hold-up could not have any serious effect whatsoever on Phileas Fogg's timetable. It had been planned. In any case, the *Mongolia*, instead of arriving in Aden only in the morning of 15 October, got there on the evening of the 14th. That meant it was fifteen hours ahead of schedule.

Mr Fogg and his servant stepped ashore. The gentleman wanted to have his passport stamped. Fix followed him without being noticed. Once the visa formalities were over, Phileas Fogg went back on board to continue the game of whist he had broken off.

Passepartout for his part strolled around as usual, mingling with this population of Somalis, Banians,[5] Parsees,[6] Jews, Arabs and Europeans that make up the 25,000 inhabitants of Aden. He admired the fortifications that make this town the Gibraltar of the Indian Ocean[7] and the magnificent water tanks[8] that British engineers are still working on, two thousand years after the engineers of King Solomon.

'Fascinating, really fascinating,' Passepartout said to himself as he went back on board. 'I realize now that there's a lot to be said for travelling if you want to see something new.'

By six o'clock in the evening the *Mongolia*'s propellers were churning up the waters of the harbour of Aden and soon the ship was in the Indian Ocean. It had a time allocation of one hundred and sixty-eight hours to complete the crossing from Aden to Bombay. As it happened, conditions in the Indian Ocean were favourable. The wind stayed in the north-west. The sails were used to supplement the ship's steam power.

Because it now had more support, the ship rolled less. The women passengers, after another change of clothes, appeared on deck once more. The singing and dancing started up again.

And so conditions for the trip were ideal. Passepartout revelled in the pleasant company that fortune had provided for him in the person of Fix.

On Sunday 20 October the coast of India was sighted. Two hours later the harbour pilot came aboard the *Mongolia*. On the horizon the outline of hills formed a harmonious backdrop. Soon the rows of palm trees covering the town could be seen, standing out clearly. The liner entered the natural harbour formed by the islands of Salsette, Kolaba, Elephanta and Butcher, and by half past four it was alongside the quays of Bombay.

Phileas Fogg was then in the process of completing the thirty-third rubber of the day and his partner and he, thanks to a bold stroke, had taken all thirteen tricks and so finished this excellent crossing with a magnificent clean sweep.

The *Mongolia* wasn't due to arrive in Bombay until 22 October. In fact, it had arrived on the 20th. This represented, then, a gain of two days, which Phileas Fogg methodically entered in the profits column of his travel schedule.

10

*In which Passepartout is only too pleased to get away
with losing just a shoe*

As is well known, India, that great upside-down triangle with its base in the north and its apex in the south, has a surface area of 1,400,000 square miles, unevenly populated by 180 million inhabitants. The British government has effective control over a certain part of this immense country. It maintains a governor-general in Calcutta, governors in Madras, Bombay and Bengal, and a lieutenant-governor in Agra.

But British India proper only accounts for an area of 700,000 square miles and a population of 100 to 110 million. The least that can be said is that a considerable part of the country is still beyond the power of Queen Victoria. It is true to say that in the case of some of the fearsome and terrifying rajahs of the interior, Indian independence is still total.

From 1756, the date of the founding of the first British trading post on the site of what is now the city of Madras, up to 1857, the year of the Indian Mutiny, the famous East India Company was all-powerful. It gradually annexed the various provinces, which it purchased from the rajahs in exchange for annuities, which it often failed to pay. It appointed its own governor-general and all the civilian and military personnel. However, it now no longer exists and the British possessions in India come under the direct authority of the Crown.

For this reason the physical appearance, the customs and the ethnographic make-up of the continent tend to vary every day. In the past travel was by all the ancient forms of transport, by foot, horse, cart, wheelbarrow, palanquin,[1] pick-a-back, coach, etc. Nowadays steamboats speed up and down the Indus and the Ganges, and thanks to a railway that crosses the whole width of India, with branch lines along its route, the journey from Bombay to Calcutta now only takes three days.

The route chosen for the railway does not cut across India in a straight line. The distance as the crow flies is only between 1,000 and 1,100 miles, and trains travelling at only medium speed would take less than three days to cross it. However, this distance is increased by a third, at least, by the detour the railway makes by going up as far as Allahabad in the north of the peninsula.

The route taken by the Great Indian Peninsular Railway is roughly as follows. After leaving the island of Bombay it crosses Salsette, joins the mainland opposite Tannah, crosses the chain of the Western Ghats, runs north-east as far as Burhampur, travels through the more or less independent territory of Bundelkhand, goes up to Allahabad, turns east to meet the Ganges at Benares, moves slightly away from it and goes back down to the south-east via Burdwan and the French possession of Chandernagore,[2] terminating in Calcutta.

It was half past four in the afternoon when the passengers from the *Mongolia* disembarked in Bombay and the train for Calcutta was leaving at exactly eight o'clock.

Mr Fogg therefore said goodbye to his partners, left the steamboat, gave his servant instructions about what to buy, emphasized the need for him to be at the station before eight o'clock and then, walking with the mechanical precision of the seconds hand of an astronomic clock, set off towards the passport office.

And so all the marvels of Bombay seemed of no interest to him: the town hall, the magnificent library, the fortifications, the docks, the cotton market, the bazaars, the mosques, the synagogues, the Armenian churches and the splendid temple on Malabar Hill with its twin polygonal towers. Not for him the masterpieces of Elephanta, with its mysterious underground burial chambers hidden to the south-east of the natural harbour, nor the caves at Kanheri on the island of Salsette, those magnificent remains of Buddhist architecture.

Absolutely nothing interested him. When he came out of the passport office Phileas Fogg went straight to the station, where he took his evening meal. Among other dishes the head-waiter made a point of recommending a fricassee made of 'jungle rabbit', which he said was delicious.

Fogg settled for the fricassee and tasted it scrupulously, but despite the spicy sauce he found it awful.

He summoned the head waiter.

'Waiter,' he said, looking him straight in the eye, 'is this what you call rabbit?'

'Yes, sir,' the character replied shamelessly, 'jungle rabbit.'

'But didn't this rabbit miaow when it was killed?'

'Miaow? Oh, sir! it's a rabbit, I swear . . .'

'Waiter,' Mr Fogg continued coldly, 'do not swear, and remember this: in the past in India cats were considered sacred animals. Those were the good old days.'

'For the cats, my lord?'

'And perhaps for travellers, too.'

After making his point Mr Fogg calmly went back to eating his meal.

A few moments after Mr Fogg, Inspector Fix also disembarked from the *Mongolia* and hurried off to see the head of the Bombay police. He explained who he was and that he was there to arrest the person suspected of theft. Had they received an arrest warrant from London? They had received nothing. In all fairness the warrant, which had been sent after Fogg had set off, could not have arrived yet.

Fix was very put out. He wanted to obtain from the police chief an arrest warrant for this man Fogg. The police chief said no. It was a matter for the Metropolitan Police and only the latter could legally issue a warrant. This sticking to principles and strict adherence to the rule of law is fully in keeping with British traditions, which, in matters of individual freedom, allow no arbitrary exercise of power.

Fix didn't press the point and accepted that he would have to wait for his warrant. But he was determined not to let out of his sights this unfathomable scoundrel for as long as the latter remained in Bombay. He was convinced and, as has been seen, so was Passepartout, that Phileas Fogg would stay on there, thus allowing time for the warrant to arrive.

But since the last instructions his master had given him as he left the *Mongolia*, Passepartout had come to realize the same would be true of Bombay as of Suez and Paris, that this was not the end of his journey, that it would go on at least as far as Calcutta, and probably further. And he began to wonder if Mr Fogg's bet wasn't for real and if, when all he wanted was a peaceful life, he wasn't condemned by fate to go around the world in eighty days.

Meanwhile, after buying some shirts and pairs of socks, he walked around the streets of Bombay. There was a large crowd of people and, in the midst of Europeans of various nationalities, Persians with pointed hats, Banians with round turbans, Sindhis[3] with square hats, Armenians in long robes and Parsees with black mitres. It was in fact the festival celebrated by the Parsees or Guebres, direct descendants of the followers of Zoroaster,[4] who are the most hard-working, civilized, intelligent and austere of the Indians and are the race to which the wealthy native merchants of Bombay currently belong. On that particular day they were celebrating a sort of religious carnival, with processions and entertainment, which included dancing girls dressed in pink gauze with silver and gold brocade, who moved beautifully but with great decorum to the sound of viols and the beating of gongs.

It is easy to understand how fascinated Passepartout was by these strange ceremonies, staring at them wide-eyed and listening intently, with a look on his face like that of a complete buffoon.

Unfortunately for him and his master, whose journey he threatened to endanger, his curiosity led him further afield than was sensible.

What happened was that, after catching sight of the Parsee carnival, Passepartout was heading towards the station when, as he passed in front of the wonderful temple on Malabar Hill, he had the foolish idea of going inside to have a look.

He was unaware of two things: firstly, that entry into certain temples is strictly forbidden to Christians and secondly, that even believers can only enter after leaving their shoes at the entrance. It should be noted here that the British government has adopted the eminently sensible policy of respecting and enforcing down to the smallest detail the religious observances of the country and punishes severely anyone who violates them.

Passepartout, who had gone in without malice, like a mere tourist, was admiring inside Malabar Hill the dazzling but fussy detail of Hindu ornamentation when suddenly he was knocked to the floor in this holy place. Three priests, their eyes blazing with anger, rushed at him, tore off his shoes and his socks and began to beat him soundly, shouting wildly as they did so.

The Frenchman, who was strong and agile, quickly got back on his feet and knocked to the ground two of his opponents, who were hampered by their long robes. Then, rushing out of the temple as fast as his legs could carry him, he soon outdistanced the third Hindu, who had set off in hot pursuit of him after alerting the local population.

At five minutes to eight, only a few minutes before the train was due to leave, Passepartout arrived at the railway station. He was without his hat, had nothing on his feet and had lost in the struggle the package containing everything he had bought.

Fix was there on the departure platform. After following that man Fogg to the station he had realized that the scoundrel was going to leave Bombay. He had immediately made up his mind to accompany him as far as Calcutta and beyond if necessary. Passepartout did not see Fix, who was standing in the shadows, but Fix overheard Passepartout's brief account of his adventures, which he gave to his master.

'I trust there'll be no repetition of this,' was all that Phileas Fogg replied as he sat down in one of the train carriages.

Barefoot and crestfallen, the poor fellow followed his master without saying a word.

Fix was about to get into a separate carriage when a thought occurred to him that suddenly made him change his plan to leave.

'No. I'm staying,' he said to himself. 'An offence committed on Indian soil. I've got my man.'

At that moment the locomotive let out a loud whistle and the train disappeared into the night.

*In which Phileas Fogg pays a phenomenal price for a
means of transport*

The train had left at the scheduled time. It was carrying a fair
number of passengers, including some officers, civil servants
and traders in opium and indigo who were travelling to the
eastern part of the subcontinent on business.

Passepartout was in the same carriage as his master. A third
traveller had taken his seat in the opposite corner.

It was Brigadier-General Sir Francis Cromarty, one of Mr
Fogg's whist partners during the crossing from Suez to Bombay,
who was rejoining his troops stationed near Benares.

Sir Francis Cromarty was a tall, fair-haired man aged about
fifty who had distinguished himself in action during the last
sepoy revolt and could justifiably be considered a native. He
had lived in India since his youth and had made only occasional
visits to the country of his birth. He was a well-educated man,
who would have been pleased to give information about the
customs, history and administration of India, if Phileas Fogg
had been the sort who would have asked for it. But the English
gentleman asked nothing. He was not travelling, he was tracing
a circle. He was matter in orbit around the globe, following the
laws of physics. At this moment in time he was working out in
his head the number of hours spent since leaving London, and
he would have rubbed his hands had it been in his nature to
make an unnecessary movement.

Sir Francis Cromarty was perfectly aware of the eccentricity
of his travelling companion, even though he had only had time
to study him while playing cards, between two rubbers. He was
quite justified, therefore, in wondering whether a human heart
did lie beneath this cold exterior, whether Phileas Fogg had any

conception of the beauty of nature or any moral aspirations. There had to be some doubt about that. Of all the odd sorts the brigadier-general had met, none of them could stand comparison with this product of the exact sciences.

Phileas Fogg had made no effort to conceal from Sir Francis Cromarty his plan of travelling around the world, nor how he intended to carry it out. The brigadier-general considered this bet to be just another example of pointless eccentricity, inevitably lacking in the principle of *transire benefaciendo*[1] that should guide the actions of all reasonable people. At the rate this odd gentleman was going, he was likely to pass through life without doing anything positive, either for himself or for others.

One hour after leaving Bombay, the train had crossed the island of Salsette over a series of viaducts and was speeding along the mainland. At Kalyan station it left behind to its right the branch line that went down via Khandala and Poona to the south-east of India and reached Panwell station. At this point it entered the extensive mountain range of the Western Ghats, a formation of trap rock and basalt, whose highest summits are densely wooded.

From time to time Sir Francis Cromarty and Phileas Fogg exchanged a few words, and at one point the brigadier-general attempted to revive the flagging conversation:

'A few years ago, Mr Fogg, you would have suffered a delay at this stage that would probably have jeopardized your whole journey.'

'And why is that, Sir Francis?'

'Because the railway stopped at the foot of these mountains and they had to be crossed in a palanquin or by pony as far as Khandala station on the other side of the mountains.'

'This delay would not have disrupted in the least the organization of my timetable,' replied Mr Fogg. 'I have been careful to take into account the possibility of encountering certain obstacles.'

'Nevertheless, Mr Fogg,' continued the brigadier-general, 'you could have had a serious problem on your hands with the business involving this man of yours.'

Passepartout, whose feet were tangled up in his travel rug,

was fast asleep, oblivious of the fact that they were talking about him.

'The British government takes a very serious view, and rightly so, of this kind of offence,' Sir Francis Cromarty went on. 'It is particularly anxious to respect the religious practices of India and if your servant had been caught –'

'Well, if he'd been caught, Sir Francis,' replied Mr Fogg, 'he would have been convicted, he would have served his sentence and then would have returned quietly to Europe. I fail to see how this business could have delayed his master!'

With that the conversation came to an end. During the night the train crossed the Ghats, went through Nasik and the following day, 21 October, sped across the relatively flat landscape of Khandesh. The countryside was well cultivated and dotted with small towns, in which the towers of temples[2] replaced the steeples of European churches. Numerous small rivers, most of them tributaries or sub-tributaries of the Godavari, irrigated this fertile land.

When he awoke, Passepartout saw to his amazement that he was crossing the Indian subcontinent in a train belonging to the Great Peninsular Railway. He couldn't believe it. And yet it really was true. The locomotive, driven by an English engineman and fuelled by English coal, poured out its smoke over plantations of cotton, coffee, nutmeg, cloves and red pepper. The steam spiralled up over clumps of palm trees, between which could be seen picturesque bungalows, a few *viharas* or monasteries, now in ruins, and some wonderful temples decorated with the inexhaustible richness of detail of Indian architecture. Then there were huge expanses of land stretching as far as the eye could see, jungles teeming with snakes and tigers frightened by the rushing of the train, and finally forests that the route of the railway had sliced through but were still the haunt of elephants, which looked on thoughtfully as the convoy swept breathlessly by.

That morning, beyond the station at Malegaon, the travellers went through the forbidding area that was so often the scene of bloody crimes committed by the votaries of the goddess Kali. Not far away they could see Ellora and its wonderful temples and also the famous city of Aurungabad, once the fearsome Aurungzeb's capital city[3] but now merely an administrative town in one of the isolated provinces of the Nizam of Hyderabad's dominions. This was the area that used to be controlled by Feringheea, the chief of the Thugs, the king of the Stranglers.[4] These assassins, who had banded together in an organization that lay beyond the reach of the law, strangled their victims, whatever their age, in honour of the goddess of death without ever shedding blood, and there was a time when it was impossible to dig below the surface of the soil without finding a dead body. The British government has, it is true, succeeded in reducing the number of murders, but this terrifying organization still exists and continues to operate.

At half past midday the train stopped in the station at Burhanpur and Passepartout was able to buy, though at considerable expense, a pair of oriental slippers decorated with imitation pearls, which he put on with no attempt to disguise his vanity.

The travellers had a quick lunch and set off again for Assurghur station after following for a short time the course of the Tapti, a small river that enters the Gulf of Kambay near Surat.

It is worth explaining at this point the thoughts that were going through Passepartout's mind. Up until his arrival in Bombay, he had believed quite reasonably that that was as far as things would go. But now, since he had been speeding across India, he had undergone a change of mind. His natural instincts had returned with a vengeance. He rediscovered all the fanciful ideas of his younger days; he took his master's plans seriously; he believed that the bet was for real, as were the journey around the world and the maximum number of days that they mustn't exceed. Already even he was worrying about possible delays and accidents that might occur on the way. He felt caught up in this bet and trembled at the thought that he might have jeopardized it the previous day by the unforgivable way he had wandered off sightseeing. Therefore, being much less phlegmatic than Mr Fogg, he was much more anxious. He counted over and over the days that had gone, cursing the train every time it halted, accusing it of being too slow, and inwardly criticizing

Mr Fogg, for not having offered the driver a reward. The dear fellow did not realize that what was possible on a steamboat was not possible on a railway where the speed is regulated.

Towards the evening the train entered the passes through the Satpura Hills, which separate the territory of Khandesh from that of Bundelkhand.

The next day, 22 October, in reply to a question from Sir Francis Cromarty, Passepartout had looked at his watch and answered that it was three o'clock in the morning. And, it is true, this famous watch, still set to the Greenwich meridian, which was almost seventy-seven degrees to the west, should have been, and in fact was, four hours slow.

Sir Francis therefore corrected the time Passepartout had given him and made the same comment to him as Fix had done. He tried to explain to him that he should set his watch according to each new meridian and that as he was going eastwards, that is towards the sun, the days became shorter by four minutes with each degree passed. It was futile. Whether the stubborn fellow understood or not the brigadier-general's remark, he solemnly refused to put his watch forward, leaving it permanently on London time. In any case, it was an innocent fixation, which couldn't harm anyone.

At eight o'clock in the morning and fifteen miles from the station at Rothal, the train stopped in the middle of a vast clearing, around which were a few bungalows and workers' huts. The guard of the train went along the carriages saying, 'Passengers should alight here.'

Phileas Fogg looked at Sir Francis Cromarty, who seemed puzzled by this stop in the middle of a forest of tamarisks and cajuput trees.

Passepartout was no less surprised and rushed out along the track, but came back almost immediately, shouting, 'Sir, the railway's come to an end.'

'What do you mean?' asked Sir Francis Cromarty.

'I mean, the train can't go any further!'

The brigadier-general immediately got out of the carriage. Phileas Fogg followed him but in no hurry. Both of them turned to the guard.

'Where are we?' said Sir Francis Cromarty.

'In the hamlet of Kholby,' replied the guard.

'Are we stopping here?'

'I assume so. The railway line isn't finished.'

'What? It isn't finished?'

'No. There's still a section of about fifty miles to complete between here and Allahabad, where the line continues.'

'But the newspapers said the railway had been completed!'

'What can I say, sir? The newspapers are wrong.'

'And yet you still make out the tickets from Bombay to Calcutta?' continued Sir Francis, who was beginning to get angry.

'Certainly,' replied the guard, 'but passengers are fully aware that they need to find another means of transport from Kholby to Allahabad.'

Sir Francis Cromarty was furious. Passepartout would have cheerfully assaulted the guard, though it really wasn't his fault. He didn't dare look at his master.

'Sir Francis,' Mr Fogg said simply, 'we shall, if you agree, decide upon a way of getting to Allahabad.'

'Mr Fogg, this is a delay that is extremely prejudicial to your interests, is it not?'

'No, Sir Francis. This had been taken into account.'

'What? You knew that the line –'

'Not at all, but I did know that some obstacle or other would crop up sooner or later on my route. In fact, nothing is in jeopardy. I have two days spare that I can use. There's a steamer that leaves Calcutta for Hong Kong on the 25th at midday. Today is only the 22nd and we shall get to Calcutta on time.'

There was nothing that could be said in reply to such a categorical statement.

It was only too true that the building of the railway had stopped at this point. Newspapers are like certain watches that insist on being fast, and they had prematurely announced the completion of the line. Most of the passengers knew that the line was not finished and when they got out of the train they had taken possession of every type of vehicle available in this small town, four-wheeled *palki-gharis*,[5] carts pulled by zebus, a sort of buffalo with a hump, carriages that looked like mobile temples, palanquins, ponies, etc. The result was that Mr Fogg and Sir Francis Cromarty, after scouring the whole town, returned empty-handed.

'I shall go on foot,' said Phileas Fogg.

Passepartout, who at this point met up with his master, winced knowingly as he looked down at his magnificent but impractical slippers. Very fortunately he had also been casting around for a solution and he said rather hesitantly, 'Sir, I think I've found a means of transport.'

'What sort?'

'An elephant! An elephant belonging to an Indian who lives only a hundred yards from here.'

'Let's go and see the elephant,' replied Mr Fogg.

Five minutes later Phileas Fogg, Sir Francis Cromarty and Passepartout arrived at a hut adjoining an enclosure surrounded by a high fence. In the hut was an Indian and in the enclosure an elephant. As requested, the Indian let Mr Fogg and his two companions into the enclosure.

There they came upon an animal that was half tamed, which his master was rearing not as a beast of burden but for combat. With this aim in mind he had begun to change the animal's naturally gentle temperament, in order to arouse him gradually to a state of excitement and frenzy, which the Indians call 'musth', and to do this he fed him for three months with sugar and butter. This treatment may seem inappropriate for the intended result, but it was none the less employed successfully by elephant trainers. Very fortunately for Mr Fogg, the elephant in question had only just been put on to this diet and had not yet reached a state of 'musth'.

Kiouni – this was the animal's name – was capable, like all members of its species, of walking long distances at considerable speed, and in the absence of another means of transport Phileas Fogg decided to use him.

Elephants are, however, expensive in India, as they are becoming rare. The males, the only ones that can be used in circus acts, are highly sought after. These animals rarely reproduce in captivity, with the result that they can only be obtained by being captured in the wild. They are therefore looked after with great

care, and when Mr Fogg asked the Indian if he could hire his
elephant, the Indian refused categorically.

Fogg persisted and offered too high a price for the beast, £10
per hour. No. £20? No again. £40? Still no. Passepartout was
more and more horrified as the price offered went up, but the
Indian would not give in.

It was a considerable amount of money, though. Assuming
that it would take fifteen hours for the animal to get to Allahabad, that was £600 that it would make for its owner.

Without betraying the least sign of emotion, Phileas Fogg
then made the Indian a proposal to buy his beast, offering him
first of all £1,000.

The Indian didn't want to sell. Perhaps the cunning fellow
had sensed he could make a very good deal.

Sir Francis Cromarty took Mr Fogg aside and urged him to
think carefully before going any further. Phileas Fogg replied to
his companion that it was not in his habit to act without careful
thought, that what was at stake was a bet of £20,000, that this
elephant was vital for him, and that, even if he had to pay twenty
times its value, he would have the animal.

Mr Fogg went back to the Indian, whose little eyes had lit up
with greed, proof that for him all that mattered was the price.
Phileas Fogg offered successively £1,200, then £1,500, then
£1,800 and finally £2,000. Passepartout, who had such a ruddy
complexion normally, was white as a sheet.

At £2,000 the Indian gave in.

'Bless my slippers!' exclaimed Passepartout. 'That's an expensive price for a piece of elephant meat.'

The deal was done and all that was left was to find a guide.
This proved easier. A young, intelligent-looking Parsee offered
his services. Mr Fogg agreed and promised him a considerable
sum of money in return, a sure way of stimulating his intelligence
even further.

The elephant was led in and got ready without delay. The
Parsee knew the job of *mahout*, or elephant driver, inside out.
He covered the elephant's back with a sort of saddle-cloth and
set up, one on each side of the animal's flanks, two rather
uncomfortable-looking baskets.

Phileas Fogg paid the Indian in banknotes, which came out of his famous bag. It really looked as if they were being surgically removed from Passepartout's insides! Then Mr Fogg offered to take Sir Francis to the station at Allahabad. The brigadier-general accepted. One extra traveller would not make any difference for this enormous animal.

They purchased provisions at Kholby. Sir Francis Cromarty took up his place in one of the baskets and Phileas Fogg in the other. Passepartout sat astride the saddle-cloth between his master and the brigadier-general. The Parsee perched himself on the elephant's neck and at nine o'clock the animal left the small town and, taking the shortest route, plunged straight into the dense forest of fan palms.

12

Where Phileas Fogg and his companions venture into the Indian jungle, and what this leads to

The guide, in order to shorten the distance to be travelled, veered away left from the intended route of the railway, which was still under construction. Because of the severe difficulties posed by the terrain of the Vindhya Mountains, this intended route was far from being the most direct, the one which would have best suited Phileas Fogg. The Parsee, who was very well acquainted with the roads and paths of the area, claimed that he could gain twenty miles by cutting across the forest, and they relied on his judgement.

Phileas Fogg and Sir Francis Cromarty, their heads barely visible above their baskets, were severely shaken about by the stiff way in which the elephant moved, urged on as fast as possible by his *mahout*. But they put up with the situation with typically British composure, though they spoke rarely and could hardly see each other.

Passepartout, for his part, perched on the beast's back, felt all the ups and downs of its movement and was careful, as his master had told him, not to put his tongue between his teeth so as not to accidentally bite it off. The dear fellow was sometimes hurled forward on to the elephant's neck and at other times thrown backward on to its rump, as if he was doing acrobatics like a clown on a trampoline. But he was joking and laughing while leaping up in the air, and from time to time he pulled out of his bag a lump of sugar, which the clever Kiouni took with the end of his trunk, without for a moment breaking his steady trot.

After travelling for two hours the guide stopped the elephant and gave him an hour's rest. The animal devoured branches and small bushes, having first quenched its thirst in a nearby pool. Sir Francis Cromarty was not sorry for the halt. He was exhausted. Mr Fogg seemed as fresh as if he had just got out of bed.

'He must be a man of iron!' said the brigadier-general, looking at him admiringly.

'A man of steel,' replied Passepartout, who was busy preparing a simple lunch.

At midday the guide gave the signal to move on. The countryside became very wild. The great forests gave way to thickets of tamarinds and dwarf palms, then to vast arid plains, bristling with stunted shrubs and dotted with huge blocks of syenite.[1] This whole, little-visited part of Upper Bundelkhand is inhabited by religious fanatics who practise the most extreme form of Hinduism. The British have not been able to assert their authority properly over the area, which is still ruled by rajahs protected by the inaccessibility of their mountain fastnesses.

Several times they caught sight of groups of fierce-looking Indians, who made angry gestures when they saw the speedy quadruped. In any case, the Parsee avoided them as far as possible, considering them unsavoury individuals. They saw few animals that day, except for the occasional monkey that ran off gesticulating wildly and making funny faces, much to Passepartout's amusement.

One thing particularly concerned the dear fellow. What would Mr Fogg do with the elephant once they had reached Allahabad? Would he take it with them? That was impossible! The cost of transporting it on top of the cost of buying it would be a financial disaster. Would it be sold, or allowed back into the wild? This admirable beast really did deserve special consideration. If by any chance Mr Fogg gave it to him as a present, he, Passepartout, would be in a very awkward position. This problem preyed on his mind constantly.

By eight o'clock in the evening the travellers had got across the main chain of the Vindhyas and halted on the northern side, at a ruined bungalow.

They had travelled that day a distance of about twenty-five miles, and they had about the same distance left before reaching the station at Allahabad.

The night was chilly. Inside the bungalow, the Parsee made a fire with dead branches and its warmth was very welcome. Supper consisted of the provisions bought in Kholby. The travellers were almost too exhausted and shaken about to eat. What began as a desultory conversation soon gave way to loud snoring. The guide kept watch over Kiouni, who slept on his feet, resting against the trunk of a large tree.

Nothing happened during the night. The roaring of the occasional cheetah and panther sometimes disturbed the silence, along with the high-pitched chattering of monkeys. But the flesh-eating animals did no more than howl and made no attempt to attack the temporary residents of the bungalow. Sir Francis Cromarty slept soundly like a good soldier worn out by combat. Passepartout, sleeping restlessly, relived all the jolts and bumps he had experienced the previous day. As for Mr Fogg, he slept as peacefully as if he was back in the quiet of his home in Savile Row.

At six o'clock in the morning they set off again. The guide hoped to arrive at the station in Allahabad that very evening. This way Mr Fogg would only lose some of the forty-eight hours that he had saved since the beginning of the journey.

They went down the final slopes of the Vindhyas. Kiouni was advancing swiftly again. Towards midday, the guide skirted around the small town of Kalinjar, situated on the Cani, one of the minor tributaries of the Ganges. He always avoided places that were inhabited, feeling more secure in the deserted countryside, the low-lying area where the catchment basin of the great river begins. The station at Allahabad was less than twelve miles to the north-east. They halted beneath a clump of banana trees. Their fruit, as wholesome as bread and 'as succulent as cream', according to travellers' reports, was greatly appreciated.

At two o'clock the guide entered the cover of a dense forest, across which he had to travel for several miles. He preferred going this way, sheltered by the woods. In any case, so far there had been no untoward event and it looked as if the journey would be completed without incident when suddenly the elephant showed signs of nervousness and stopped in its tracks.

It was then four o'clock.

'What's the matter?' asked Sir Francis Cromarty, raising his head above the basket.

'I don't know, sir,' said the Parsee, trying to make out a strange noise that was coming through the thick foliage.

A few minutes later, the noise became easier to identify. It sounded like a concert, still a long way off, with human voices and brass musical instruments.

Passepartout was all eyes and ears. Mr Fogg waited patiently, without saying a word.

The Parsee jumped to the ground, tied the elephant to a tree and went into the depths of the undergrowth. A few minutes later he came back, saying:

'It's a procession of Hindu priests, heading towards us. Let's try to avoid being seen.'

The guide untied the elephant and led it to a copse, urging the travellers not to get down. He himself stood ready to jump quickly back on to the animal if it became necessary to make a hasty retreat. But he thought that the group of worshippers would go past without noticing him, because he was completely hidden by the thick foliage.

The grating noise of the voices and instruments was getting nearer. Monotonous chanting mingled with the sound of drums and cymbals. Soon the head of the procession appeared beneath the trees about fifty yards from Mr Fogg and his companions. They could easily make out through the branches the strange celebrants of this religious ceremony.

At the front came the priests, wearing mitres and long, brightly decorated robes. They were surrounded by men, women and children, who were chanting a sort of funeral hymn, interrupted at regular intervals by the playing of gongs and cymbals. Behind them, on a cart with large wheels, the spokes and rims of which represented intertwined snakes, there appeared a hideous statue pulled by two pairs of zebus richly decked out. The statue had four arms. Its body was dark red, its eyes wild and staring, its hair tangled, its tongue lolling and its lips dyed with henna and betel juice. Around its neck was draped a garland of death's heads and around its waist a girdle of severed hands. It was standing over a felled giant, whose head had been cut off.

Sir Francis Cromarty recognized the statue.

'The goddess Kali,' he murmured, 'the goddess of love and death.'

'The goddess of death, I agree, but the goddess of love, never!' said Passepartout. 'What an ugly-looking woman.'

The Parsee motioned to him to be quiet.

Around the statue a group of elderly fakirs were working themselves up into a furious frenzy. Their bodies were streaked with bright yellow markings and covered with cross-shaped incisions from which blood was oozing. These are the same mindless fanatics who in the great Hindu ceremonies still throw themselves under the wheels of the Car of Juggernaut.[2]

Behind them a few Hindu priests, in the full splendour of their oriental costumes, were dragging along a woman who could barely stay on her feet.

The woman was young and with a skin as white as a European's. Her head, neck, shoulders, ears, arms, hands and toes were laden with jewels, necklaces, bracelets, earrings and rings. A tunic spangled with gold and covered with a thin muslin veil revealed the beauty of her figure.

Behind this young woman, in stark contrast, guards armed with bare sabres sticking out of their belts and long inlaid pistols carried a body on a litter.

It was the body of an elderly man, dressed in the sumptuous clothes of a rajah, wearing as in life a turban embroidered with pearls, a flowing robe woven with silk and gold, a sash of diamond-studded cashmere and the magnificent weapons of an Indian prince.

The procession ended with a group of musicians and a rear-guard of fanatics, whose shouts sometimes drowned out the deafening din of the instruments.

Sir Francis watched all this pomp and ceremony with a particularly sad expression and, as he turned towards his guide, he said, 'It's a suttee!'[3]

The Parsee nodded in agreement and put a finger to his lips. The long procession wound its way slowly among the trees and soon its last members disappeared into the depths of the forest.

Gradually the singing died away. There were still some occasional distant shouts, but finally all this commotion gave way to a deep silence.

Phileas Fogg had heard what Sir Francis Cromarty had said and, as soon as the procession had disappeared, he asked, 'What is a suttee?'

'A suttee, Mr Fogg,' replied the brigadier-general, 'is a human sacrifice, but a voluntary sacrifice. The woman you have just seen will be burnt tomorrow at first light.'

'Oh, the wretches!' exclaimed Passepartout, unable to hold back this cry of indignation.

'And what about the corpse?' asked Mr Fogg.

'It's her husband, the prince,' replied the guide, 'an independent rajah from Bundelkhand.'

'What!' continued Phileas Fogg, without letting the slightest sign of emotion show in his voice. 'Are these barbaric customs still practised in India without the British being able to stamp them out?'

'In most of India,' replied Sir Francis Cromarty, 'these sacrifices are no longer carried out, but we have no influence in these savage parts and especially in this region of Bundelkhand. The whole of the area to the north of the Vindhyas is the scene of constant acts of murder and plunder.'

'The poor woman!' murmured Passepartout. 'Burnt alive!'

'Yes,' continued the brigadier-general, 'and if she wasn't, you wouldn't believe what a terrible fate would await her at the hands of her relatives. She would have her head shaved, be given only a few handfuls of rice to eat, be disowned, considered unclean and left to die in some corner like a mangy dog. So it's the prospect of such an appalling existence that often drives these unfortunate women to sacrifice themselves, rather than love or religious fanaticism. Sometimes, however, the sacrifice really is voluntary and it takes the energetic intervention of the governor to prevent it. For example, a few years ago, when I was living in Bombay, a young widow came to ask the governor permission to be burnt along with the body of her husband. As you might imagine, the governor said no. So the widow went away and sought refuge with an independent rajah and there she went through with her sacrifice.'

While the brigadier-general was telling this story the guide shook his head, and after it was finished, he said, 'The sacrifice taking place tomorrow is not voluntary.'

'How do you know?'

'Everybody in Bundelkhand knows about this business,' replied the guide.

'Nevertheless, the poor woman didn't seem to be putting up any resistance,' remarked Sir Francis Cromarty.

'That's because they've drugged her by making her inhale hashish and opium fumes.'

'But where is she being taken to?'

'To the temple at Pillagi, two miles from here. She'll spend the night there, waiting until the time comes for the sacrifice.'

'Which will be . . . ?'

'Tomorrow, at first light.'

After this reply the guide led the elephant out from the thick undergrowth and hoisted himself on to the elephant's neck. But just when he was about to get the animal going by making a particular whistling sound, Mr Fogg stopped him and, turning to Sir Francis Cromarty, said, 'What if we rescued this woman?'

'Rescued this woman, Mr Fogg!' exclaimed the brigadier-general.

'I still have twelve hours spare. I can certainly devote them to this.'

'Well, well! So you do have feelings after all!' said Sir Francis Cromarty.

'Sometimes,' replied Phileas Fogg simply. 'When I have the time.'

13

In which Passepartout proves once again that fortune favours the bold

The plan was daring, fraught with difficulty and perhaps imposs-ible. Mr Fogg was going to risk his life, or at least his freedom, and thereby the success of his project, but he had no hesitation. In any case he had in Sir Francis Cromarty a staunch ally.

Passepartout, for his part, was ready for action and he was at their command. His master's idea filled him with enthusiasm. He realized there was a heart and a soul beneath this cold exterior. He was beginning to take to Phileas Fogg.

There remained the guide. Whose side would he take in this business? Wouldn't he be for the Indians? Even if he wouldn't help them, they needed to make sure he remained neutral.

Sir Francis Cromarty asked the question point blank.

'Sir,' replied the guide, 'I'm a Parsee and this woman is a Parsee. I'm at your command.'

'Good,' replied Mr Fogg.

'Nevertheless, you must realize,' continued the Parsee, 'that we're in danger not only of losing our lives, but also of being horribly tortured if we're captured. So think about it.'

'We have,' answered Mr Fogg. 'I feel we must wait until nightfall before taking action.'

'So do I,' said the guide.

The worthy Indian then gave some details about the victim. She was an Indian lady famous for her beauty, a Parsee by race and the daughter of a wealthy family of Bombay merchants. She had received a thoroughly English upbringing in the city and from her manners and her schooling she could have been taken for a European. Her name was Aouda.[1]

After being orphaned she had been married against her will

to this elderly rajah from Bundelkhand. Three months later she was widowed. Knowing the fate that awaited her, she ran away but was immediately caught, and the relatives of the rajah, who would benefit from her death, condemned her to this punishment, from which she seemed to have no escape.

This story could only strengthen Mr Fogg and his companions in their generous resolve. It was decided that the guide would lead the elephant towards the temple of Pillagi, which he would get as near to as possible.

Half an hour later they came to a halt in a thicket, 500 yards from the temple, which they could not see, but the howling of the fanatics could be clearly heard.

They then discussed how to reach the victim. The guide knew this temple, in which he said the young woman was being held prisoner. Would it be possible to get in through one of the doors while the group were deep in a drugged stupor, or would they have to make a hole in the wall? It was not possible to come to a decision there and then. But what was beyond doubt was that the rescue would have to take place that night, and not the next day when the victim was being taken to her death. By that time no human intervention would be able to save her.

Mr Fogg and his companions waited for night to fall. As soon as the light began to fade, towards six in the evening, they decided to reconnoitre the area around the temple. The final shouts of the fakirs were dying away as they did so. As was their habit, the Indians must have been in a drug-induced stupor, the result of taking *bhang*, liquid opium mixed with an infusion of hashish. It would perhaps therefore be possible to slip past them to get to the temple.

Guiding Mr Fogg, Sir Francis Cromarty and Passepartout, the Parsee advanced through the forest without making a sound. After crawling for about ten minutes through the thick undergrowth, they reached the edge of a small river and there by the light of iron torches tipped with burning resin, they glimpsed a carefully constructed wood pile. It was the funeral pyre, made from precious sandalwood, and already soaked in sweet-smelling oils. On the upper part rested the embalmed body of the rajah, which was to be burnt at the same time as his widow.

A hundred yards from the pyre stood the temple, whose towers reached up into the darkened treetops.

'Come on,' whispered the guide.

Then, taking even more care and with his companions following him, he crept silently through the tall grass.

The silence was now broken only by the soughing of the wind in the branches.

Soon the guide stopped at the edge of a clearing. A few torches lit up the area. The ground was strewn with groups of people asleep, sunk in a drug-induced stupor. It looked like a battlefield covered with corpses. Men, women and children were all lying together. Here and there a few drunken bodies let out groans.

In the background, between the mass of trees, the temple of Pillagi could be dimly seen. But to the great disappointment of the guide, the rajah's guards, illuminated by the smoke-blackened torches, were keeping watch at the doors and were walking around with their sabres drawn. It could safely be assumed that inside the priests were also keeping watch.

The Parsee did not move any further forward. He had realized the impossibility of forcing their way into the temple, and he made his companions move back.

Phileas Fogg and Sir Francis Cromarty had understood, like him, that they couldn't attempt anything on that side.

They stopped and spoke to one another in a whisper.

'Let's wait,' said the brigadier-general, 'it's still only eight o'clock and it's possible that the guards will also fall asleep.'

'Yes, that's quite possible,' replied the Parsee.

So Phileas Fogg and his companions lay down at the foot of a tree and waited.

To them time seemed to go by very slowly. The guide left them from time to time and went to look at the edge of the wood. The rajah's guards were still keeping watch by the glare of the torches, and a faint trickle of light was coming through the windows of the temple.

They waited like this until midnight. There was no change in the situation and the guards remained outside. It was obvious that the guards couldn't be relied on to succumb to drowsiness. They had probably been spared the effects of the *bhang*. So there would have to be another solution, getting in through an opening that would have to be made in the temple walls. There remained the problem of knowing whether the priests were keeping as careful a watch over their victim as were the soldiers at the gate of the temple.

After a final conversation, the guide said he was ready to move. Mr Fogg, Sir Francis and Passepartout followed him. They made quite a long detour in order to reach the temple by the back of the building.

At about half past midnight they arrived at the foot of the walls without encountering anyone. No attempt had been made to guard this side, but it must be said that there were absolutely no windows or doors.

The night was dark. The moon, then in its final quarter, was hardly above the horizon and was obscured by heavy clouds. The height of the trees further increased the darkness.

But getting to the foot of the walls wasn't the end of it. They still had to make an opening in them. For this operation Phileas Fogg and his companions had absolutely nothing except their pocket knives. Very fortunately the temple walls were made of a mixture of brick and wood that couldn't be difficult to get through. As soon as one brick had been removed the others would come away easily.

They got down to work, making as little noise as possible. The Parsee on one side and Passepartout on the other set about dislodging the bricks, in order to make an opening two feet wide.

The work was progressing when suddenly a shout rang out inside the temple and almost immediately there was more shouting in reply from outside.

Passepartout and the guide broke off what they were doing. Had they been spotted? Had someone raised the alarm? The most basic common sense dictated that they should move away, which is what they did, at the same time as Phileas Fogg and Sir Francis Cromarty. They crouched back down under the cover of the wood, waiting for the alarm, if that is what it was, to be over, and ready in that case to resume their work.

But by an unfortunate turn of events some guards showed up

at the back of the temple and took up position there in order to prevent anyone getting near.

It would be hard to describe the disappointment of the four men, stopped before their task was complete. Now that they couldn't reach the victim how could they rescue her? Sir Francis Cromarty was fuming. Passepartout was beside himself with anger, and the guide had difficulty restraining him. The impassive Fogg waited without showing his feelings.

'All we can do is go away, isn't it?' whispered the brigadier-general.

'All we can do is go away,' replied the guide.

'Wait,' said Fogg. 'All I need is to be in Allahabad by midday.'

'But what are you hoping for?' asked Sir Francis. 'In a few hours it will be daylight, and –'

'Our luck may change at the vital moment.'

The brigadier-general would have liked to have been able to read the expression on Phileas Fogg's face.

So what was this cold Englishman counting on? Did he want, just as the young woman was to be sacrificed, to rush towards her and snatch her from the grasp of her executioners in full view of everyone?

It would have been an act of madness, and how could anyone think him as mad as that? Nevertheless, Sir Francis Cromarty agreed to wait until the final act of this horrible drama. However, the guide did not allow his companions to stay in the place where they had sought refuge and he led them back to another part of the clearing. From there, under the shelter of a clump of trees, they would be able to observe the groups of people asleep.

Meanwhile Passepartout, perched on the lowest branches of a tree, was turning over in his mind an idea that had first occurred to him in a flash and that had now taken a firm hold.

He had said to himself at first, 'This is madness,' and now he kept on repeating to himself, 'Why not, after all? It's a possibility, perhaps the only one, and with maniacs like these around . . .'

In any case, Passepartout spent no more time organizing his thoughts, but instead, with the agility of a snake, he slithered along the lower branches of the tree, which reached almost down to the ground.

Time was passing and soon a few hints of light suggested that dawn was on its way. However, it was still quite dark.

Now was the moment. The sleeping crowd showed signs of coming back to life. People were stirring. The striking of gongs could be heard. Chanting and shouting burst out again. The time had come for the unfortunate woman to die.

At that very moment the doors of the temple opened. The light coming from inside became brighter. Mr Fogg and Sir Francis were able to see the victim, now clearly illuminated, being dragged out by two priests. They even thought that by a supreme effort of self-preservation, the unfortunate woman was shaking off the effects of her drug-induced drowsiness and attempting to escape from her executioners. Sir Francis Cromarty's heart leapt and, impulsively seizing Phileas Fogg's hand, he realized that the latter was holding an open knife.

At that point the crowd began to move forward. The young woman had relapsed into the torpor induced by the hashish fumes. She went past the fakirs, who were accompanying her with their religious incantations.

Phileas Fogg and his companions, merging with those at the back of the crowd, followed her.

Two minutes later they reached the edge of the river and stopped less than fifty yards from the funeral pyre, where the rajah's body was laid out. In the semi-darkness they could see the victim looking absolutely lifeless, lying next to her husband's corpse.

Then a torch was brought forward and the wood, which had been soaked with oil, caught fire immediately.

At that moment, Sir Francis Cromarty and the guide attempted to restrain Phileas Fogg, who in a moment of generous insanity began to rush towards the pyre.

But Phileas Fogg had already pushed them back when the scene suddenly changed. A cry of terror rang out. The whole crowd flung themselves to the ground in fear.

So the old rajah was not dead after all? Suddenly he rose to his feet like a ghost, lifted the young woman up in his arms and stepped down from the pyre amid the swirling smoke, looking like a ghostly apparition.

The fakirs, guards and priests were overcome with a sudden terror and remained prostrate, not daring to raise their eyes to behold this supernatural event.

The unconscious victim was taken up and carried away by a pair of strong arms as if she were as light as a feather. Mr Fogg and Sir Francis Cromarty had remained standing. The Parsee had bowed his head and no doubt Passepartout was equally amazed.

So it was that the ghostly apparition got near to where Mr Fogg and Sir Francis Cromarty were standing and there it said curtly, 'Let's get out of here!'

It was Passepartout himself who had crept towards the pyre in the midst of the thick smoke! It was Passepartout who, taking advantage of the fact that it was still pitch dark, had snatched the young woman from her death. It was Passepartout who, playing his role with consummate daring, had walked through the terror-struck crowd!

A moment later the four disappeared into the wood and the elephant carried them swiftly away. But shouting and screaming and even a bullet, which went through Phileas Fogg's hat, were proof that their ruse had been discovered.

The body of the old rajah could now be clearly seen on the burning pyre. The priests had recovered from their fright and now realized that a rescue had just taken place.

Immediately they rushed into the forest, followed by the guards. A volley of shots rang out, but the rescuers fled rapidly and within a few moments they were beyond the range of the bullets and arrows.

14

In which Phileas Fogg travels the whole length of the wonderful valley of the Ganges without thinking it worth a look

The bold rescue plan had come off. An hour later Passepartout was still revelling in his success. Sir Francis Cromarty had shaken the intrepid fellow's hand. His master had said to him 'well done', which, coming from the gentleman in question, was the equivalent of the highest praise, to which Passepartout had replied that all the credit lay with his master. All that he had done was to have a 'daft' idea and he was still amused by the thought that for a few moments he, Passepartout, the former gymnast and ex-fireman, had been this charming lady's widower, an elderly embalmed rajah.

As for the young Indian lady, she had not been aware of what had happened. Wrapped in travel rugs, she was resting in one of the baskets.

Meanwhile the elephant, under the expert guidance of the Parsee, was advancing rapidly through the forest, where it was still dark. An hour after leaving the temple of Pillagi the elephant began to cross an immense plain. At seven o'clock they made a halt. The young woman was still completely prostrate. The guide gave her a few drops of water and brandy to drink, but her drugged state would last some time longer.

Sir Francis Cromarty, who was well aware of the effects of inhaling the hashish fumes, had no worries on her score.

However, if the young Indian woman's recovery was not in doubt, her safety was, in the brigadier-general's mind, quite another matter. He was not afraid to say to Mr Fogg that if she remained in India she would inevitably fall into the hands of her would-be executioners. These fanatics were to be found over the whole of the subcontinent, and it was certain that despite the best efforts of the British police they would succeed in recapturing their victim, whether it be in Madras, Bombay or Calcutta. To back up his argument Sir Francis quoted a similar recent case. In his opinion the young woman would only really be safe once she had left India.

Phileas Fogg replied that he would take account of these remarks and would then make up his mind accordingly.

At about ten o'clock the guide announced that they had arrived at the station in Allahabad. This was where the railway line picked up again and from where trains took less than a day and a night to cover the distance between Allahabad and Calcutta.

Phileas Fogg should therefore arrive in time to catch a steamer that didn't leave for Hong Kong until midday the following day, 25 October.

They installed the young woman in a waiting-room at the station. Passepartout was given the task of going out to buy her various items of clothing, a dress, a shawl, furs, etc., whatever he could find. His master set no limit on how much he could spend.

Passepartout left immediately and went all around the town. Allahabad is the city of God, one of the holiest cities in India, because it is built where two sacred rivers meet, the Ganges and the Jumna, whose waters attract pilgrims from the whole subcontinent. In addition, it is well known that, according to the legends of the *Ramayana*,[1] the Ganges has its source in the heavens from where, thanks to Brahma, it comes down to this earth.

As he made his purchases it didn't take Passepartout long to see the whole of the town, which in the past had been defended by a magnificent fort that is now a state prison. There were no longer any businesses or industries in what had previously been an important commercial and industrial centre. Passepartout searched in vain for a department store as if he was in Oxford Street, but he had to go to a second-hand shop run by a pernickety old Jew to find the items he needed, a tartan dress, a large cloak and a magnificent fur coat made out of otter's skin, which he had no hesitation in paying £75 for. Then he returned in triumph to the station.

Mrs Aouda was beginning to come round. The effect of the drug administered by the priests of Pillagi was gradually wearing off, and her beautiful eyes were recovering all their gentle Indian charm.

Celebrating the beauty of the queen of Ahmadnagar, the poet-king Yusuf Adil[2] wrote as follows:

Her glistening hair, carefully parted, frames the gently flowing outline of her delicate white cheeks that gleam with a smooth sheen. Her eyebrows, dark as ebony, have the shape and strength of the bow of Kama, the god of love, and beneath her silky long eyelashes, in the dark pupils of her large clear eyes, there shimmer, as in the sacred lakes of the Himalayas, the purest reflections of celestial light. Her delicate, perfect white teeth shine out between smiling lips, like dewdrops in the half-closed cups of a pomegranate flower. Her dainty, perfectly shaped ears, her rose-red hands, her tiny feet, rounded and delicate like lotus buds, sparkle like the finest Ceylon pearls and the most dazzling Golconda diamonds. Her slender, supple waist, which a single hand could enclasp, sets off the elegant curve of her back and the fulsomeness of her bosom, in which the flowering of youth spreads forth its most perfect treasures, and, beneath the silken folds of her garments, she seems as if crafted in pure silver by the divine hand of Viswakarma,[3] the sculptor of the gods.

Putting aside these rhetorical flourishes, it is enough to say that Mrs Aouda, the widow of the rajah of Bundelkhand, was a charming woman, in the full European sense of the word. She spoke perfect English and the guide had certainly not been exaggerating when he said that this young Parsee woman had been transformed by her education.

Meanwhile the train was about to leave Allahabad station. The Parsee was waiting. Mr Fogg paid him his wages at the agreed rate, and not a penny extra. Passepartout was surprised at this because he realized how much his master owed to the guide's devotion to duty. After all the Parsee had willingly risked his life in the Pillagi business, and if he was later caught by the Hindus, he was unlikely to escape their vengeance.

There remained the question of Kiouni. What was to be done with an elephant that had cost so much?

But Phileas Fogg had already made up his mind about this matter.

'Parsee,' he said to the guide, 'you have been helpful and devoted. I have paid for your help but not for your devotion. Would you like this elephant? If so, he is yours.'

The guide's eyes lit up.

'Your honour is giving me a fortune!' he exclaimed.

'Take it, guide,' replied Mr Fogg, 'but even then I shall still be in your debt.'

'Well done!' exclaimed Passepartout. 'Take it, my friend! Kiouni is a trusty and courageous animal!'

Then he went up to the beast and gave him a few lumps of sugar, saying:

'Here, Kiouni. Here.'

The elephant gave out a few grunts of satisfaction. Then he took Passepartout by the waist and, wrapping his trunk around him, lifted him as high as his head. Passepartout showed no sign of fear and stroked the animal, which put him gently back on the ground. So, having received from the faithful Kiouni an elephant handshake, the dear fellow returned the compliment by taking the animal by the trunk and giving him a hearty human one.

A few minutes later Phileas Fogg, Sir Francis Cromarty and Passepartout were installed in a comfortable carriage, in which Mrs Aouda had the best seat, and were speeding towards Benares.

It is only eighty miles at the outside between the latter and Allahabad and it took just two hours to cover them.

During the journey the young woman came round completely. The effects of the hashish fumes had fully worn off.

It is easy to imagine her surprise at finding herself on a railway, in this compartment, wearing European clothes and surrounded by travellers who were total strangers!

First of all her companions showed her every care and attention and revived her with a few drops of spirits. Then the brigadier-general recounted what had befallen her. He stressed the devotion of Phileas Fogg, how he had not hesitated to put his own life at risk to rescue her, and the final outcome of the adventure, thanks to Passepartout's bold stroke.

Mr Fogg added nothing to the account. Passepartout looked very embarrassed and kept saying, 'It was nothing.'

Mrs Aouda thanked her rescuers profusely, by her tears more than by her words. More than her lips it was her beautiful eyes that expressed her gratitude. Then, as her thoughts returned to the scene of the suttee and as she looked out again on the land of India, where so many dangers still awaited her, she suddenly shuddered with fear.

Phileas Fogg realized what was going through Mrs Aouda's mind and to reassure her he offered, albeit without showing any sign of emotion, to accompany her to Hong Kong, where she would stay until this whole business died down.

Mrs Aouda gratefully accepted the offer. It was in Hong Kong in fact that one of her relatives lived, a Parsee like her, and one of the most important merchants in this city, which is thoroughly English, even though it is off the coast of China.

At half past midday, the train stopped in the station at Benares. Hindu legend has it that the present city stands on the site of the ancient Kasi, which was formerly suspended in space between the zenith and the nadir, like Mohammed's tomb.[4] But in these more prosaic times Benares, the Athens of India according to orientalists, had come back down to earth with a jolt, and for a moment Passepartout was able to glimpse its brick houses and its wattle huts, which give it an absolutely desolate appearance, devoid of all local colour.

This is where Sir Francis Cromarty was due to end his journey. The troops he was returning to were encamped a few miles to the north of the town. The brigadier-general therefore said his farewells to Phileas Fogg, wished him every success, and expressed the hope that he would continue his journey in a less eccentric but more profitable way. Mr Fogg lightly shook his companion's hand. Mrs Aouda's leave-taking showed far more affection. She would never forget what she owed Sir Francis Cromarty. As for Passepartout, he was given the honour of a real handshake by the brigadier-general. Visibly moved, he wondered where and when and how he might be able to be of service to him. Then they went their separate ways.

After Benares the railway went through part of the valley of the Ganges. When the weather was clear they could see, out of the windows of the carriage, the varied landscape of Bihar, then green-clad mountains, fields of barley, maize and wheat, rivers and pools infested with greenish alligators, well-kept villages and luxuriant forests. Some elephants and zebus with big humps went down to bathe in the waters of the sacred river, as did, despite the late time of year and the already low temperature, groups of Hindus of both sexes, who were ritually purifying themselves. These believers, sworn enemies of Buddhism, are faithful followers of the religion of Brahma, who is incarnated in three forms: Vishnu, the sun-god, Shiva, the divine personification of the forces of nature, and Brahma, the supreme ruler of priests and law-givers. But what could Brahma, Shiva and Vishnu be thinking of the now 'Britannicized' India that they looked on from above as a steamboat shrilly chugged past, disturbing the holy waters of the Ganges and scaring away the gulls that flew over its surface, the tortoises swarming along the riverbank and the faithful lying along its shores!

This whole panorama went past in a flash, and often its details were hidden by a cloud of smoke. The travellers scarcely managed a glimpse of the fort at Chunar, twenty miles south-west of Benares, the former stronghold of the rajahs of Bihar, Ghazipur and its large rosewater factories, the tomb of Lord Cornwallis,[5] erected on the left bank of the Ganges, the fortified town of Buxar, the large manufacturing and trading centre of Patna, with the largest opium market in India, and Monghyr, a town that is not merely European but as English as Manchester or Birmingham,[6] famous for its iron foundries, its hardware and arms factories, and whose tall chimneys belch out black smoke into Brahma's heavens – an affront to this idyllic landscape.

Then night came, and amid the howling of the tigers, bears and wolves that fled from the locomotive, the train went along at full speed, and nothing more could be seen of the beauties of Bengal, such as Golconda, the ruins of Gour, Murshidabad, its former capital, Burdwan, Hoogli or Chandernagore, a French outpost on Indian soil, over which Passepartout would have been proud to see the flag of his native land flying.

Finally at seven o'clock in the morning they reached Calcutta. The steamer bound for Hong Kong was not due to sail until midday. Phileas Fogg therefore had five hours in front of him.

According to his travel plan the gentleman had been due to arrive in the Indian capital on 25 October, twenty-three days after leaving London, and he had arrived on the appointed day. So he was neither behind nor ahead of schedule. Unfortunately the two days he had gained between London and Bombay had been lost, as has been seen, during the crossing of the Indian subcontinent. However, it can be safely assumed that Phileas Fogg did not regret them.

15

Where the bag of banknotes becomes another several thousand pounds lighter

The train had stopped at the station. Passepartout was the first to get out of the carriage, followed by Mr Fogg, who helped his young female companion to step down on to the platform. Phileas Fogg was intending to go straight to the steamer for Hong Kong, in order to see that Mrs Aouda was comfortably settled in, as he did not want to leave her on her own as long as she remained in this country where her safety was in danger.

Just as Mr Fogg was about to leave the station, a policeman came up to him and said, 'Mr Phileas Fogg?'

'Yes.'

'Is this man your servant?' added the policeman, pointing to Passepartout.

'Yes.'

'Would both of you please follow me.'

Mr Fogg did not betray the least sign of surprise. The officer was a representative of the law and for any Englishman the law is sacrosanct. Passepartout, reacting like a Frenchman, wanted to argue, but the policeman tapped him with his truncheon and Phileas Fogg motioned to him to obey.

'May this young lady come with us?' asked Mr Fogg.

'She may,' replied the policeman.

The policeman led Mr Fogg, Mrs Aouda and Passepartout towards a *palki-ghari*, a sort of four-wheeled, four-seater carriage, drawn by two horses. They set off. No one spoke during the journey, which lasted about twenty minutes.

The carriage first of all went through the Indian quarter, with its narrow streets, on either side of which stood huts swarming with a cosmopolitan, dirty and ragged population, then it entered the European quarter, with its attractive brick houses, shaded by coconut trees and bristling with ship masts. There, although it was still early in the morning, elegant riders and magnificent horse-drawn carriages were out and about.

The *palki-ghari* stopped in front of a plain-looking building, one that could not have been a private house. The policeman made his prisoners – there was no other word for them – get out and he led them into a room with bars on the windows, saying to them, 'At half past eight you will appear before Judge Obadiah.'

Then he withdrew and closed the door.

'That's it. We've been caught!' exclaimed Passepartout, collapsing on to a chair.

Mrs Aouda turned towards Mr Fogg and said to him in a voice that could not disguise her emotion:

'Sir, you must leave me behind. It's because of me that you're being prosecuted. It's because you came to my rescue.'

Phileas Fogg replied only that it was not possible. To be prosecuted for the business of the suttee! That was unacceptable. How could the plaintiffs dare to show themselves? There must be a mistake. Mr Fogg added that in any case he would not leave the young woman behind and would take her to Hong Kong.

'But the boat leaves at midday!' Passepartout pointed out.

'We'll be on board before twelve,' was all the impassive gentleman said in reply.

The statement was so categorical that Passepartout couldn't help saying to himself: 'Goodness me! There's no doubt about it. By midday we'll be on board!' But in fact he was far from convinced.

At half past eight the door in the room opened. The policeman reappeared and showed the prisoners into the adjoining room. It was a courtroom and a fairly large public, made up of Europeans and natives, was already inside.

Mr Fogg, Mrs Aouda and Passepartout sat down on a bench opposite the seats reserved for the magistrate and the clerk to the court.

The magistrate, Judge Obadiah, came in almost immediately, followed by the clerk of the court. He was a stout man with a roundish face. He took his wig down from a peg and put it on his head briskly.

'Call the first case,' he said.

Then, putting his hand, on his head, he exclaimed, 'Wait a minute. This isn't my wig!'

'Quite right, Mr Obadiah. It's mine,' replied the clerk.

'My dear Mr Oysterpuf, how do you expect a judge to pass judgment properly if he's wearing a clerk's wig?'

An exchange of wigs duly took place. During these preliminaries Passepartout could scarcely contain his impatience, because the hand on the large courtroom clock seemed to be moving extremely quickly.

'The first case,' repeated Judge Obadiah.

'Phileas Fogg?' said the clerk.

'Here I am,' replied Mr Fogg.

'Passepartout?'

'Present,' replied Passepartout.

'Good,' said the judge. 'Prisoners at the bar, for two days the police have been looking out for you on every train from Bombay.'

'But what are we accused of?' Passepartout cried out impatiently.

'You will soon find out,' replied the judge.

'Your Honour,' Mr Fogg then said, 'I am a British citizen and I have the right to –'

'Have you been treated disrespectfully?' asked Judge Obadiah.

'Not in the least.'

'Good! Bring in the plaintiffs.'

On the judge's orders a door opened and three Hindu priests were shown in by a doorman.

'Just as I thought,' mumbled Passepartout. 'These are the scoundrels who wanted to burn our young lady.'

The priests stood before the judge, and the clerk read out aloud the charge of sacrilege, brought against Phileas Fogg, Esq., and his servant, both accused of having violated a place sacred to the Hindu religion.

'Have you heard the charge?' the judge asked Phileas Fogg.

'Yes, my lord,' replied Mr Fogg, looking at his watch, 'and I plead guilty.'

'Ah, you plead guilty . . .'

'I plead guilty to the charge and I expect these three priests to plead guilty in turn to what they attempted to do at the temple of Pillagi.'

The priests looked at one another. They didn't seem to understand a word of what the accused was talking about.

'Certainly,' exclaimed Passepartout impetuously, 'at the temple of Pillagi, in front of which they were about to burn their victim!'

The priests looked even more mystified and the judge extremely surprised.

'What victim?' he asked. 'Burning who? In the middle of Bombay?'

'Bombay?' cried out Passepartout.

'Certainly. It's got nothing to do with the temple at Pillagi but the temple at Malabar Hill, in Bombay.'

'And as evidence of his guilt here are the shoes used by the perpetrator of that act of desecration,' added the clerk, placing a pair of shoes on his desk.

'My shoes!' shouted out Passepartout, who was surprised beyond belief and unable to prevent himself from coming out with this exclamation.

It is easy to understand the confusion in the minds of both master and servant. They had forgotten about the incident in the temple at Bombay, but this was what had brought them to court in Calcutta.

What had happened was that Fix had realized the advantage he could gain from this unfortunate business. Delaying his departure by two hours, he had given legal advice to the priests of Malabar Hill and had promised them a large sum in damages, knowing full well that the British government was very severe on this type of offence. Then he had sent them off by the next train hot in pursuit of the perpetrator of the sacrilege. However, as a result of the time it had taken to rescue the young widow, Fix and the Hindus arrived in Calcutta before Phileas Fogg and his servant, who were supposed to be arrested as soon as they stepped off the train after the magistrates had been alerted by telegram. It is easy to imagine Fix's disappointment when he discovered that Phileas Fogg had not yet arrived in the Indian capital. He must have thought that his thief had stopped off at one of the stations along the Peninsular Railway and taken refuge in the northern provinces. For twenty-four hours Fix had watched out for him at the station, beset with anxiety. Imagine, then, his joy when that very morning he saw him get out of the carriage, accompanied, it is true, by a young woman whose presence was a mystery to him. He immediately sent a policeman off to follow him and this is how Mr Fogg, Passepartout and the widow of the rajah from Bundelkhand were brought before Judge Obadiah.

What is more, if Passepartout had not been so taken up by his own situation he would have noticed in the corner of the courtroom the presence of the detective, who was following the proceedings with understandable interest, since here in Calcutta, as in Bombay and Suez, he was still without his arrest warrant.

However, Judge Obadiah had taken note of the admission of guilt that Passepartout had blurted out, though the latter would have given all he possessed to take back his reckless words.

'Are the facts admitted?' said the judge.

'Admitted,' Mr Fogg replied coldly.

'In so far as,' continued the judge, 'in so far as English law seeks to protect equally and strenuously all the religions of the peoples of India, the offence having been admitted by Master Passepartout, here convicted of having violated with his shoes the sanctity of the precincts of the temple of Malabar Hill during the day of 20 October, the court hereby condemns the aforesaid Passepartout to fifteen days' prison and a fine of £300.'

'£300!' exclaimed Passepartout, who was only really concerned about the fine.

'Silence,' barked the usher.

'And,' added Judge Obadiah, 'in so far as it has not been materially proven that there was no complicity between the servant and his master and in that in any case the latter must be held responsible for the deeds and actions of a servant in his employ, the court hereby detains the aforesaid Phileas Fogg and condemns him to eight days' prison and a fine of £150. Clerk, call the next case!'

Fix, in his corner, felt an inexpressible sense of satisfaction. Detaining Phileas Fogg for eight days in Calcutta gave more than enough time for the warrant to reach him.

Passepartout was dumbfounded. This sentence meant that his master was ruined. A £20,000 bet had been lost, all because he had casually wandered into that wretched temple!

Phileas Fogg, as firmly in control of himself as if the sentence concerned someone else, didn't raise an eyebrow. But just at the moment when the clerk was calling the next case, he rose to his feet and said, 'I wish to put up bail.'

'You are quite entitled to do so,' replied the judge.

Fix felt a shiver run down his spine, but he regained his composure when he heard the judge say that 'in so far as Phileas Fogg and his servant had the status of foreigners' he was fixing bail for each of them at the enormous sum of £1,000.

It would cost Mr Fogg £2,000 if he failed to serve his sentence.

'I shall pay,' the gentleman said.

With that he took from the bag that Passepartout was carrying a wad of banknotes and put them down on the clerk's desk.

'This sum of money will be returned to you when you leave prison,' said the judge. 'In the meantime you are free on bail.'

'Come on,' said Phileas Fogg to his servant.

'Let me at least have my shoes back!' exclaimed Passepartout angrily.

His shoes were given back to him.

'They're an expensive pair of shoes,' he muttered. 'More than a £1,000 each. Not to mention the fact that they're killing me!'

Passepartout was absolutely crestfallen as he followed Mr Fogg, who had offered Mrs Aouda his arm. Fix was still hoping that the thief would never be prepared to write off this sum of £2,000 and that he would do his eight days in prison. He therefore set off, following in Fogg's footsteps.

Mr Fogg called for a carriage, which Mrs Aouda, Passepartout and he got into straightaway. Fix ran behind the carriage, which soon came to a stop at one of the quaysides in the town.

Moored in the harbour half a mile offshore stood the

Rangoon, ready to sail. Eleven o'clock struck. Mr Fogg was an hour early. Fix saw him get out of the carriage and into a small boat along with Mrs Aouda and his servant. The detective kicked the ground with his foot.

'The wretch!' he exclaimed. 'He's off. £2,000 down the drain. A money-waster as well as a thief. Well, I shall follow him to the ends of the earth if necessary, but at this rate all the money stolen will have gone by then!'

The police inspector was justified in thinking this. It was certainly true that since leaving London, between the cost of travel, the money spent on rewards, buying an elephant and paying the bail and the fines, Phileas Fogg had already used up more than £5,000 to get this far, and the proportion of the amount recovered, which would go to the detectives, was getting smaller all the time.

16

Where Fix appears to have no knowledge at all of
what he's being told

The *Rangoon*, one of the steamers that the Peninsular and Oriental Company uses on its service over the China Seas and the Sea of Japan, was an iron-hulled, propeller-driven ship, weighing 1,770 tons unloaded with a nominal 400 horsepower. It was as fast as the *Mongolia* but not as comfortable. Mrs Aouda's needs were not therefore as well catered for as Phileas Fogg would have liked. It was, though, only a crossing of 3,500 miles, in other words eleven or twelve days, and the young woman did not prove to be a very demanding passenger.

Over the first few days of the crossing Mrs Aouda got to know Phileas Fogg better. At every opportunity she showed him the warmest gratitude. The phlegmatic gentleman listened to her with total detachment, or so it seemed, without betraying in his tone of voice or his reactions the slightest emotion. He saw to it that the young woman had everything she wanted. He would regularly come, at set times, if not to talk to her then at least to listen to her. He treated her with a scrupulous respect for the rules of politeness, but his method had all the charm and spontaneity of an automaton whose movements had been specifically designed for this purpose. Mrs Aouda didn't know exactly what to make of it, but Passepartout had explained to her a bit about his master's eccentric behaviour. He had told her about the bet, which was the reason for the gentleman's journey around the world. Mrs Aouda found this amusing, but after all she owed him her life, and this gratitude to her saviour could only further endear him to her.

Mrs Aouda confirmed the Hindu guide's account of her touching story. She did indeed belong to the highest social class in

Indian society. Several Parsee traders have made huge fortunes in India in the cotton trade. One of them, Sir James Jejeebhoy had been knighted by the British government and Mrs Aouda was related to this wealthy individual, who lived in Bombay. It was a cousin of this very Sir James, the Honourable Jejeeh, that she was expecting to meet up with in Hong Kong. Would he offer to take her in and help her? She couldn't say for sure. To which Mr Fogg replied that she shouldn't worry and that everything would turn out mathematically! That was the very word he used.

Did the young woman understand this appalling adverb? It is impossible to say. However, she looked at him with those great eyes of hers, eyes 'as clear as the sacred lakes of the Himalayas'. But the unyielding Mr Fogg, more buttoned up than ever, did not seem to be the sort of man who would plunge into such waters.

The first part of the crossing on board the *Rangoon* went perfectly. The weather was kind to them. All this part of the immense bay that sailors call 'the fathoms of Bengal' favoured the progress of the steamer. The *Rangoon* was soon within sight of Grand Andaman, the main island in the group, easily recognizable to navigators thanks to the picturesque mountain of Saddle Peak, 2,400 feet high.

They stayed quite close to the coast. The savage inhabitants of the island were nowhere to be seen. They stand at the very bottom of the human scale, but it is wrong to call them cannibals.

The panoramic view of the islands was magnificent. Immense forests of fan palms, areca palms, bamboo, nutmeg, teaks, giant mimosas and tree-ferns made up the landscape to the foreground and behind it stood the majestic backdrop of the mountains. The coastline was swarming with thousands of these precious sea-swallows whose edible nests provide the Chinese with one of their most sought after delicacies. But the whole of this diverse spectacle offered by the view of the Andaman Islands soon came to an end and the *Rangoon* headed swiftly for the Strait of Malacca, which led on to the China Seas.

Meanwhile, what had become of Inspector Fix, who had been so unfortunately caught up in this journey of circumnavigation?

As he was leaving Calcutta he gave orders for the arrest warrant, if it eventually arrived, to be sent to him in Hong Kong. He had been able to get on board the *Rangoon* without being noticed by Passepartout and he hoped to remain undiscovered until the steamer arrived. It would indeed have been difficult for him to explain his presence on board without arousing Passepartout's suspicions, since the latter must have thought he was in Bombay. But, as it turned out, he was destined to meet up with the dear fellow once again in circumstances that will soon be explained.

All the police inspector's hopes and desires were now concentrated on one single spot, Hong Kong, since the steamer did not stop in Singapore long enough for him to be able to do anything there. So it was in Hong Kong that the thief's arrest had to take place. Otherwise the thief would escape him for good, so to speak.

Hong Kong was, it must be remembered, another British possession, but it was the last one on the journey. After that, China, Japan and America offered a more or less safe haven to this man Fogg. In Hong Kong, if he finally got hold of the arrest warrant that must surely be on its way, Fix could arrest Fogg and hand him over to the local police. There was no problem about that. But after Hong Kong a straightforward arrest warrant would no longer be enough. Extradition papers would be needed. That would lead to further delay, lengthy procedures and obstacles of all sorts, which the scoundrel would take advantage of to get away once and for all. If the operation failed in Hong Kong, it would be, if not downright impossible, at least very difficult to repeat it with any real chance of success.

'So,' Fix kept saying to himself during the long hours he spent in his cabin, 'so, either the warrant is in Hong Kong and I can arrest my man, or it isn't and in that case I'll have to delay his departure at all costs. I failed in Bombay and I failed in Calcutta. If things don't work out in Hong Kong my reputation will be ruined. Whatever happens I must succeed. But what's the best way of delaying, if necessary, the departure of this wretched man Fogg?'

As a last resort Fix was quite determined to reveal everything to Passepartout, to make him realize the truth about the master he served, even though he definitely wasn't his accomplice. After being enlightened by these revelations, Passepartout would fear being implicated and would certainly side with him, Fix. Nevertheless, this was a risky tactic and one only to be used when all else had failed. One word from Passepartout to his master would be enough to completely wreck the whole plan.

The police inspector was therefore in a very awkward position, until the presence of Mrs Aouda on board the *Rangoon* opened up some new possibilities for him.

Who exactly was this woman? What was the combination of circumstances that had made her Fogg's companion? The meeting must obviously have taken place between Bombay and Calcutta. But where exactly on the Indian subcontinent? Was it chance that had brought together Phileas Fogg and the young woman traveller? Or on the contrary had the gentleman undertaken his trip to India in order to meet up with this delightful person? And delightful she certainly was. Fix had realized this well enough in the courtroom in Calcutta.

It is easy to understand how intriguing all this must have been for the detective. He wondered if there might not be an element of criminal abduction about this business. Yes! That must be it! This idea took a firm hold in Fix's mind and he realized all the advantage he could derive from the situation. Whether the young woman was married or not, it was still an abduction, and in Hong Kong it was possible to stir up enough trouble for the abductor for him not simply to buy his way out.

But something had to be done before the *Rangoon* reached Hong Kong. This man Fogg had the unpleasant habit of hopping from one boat to another, and before the operation got going he might already be far away.

So the main thing was to alert the British authorities, and to inform them that the *Rangoon* was on its way before it actually arrived. In fact, nothing could be simpler, since the steamer was due to put in at Singapore and Singapore is linked to the Chinese mainland by telegraph.

However, before doing anything, and just to be on the safe side, Fix made up his mind to question Passepartout. He knew that it wasn't very difficult to get this chap to talk, and so he decided to drop his disguise. There was therefore no time to lose. It was 30 October and the following day the *Rangoon* was due to put in at Singapore.

Accordingly, that very day Fix left his cabin and went up on deck with the intention of going up to Passepartout and making great play of how surprised he was to see him. Passepartout was walking around the fore of the ship when the detective inspector rushed towards him, exclaiming, 'Fancy seeing you on the *Rangoon*.'

'Mr Fix on board!' replied Passepartout, completely taken by surprise, recognizing his companion from the crossing on the *Mongolia*. 'Amazing! I left you in Bombay and I meet up with you again on the way to Hong Kong! Are you going around the world, too?'

'No, no. I'm intending to stop in Hong Kong – at least for a few days.'

'Oh,' said Passepartout who seemed taken aback for a moment. 'But how come I haven't seen you on board since we left Calcutta?'

'Well, I didn't feel too good ... seasickness ... I was lying down in my cabin ... the Bay of Bengal didn't suit me as much as the Indian Ocean. What about your master, Mr Phileas Fogg?'

'In perfect health, and as punctual as his travel plan. Not a day late! Oh, Mr Fix, you won't know this, but we have a young lady with us.'

'A young lady?' replied the detective, giving a perfect imitation of someone who didn't understand what he was being told.

But Passepartout had soon put him in the picture. He recounted the incident at the temple in Bombay, the purchase of an elephant for £2,000, the business of the suttee, the rescue of Mrs Aouda, the conviction at the court in Calcutta and the release on bail. Fix, who knew the last part of the story, pretended not to know any of it and Passepartout let himself get carried away, relishing the opportunity to relate his adventures to a listener who showed so much interest in what he had to say.

'But, when it comes down to it,' asked Fix, 'does your master intend to take this young lady to Europe?'

'Certainly not, Mr Fix. Certainly not. We simply intend to hand her over safely to one of her relatives, a wealthy business-man in Hong Kong.'

'Nothing doing,' the detective said to himself, disguising his disappointment. 'How about a glass of gin, Mr Passepartout?'

'Delighted, Mr Fix. The least we can do is drink to our meeting on board the *Rangoon*.'

17

*In which various matters are dealt with during the
crossing from Singapore to Hong Kong*

From that day on Passepartout and the detective met each other
frequently, but the policeman was extremely guarded towards
his companion and made no attempt to make him talk. On one
or two occasions only did he catch sight of Mr Fogg, who was
happy to remain in the main lounge of the *Rangoon*, either
because he was keeping Mrs Aouda company or because he was
playing whist, an unvarying part of his daily routine.

Passepartout, for his part, had begun to think very hard about
the strange coincidence that had resulted once again in Fix
meeting up with his master during their travels and, all in
all, that was hardly surprising. This gentleman, who was very
friendly and certainly very obliging, who had turned up in Suez
then embarked on the *Mongolia* and disembarked at Bombay,
where he said he had to stay, who then showed up again on the
Rangoon, on the way to Hong Kong, who in a word was
following Mr Fogg step by step on his journey: all this really
was something to think about. There was something strange, at
the very least, about all these coincidental meetings. Who was
this Fix after? Passepartout was ready to bet his oriental slippers
– he had taken great care of them – that this Fix fellow would
leave Hong Kong at the same time as them and probably by the
same steamer.

Passepartout could have gone on thinking for a hundred years
and still not have guessed what business Fix was about. He
would never have imagined that Phileas Fogg was being trailed
by a detective all around the world like a common thief. But as
it is only human nature to attempt to find an explanation for
everything, this is how Passepartout, in a sudden flash of illumi-

nation, interpreted the fact of Fix's permanent presence, and in all fairness his interpretation was perfectly plausible. According to him, then, Fix was, and could only be, a private investigator set on Mr Fogg's trail by his colleagues from the Reform Club, in order to check that he followed the agreed route in his journey around the world.

'It's obvious! It's obvious!' the dear fellow repeated to himself, proud of how clever he was. 'He's a spy that these gentlemen have set on our trail. It's just not fair! Mr Fogg is so upright and honourable. To have him spied on by a private investigator! Well, members of the Reform Club, you're really going to pay for this!'

Passepartout, though he was delighted by his discovery, decided to say nothing about it to his master, in case the latter felt justifiably hurt at the way his opponents distrusted him. But he swore that he would take the mickey out of Fix when the opportunity arose, but discreetly and without showing that he was in the know.

On the afternoon of Wednesday 30 October, the *Rangoon* entered the Strait of Malacca, which separates the Malaya peninsula from the island of Sumatra. The main island was hidden from view by very picturesque small islands with steeply sloping mountains.

The next day, at four o'clock in the morning, the *Rangoon*, which was half a day ahead of schedule on the crossing put in at Singapore,[1] in order to take on a new supply of coal.

Phileas Fogg noted this gain in the plus column of his ledger and this time went ashore to accompany Mrs Aouda, who had indicated that she would like to look around for a few hours.

Fix, who was suspicious of everything Fogg did, followed without being seen. Passepartout, for his part, laughing to himself at Fix's antics, went off to do his usual shopping.

The island of Singapore is not particularly large or impressive. It lacks mountains to make it attractive. However, there is a certain charm to its compactness. It resembles a park with fine roads going through it. A handsome carriage drawn by elegant horses specially brought from Australia transported Mrs Aouda and Phileas Fogg through groves of luxuriant palm trees and clove trees, the fruit of which comes from the blossom of the half-opened flower. Instead of the prickly hedges to be found in the countryside of Europe, here there were pepper bushes. Sago trees, large ferns with their magnificent fronds, gave variety to the tropical vegetation and the air was thick with the intense perfume of nutmeg trees, with their shiny green foliage. Hordes of lively, grinning monkeys roamed around the woods, and there were probably tigers, too, in the jungle. Anyone surprised at the idea that these terrifying carnivores had not been eliminated on such a relatively small island should realize that they come from Malacca, by swimming across the strait.

After travelling around the countryside for a couple of hours, Mrs Aouda and her companion – who took little notice of what he saw – went back into the town, a large concentration of squat houses surrounded by delightful gardens in which grow mangosteens, pineapples and all the most delicious kinds of fruits. At ten o'clock they arrived back at the steamer, having been followed, without realizing it, by the inspector, who had also had to go to the expense of hiring a carriage.

Passepartout was waiting for them on the deck of the *Rangoon*. The dear fellow had bought a few dozens mangosteens, the size of an average apple, dark brown on the outside and bright red inside. The white flesh melts between the lips and is a source of unique pleasure to the true connoisseur. Passepartout was only too pleased to present them to Mrs Aouda, who graciously accepted them.

At eleven o'clock the *Rangoon*, having filled up with coal, slipped its moorings, and a few hours later the passengers lost sight of the high mountains of Malacca, whose forests are home to the finest tigers in the world.

There are about 1,300 miles between Singapore and the island of Hong Kong, a small British possession separated from the Chinese mainland. Phileas Fogg needed to cover this distance in six days at the most in order to be in Hong Kong in time to catch the boat that was due to leave on 6 November for Yokohama, one of the main ports in Japan.

The *Rangoon* was heavily loaded. A large number of passengers had boarded at Singapore, Indians, Singhalese, Chinese,

Malays and Portuguese, most of whom were in the second-class accommodation.

The weather, which had been generally fine up to then, changed as the moon entered its last quarter. The sea became rough. The wind sometimes got up, but very fortunately it was blowing from the south-east, which helped the steamer to go faster. When the wind was moderate the captain put up the sails. The *Rangoon*, which had the rigging of a brig, often sailed with its two topsails and its foresail, and its speed increased under the combined effect of steam and wind. And so it was that they followed the coastline of Annam and Cochin China[2] on a choppy and very tiring sea.

But the fault for this lay with the *Rangoon* rather than the sea and it was the steamer that the passengers, most of whom were seasick, should have blamed for their exhaustion.

The truth is that the ships of the P&O line which sail the China Seas have a serious design fault. The ratio between their draught when laden and their depth has been wrongly calculated and as a result they lack stability in heavy seas. The volume of the ship that is enclosed and watertight is insufficient. The ships are 'drowned', to use the sailing term, and because of this lay-out, a few heavy waves washing over the deck are enough to slow them down. These ships are therefore far inferior – if not by their engines and their steam apparatus, then at least in their design – to the sorts of ships used by the French mail service, such as the *Impératrice* and the *Cambodge*. Whereas, according to the engineers' calculations, the latter can take on board a weight of water equal to their own weight before sinking, the P&O ships, the *Golconda*, the *Korea* and lastly the *Rangoon*, could not take on board a sixth of their weight without going down.

Thus, when the weather was bad, extreme caution was needed. It was sometimes necessary to heave to at low steam. The resulting loss of time did not seem to affect Phileas Fogg in the least, but Passepartout got extremely annoyed. At such times he blamed the captain, the chief engineer and the Company, and he cursed all those involved in transporting passengers. Perhaps, too, the thought of the gas bill he would have to pay back in Savile Row had something to do with his impatience.

'Are you really in such a hurry to get to Hong Kong?' the detective asked him one day.

'Very much so,' replied Passepartout.

'Do you think Mr Fogg is in a rush to catch the steamer to Yokohama?'

'A terrible rush.'

'Do you really believe in this bizarre journey around the world?'

'Absolutely. What about you, Mr Fix?'

'Me? I don't believe a word of it.'

'You're a real jester,' replied Passepartout, winking at him.

This word gave the detective food for thought. The choice of the term worried him, though he wasn't too sure why. Had the Frenchman seen through him? He wasn't sure what to think. But how could Passepartout have realized that he was a detective when he had been careful to keep it secret? Nevertheless, when speaking to him like that, Passepartout must certainly have had something at the back of his mind.

In the event, the dear fellow went even further another day. He just couldn't help himself. He couldn't hold his tongue.

'Come on, Mr Fix,' he said to his companion mischievously. 'Is it true that after we get to Hong Kong we will no longer have the pleasure of your company?'

'Well,' replied Mr Fix, looking rather embarrassed, 'I'm not sure. Perhaps I . . .'

'Oh,' said Passepartout, 'if you were to stay with us, I would be delighted. Why on earth would an employee of P&O want to break off his journey? You were only going to Bombay and now you are almost in China. America's not far away, and from America to Europe is no distance at all.'

Fix looked carefully at his fellow passenger, who had the friendliest of expressions on his face, and decided to laugh along with him. However, the latter, who was in good spirits, asked him if this job of his was 'a good little earner'.

'Yes and no,' said Fix without batting an eyelid. 'There are times when it is and times when it isn't. But, as you will quite understand, it's not me who's paying for the trip.'

'Oh, I'm quite sure of that!' exclaimed Passepartout, laughing even more.

That was the end of the conversation. Fix went back to his cabin and began to think things over. It was obvious that he'd been found out. One way or another, the Frenchman had worked out that he was a detective. But had he warned his master? What was his role in all this? Was he an accomplice or not? The secret was out and the game was up. The detective spent a few difficult hours, sometimes believing that all was lost, sometimes hoping that Fogg was not aware of the situation, and in the end not knowing what to do next.

However, after a while his mind became more settled and he decided that he would come clean with Passepartout. If it did not prove possible to arrest Fogg in Hong Kong and if Fogg was preparing to leave British soil once and for all, then he, Fix, would tell Passepartout everything. Either the servant was his master's accomplice and Fogg knew everything – in which case the game was definitely up – or the servant had nothing to do with the theft – and then it would be to his advantage to give up on the thief.

This, then, was the situation between the two men, while Phileas Fogg, for his part, sailed on, majestically indifferent. He continued on his scientifically calculated orbit around the world, without bothering about the asteroids gravitating around him.

And yet in the vicinity there was – to use a term from astronomy – a 'disturbing' star, one that should have produced a certain amount of disturbance in the gentleman's heart. But no. Mrs Aouda's charm had no such effect, much to Passepartout's surprise, and such disturbances, if they did exist, would have been more difficult to detect than those on Uranus that had led to the discovery of Neptune.[3]

Yes. This was an unfailing source of amazement to Passepartout, who read all that gratitude towards his master in the young woman's eyes. It was clear that Phileas Fogg had what it took to be a hero, but certainly not what was needed to be a lover. As for concern about the success of the journey, he gave no sign of any. Passepartout, however, was constantly on tenterhooks. One day when he was leaning on the handrail of the engine room, he watched the powerful machinery race away from time to time as the boat pitched suddenly, making the propeller spin

wildly clean out of the water. Steam then came pouring out of
the valves, making the dear fellow very angry.

'These valves aren't properly weighted down,' he exclaimed.
'We aren't going fast enough. That's the English for you! If only
it was an American boat. We might go up in smoke, but at least
we'd be travelling faster!'

18

In which Phileas Fogg, Passepartout and Fix all go about their business, but separately

In the final days of the crossing the weather was quite bad. The wind became very strong, and because it was blowing from the north-west it slowed down the steamer's progress. The *Rangoon*, because of its lack of stability, rolled heavily and the passengers were entitled to feel a certain resentment towards the high waves that were whipped up by the wind from the open sea and that made them feel sick.

During 3 and 4 November there was quite a storm. Fierce gusts of wind lashed the sea. The *Rangoon* had to heave to for half a day, with its engine only ticking over so as to ride out the storm. All the sails had been furled, but even then the rigging whistled in the high wind.

As can well be imagined, the speed of the steamer was considerably reduced, and it was reasonable to assume that the arrival time in Hong Kong would be twenty hours later than scheduled, or even more if the storm did not abate.

Phileas Fogg observed this spectacle of a raging sea, which seemed to have been unleashed against him in particular, with his usual impassiveness. His expression showed no sign of anxiety, and yet a delay of twenty hours could put the whole journey in jeopardy by making him miss the departure of the steamer for Yokohama. But this man, who seemed totally imperturbable, felt neither impatience nor boredom. It really seemed as if the storm was part of his plan, that it had been taken into account. When discussing this setback with her companion, Mrs Aouda found him as calm as before.

Fix didn't see things in the same light. Far from it. This storm was exactly what he wanted. His satisfaction would have known no bounds if the *Rangoon* had been forced to run before the storm. Any delay like this suited him because it would force this man Fogg to spend a few days in Hong Kong. At last the weather, in the form of gusts and gales, was on his side. Admittedly he wasn't well, but what did that matter! He lost count of the number of times he'd been sick, but when his body was writhing from the effects of seasickness his mind was revelling in an immense sense of satisfaction.

As for Passepartout, it is easy to imagine what little effort he made to disguise his anger during this ordeal. Up until then everything had gone so well. Land and sea seemed at his master's command. Steamers and railways obeyed him. Wind and steam united to further his progress. Was this the turning-point with things starting to go wrong? Passepartout was on tenterhooks, as if the £20,000 for the bet had come out of his own pocket. The storm got on his nerves, the gale infuriated him and he would happily have whipped the sea for its disobedience.[1] Poor chap! Fix was careful to conceal from him his personal satisfaction and that was the sensible thing to do, because if Passepartout had sensed his secret enjoyment of the situation, Fix would have been in for it.

Passepartout stayed outside on the *Rangoon* all the time the gale lasted. He wouldn't have been able to remain below deck. He climbed aloft, to the surprise of the crew, and, with the agility of a monkey, helped out with everything. He constantly questioned the captain, the officers and the men, who couldn't help laughing when they saw how put out the fellow was. Passepartout wanted to know how long the storm would last. So they told him to go and look at the barometer, which stubbornly refused to rise. Passepartout shook the barometer, but nothing had any effect, neither shaking it nor hurling insults at the irresponsible instrument.

Finally the storm abated. The state of the sea changed during the day of 4 November. The wind shifted two points to the south and helped their progress again.

Passepartout calmed down like the weather. It was possible to put back the topsails and the lower sails, and the *Rangoon* continued its journey at an impressive rate of knots.

But it was not possible to make up all the time lost. The situation had to be accepted and land was not sighted until the 6th at five o'clock in the morning. The entry in Phileas Fogg's travel plan gave the steamer's date of arrival as the 5th, but the ship would not be there until the 6th. That meant that they would be twenty-four hours late and bound to miss the departure for Yokohama.

At six o'clock the pilot came on board the *Rangoon* and took his place on the bridge in order to guide the ship through the approaches to the port of Hong Kong.

Passepartout was dying to question this man and to ask him if the steamer for Yokohama had already left Hong Kong. But he didn't dare to, preferring to retain a glimmer of hope until the last minute. He had confessed his concerns to Fix, who, the sly old fox that he was, attempted to console him by saying that all Mr Fogg had to do was to catch the next boat. This only made Passepartout even more angry.

However, if Passepartout wasn't so bold as to question the pilot, Mr Fogg, on the other hand, after looking in his *Bradshaw*, asked the said person in that calm way of his if he knew when there'd be a boat from Hong Kong to Yokohama.

'Tomorrow, on the morning tide,' replied the pilot.

'Oh!' said Mr Fogg without showing any sign of surprise.

Passepartout, who was present at this exchange, would have liked to embrace the pilot, whereas Fix would have liked to wring his neck.

'What's the name of the steamer?' asked Mr Fogg.

'The *Carnatic*,' replied the pilot.

'But wasn't it due to leave yesterday?'

'Yes, sir, but it needed repairs to one of its boilers, and so its departure has been put back until tomorrow.'

'Thank you,' replied Mr Fogg, who with his machine-like walk went back down into the lounge of the *Rangoon*.

As for Passepartout, he grabbed the pilot's hand and shook it vigorously, saying, 'Pilot, you really are a good man.'

The pilot no doubt never understood why his replies produced such a warm-hearted response. When the whistle sounded he went back to the bridge and guided the steamer in through the armada of junks, tankas,[2] fishing boats and ships of all sorts that cluttered up the approaches to Hong Kong.

By one o'clock the *Rangoon* had docked and the passengers were disembarking.

In the event, it must be said that things really had worked out in Phileas Fogg's favour. If it hadn't been for the need to repair the boilers, the *Carnatic* would have left on 5 November and anyone travelling to Japan would have had an eight-day wait for the next steamer to leave. Admittedly Mr Fogg was twenty-four hours behind schedule, but this delay couldn't have serious repercussions on the rest of the journey.

As it happened, the steamer that did the crossing from Yokohama to San Francisco was a direct connection for the steamer from Hong Kong and it couldn't leave before the latter had arrived. Of course, they would be twenty-four hours behind in reaching Yokohama, but it would be easy to make this time up during the twenty-two days it took to cross the Pacific. So Phileas Fogg was, give or take twenty-four hours, on schedule thirty-five days after leaving London.

As the *Carnatic* was not due to leave until five o'clock the next morning, Mr Fogg had sixteen hours in front of him to sort out his affairs, those concerning Mrs Aouda, that is. As they got off the ship he offered the young woman his arm and escorted her to a palanquin. He asked the porters for the name of a hotel and they suggested the Club Hotel. The palanquin set off, with Passepartout following, and twenty minutes later it arrived at its destination.

Phileas Fogg booked a suite for the young woman and saw to it that she had everything she wanted. Then he said to Mrs Aouda that he was going off immediately in search of this relative of hers, in whose safe-keeping he would leave her in Hong Kong. At the same time he told Passepartout to stay in the hotel until he came back, so that the young woman was not left on her own.

The gentleman then had himself driven to the Stock Exchange, where everyone was sure to know someone as important as the Honourable Jejeeh, one of the richest businessmen in the city.

The broker who Mr Fogg spoke to did indeed know the Parsee

businessman. However, the latter had not lived in China for the past two years. After making his fortune he had settled in Europe – probably Holland, which was understandable given the large number of trading connections he had had with that country during his time as a businessman.

Phileas Fogg went back to the Club Hotel. He immediately asked Mrs Aouda's permission to go up to see her and, getting straight to the point, informed her that the Honourable Jejeeh no longer lived in Hong Kong and that he was probably in Holland.

At first Mrs Aouda made no reply. She put her hand to her forehead and thought for a few moments. Then she said in that gentle voice of hers, 'What should I do, Mr Fogg?'

'It's quite simple,' the gentleman replied. 'Come to Europe.'

'But I can't take advantage –'

'You are not taking advantage and your presence will not harm my plans in the least . . . Passepartout?'

'Sir?' replied Passpartout.

'Go along to the *Carnatic* and reserve three cabins.'

Passepartout, delighted to be able to continue the journey in the company of the young woman, who was so considerate towards him, left the Club Hotel immediately.

19

*Where Passepartout takes too keen an interest in his
master and what that leads to*

Hong Kong is only a small island, ceded to Great Britain by the
Treaty of Nanking[1] after the war of 1842. Within the space of
a few years the colonizing spirit of the British was responsible
for the building of a large town and the creation of a port,
Victoria Harbour. The island is situated at the mouth of the
Canton River and only sixty miles separate it from the Portuguese possession of Macao, which stands on the opposite bank.
It was inevitable that Hong Kong would be the victorious rival
of Macao as a trading centre,[2] and now most Chinese goods
for export transit via the British possession. Docks, hospitals,
wharves, warehouses, a Gothic cathedral, a government house
and tarmacked roads all give the visitor the impression that
a typical busy town in the south-east of England has been
transported halfway across the globe and has landed here in
China, almost at the antipodes.

So Passepartout, with his hands in his pockets, went along to
Victoria Harbour, watching on his way the palanquins, the
sail-powered wheelbarrows, still popular in the Celestial
Empire,[3] and this whole crowd of Chinese, Japanese and Europeans thronging the streets. Give or take a few differences, the
dear fellow found it was like walking through Bombay, Calcutta
or Singapore. The English have left a trail of similar cities around
the world.

Passepartout reached Victoria Harbour. There, at the mouth
of the Canton River, he saw a heaving mass of ships from all
over the world, English, French, American, Dutch, warships
and trading vessels, Japanese or Chinese boats, junks, sampans,
tankas and even flower-boats that looked like gardens floating

on water. As he walked around, Passepartout noticed that some of the native inhabitants were dressed in yellow, all of them very elderly. After going into a barbershop to have a Chinese-style shave, he was told by the local barber, who spoke quite good English, that these elderly men were at least eighty years old, and from that age on they were given the privilege of wearing yellow, the imperial colour. Passepartout found this very amusing, without quite knowing why.

Once his beard was shaved he went along to the quay from where the *Carnatic* was due to depart and there he caught sight of Fix, who was walking up and down, which didn't surprise him. However, the inspector's face bore the sign of severe disappointment.

'Good!' thought Passepartout. 'Things must be going badly for those gentlemen members of the Reform Club.'

So he went up to Fix with a broad smile, pretending not to notice his companion's look of annoyance.

The detective really had every reason to curse the appalling bad luck that dogged him. There was still no sign of the warrant. It was obvious that the warrant was still on its way and could only reach him if he stayed put for a few days. Since Hong Kong was indeed the last British territory on the route, this Fogg fellow would get away once and for all unless he found some way of keeping him here.

'Well then, Mr Fix, have you made up your mind to come to America with us?' asked Passepartout.

'Yes,' replied Fix, gritting his teeth.

'Now, now!' exclaimed Passepartout, in a joyful burst of laughter. 'I was sure you wouldn't be able to let us go off like that on our own. Come and book your seat. Come on!'

So the two men went into the shipping office and booked cabins for four people. But the employee pointed out that as the repairs to the *Carnatic* had been completed, the steamer would be leaving that evening at eight o'clock and not the following morning, as had been announced.

'Very good!' replied Passepartout. 'That will suit my master. I'll go and tell him.'

At that moment Fix decided on an extreme course of action.

He would tell Passepartout everything. It was perhaps the only way to keep Phileas Fogg in Hong Kong for a few more days.

After they had left the office Fix offered to take his companion for a drink in a nearby tavern. Passepartout had time, so he accepted Fix's invitation.

There was a tavern fronting on to the quayside. It looked inviting and both men went in. There was a large, well-decorated room, at the back of which stood a camp-bed, scattered with cushions. On the bed a number of men were stretched out, asleep.

Thirty or so customers were in the main room sitting at small rattan tables. Some of them were downing pints of English beer, ale or porter, others flagons of spirits, gin or brandy. In addition most of them were smoking long pipes made of red clay, stuffed with small pellets of opium mixed with attar of roses. Then, from time to time, some helpless smoker collapsed under the table and the barmen would take him by the head and feet and carry him on to the camp-bed near a fellow smoker. About twenty of these drunkards were thus laid out side by side, in an advanced state of drugged stupor.

Fix and Passepartout realized that they had walked into a den frequented by the drugged, emaciated, stupefied wretches to whom England sells annually for its commercial gain more than £11,000,000 of that fateful drug called opium. What a terrible source of wealth, one derived from exploiting one of the most deadly of human vices!

The Chinese government has attempted to tackle this problem by introducing strict laws, but to no avail. The use of opium has spread from the upper classes, for whom it was at first exclusively reserved, to the lower classes, and since then its disastrous effects have proved unstoppable. Opium is smoked everywhere and at any time in the Middle Kingdom. Both men and women are addicted to this deplorable habit and once they have become used to taking the drug they cannot go without it without experiencing severe stomach pains. A heavy opium smoker may smoke as many as eight pipes a day but will die within five years.

Their search for a drink had, then, led Fix and Passepartout into one of the many dens of this type that have sprung up even in Hong Kong. Passepartout didn't have any money, but he was happy to accept his companion's offer of a drink, though he insisted on returning the compliment at the right time and place.

They ordered two bottles of port, which the Frenchman proved very keen on, whereas Fix was more circumspect and observed his companion very carefully. They talked about this and that and especially about Fix's brilliant idea of travelling with them on the *Carnatic*. After this mention of the *Carnatic*, which was due to leave several hours earlier than planned, Passepartout got to his feet, now that the bottles were empty, in order to go off to inform his master of the situation.

Fix held him back.

'Just a moment,' he said.

'What do you want, Mr Fix?'

'I need to speak to you about some serious matters.'

'Serious matters!' exclaimed Passepartout as he drank up a few drops that had remained at the bottom of his glass. 'Well, we'll discuss them tomorrow. I don't have time today.'

'Stay a minute,' replied Fix. 'It's about your master.'

At the mention of this word Passepartout looked carefully at the expression on Fix's face.

He had a strange look, Passepartout thought. He sat down again.

'So what exactly have you got to say to me?' he asked.

Fix put his hand on his companion's arm and whispered, 'Have you worked out who I am?'

'I should say so,' said Passepartout, smiling.

'In that case I'm going to come clean with you . . .'

'Now that I already know everything, old chum! Well, so much for that! On the other hand, why not? But before you do so, let me just tell you that these gentlemen from the club have been wasting their money.'

'Wasting their money?' said Fix. 'It's easy for you to talk. You obviously don't have any idea of the amount of money involved.'

'But I certainly do,' replied Passepartout. '£20,000!'

'£55,000!' continued Fix, squeezing the Frenchman's hand.

'What!' exclaimed Passepartout. 'Fancy Mr Fogg daring to go so far! £55,000! Well, that's all the more reason not to lose a second,' he said as he got to his feet again.

'£55,000,' Fix went on, forcing Passepartout to sit down again after ordering another flagon of brandy. 'And if I'm successful I earn a reward of £2,000. Would you fancy £500, if you agree to help me?'

'To help you?' cried out Passepartout, whose eyes were popping out of his head.

'Yes, to help me keep this Fogg fellow in Hong Kong for a few days.'

'Hey!' said Passepartout. 'What are you talking about? What? Not only do these gentlemen have my master followed, and doubt his honesty, but they also want to put obstacles in his path! I feel ashamed for them.'

'Hang on. What do you mean?' asked Fix.

'I mean that it's completely unacceptable behaviour. You might as well strip Mr Fogg of his belongings and take the money out of his pocket.'

'Well, that's exactly what we expect it to come to.'

'But it's a trap!' exclaimed Passepartout, excited by the effects of the brandy that Fix was serving him and that he was drinking without realizing it. 'A real trap, set by so-called gentlemen and colleagues!'

Fix was beginning to lose track.

'Call them colleagues!' shouted Passepartout. 'Members of the Reform Club! Remember this, Mr Fix. My master is an honourable man and when he's made a bet he intends to win it fairly.'

'But who do you think I am?' asked Fix, looking straight at Passepartout.

'I'll tell you, all right. You're a private investigator for the members of the Reform Club, given the job of checking up on the route my master's taking. It's a disgrace! So, although I guessed what you were some time ago, I've been careful not to tell Mr Fogg.'

'He doesn't know anything about this, does he?' Fix asked sharply.

'Nothing,' replied Passepartout downing another glass of brandy.

The police inspector scratched his forehead. He waited before going on. What was he to do? Passepartout's mistake seemed genuine, but it made his plan more difficult. It was obvious that this fellow was speaking in complete good faith and that he wasn't his master's accomplice – something which Fix might have feared.

'Well,' he said to himself, 'if he's not his accomplice he'll be prepared to help me.'

The detective had come to a second decision. In any case, he had no time to lose. Phileas Fogg had to be arrested in Hong Kong at all costs.

'Listen,' said Fix curtly, 'listen to me carefully. I'm not what you think. I'm not a private detective for the members of the Reform Club.'

'Huh!' said Passepartout, looking at him mockingly.

'I'm a police inspector, working for the Metropolitan Police.'

'You . . . A police inspector!'

'Yes, and I can prove it. Here's my commission.'

With that, the detective took a piece of paper from his wallet and showed to his companion a commission signed by the head of the Metropolitan Police. Passepartout was dumbfounded and unable to say a word.

'Mr Fogg's bet is just a front, which you've fallen for, you and his colleagues from the Reform Club, because it was important for him to make you his accomplices without you realizing it.'

'But why?' cried out Passepartout.

'Listen. On 28 September a theft involving £55,000 was committed at the Bank of England by an individual whom we have a description of. That description fits exactly this man Fogg.'

'Come off it!' exclaimed Passepartout, banging the table with his hefty fist. 'My master is the most honest man in the world.'

'How can you tell?' replied Fix. 'You don't even know him. You started to work for him the day you set off and he left in a considerable hurry with a madcap excuse, without any luggage, and taking with him a large amount of money in banknotes. And you still maintain that he's an honest man!'

'I do. I do,' the poor fellow repeated, like a machine.

'Do you want to be arrested as his accomplice, then?'

Passepartout had his head in his hands. He was unrecognizable. He didn't dare look at the police inspector. Phileas Fogg, a thief? The very man who had rescued Mrs Aouda, a good and a generous man? And yet there was no denying the evidence against him. Passepartout tried to brush aside the suspicions that were creeping into his mind. He refused to believe his master was guilty.

'Well then, what do you want from me?' he said to the policeman with a supreme effort of self-restraint.

'Just this,' replied Fix. 'I've trailed this fellow Fogg all this way, but I still haven't received the arrest warrant that I've requested from London. I need you to help me to keep him in Hong Kong.'

'What! You want me to –'

'And then I'll give you a share of the £2,000 reward put up by the Bank of England.'

'Never,' replied Passepartout, who wanted to get up but fell back down, feeling both his wits and his strength deserting him at the same time. 'Mr Fix,' he stammered, 'even if everything you say is true . . . even if my master was the thief you're after . . . which I don't believe for a moment . . . I've worked for him . . . I still work for him . . . I know how kind and generous he is . . . Betray him . . . never . . . no, not for all the money in the world. Where I come from, that's just not the sort of thing people go in for . . .'

'So you refuse?'

'I refuse.'

'Let's just forget everything I've said,' replied Fix, 'and have a drink.'

'Yes. Let's have a drink.'

Passepartout was feeling the effects of the alcohol more and more. Fix realized that he needed to separate him from his master at all costs and wanted to finish the job off. On the table were a few pipes, stuffed with opium. Fix slipped one into

Passepartout's hand and the latter took it, put it in his mouth, lit it, took a few puffs and fell back, his mind befuddled by the drug.

'At last,' said Fix, seeing Passepartout senseless. 'This man Fogg won't find out in time about the departure of the *Carnatic*, and even if he does leave at least it'll be without this wretched Frenchman.'

Then he paid the bill and walked out.

20

In which Fix comes into direct contact with Phileas Fogg

While events were taking place in the opium den with potentially disastrous consequences for his future plans, Mr Fogg was accompanying Mrs Aouda around the streets of the English quarter. Since Mrs Aouda had accepted his offer of being taken to Europe he had had to think of the detailed preparations necessary for such a long trip. It was just about acceptable for an Englishman like himself to travel around the world with only one bag, but it was unthinkable for a woman to undertake such a journey like that. Hence the need to buy clothes and other items necessary for the journey. Mr Fogg performed this task with his usual composure and, in response to all the apologies or protestations of the young widow, who was embarrassed by so much care and attention, he invariably replied, 'It's good for my journey. It's part of my plan.'

When they had bought what was needed, Mr Fogg and the young woman returned to the hotel and enjoyed a splendid meal served in the restaurant. Then Mrs Aouda, who was feeling rather tired, went up to her suite after giving her imperturbable saviour a typically English handshake. The honourable gentleman, for his part, spent the whole evening engrossed in *The Times* and the *Illustrated London News*.

If he had been the sort of man who was capable of expressing surprise, that is how he would have reacted at not seeing his servant at bedtime. But since he knew that the steamer for Yokohama wasn't due to leave until the following morning, he didn't seem particularly concerned. The next day Passepartout failed to turn up when Mr Fogg rang for him.

No one can say what went through the honourable gentleman's mind when he learnt that his servant hadn't returned to the hotel. Mr Fogg merely picked up his bag, informed Mrs Aouda and ordered a palanquin.

It was then eight o'clock, and high tide, which the *Carnatic* had to take advantage of to get through the channels, was due for half past nine.

When the palanquin arrived in front of the hotel Mr Fogg and Mrs Aouda got into this comfortable means of transport and their luggage followed behind in a wheelbarrow.

Half an hour later the travellers arrived at the quayside, and it was there that Mr Fogg was told that the *Carnatic* had left the previous day.

Mr Fogg, who had been expecting to find both the steamer and his servant waiting for him, was now in the position of having to do without both. But there was no sign of disappointment visible on his face, and when Mrs Aouda looked at him anxiously he merely replied, 'It's just a minor problem, madam, nothing more.'

At that moment a figure who had been watching him intently came up to him. It was Inspector Fix, who greeted him and said, 'Are you not, sir, like me, one of the passengers from the *Rangoon*, which arrived yesterday?'

'Yes, sir,' replied Mr Fogg coldly, 'but I do not have the honour of –'

'Excuse me, but I was expecting to find your servant here.'

'Do you know where he is, sir?' asked the young woman eagerly.

'What!' answered Fix, pretending to be surprised. 'Isn't he with you?'

'No,' said Mrs Aouda. 'He hasn't reappeared since yesterday evening. Could he have gone off on the *Carnatic* without us?'

'Without you, madam?' replied the detective. 'Pardon me for asking, but were you intending to catch this steamer?'

'Yes, sir.'

'So was I and, as you can see, I'm very disappointed. The *Carnatic* had finished its repairs, and it left Hong Kong twelve hours early without informing anyone. Now we'll have to wait a whole week until the next sailing!'

As he said the words 'a whole week' Fix felt his heart leap for joy. A whole week. Fogg held up for a whole week in Hong Kong. That would be enough time for the warrant to arrive. At last luck was on the side of the representative of the law.

It is easy to imagine, then, the hammer blow he received when he heard Phileas Fogg say in his calm voice, 'But the *Carnatic*'s not the only boat, I believe, in Hong Kong harbour.'

And so, with Mrs Aouda at his arm, he went off towards the docks in search of a boat that was ready for departure. A dumbfounded Fix followed him. It was as if he was bound to this man by an unseen thread.

Nevertheless, it looked as if luck, which had served Phileas Fogg so well up to then, really had deserted him now. For three hours he went all around the port, prepared if necessary to charter a vessel to take him to Yokohama, but all he could see were ships loading and unloading which were not therefore ready to sail. Fix began to hope again.

However, Mr Fogg was not in the least put out and he was intent on continuing his efforts, even if he had to go as far afield as Macao, when a sailor came up to him in the outer harbour.

'Is your honour after a boat?' the sailor said to him, taking his cap off.

'Do you have a boat ready to sail?' asked Mr Fogg.

'Yes, your honour, a pilot boat, number 43, the best of the whole lot.'

'Is it fast?'

'Between eight and nine knots, as near as makes no difference. Do you want to see it?'

'Yes.'

'Your honour couldn't ask for more. Is it for a boat trip?'

'No, for a voyage.'

'A voyage?'

'Are you prepared to take me to Yokohama?'

The sailor couldn't believe what he'd just heard. He just stood there, aghast.

'Your honour must be joking!' he said.

'No. I've missed the *Carnatic* and I must be in Yokohama by the 14th at the latest, to catch the steamer for San Francisco.'

'Sorry,' replied the sailor, 'but it's impossible.'

'I'm offering you £100 a day and a bonus of £200 if you get me there on time.'

'Are you serious?' asked the sailor.

'Deadly serious,' replied Mr Fogg.

The pilot stepped away. He looked at the sea, obviously torn between the desire to earn a huge amount of money and the fear of venturing so far. Fix was on tenterhooks.

Meanwhile Fogg turned towards Mrs Aouda and asked her, 'Does this frighten you, madam?'

'Not if I'm with you, Mr Fogg,' the young woman replied.

The pilot went up to the gentleman once more and started fidgeting with his cap.

'Well then, pilot?' said Mr Fogg.

'Well then, your honour,' replied the pilot, 'I can't take the risk, either with my men, myself, or you on such a long crossing in a boat that weighs hardly twenty tons, and especially at this time of year. In any case, we wouldn't arrive in time because it's 1,650 miles from Hong Kong to Yokohama.'

'Only 1,600,' said Mr Fogg.

'Makes no difference.'

Fix breathed again.

'But,' added the pilot, 'maybe we can come to some other arrangement.'

Fix held his breath.

'How?' asked Phileas Fogg.

'By going to Nagasaki, in the far south of Japan, 1,100 miles away, or to Shanghai, which is 800 miles from Hong Kong. If we went the second way we could stay close to the Chinese coast, which would be a considerable advantage, especially as the currents run north.'

'Pilot,' said Phileas Fogg, 'it's from Yokohama, not Shanghai or Nagasaki, that I've got to catch the American mail boat.'

'Why?' replied the pilot. 'The steamer for San Francisco doesn't start from Yokohama. It puts in at Yokohama and Nagasaki, but its home port is Shanghai.'

'Are you sure what you're saying is correct?'

'Yes, I am.'

'So when does the steamer leave Shanghai?'

'On the 11th at seven in the morning. So we've got four days ahead of us. Four days makes ninety-six hours and at an average rate of eight knots if all goes well, with the wind staying in the south-west and a calm sea, we can cover the 800 miles between here and Shanghai.'

'When could you set sail?'

'In an hour. The time it takes to get provisions on board and the ship under sail.'

'Consider it a deal . . . Are you the skipper of this boat?'

'Yes, John Bunsby, the skipper of the *Tankadère*.'

'Do you want a deposit?'

'If you would be so kind, your honour.'

'Here's an advance of £200. Sir,' he added, turning towards Fix, 'if you would like to avail yourself of the opportunity . . .'

'Sir,' Fix replied without flinching, 'I was about to ask you this favour.'

'Good. In half an hour we'll be on board.'

'But the poor fellow . . .' said Mrs Aouda, who was very concerned about Passepartout's disappearance.

'I shall do all I can for him,' replied Phileas Fogg.

And so, while Fix went towards the pilot boat in a jittery, feverish and furious state, the other two headed for the main police station in Hong Kong. When they got there Phileas Fogg gave a description of Passepartout and left enough money to cover the cost of his repatriation. He went through the same formalities at the French consulate and then the palanquin took the travellers back to the outer harbour, after previously stopping at the hotel to pick up the luggage.

Three o'clock struck. The pilot boat number 43, with its crew on board and supplies loaded, was ready to set sail.

The *Tankadère* was an attractive little schooner of twenty tons, long in the beam, with fine bows and elegant lines. It looked like a racing yacht. Its shiny brass fittings, its galvanized-iron features and its spotless white deck showed that skipper John Bunsby was determined to look after it properly. Its two masts leaned slightly backwards. It carried a spanker, a mizen, a forestay, a jib and topsails and was rigged to take full advantage of a following wind. It clearly had an excellent turn of speed, and it had in fact won several prizes in pilot-boat competitions.

The crew of the *Tankadère* consisted of John Bunsby and four seamen. They were the sort of fearless sailors ready to go out whatever the weather to bring ships in to port and were very familiar with the conditions. John Bunsby was a man of about forty-five, sturdy, weatherbeaten, keen-eyed, energetic-looking, steady as a rock and in full control of the situation. He could inspire confidence in the most timid of people.

Phileas Fogg and Mrs Aouda went on board. Fix was already there. The rear hatch of the schooner led down into a square cabin, containing bunks recessed into the walls and a round-shaped sofa. In the middle stood a table lit by a hurricane lamp. The accommodation was small but clean.

'I'm sorry I have nothing better to offer you,' said Mr Fogg to Fix, who bowed without making any reply.

The police inspector felt a sort of humiliation at being the recipient of this fellow Fogg's kindness like this.

'One thing's sure,' he thought, 'he's a very polite crook, but he's a crook all the same.'

At ten past three the sails were hoisted. The Union Jack was flying from the schooner's gaff. The passengers were sitting out on deck. Mr Fogg and Mrs Aouda gave a last look at the quayside in case Passepartout had reappeared.

Fix was feeling somewhat apprehensive, because there was still a chance that the unfortunate chap he had treated so shabbily might show up and that would have led to an argument in which Fix would have been the likely loser. But the Frenchman did not turn up, and doubtless the overpowering effects of the drug had still not worn off.

At last the skipper reached the open sea and, as it caught the wind in its spanker, foresail and jibs, the *Tankadère* leapt forward over the waves.

21

Where the skipper of the Tankadère *is in serious danger of losing a £200 bonus*

To attempt an 800-mile voyage on a vessel weighing twenty tons was a hazardous undertaking, and particularly at that time of year. The China Seas are generally rough and subject to frequent heavy squalls, especially at the time of the equinoxes, and it was still early November.

It would obviously have been to the pilot's advantage to take his passengers as far as Yokohama, because he was being paid by the day. But it would have been reckless of him to attempt such a crossing in the prevailing conditions, and even going up to Shanghai was already a bold, not to say foolhardy, thing to do. However, John Bunsby had every faith in his *Tankadère*, which rose to the waves like a seagull, and perhaps he was right to be confident.

As the day came to a close, the *Tankadère* navigated its way through the treacherous channels around Hong Kong, performing admirably, whatever the setting of the sails, whether going close to the wind or with the wind behind it.

'It goes without saying, captain,' said Phileas Fogg just as the schooner was heading for the open sea, 'that time is of the essence.'

'Your honour may rely on me,' replied John Bunsby. 'As far as the sails are concerned, we've put out everything the wind will allow. Our topsails wouldn't be any help at all. They would only slow us down.'

'You're the expert, captain, not me, and I have every trust in you.'

Phileas Fogg, his back straight, his legs apart, and firm on his feet like a seasoned sailor, looked unflinchingly out at the stormy sea. The young woman, who was sitting at the stern, felt moved as, in the gathering dusk, she gazed out over this dark ocean that she was braving on such a frail craft. Above her head spread the sails that carried it through space as if they were great wings. The schooner, lifted up by the wind, seemed to be flying through the air.

Night came. The moon was entering its first quarter and its faint light would soon be extinguished by the mist on the horizon. Clouds were blowing in from the east and were already filling part of the sky.

The captain had set up his navigation lights – a necessary precaution in these busy waters where vessels were making for port. Collisions between ships were quite common, and at the speed the schooner was travelling it would have broken up on the slightest impact.

Fix was daydreaming at the fore of the vessel. He kept to himself, since he knew that Fogg was not very talkative by nature. In any case, he strongly disliked talking to this man, whose help he had accepted. He was also thinking about the future. It seemed certain to him that Fogg would not stop in Yokohama and that he would immediately catch the steamer for San Francisco in order to get to America, whose vastness would ensure that he was safe and beyond the reach of the law. Phileas Fogg's plan seemed to him to be perfectly straightforward.

Instead of leaving England for the United States, like any ordinary criminal, this man Fogg had gone the long way round and crossed three-quarters of the globe in order to have a better chance of getting to America where he would quietly get through all the Bank's money once the police were off his trail. But what would Fix do once he was in the United States? Would he give up on his man? No way. Until he received the extradition papers he wouldn't let Fogg out of his sight. It was his duty and he would see things through to the bitter end. In any case, one thing had worked in his favour: Passepartout was no longer there to help his master, and, above all, after the secrets Fix had already given away, it was vital that master and servant should not see each other ever again.

Phileas Fogg was also thinking about his servant, who had disappeared in such mysterious circumstances. All things considered, he thought it still quite possible that as a result of some misunderstanding the poor fellow might have got on board the *Carnatic* at the last minute. Mrs Aouda was of the same opinion, and she greatly missed this trusty servant, to whom she owed so much. It was possible, therefore, that they might meet up with him again in Yokohama, and it would be easy to find out if he had got there on the *Carnatic*.

At about ten o'clock the wind began to freshen. It would have perhaps been safer to reef the sails, but the captain, after carefully considering the look of the sky, decided to leave them as they were. In any case, the *Tankadère* was a very stable vessel with a good draught and the sails could be taken down quickly in the event of a squall.

At midnight Phileas Fogg and Mrs Aouda went down to the cabin. Fix had got there before them and was stretched out on one of the bunks. As for the captain and his men, they stayed out on deck all night.

By sunrise the following morning, 8 November, the schooner had done more than a hundred miles. The log,[1] which was frequently dropped into the water, showed that the average speed was between eight and nine knots. The *Tankadère* had slack in its sails, which were all out, and with this setting it could reach its maximum speed. If the wind held, all would be well.

For the whole of that day the *Tankadère* stayed close to the coast, where the currents were favourable. The coast was no more than five miles away on the port quarter and its irregular outline could sometimes be seen through breaks in the fog. As the wind was coming from the land, the sea was less rough for that very reason. This was fortunate for the schooner, because vessels of low tonnage are particularly affected by the swell, which cuts down their speed or, to use a nautical term, 'kills' them.

Around midday the wind slackened a little and shifted southeast. The pilot put up the topsails, but two hours later he had to bring them down because the wind was freshening again.

Mr Fogg and the young woman, who very fortunately were not susceptible to seasickness, had a healthy appetite for the rations aboard. Fix was invited to share their meal and had to accept, well aware that his stomach, like a boat, needed some form of ballast, but he found it galling. He felt it somehow disloyal to be travelling at this man's expense and to eat his provisions. Nevertheless, eat is what he did, even if it was really more of a snack than a meal.

When they'd finished eating, however, he thought it necessary to take this man Fogg to one side and say to him, 'Sir . . .'

This 'sir' really stuck in his gullet and he had to restrain himself not to take this 'sir' by the scruff of the neck!

'Sir, you have been so kind as to offer me a place on board. But, although my means are much more modest than your own, I do intend to pay my way –'

'Don't mention it, sir,' replied Mr Fogg.

'But I insist –'

'No, sir,' repeated Fogg in a tone of voice that allowed no further discussion. 'It comes under the running costs.'

Fix bowed. He could hardly breathe and so he went to lie down at the fore of the schooner, and didn't say a word for the rest of the evening.

Meanwhile the boat was making rapid progress. John Bunsby was feeling very optimistic. Several times he said to Mr Fogg that they would arrive in good time. Mr Fogg merely replied that that was what he expected. In any case the whole crew of the little schooner were doing their utmost. The prospect of a bonus spurred these good fellows on. And so every single rope was carefully tightened, every sail was vigorously hoisted taut, and the helmsman was careful to ensure the vessel did not veer off course. The standard of sailing couldn't have been any higher in a Royal Yacht Club regatta.

By the evening the pilot could tell from the log that they had covered 220 miles since Hong Kong and Phileas Fogg had grounds for hoping that when he arrived in Yokohama he would still be on schedule. If this proved to be the case, the first serious setback he had encountered since leaving London would probably not have any harmful effect.

During the night, towards the early hours of the morning, the *Tankadère* was well on its way through the Fokien Strait, which separates the large island of Formosa[2] from the mainland of China, and it was now crossing the Tropic of Cancer. The sea was very difficult in this strait, which was full of eddies formed by different currents meeting. The schooner laboured a lot. The choppy waves slowed down its progress. It became almost impossible to stand up on deck.

At daybreak the wind freshened further. The sky gave signs of a gale coming. In addition, the barometer showed that a change of atmospheric pressure was in the offing. Its day time readings were irregular and the mercury oscillated unpredictably. Towards the south-east they could see a heavy swell developing, which suggested that a storm was brewing. The previous evening the sun had set against a red mist, in an ocean glowing like fire.

The captain spent a long time examining the lowering sky and mumbling unintelligibly to himself. A little later, finding himself next to his passenger, he whispered to him:

'Can I tell your honour the truth?'

'Of course,' replied Phileas Fogg.

'Well, we're in for a storm.'

'Is it coming from the north or the south?' was all Mr Fogg wanted to know.

'From the south. Look. There's a typhoon on the way.'

'I don't mind about a typhoon if it's from the south. It'll help us on our way,' replied Mr Fogg.

'If that's how you take it, then it's fine by me,' retorted the captain.

John Bunsby's predictions proved only too accurate. At an earlier time of year the typhoon, would, in the words of a famous meteorologist, have spent itself in a spectacular electrical display, but now at the winter equinox it was likely that it would turn out to be extremely violent.

The captain took every advance precaution. He had all the schooner's sails furled and the yards brought down on deck. The topmasts were struck and the boom taken in. The hatches were securely battened down, so that not a drop of water could get into the vessel's hull. A single triangular sail, a storm-jib of strong canvas, was hoisted as a foretop stay-sail, to enable the schooner to stay stern to the wind. Then all they could do was wait.

John Bunsby had urged the passengers to go down into the cabin, but to be cooped up in such a confined space with hardly any air and shaken about by the swell was not a very appealing prospect. Neither Mr Fogg, nor Mrs Aouda, nor even Mr Fix agreed to leave the deck.

Towards eight o'clock a squall of rain and gusting wind hit the ship. Even with the small amount of sail it had out the *Tankadère* was tossed about like a feather in this indescribably strong wind. To say that it was four times the speed of a locomotive going at full steam would be an understatement.

So, for the whole of that day, the vessel headed north, swept along by the monstrous waves but fortunately going at the same speed as them. Many times it was almost engulfed by one of these mountains of water that reared up behind it, but the captain's deft touch at the helm prevented disaster. The passengers were sometimes soaked by spray but reacted stoically. Fix was grumbling away, it was true, but the intrepid Mrs Aouda kept her eyes firmly fixed on her companion, whose composure she couldn't help admiring, and proved herself worthy of him as she stood by his side to face the storm. As for Phileas Fogg himself, he made it look as if the typhoon had been part of his plan.

Up until then the *Tankadère* had been sailing north, but towards evening, as was to be feared, the wind veered three-quarters and blew instead from the north-west. The schooner, now broadsides on to the waves, was severely tossed around. The waves struck with a violence that would have been terrifying for anyone who did not realize how securely the different parts of a boat are put together.

As night came the storm grew even stronger. Seeing the darkness descend and with it the gale increase, John Bunsby became extremely worried. He wondered if the time had come to put into port and consulted his crew.

After consulting them John Bunsby went up to Phileas Fogg

and said to him: 'Your honour, I think it would be advisable to put in at one of the ports along the coast.'

'I think so, too,' replied Phileas Fogg.

'Right,' said the captain, 'but which one?'

'I only know of one,' Mr Fogg answered calmly.

'And that one is . . .'

'Shanghai.'

For a few moments the captain did not understand what this reply meant, the obstinacy and tenacity it contained. Then he exclaimed, 'Well then, yes. Your honour is right. Shanghai it is!'

So the *Tankadère* stayed determinedly on course to the north.

It was a truly terrifying night. It was a miracle that the little schooner didn't capsize. Twice it was swamped by the waves and everything would have been swept overboard if the lashings hadn't held. Mrs Aouda was exhausted, but she didn't make the slightest complaint. On more than one occasion Mr Fogg had to rush towards her to protect her from the violence of the waves.

Daylight returned. The storm was still raging fiercely. However, the wind fell back to the south-east. This improved things and the *Tankadère* could again make headway over this stormy sea, whose waves came up against those produced by the new direction of the wind. The resulting clash of opposing swells would have crushed a less sturdily built vessel.

From time to time they could glimpse the coastline through breaks in the mist, but there wasn't a ship in sight. The *Tankadère* was the only one out at sea.

By midday there were signs that it was becoming calm again and, as the sun went down, these signs became clearer.

The storm was short-lived because of its very intensity. The passengers, who were by now absolutely exhausted, were able to eat a little and have some rest.

The night was relatively peaceful. The captain was able to unfurl his sails partially. The vessel was travelling at considerable speed. By dawn of the following day, 11 November, John Bunsby could tell from looking at the coastline that they were about a hundred miles from Shanghai.

There were a hundred miles to go and only one day left. Mr Fogg had to be in Shanghai by that very evening if he was to catch the steamer leaving for Yokohama. Without the storm, which had made him lose several hours, he wouldn't still have been thirty miles from the port.

The wind slackened noticeably, but fortunately the sea fell at the same time. The schooner unfurled all its sails. The topsails, staysails and foretop staysails were all out and the sea was foaming beneath the stem of the ship.

By midday the *Tankadère* was only about forty-five miles from Shanghai. It had six hours left to reach the port before the steamer for Yokohama departed.

There was great anxiety on board. They wanted to arrive at all costs. All of them – with the exception of Phileas Fogg – felt their hearts pounding with impatience. The little schooner needed to keep up its rate of nine knots, but the wind kept on slackening. The breeze blew fitfully, with unpredictable gusts coming off the coast. Once they had passed, the sea immediately became calm.

However, the vessel was very light and its tall sails, made from very fine cloth, captured the wayward breezes so well that, with the help of the current, John Bunsby calculated that it was only ten miles to the Shanghai River, though the town itself is situated at least twelve miles above the mouth.

By seven o'clock they were still three miles from Shanghai. The captain let out a crude expletive. He was bound to forfeit the £200 bonus. He looked at Mr Fogg. Mr Fogg was impassive and yet his whole fortune was at stake at that very moment.

At that moment also a long black tapering shape, accompanied by a plume of smoke, appeared on the waterline. It was the American steamer, which was leaving on schedule.

'Damn it!' exclaimed John Bunsby, pushing away the helm in a gesture of despair.

'Send a signal,' was all Phileas Fogg said.

A small brass cannon was lying on the foredeck of the *Tankadère*. Its purpose was to send signals when visibility was poor.

So the cannon was loaded to the muzzle, but just when the captain was going to fire it Mr Fogg said, 'Put the flag at half mast.'

The flag was duly lowered. It was a distress signal and it was to be hoped that on seeing it the American steamer would change course momentarily and make towards the vessel.

'Fire,' said Mr Fogg.

And a blast from the small brass cannon rang out.

22

Where Passepartout comes to realize that, even on the other side of the world, it is sensible to have some money in your pocket

After leaving Hong Kong on 7 November at half past six in the evening, the *Carnatic* headed at full steam for Japan. It was carrying a full load of goods and passengers. Two cabins at the aft remained empty. They were the ones booked in the name of Mr Phileas Fogg.

The next morning, the crew at the fore of the ship were presented with rather a strange sight, a half-dazed passenger, unsteady on his feet and totally dishevelled, who was emerging from the second class hatchway and staggering across to a pile of spare masts, which he sat down on.

This passenger was none other than Passepartout. What had happened was as follows:

A few moments after Fix had walked out of the opium den, two attendants had picked up Passepartout, who had fallen into a deep sleep, and laid him out on the bed reserved for the smokers. But three hours later, Passepartout, haunted even in his nightmares by a single idea, woke up struggling against the stupefying effects of the drug. The thought of a duty unfulfilled roused him from his torpor. He left this bed for addicts and, clinging to the walls, falling then getting up again, but all the time driven by a sort of irresistible impulse, he staggered out of the opium den, shouting as if still in a dream, 'The *Carnatic*, the *Carnatic*!'

The *Carnatic* was there with its steam up, ready to depart. Passepartout only had a few steps to take. He rushed up the gangway, crossed on to the fore of the ship and fell down senseless, just as the *Carnatic* was slipping its moorings.

Used as they were to this sort of spectacle, a few of the sailors took the poor fellow down to a second-class cabin, and

Passepartout didn't wake up until the following morning, by which time they were 150 miles off the Chinese coast.

This, then, is how that morning Passepartout came to on the deck of the *Carnatic*, filling his lungs with fresh sea breeze. The pure air sobered him up. He tried to collect his thoughts, but it was not easy. Still, in the end he remembered what had happened the previous evening, the secrets Fix had let him in on, the opium den, etc.

'It's obvious,' he said to himself, 'that I must have got horribly drunk! What will Mr Fogg have to say about it? In any case, I didn't miss the boat and that's the main thing.'

Then, with Fix in mind, he said to himself, 'Well, I hope that's the last we ever hear of him and that after the suggestions he made to me he hasn't had the nerve to follow us on the *Carnatic*. A police inspector, a detective on the trail of my master, who's accused of robbing the Bank of England! Come off it! If Mr Fogg's a thief, then I'm a murderer!'

Should Passepartout tell all this to his master? Was it right to explain to him Fix's role in this business? Wouldn't it be better to wait until they got to London to tell him that an inspector from the Metropolitan Police had trailed him all the way around the world, so that they could laugh about it together? Yes, that must be it. In any case, it was something to think about. The most urgent thing was to meet up with Mr Fogg and present his apologies for his unspeakable behaviour.

So Passepartout got up. The sea was rough and the steamer was rolling heavily. The worthy fellow, who was still not very steady on his feet, made his way as best he could to the rear of the ship.

On the deck he could see no one resembling either his master or Mrs Aouda.

'Good,' he said. 'Mrs Aouda must still be asleep now. Mr Fogg, for his part, will have found himself a whist partner and true to form . . .'

With this, Passepartout went into the lounge. Mr Fogg wasn't there. There was only one thing left for it: to ask the purser which was Mr Fogg's cabin. The purser replied that there was no passenger of that name.

'Excuse me,' said Passepartout, not taking no for an answer. 'He's a tall gentleman, stand-offish, not very communicative, accompanied by a young lady –'

'There isn't a young lady aboard,' replied the purser. 'What's more, here is the passenger list. You can look at it for yourself.'

Passepartout looked at the list. His master's name wasn't on it.

He was completely dazed. Then an idea flashed through his mind.

'Wait a minute. I am on the *Carnatic*, aren't I?' he let out.

'Yes,' replied the purser.

'On the way to Yokohama?'

'Absolutely.'

For a moment Passepartout had thought that he was on the wrong ship. But if he really was on the *Carnatic*, then it was definite that his master wasn't.

Passepartout collapsed into an armchair. It was a bolt from the blue. Then suddenly in a flash everything became clear to him. He remembered that the *Carnatic*'s departure had been brought forward, that he was supposed to inform his master, and that he hadn't done so. It was his fault that Mr Fogg and Mrs Aouda were not on the boat!

It was his fault certainly, but even more it was the fault of that double-crosser who had got him drunk in order to separate him from his master and to keep Mr Fogg in Hong Kong. At last he understood the police inspector's game. And now his master was without doubt financially ruined, he had lost his bet, been arrested and perhaps imprisoned ... Passepartout was beside himself at the thought of all this. If ever he came across that man Fix again, he really would have a score to settle.

In the end, after his initial feeling of dejection, Passepartout recovered his composure and considered the situation. It was certainly not enviable. The Frenchman was on his way to Japan. He would get there all right but how would he get back? His pockets were empty. He didn't have a shilling, not even a penny. On the other hand, his passage and his food on board had already been paid for. So he had five or six days to make up his mind about what to do. It would be impossible to describe how much he ate and drank during the crossing. He ate for his master, for Mrs Aouda and for himself. He ate as if Japan, the country he was heading for was a desert island, totally devoid of anything edible.

On the 13th the *Carnatic* entered Yokohama harbour on the morning tide.

Yokohama is an important stopping-off point in the Pacific, used by all the steamers that transport mail and passengers between North America, China, Japan and Malaya. Yokohama is situated in Tokyo Bay, quite close to that enormous town, which is the second capital of the Japanese empire and where the Shogun[1] used to live in the days when this title of civil emperor existed. Tokyo is also the rival of Kyoto, the great city where the Mikado, the holy emperor descended from the gods, lives.

The *Carnatic* docked in Yokohama, near the jetties of the port and the customs sheds, amid a large number of ships from all over the world.

Passepartout set foot in the mysterious Land of the Rising Sun without the slightest enthusiasm. He had nothing better to do than trust his luck and wander around the streets of the city.

Passepartout found himself to begin with in a truly European-style city, with houses with low façades, decorated with verandas beneath which spread elegant colonnades. Its streets, squares, docks and wharves covered the whole area between the Treaty Promontory and the river. There, as in Hong Kong or Calcutta, was a swarming mass of people of all races, Americans, English, Chinese and Dutch, merchants prepared to buy and sell anything under the sun. Amid all these a French person would have looked as much of an outsider as if he'd been abandoned among savages.

Passepartout had one possible solution: to seek the help of the French or British consulates in Yokohama. However, he was reluctant to tell his story because it was so closely connected to his master's, and before having to resort to this he wanted to explore all the other options.

So, after going through the European quarter without anything positive turning up he went into the Japanese quarter, determined if necessary to carry on as far as Tokyo.

This native part of Yokohama is called Benten, after the name of a goddess of the sea worshipped on the neighbouring islands. It contained wonderful avenues of fir trees and cedars, sacred doorways with strange architectural forms, bridges hidden amid bamboo and reeds, temples sheltering under the immense and melancholy cover of ancient cedars, monasteries in the depths of which Buddhist priests and the followers of Confucius vegetated.[2] The unending streets were crowded with groups of children with rosy complexions and red cheeks. These youngsters, who looked as if they were cut-outs from a Japanese screen, were playing among short-legged poodles and yellowish cats that had no tails and were very lazy and affectionate.

The streets were teeming with people and there was an incessant coming and going: bonzes[3] going past in procession monotonously striking their drums and tambourines, *yakunin*, customs and police officers, with lacquer-incrusted pointed hats, carrying two sabres in their belts,[4] soldiers dressed in blue cotton uniforms with white stripes and armed with percussion guns; men from the Mikado's guard with their tight-fitting silk doublets, chain-mail tunics and coats of mail, and many other soldiers of various ranks because the military profession is as highly regarded in Japan as it is looked down on in China. Then came mendicant friars, pilgrims in long robes, ordinary civilians, with sleek, jet-black hair, large heads, long torsos and thin legs, short in stature, with complexions varying in colour from the darkest shades of copper to dull white, but never as yellow as that of the Chinese, from whom the Japanese differ considerably. Finally, among the carriages, the palanquins, the horses, the porters, the wind-powered wheelbarrows, the *norimons* with their lacquered sides, the comfortable *cangos*, proper litters made of bamboo,[5] could be seen some plain-looking women. They walked around taking small steps with their tiny feet, wearing canvas shoes, straw sandals or elaborately carved wooden clogs. They had slanting eyes, flattened breasts and blackened teeth, as was the fashion of the day, but they wore with great elegance the national dress, the kimono, a sort of combination of dressing gown and silk sash, with a wide belt that opened out behind into an elaborate bow, a design that modern Parisian women seem to have borrowed from the Japanese.

Passepartout spent a few hours walking among this colourful crowd, looking as he went at the strange and expensive-looking shops, the bazaars crammed with flashy items of Japanese jewellery, the eating-houses decorated with streamers and banners, which he couldn't afford to go into, and the tea-houses that serve the hot, sweet-smelling liquid by the cupful, along with sake, an alcoholic drink made from fermenting rice, and the comfortable smoking dens, where they smoke a very fine kind of tobacco and not opium, whose use is practically unknown in Japan.

Then Passepartout found himself in the countryside, surrounded by immense rice fields. Here camellias the size not of shrubs but trees provided a brilliant display with flowers that showed their fading colours and exuded fading fragrances, and inside bamboo enclosures were cherry trees, plum trees and apple trees, which the inhabitants grow more for their blossom than their fruit and which are protected by fierce-looking scarecrows and noisy whirligigs from the beaks of sparrows, pigeons, crows and other ravenous birds. There was not a single majestic cedar without its great eagle, not a single weeping willow without a heron sheltering in its foliage, balancing melancholically on one leg. Finally there were everywhere rooks, ducks, sparrow-hawks, wild geese and a large number of the type of crane the Japanese call 'lordships', which are for them symbols of longevity and happiness.

As he wandered around like this, Passepartout noticed some violets growing among the grass.

'Good,' he said, 'here's my supper.'

But after smelling them he thought they had no fragrance.

'No luck,' he said to himself.

Admittedly the trusty fellow had taken the precaution of having a hearty meal before leaving the *Carnatic*, but after a day's walk, he felt pretty hungry. He had been quick to notice that there was absolutely no mutton, goat or pork on the stands of the local butchers, and because he knew that it was against their religion to kill cattle, which were used only for agricultural purposes, he had come to the conclusion that meat was very scarce in Japan. He was quite right about this but if he couldn't eat butcher's meat his stomach would have made do quite happily with a joint or two of wild boar or deer, a few partridges or quails, some poultry or fish, which together with rice make up the staple diet of the Japanese. However, he had to make the best of things and so he put off until the next day the question of finding something to eat.

Night came. Passepartout returned to the native quarter and wandered about the streets amid the multicoloured lanterns, watching the groups of travelling acrobats perform their amazing tricks and the outdoor astrologers getting crowds of people to gather around their telescopes. Then he saw the harbour again, sparkling with the lights of fishermen, who attracted the fish by the glow of their burning torches.

Finally the streets emptied. The crowd gave way to the *yakunin* on their rounds. These officers, in their magnificent uniforms and surrounded by their retinue, looked like ambassadors, and each time he encountered one of these splendid-looking patrols Passepartout joked to himself, 'Here we go. Another Japanese delegation off to Europe.'[6]

23

In which Passepartout grows an exceedingly long nose

The following day an exhausted, starving Passepartout said to himself that he had to have something to eat at all costs, and the sooner the better. He did have the option of selling his watch, but he would rather have died of hunger. Now was the ideal opportunity for the dear fellow to use the loud if not harmonious voice with which nature had endowed him.

He knew a few French and English popular songs and he made up his mind to try them out. The Japanese must certainly be keen on music since they did everything to the accompaniment of cymbals, drums and tambourines, and they were bound to appreciate the talents of a European virtuoso.

However, it was perhaps too early in the morning to organize a concert and the music lovers, if awakened unexpectedly, might not have shown themselves too grateful for the privilege.

Passepartout decided therefore to wait a few hours, but as he walked around the thought struck him that he looked too well dressed for a travelling musician, so he had the idea of exchanging his clothes for a get-up more in keeping with his position. In addition this exchange would produce a small profit, which he could immediately put to use to satisfy his appetite.

Once he had taken this decision, all that remained was for him to put it into practice. After a considerable amount of searching he eventually found a local second-hand dealer, to whom he made his proposal. The second-hand dealer liked the European clothes and soon Passepartout left the shop wearing old Japanese robes and a sort of ribbed turban, which had faded over time. But in exchange he had a few silver coins jangling in his pocket.

'Good,' he thought, 'I'll just pretend to myself that it's carnival time.'

Passepartout's first concern, now that he had been 'Japanesed', was to go into a modest-looking tea-house, and there he ate chicken leftovers and a few handfuls of rice like a man who didn't know where his next meal was coming from.

'Now,' he said to himself after his hearty meal, 'the main thing is to keep a cool head. I no longer have the option of selling this get-up for an even more Japanese-looking one. So I'll have to devise the quickest means I can of getting out of the Land of the Rising Sun, which I won't have very fond memories of.'

Passepartout then had the idea of going to see the steamers due to leave for America. He was planning to offer his services as a cook or servant, and wanted in return only his food and passage. Once he'd reached San Francisco he'd see about sorting out his other problems. The main thing was to get across the 4,700 miles of Pacific Ocean that lay between Japan and the New World.

Passepartout was not the type who would let an idea go to waste and so he headed for Yokohama harbour. But the closer he got to the docks, the more his plan, which had looked so simple on the spur of the moment, seemed impractical. Why would they need a cook or servant on board an American steamer, and how would anyone trust him in his present get-up? What recommendations or references did he have?

Just as these thoughts were going through his mind, he noticed quite by accident a huge poster that a sort of clown was carrying through the streets of Yokohama. The poster, written in English, read as follows:

THE JAPANESE ACROBATICS TROUPE

OF THE HONOURABLE WILLIAM BATULCAR

LAST PERFORMANCES

Before their departure for the United States of America

OF THE LONG-NOSES-LONG-NOSES

DEDICATED TO THE GOD TENGU[1]

Great Attraction!

'The United States of America!' exclaimed Passepartout. 'That's right up my street!'

He followed the sandwichman and by doing so soon found himself back in the Japanese quarter. Fifteen minutes later he stopped in front of a large square building decorated on top with several garlands of streamers. On the outside wall was a painting, lacking all sense of perspective but with gaudy colours, showing a large group of jugglers.

It was the establishment belonging to the Honourable Batulcar, an American showman who was the director of a troupe of tumblers, jugglers, clowns, acrobats, tight-rope walkers and gymnasts who, according to the poster, were giving their last performances before leaving the Land of the Rising Sun for the United States.

Passepartout entered the colonnade in front of the building and asked for Mr Batulcar. Mr Batulcar appeared in person.

'What do you want?' he said to Passepartout, taking him at first for a native.

'Do you need a servant?' asked Passepartout.

'A servant!' exclaimed the showman, stroking the bushy grey beard under his chin. 'I've got two of them, obedient and trusty. They've never left me and they work for nothing provided I feed them. There they are,' he added, pointing to his two sturdy arms, scored by veins as thick as the strings of a double-bass.

'So I can't be of any use to you, can I?'

'None at all.'

'Damn! It would've been really convenient for me to travel with you.'

'Well, well,' said the Honourable Batulcar. 'If you're Japanese, then I'm a monkey. Why are you wearing that get-up?'

'You wear what you can get hold of.'

'That's true. Are you French?'

'Yes, I am. A Parisian through and through.'

'Well in that case you must know how to pull funny faces.'

'Wait a minute,' replied Passepartout, annoyed at this reaction to the discovery of his nationality. 'We French people may know how to make funny faces, but no more so than you Americans.'

'Fair enough. Well, if I don't take you on as a servant, I can take you on as a clown. Do you understand, my dear fellow? In France they use foreigners to make people laugh and abroad they use Frenchmen.'

'Oh!'

'Are you strong, by the way?'

'Especially after I've had a good meal.'

'Can you sing?'

'Yes,' answered Passepartout, who in the past had taken part in some street concerts.

'But can you sing upside down, spinning a top on the sole of your left foot and balancing a sword on the sole of your right foot?'

'You bet,' replied Passepartout, with memories of the first tricks he performed in his youth coming back to him.

'That's what it's all about,' said the Honourable Batulcar.

The deal was done there and then.

At last Passepartout had found himself a job. He'd been taken on as a dogsbody in the famous Japanese troupe. It was a bit demeaning, but it meant that within a week he would be on his way to San Francisco.

The performance, loudly advertised by the Honourable Batulcar, was to begin at three o'clock, and soon the noisy instruments of a Japanese orchestra, drums and tam-tams were blaring away at the door. Understandably, Passepartout hadn't been able to prepare for the performance, but he was supposed to lend the support of his sturdy shoulders to the famous act known as 'the human pyramid' performed by the Long-Noses of the god Tengu. This 'great attraction' was the climax of the whole show.

By three o'clock, the audience had filled the huge building. Europeans and Asians, Chinese and Japanese, men, women and children rushed in to occupy the narrow benches and the boxes opposite the stage. The musicians had come inside and the complete orchestra, with gongs, tam-tams, castanets, flutes, tambourines and bass drums, was playing away for all it was worth.

It was the usual sort of acrobatic display, but it must be admitted that the Japanese have the best balancing acts in the world. One of the performers, equipped with his fan and small pieces of paper, gracefully imitated the movement of butterflies and flowers. Another, using the sweet-smelling smoke from his pipe, traced a rapid series of blue-coloured words in the air, spelling out compliments to the audience. Another juggled with lighted candles, which he extinguished one by one as they passed in front of his lips and then relit one from the other without interrupting for a moment his wonderful feat of juggling. Another managed to make spinning-tops perform the most amazing figures. In his hands these whirring machines seemed to take on a life of their own in their unending girations. They ran along pipe-stems, sabre blades and wires as thin as wisps of hair, which stretched from one side of the stage to the other. They went around the rims of large crystal vases, climbed up bamboo ladders and then scattered to every corner, producing strange sound effects by the combination of their different tones. The jugglers juggled with them and they spun in the air. They threw them up like shuttlecocks by means of wooden rackets and they continued to spin. They stuffed them in their pockets and when they took them out the tops were still spinning – until the moment when, at the release of a spring, they burst out into a dazzling firework display.

There is no need here to describe the astonishing acts performed by the acrobats and gymnasts of the troupe. The tricks they did with a ladder, pole, ball, barrels, etc., were carried out with remarkable precision. But the main attraction was the appearance of the Long-Noses, an astonishing balancing act that has not yet been seen in Europe.

The Long-Noses made up a special corporation dedicated to the god Tengu. Dressed like heralds in the Middle Ages, they wore on their shoulders a magnificent pair of wings. But their most distinctive feature was a long nose and in particular the use they put it to. Their noses were made of bamboo and were about five, six or even ten feet long, some straight, others curved, some smooth, others knobbly. These firmly fixed appendages were in fact what they used for all their balancing acts. A dozen or so of these followers of Tengu lay on their backs and their companions sported themselves on their noses, which stuck up in the air like lightning conductors, leaping about and vaulting from one to the other, performing the most extraordinary tricks.

The show was to end with a special performance of the human pyramid, in which about fifty Long-Noses were supposed to represent the Car of Juggernaut. But, instead of forming this pyramid by standing on one another's shoulders, the Honourable Batulcar's artistes were to be linked to one another only by their noses. As it happened, one of those who formed the base of the cart had left the troupe and, since all that was needed was to be strong and agile, Passepartout had been chosen to replace him.

Admittedly, the dear fellow felt rather sorry for himself after putting on his medieval costume, decorated with multicoloured wings, and a six-foot-long nose that was fixed on to his face. It all reminded him too much of his youth. But in the end this nose was his livelihood, so he put up with it.

Passepartout came on stage and went to stand with the other performers who were to make the base of the Car of Juggernaut. They all lay down on the floor with their noses pointing upwards. A second group of performers got into position on top of their long appendages, a third group formed another layer, then a fourth group, and with these noses that only touched one another at the ends they built up a human structure that soon reached almost up to the ceiling of the theatre.

By now, the applause was getting louder and louder and the instruments in the orchestra were blasting out when suddenly the pyramid wobbled, lost its balance, one of the noses at the base disappeared and the whole structure came tumbling down like a pack of cards.

The cause of it all was Passepartout, who abandoned his post, got across the floodlights without even using his wings, climbed up to the right-hand gallery and then threw himself down at the feet of someone in the audience, shouting, 'Oh, my master, my master!'

'Is it you?'

'Yes, it's me!'

'Well, in that case let's get to the steamer, my fellow!'

Mr Fogg, Mrs Aouda, who was accompanying him, and

Passepartout had rushed along the corridors and out of the building. But there they came upon a furious Honourable Batulcar, who was asking for compensation for the 'breakage'. Mr Fogg calmed him down by stuffing some banknotes into his hand. And so, at half past six, just when the ship was about to leave, Mr Fogg and Mrs Aouda set foot on the American steamer, followed by Passepartout with his wings on his back and a six-foot-long nose that he hadn't yet been able to remove from his face.

24

*During which the crossing of the Pacific Ocean
takes place*

What had happened off Shanghai is easy to work out. The signals from the *Tankadère* had been spotted from the Yokohama steamer. Its captain, seeing the flag at half mast, had made for the little schooner. A few moments later Phileas Fogg paid for his voyage at the agreed rate, making the skipper John Bunsby richer to the tune of £550. Then the honourable gentleman, Mrs Aouda and Fix went on board the steamer, which immediately headed off in the direction of Nagasaki and Yokohama.

After arriving that very morning, 14 November, at the scheduled time, Phileas Fogg left Fix to his own business, went on board the *Carnatic* and there learnt, to the great joy of Mrs Aouda – and perhaps to his own, though he didn't let it show – that the Frenchman Passepartout had in fact arrived in Yokohama the previous day.

Phileas Fogg, who was due to leave again that very evening for San Francisco, at once set about looking for his servant. He turned in vain to the French and British consulates and, after unsuccessfully going around the streets of Yokohama, he had almost given up hope of finding Passepartout when chance or a sort of premonition led him to the building of the honourable Batulcar. He would certainly not have recognized his servant in the bizarre attire of a herald, but the latter, as he was standing upside down, noticed his master in the gallery. He couldn't stop himself from moving his nose. Hence the loss of balance and all that followed.

This is what Passepartout learnt directly from Mrs Aouda, who also told him how they had done the crossing from Hong

Kong to Yokohama in the company of a man called Fix, on the schooner the *Tankadère*.

At the mention of the name Fix, Passepartout didn't bat an eyelid. He thought the moment had not yet come for him to tell his master what had transpired between the detective and himself. And so, in the version Passepartout gave of his adventures, he put all the blame on himself for having been overcome by the effects of opium in a smoking den in Hong Kong,[1] for which he apologized.

Mr Fogg listened to this story impassively and made no reply. Then he gave his servant enough cash to buy some more suitable clothes on board. Sure enough, less than an hour later, once he had cut off his nose and clipped his wings, the trusty fellow had nothing about him of a follower of the god Tengu.

The steamer that was doing the crossing from Yokohama to San Francisco belonged to the Pacific Mail Steam Company and was called the *General Grant*.[2] It was a large paddle steamer, weighing 2,500 tons, well equipped and capable of high speed. A huge beam moved alternatively up and down above the deck. One end was fitted to a piston rod and the other to a push rod, which by converting rectilinear into circular motion directly operated the wheel shaft. The *General Grant* had the rigging of a three-masted schooner and it had a great expanse of sail, which gave a considerable boost to its steam power. At a steady rate of twelve knots, the steamer should not take more than twenty-one days to cross the Pacific. Phileas Fogg could therefore confidently predict that after reaching San Francisco by 2 December he would be in New York by the 11th and London by the 20th, thereby beating the fateful deadline of 21 December by several hours.

There were quite a few passengers on board the steamer, English people, a lot of Americans, a veritable flood of coolies emigrating to America and a number of officers from the British army in India, who were using their leave to go around the world.

During the crossing there were no problems from a nautical point of view. Because it was supported by its large paddles and steadied by its large expanse of sail, the steamer did not roll.

The Pacific Ocean lived up to its name. Mr Fogg, too, was as calm and as uncommunicative as usual. His young female companion increasingly experienced towards him feelings that went beyond gratitude. His silent nature, which was so generous in its own way, made more of an impression on her than she cared to admit, and it was almost against her own will that she began to give in to emotions to which the mysterious Mr Fogg seemed quite impervious.

In addition, Mrs Aouda was becoming extremely interested in the gentleman's plans. She worried about what could go wrong and threaten the success of the journey. She often talked to Passepartout, who was not unaware of Mrs Aouda's real feelings. The dear fellow now had total faith in his master. He never stopped praising the honesty, generosity and selflessness of Phileas Fogg. Then he would reassure Mrs Aouda about the outcome of the journey, telling her repeatedly that the hardest part was already over, that they had left behind strange countries like China and Japan and were now returning to civilization, and finally that a train from San Francisco to New York and a transatlantic steamer from New York to London would undoubtedly enable them to complete this impossible journey around the world within the allotted time.

Nine days after leaving Yokohama, Phileas Fogg had gone exactly halfway around the globe.

So it was that on 23 November the *General Grant* reached the 180th meridian, the one which in the southern hemisphere stands at the antipodes of London. Of the eighty days he had available, it is true that Mr Fogg had used up fifty-two and had only twenty-eight left. But it should be remembered that if the gentleman was only halfway in terms of the difference of meridians, in reality he had completed more than two-thirds of his total journey. This was the result of all those enforced detours between London and Aden, between Aden and Bombay, between Calcutta and Singapore and between Singapore and Yokohama. If he had followed all the way the fiftieth parallel, the one which runs through London, the distance would only have been about 12,000 miles, whereas Phileas Fogg was obliged by the vagaries of his means of transport to cover 26,000 miles,

of which he had done about 17,500 by this date of 23 November.
But now the route was direct and Fix was no longer around to
put more obstacles in their way.

Something also happened on this day of 23 November that
made Passepartout a very happy man. It will be remembered
that the stubborn fellow had insisted on keeping London time
on that famous family watch of his, since he thought that the
time in all the countries he went through was wrong. On that
particular day, then, although he hadn't put it forward or backward his watch was in agreement with the ship's chronometers.

It is quite understandable that Passepartout should have had
such a feeling of triumph. He would dearly have loved to know
what Fix would have made of this if he'd been around.

'What a load of nonsense this scoundrel talked about the
meridians, the sun and the moon!' Passepartout repeated. 'Huh!
If people like that had their way we'd have some clever sorts of
clocks and watches around! I knew for sure that one day or the
other the sun would make up its mind to set itself by my watch.'

What Passepartout didn't know was that if he'd had a watch
with a twenty-four-hour face, like Italian watches, he would
have had no reason to be so triumphant, because the hands on
his instrument would have shown nine o'clock in the evening,
that is the twenty-first hour since midnight, whereas the time on
board was nine o'clock in the morning. This was exactly the
same difference as that between London time and the 180th
meridian.

But even supposing that Fix had been capable of explaining
this scientific fact, Passepartout would almost certainly have
been incapable, if not of understanding it, then at least of
accepting it. And in any case if, assuming the impossible, the
police inspector had unexpectedly appeared on board, it is
probable that a justifiably resentful Passepartout would have
had something quite different to discuss with him and would
have gone about it in quite a different way.

Where exactly, then, was Fix at that moment in time?

Quite simply, he was on board the *General Grant*!

What had happened was that after arriving in Yokohama the
detective left Mr Fogg, expecting to meet up with him again

later in the day, and went straight to the English consul's office. There at last he found the warrant that had been following him all the way from Bombay and that was already forty days old. The warrant had been sent from Hong Kong via this same *Carnatic*, which Fogg was thought to be aboard. Fix's disappointment is easy to imagine. The warrant was useless. This man Fogg was no longer on British territory. An extradition order was now what was needed to arrest him.

'Too bad,' Fix said to himself, when his anger subsided. 'My warrant is no use here but it will be in England. It looks as if the scoundrel intends to return to his native country, in the belief that he has thrown the police off his trail. Good. I'll follow him until he gets there. As far as the money is concerned, I just hope to goodness there'll be some left. Nevertheless, between the cost of the journey, the bonuses, the court case, the fines, the elephant and assorted expenses, my man must already have spent £5,000 during his travels. Never mind. The Bank's not short of money!'

Having made up his mind, he immediately went on board the *General Grant*. He was already on the ship when Mr Fogg and Mrs Aouda arrived. To his great surprise he recognized Passepartout in his herald's costume. He at once hid himself away in his cabin, in order to avoid an angry scene which might jeopardize everything. Thanks to the number of passengers on board he expected that his enemy wouldn't notice him, when suddenly that very day he came face to face with him at the fore of the ship.

Passepartout leapt at Fix, seizing him by the throat without any attempt at explanation, and much to the delight of some of the Americans on board, who immediately put their money on him, struck the unfortunate inspector a series of mighty blows, thus proving how much superior French boxing is to the English version of the sport.[3]

By the time Passepartout had finished he had calmed down and looked almost relieved. Fix staggered to his feet and, looking straight at his adversary, said to him coldly: 'Is that it?'

'Yes, for the moment.'

'Then I'd like to have a word with you.'

'Just let me –'

'For the benefit of your master.'

Passepartout, as if overpowered by this show of composure, followed the police inspector and the two men sat down at the fore of the ship.

'You've given me a real beating,' said Fix. 'Fine. But now listen to me. So far I've been Mr Fogg's opponent but from now on I'm on his side.'

'About time, too!' exclaimed Passepartout. 'So you believe he's an honest man, then?'

'No,' Fix replied coldly. 'I think he's a crook . . . Quiet! Don't move and let me do the talking. All the time Mr Fogg was on British soil it was in my interest to hold him up while I waited for an arrest warrant. I did everything I could for that to happen. I sent the Bombay priests after him, I got you drunk in Hong Kong, I separated you from your master and I made him miss his steamer in Yokohama.'

Passepartout listened to him, fists clenched.

'Now,' continued Fix, 'Mr Fogg looks as if he's going back to England. That's fine by me. I'll follow him there. But from now on I'll be as careful to remove any obstacles that may be in his way as I was before to put them there. As you can see, my game has changed and it's changed because that's how I want it. I should add that this is what you should want as well, because it's only when you get to England that you'll know whether you've been working for a criminal or an honest man.'

Passepartout had listened very intently to Fix, and he was convinced that Fix was completely sincere in what he was saying.

'Are we friends?' asked Fix.

'Friends, no,' replied Passepartout. 'Allies, yes, but even that could change, because at the slightest hint of treachery I'll wring your neck.'

'Agreed,' said the police inspector calmly.

Eleven days later, on 3 December, the *General Grant* entered Golden Gate Bay and arrived in San Francisco.

Mr Fogg still had neither gained nor lost a single day.

25

Which gives an idea of what San Francisco is like on
the day of a political rally

It was seven o'clock in the morning when Phileas Fogg, Mrs
Aouda and Passepartout set foot on American soil – if this is
what you can call the floating quays on to which they stepped.
These quays, which move up and down according to the tide,
make it easier for ships to load and unload. Here can be seen at
their moorings clippers of all sizes, steamers from every country
under the sun and steamboats with several decks, which serve
the Sacramento and its tributaries. Here too can be seen stock
piles of goods, the produce of trade from as far afield as
Mexico, Peru, Chile, Brazil, Europe, Asia and all the islands in
the Pacific Ocean.

Passepartout was so delighted to reach American soil at last
that he felt obliged to mark his arrival by performing a perfectly
executed somersault. But when he came down on the quay with
its rotten planks he almost went right through it. Somewhat
put out by the way in which he had landed in the New World,
the dear fellow let out an enormous shout, which scared away
a large flock of cormorants and pelicans, which normally
frequented these mobile quays.

As soon as Mr Fogg had disembarked he found out the time
of the next train to New York. It was due to leave at six o'clock
in the evening. Mr Fogg therefore had a whole day to spend in
the Californian capital.[1] He ordered a carriage for Mrs Aouda
and himself. Passepartout climbed up on to the outside seat and
the vehicle, which cost three dollars to hire, set off towards the
International Hotel.

From his elevated position Passepartout was able to satisfy
his curiosity as he observed this large American city: wide streets,

neat rows of low houses, neo-Gothic churches and chapels, huge docks and palatial-looking warehouses, some in wood, others in brick. In the streets there were a large number of carriages, omnibuses and tramcars, and on the crowded pavements there were not only Americans and Europeans but also Chinese and Indians, who together made up a population of more than 200,000 people.

Passepartout was quite surprised by what he saw. He still had in his mind the image of the legendary city of 1849, a town of bandits, arsonists and murderers all attracted by the lure of gold, an immense confusion of social misfits, where people betted in gold dust with a revolver in one hand and a knife in the other. But these 'good old days' were gone. San Francisco looked like any other large commercial town. The tall tower of the townhall, where men on guard kept watch, looked down on this grid plan of intersecting streets and avenues that were interspersed with spacious green squares. Then came the Chinese quarter, which looked as if it had been imported from China in a toy box. There were no longer any sombreros to be seen, no red shirts like those worn by the gold-diggers, no Indian tribes in feathered head-dresses, but silk hats and black suits, worn by a large number of gentlemen rushing about their business. Some of the streets, such as Montgomery Street, the equivalent of Oxford Street in London or the Champs-Élysées in Paris or Fifth Avenue in New York, were lined with impressive-looking shops, displaying goods from all over the world.

When Passepartout arrived in the International Hotel he felt as if he had never left England.

On the ground floor of the hotel there was a huge bar, a sort of buffet area, free to anyone who went in. Cured meats, oyster soup, biscuits and cheese could be consumed without it costing anything. All that the customers had to pay for was what they had to drink, if they felt thirsty enough, beer, port or sherry. Passepartout thought this was 'very American'.

The hotel's restaurant was comfortable. Mr Fogg and Mrs Aouda sat down at a table and were treated to a copious meal served on miniature plates by Blacks with beautiful dark skin.

After lunch Phileas Fogg, accompanied by Mrs Aouda, left

the hotel to go to the British consulate in order to have his passport stamped. On the pavement he met his servant, who asked him if before taking the Pacific railroad it wouldn't be advisable to buy a dozen or so Enfield rifles and some Colt revolvers. Passepartout had heard about the Sioux and the Pawnees, who held up trains as if they were mere stagecoaches like Spanish highwaymen. Mr Fogg replied that there was no real need for such precautions, but he said that Passepartout could do as he saw fit. Then he headed off towards the consulate.

Phileas Fogg had hardly gone more than about 200 yards when by 'sheer coincidence' he bumped into Fix. The inspector pretended to be very surprised. How could it be that Mr Fogg and he had done the crossing of the Pacific together and not come upon each other on board? In any case, Fix was extremely honoured to see once more the gentleman to whom he owed so much, and since he had to go back to England on business he would be delighted to continue his journey in such pleasant company.

Mr Fogg replied that the honour was all his, and Fix, who was anxious not to let him out of his sight, asked permission to accompany him around this fascinating city of San Francisco. Permission was duly granted.

And so Mrs Aouda, Phileas Fogg and Fix strolled through the streets. They soon found themselves in Montgomery Street, where there were huge crowds. There were people everywhere: on the pavements, in the middle of the road, on the rails of the tramway, despite the constant traffic of coaches and omnibuses, outside shops, at the windows of all the houses and even on the rooftops. Sandwich men were walking around in the midst of the gathering. Banners and streamers were flying in the wind. There was shouting from all sides.

'Hooray for Kamerfield.'

'Hooray for Mandiboy.'

It was a political rally. At least that was what Fix thought and he said so to Mr Fogg, adding: 'We would be well advised, sir, to keep well away from this mob. There's bound to be a punch-up in the end.'

'Quite right,' replied Phileas Fogg, 'and a punch-up, even if it's about politics, is still a punch-up.'

Fix felt it appropriate to smile when he heard this comment and, in order not to get caught up in the brawl, Mrs Aouda, Phileas Fogg and he positioned themselves on the top of a flight of steps leading to a terrace that overlooked Montgomery Street. In front of them, on the other side of the street between a coal depot and a petroleum store stood a large open-air committee room, on which the various sections of the crowd seemed to be converging.

So what exactly was the purpose of this rally? Why was it taking place at this particular time? Phileas Fogg had absolutely no idea. Was it to do with making an important military or civilian appointment or electing a State governor or a member of Congress? This was a reasonable supposition, judging from the tremendous state of excitement throughout the town.

At that moment there was considerable activity among those present. Everywhere hands shot up in the air. Some, firmly clenched, seemed to be raised then quickly lowered amidst the shouting, presumably an energetic way of casting a vote. The mass of people surged backward and forward. Banners were being waved in the air, disappearing briefly and then reappearing in tatters. The swaying crowd swept along to the flight of steps, heads bobbing up and down like the surface of the sea suddenly stirred up by a squall. The number of black hats visibly decreased and most of them seemed to have become noticeably less tall.

'It's obviously a political rally,' said Fix, 'and whatever it's about has really got people worked up. I wouldn't be surprised if it wasn't about that *Alabama* business, even though it's been officially settled.'

'Perhaps,' was all Mr Fogg said in reply.

'In any case,' continued Fix, 'there are two opposing candidates, the Honourable Kamerfield and the Honourable Mandiboy.'

Mrs Aouda, who was holding on to Mr Fogg's arm, looked surprised as she watched these angry scenes and Fix was about to ask one of his neighbours the reason for all this commotion when there was another sudden surge. The cheers increased, accompanied by shouting and booing. The poles carrying the banners were turned into offensive weapons. Hands gave way to fists everywhere. On the tops of carriages that had stopped and omnibuses that had been brought to a standstill, people were trading punches. Everything served as a missile. Boots and shoes came flying through the air and it even seemed as if a few revolvers were being fired, giving an added touch of local colour to the shouting of the crowd.

The mob got closer to the flight of stairs and poured out on to the bottom steps. One side was obviously being pushed back, but it was impossible for mere spectators to say who had the upper hand, Mandiboy or Kamerfield.

'I think it would be wise to withdraw,' said Fix, who certainly didn't want his man to be hurt or to get into trouble. 'If this has got anything to do with Britain and they recognize us, then we are bound to get caught up in the brawl.'

'A British subject –' replied Phileas Fogg.

But the gentleman was unable to complete his sentence. Behind him, from the terrace in front of the flight of stairs, came a terrifying roar. There were shouts of 'Hip! hip! hooray! Mandiboy!' It was a contingent of his voters joining the fray, outflanking the supporters of Kamerfield.

Mr Fogg, Mrs Aouda and Fix were caught in the middle. It was too late to escape. The flood of men, armed with leaded sticks and clubs, carried all before them. Phileas Fogg and Fix, in attempting to protect the young woman, were severely jostled. Mr Fogg with his usual composure sought to defend himself with the two natural weapons with which nature has equipped every trueborn Englishman, his fists, but to no avail. An enormous fellow with a red goatee beard, a ruddy complexion and broad shoulders, who looked like the ringleader, raised his huge fist against Mr Fogg and would have inflicted serious injury on the gentleman had not Fix nobly received the blow in his place. An enormous bump soon appeared under the detective's silk hat, which had been reduced to the size of a cap.

'Yankee,' said Mr Fogg, giving his opponent an extremely contemptuous look.

'Limey,' replied the other.

'We shall meet up again!'

'Whenever you like. What's your name?'

'Phileas Fogg. What's yours?'

'Colonel Stamp W. Proctor.'

With that the human tide swept past. Fix was knocked to the ground and got to his feet again, with his clothes torn but no serious injury. His coat had been divided into two unequal parts and his trousers looked like the breeches that some Indians consider it fashionable to wear only after first removing the seat. But in a word, Mrs Aouda had been spared and only Fix had been at the receiving end of a punch.

'Thank you,' said Mr Fogg to the inspector, as soon as they had got away from the crowd.

'Don't mention it,' replied Fix, 'but let's get out of here.'

'Where to?'

'To a clothes shop.'

This was indeed an appropriate port of call. Phileas Fogg and Fix both had their clothes in tatters, as if the two gentlemen had themselves come to blows over Messrs Kamerfield and Mandiboy.

An hour later they were properly dressed, with new clothes and hats. Then they went back to the International Hotel.

There Passepartout was waiting for his master, armed with half a dozen six-shot, central-fire revolvers with mounted daggers. When he noticed that Fix was accompanying Mr Fogg his face fell, but he perked up after hearing Mrs Aouda's brief account of what had happened. Clearly Fix was no longer an enemy but an ally. He had kept his word.

After dinner a coach was ordered, to take the travellers and their luggage to the station. Just when he was getting into the carriage Mr Fogg said to Fix:

'You haven't seen that Colonel Proctor again, I suppose?'

'No,' replied Fix.

'I shall come back to America to find him,' said Phileas Fogg coldly. 'It is not acceptable for a British citizen to allow himself to be insulted in such a way.'

The inspector smiled and didn't answer. But, as can be seen, Mr Fogg was the sort of Englishman who, even though they don't put up with duels in their own country, are quite happy to fight them abroad, when their honour is at stake.

At a quarter to six the travellers reached the station and found the train ready to leave.

Just as Mr Fogg was about to get on the train he spotted a porter and went up to him, saying:

'My dear fellow, there've been some disturbances in San Francisco today, haven't there?'

'It was a political rally, sir,' replied the employee.

'Nevertheless, I seem to have noticed quite a lot of excitement on the streets.'

'It was only an election rally.'

'For electing a commander-in-chief, I assume?' asked Mr Fogg

'No, sir. For a justice of the peace.'[2]

After receiving this answer Phileas Fogg got into the carriage and the train set off at full speed.

26

In which the express train travels the Pacific Railroad

'Ocean to ocean' is how the Americans put it – and this phrase really should be the best way of referring to the grand trunk line that crosses the United States of America at its widest point. But in fact the Pacific Railroad is divided into two quite distinct sections, the 'Central Pacific' between San Francisco and Ogden, and the 'Union Pacific' between Ogden and Omaha. That is where five different lines meet up, making regular travel possible between Omaha and New York.

New York and San Francisco are therefore now linked by an uninterrupted metal strip stretching for no less than 3,786 miles. Between Omaha and the Pacific the railroad crosses territory that is still the haunt of Native Americans and wild animals, a vast tract of land that the Mormons began to colonize around 1845 after being driven out of Illinois.

In the past it took at best six months to go from New York to San Francisco. Now it takes seven days.

It was in 1862 that, despite the opposition of representatives from the southern states, who wanted a line further to the south, it was decided that the route for the new railroad would run between the forty-first and forty-second parallels. The late, lamented President Lincoln himself chose the town of Omaha in the state of Nebraska as the starting-point of the new network. Work began immediately and was carried out in typical American style, without too much paperwork or bureaucratic fuss. The speed with which the track was laid would not at all affect the quality of its contruction. Over the prairies the work progressed at a mile and a half per day. A locomotive running along the track that had been laid the previous day transported the rails for the day after and worked its way along them as they were being laid.

The Pacific Railroad has various junctions along its length, with branch lines going off into the states of Iowa, Kansas, Colorado and Oregon. After leaving Omaha it follows the south bank of the Platte River as far as the mouth of the North Platte, follows the South Platte, crosses the territory of Laramie and the Wasatch Mountains, skirts the Great Salt Lake, arrives in Salt Lake City, the Mormon capital, goes deep into the Tuilla Valley, runs along the edge of the Great Salt Lake Desert, Mounts Cedar and Humboldt, the Humboldt River and the Sierra Nevada and goes back down to the Pacific via Sacramento, and over its whole length the gradient never exceeds one in fifty, even when it crosses the Rocky Mountains.

This was the long line of communication that trains took seven days to travel and that would enable Phileas Fogg, Esq. – at least that was what he hoped – to be in New York by 11 December to catch the Liverpool steamer.

The carriage in which Phileas Fogg was sitting was a sort of long omnibus resting on two undercarriages, each with four wheels, which because of their mobility made it possible to negotiate tight bends. Inside there were no separate compartments. Instead there were two rows of seats facing each other, situated at right angles to the axle and separated by a passageway that led to the washroom and toilet with which every carriage was provided. Throughout the train there were platforms that connected the carriages,[1] so the passengers were able to go from one end of the train to another, with at their disposal saloon cars, observation cars, restaurant cars and buffet cars. All that was missing were theatre cars, and even they must only be a matter of time.

People were constantly moving up and down the platforms, selling books and newspapers, spirits, food and cigars, all doing good business with no shortage of customers.

The travellers had left Oakland station at six o'clock in the evening. Darkness had already fallen: a cold, thick night with overcast skies and clouds that were threatening snow. The train was not going very quickly. Allowing for the stops, it wasn't doing more than twenty miles per hour, but this was still fast enough to enable it to cross the United States on schedule.

There was little talking in the carriage. In any case, the travellers would soon be asleep. Passepartout found himself sitting next to the police inspector, but he didn't speak to him. Since recent events, relations between them had noticeably cooled. There was no longer any fellow feeling or closeness between them. Fix's manner hadn't changed at all, but Passepartout on the contrary was extremely reserved, ready to strangle his former friend on the least suspicion.

An hour after the train had left it began to snow. It was a fine snow, which very fortunately would not slow down the train's progress. All that could be seen through the windows was an immense white covering of snow, which made the unfurling coils of steam from the locomotive seem positively grey.

At eight o'clock a steward came into the carriage and informed the passengers that it was time to go to bed. The carriage they were in was a sleeping car, which in the space of a few minutes was transformed into a dormitory. The backs of the seats folded down, carefully made-up couchettes opened out thanks to an ingeniously devised system, and within the space of a few minutes a series of cabins had been put together so that each traveller could enjoy a comfortable bed with thick curtains to protect their privacy. The sheets were white and the pillows soft. All that remained was for them to get into bed and go to sleep, which they all proceeded to do as if they were in the comfort of a cabin on a steamship. Meanwhile the train sped along at full steam across the state of California.

In this part of the country between San Francisco and Sacramento the land is fairly flat. This section of the line, called the Central Pacific Railroad, first took Sacramento as its starting-point and then went east to meet up with the line coming from Omaha. From San Francisco to Sacramento the line headed directly north-east along the American River, which enters San Pablo Bay. The distance of 120 miles between these two large towns was covered in six hours and towards midnight, while the travellers slept soundly, they went through Sacramento. They therefore saw nothing of this sizeable city, the seat of the legislature of the state of California, with its handsome wharves, its wide streets, its splendid-looking hotels, its squares and churches.

After Sacramento the train, once it had gone past the stations at Junction, Rochin, Auburn and Colfax, entered the Sierra Nevada mountain range. It was seven o'clock in the morning when it went through the station at Cisco. One hour later the dormitory was once again an ordinary carriage and the travellers were able to catch a glimpse through the windows of the pictur-esque panoramas of this mountainous region. The route taken by the train followed the twists and turns of the Sierra, at times clinging to the mountainside, at others hanging over precipices, avoiding tight corners by cutting bold curves, rushing into nar-row gorges with apparently no way through. The locomotive sparkled like a box of jewels, with its great lantern that gave off a yellowish light, its silver bell and its cowcatcher that jutted out like a spur, and as it went the noise of its whistling and roaring mingled with the sound of the streams and waterfalls and its smoke twisted itself around the black branches of the fir trees.

Tunnels and bridges were few and far between on the route. The railroad went around the sides of mountains making little attempt to go in a straight line or to find the shortest distance between two points, thereby respecting the natural sur-roundings.

Towards nine o'clock the train entered the state of Nevada through the Carson Sink, continuing in a north-easterly direc-tion. At midday it left Reno, where the travellers had twenty minutes to eat their lunch.

From this point the railway line, running alongside the Hum-boldt River, headed up towards the north. Then it turned east-wards but still following the course of the river as far as the Humboldt Ranges, where the river takes its source, almost at the easternmost point of the state of Nevada.

After eating their lunch Mr Fogg, Mrs Aouda and their com-panions went back to their seats in the carriage. Phileas Fogg, the young woman, Fix and Passepartout were comfortably seated and were looking out at the varied scenery that went past them: vast prairies, a backdrop of mountains and creeks that poured forth their foaming waters. Sometimes a large herd of bison gathered in the distance, forming what seemed like an encroaching tide. These innumerable armies of ruminants often present an insurmountable obstacle to passing trains. It has been known for thousands of animals to take hours to move across the railroad. The locomotive is forced in such cases to stop and to wait for the line to become clear again.

This is precisely what happened on this occasion. Towards three o'clock in the afternoon a herd of 10,000 to 12,000 head of cattle blocked the railroad. The locomotive reduced speed and attempted to drive its ram into the side of the immense column, but it had to stop in the face of this impenetrable mass.

These ruminants, which the Americans wrongly call buffaloes, could be seen lumbering along, sometimes bellowing loudly. They are bigger in size than a European bull, with short legs and tail, prominent withers that form a muscular hump, horns that are set well apart at the base, and a head, neck and shoulders that are covered with a thick mane. It was pointless to even think of stopping this migration. When bison have decided which way to go, nothing can stop them or alter their path. They are an advancing tide of living flesh that no barrier could hold back.

The travellers watched this curious spectacle from the vantage point of the platforms. But the person who was in the greatest hurry of all, Phileas Fogg, had remained in his seat and was calmly waiting for the buffaloes to agree to let him through. Passepartout was furious about the delay caused by this congregation of beasts. He would have liked to empty the contents of his whole arsenal of revolvers on them.

'What a country!' he exclaimed. 'Trains brought to a standstill by a few bulls, which wander off in procession without being in the least hurry, as if they weren't holding up the traffic . . . Good heavens! I'd like to know if this setback was catered for in Mr Fogg's schedule! And what about this engine driver, who doesn't have the courage to drive his machine straight through these obstructive beasts!'

The engine driver was certainly not tempted to remove the

obstruction and this was wise of him. He would certainly have managed to crush the first bison with the ram of his locomotive, but, however powerful it may have been, the engine would have been brought to a standstill before long, a derailment would have been inevitable and the train would have been left stranded.

The best thing was therefore to wait patiently, even if that meant having to make up for lost time by driving faster afterwards. The procession of bison lasted for a good three hours and the track was not clear again until midnight. Only then did the rearguard of the herd cross the rails while those at the front were disappearing below the southern horizon.

And so it was eight o'clock by the time the train crossed the narrow passes of the Humboldt Ranges and half past nine by the time it entered the territory of Utah,[2] the area of the Great Salt Lake and the strange land of the Mormons.

27

In which Passepartout receives a lecture on Mormon history[1] while travelling at a speed of twenty miles per hour

During the night of 5 to 6 December, the train headed south-east over a distance of about fifty miles, then travelled about as far again towards the north-east, in the direction of the Great Salt Lake.

At about nine o'clock in the morning Passepartout went out on to the platform for a breath of air. The weather was cold and the sky was grey, but it had stopped snowing. The orb of the sun, swollen by the mist, looked like a huge gold coin, and Passepartout was busy calculating its value in pounds sterling when he was interrupted in this useful activity by the arrival of a rather odd-looking character.

The man, who had got on to the train at Elko station, was tall in stature, with a dark brown complexion, a black moustache, black stockings, a black silk hat, a black waistcoat, black trousers, a white tie and dog-skin gloves. He looked like a clergyman. He was going from one end of the train to the other, sticking up handwritten notices on the doors of each carriage.

Passepartout went closer and read on one of these notices that the church elder Mr William Hitch, a Mormon missionary, would be taking advantage of being on train no. 48 to give a lecture on Mormonism from eleven o'clock to midday in car no. 117. He invited all those gentlemen anxious to be instructed in the mysteries of the religion of the Church of Latter-Day Saints to come to listen to him.

'I'm definitely going,' Passepartout said to himself, although he knew hardly anything about Mormonism except that polygamy was the basis of its society.

The news spread quickly through the train, which was carrying about a hundred passengers. Of these, thirty at the most were by eleven o'clock seated on the benches in car no. 117, attracted by the prospect of the lecture. Passepartout was sitting in the front row of the congregation. Neither his master nor Fix had thought it worth making the effort to attend.

At the appointed time the elder William Hitch rose to his feet and in rather an angry tone of voice, as if he had already been contradicted, exclaimed: 'I say unto you, brethren, that Joe Smith is a martyr, that his brother Hyrum is a martyr, and that the manner in which the federal government is persecuting our prophets will also make a martyr out of Brigham Young. Who would dare claim otherwise?'

No one had the temerity to contradict the missionary, whose state of excitement was in sharp contrast to the naturally calm expression on his face. But his anger was in all probability due to the fact that the Mormons were at present suffering trials and tribulations, since the government of the United States had only recently, and with considerable difficulty overcome these fanatics for independence. It had taken control of Utah and had made it subject to federal law after imprisoning Brigham Young for insurrection and polygamy. Since then, the prophet's disciples had become even more active and, before resorting to more extreme measures, were using the spoken word to oppose the demands of Congress.

As can be seen, the elder William Hitch was seeking to make converts even on the railroad.

He then proceeded to recount the history of Mormonism from biblical times, enlivening the narrative by raising his voice and making dramatic gestures. He told how in Israel a Mormon prophet from the tribe of Joseph proclaimed the records of the new religion and bequeathed them to his son Moroni. How, many centuries later, a translation of this priceless book, which had been written in Egyptian hieroglyphics, was made by Joseph Smith Jr, a farmer from the state of Vermont, who in 1825 assumed the status of a mystical prophet. How, finally, a heavenly messenger appeared to him in the midst of a forest filled with light and handed to him the records of the Lord.

At that point a few listeners, who had little interest in the missionary's historical overview, left the carriage, but William Hitch carried on. He recounted how Smith Jr gathered together his father, his two brothers and a few disciples to found the religion of the Latter-Day Saints, a religion which was taken up not only in America but also in England, Scandinavia and Germany and which counts among its members craftsmen and also many professional people. How a colony was founded in Ohio. How a church was erected at a cost of $200,000 and a town built at Kirkland. How Smith became an adventurous banker and was given by a humble tourist guide in Egypt a papyrus containing a handwritten account by Abraham and other famous Egyptians.[2]

As the tale was rather long-winded, the ranks of listeners grew thinner and thinner until no more than twenty people were left in the audience.

But the elder, undaunted by the number of defections, recounted in detail how Joe Smith went bankrupt in 1837. How he was tarred and feathered by his shareholders, who were financially ruined. How a few years later he emerged, more respectable and more respected than ever, in Independence, Missouri, and became the head of a thriving community of no fewer than 3,000 disciples. How then he fell victim to the hatred of the Gentiles and was forced to flee to the American Far West.

By now there were ten people still listening, among them the trusty Passepartout, who was all ears. It was in this way that he learnt how after much persecution Smith reappeared in Illinois and in 1839 founded on the banks of the Mississippi Nauvoo-la-Belle with a population of as many as 25,000 souls. How Smith became its mayor, chief magistrate and commander-in-chief. How in 1843 he was a candidate for the presidency of the United States and how finally he was drawn into an ambush in Carthage, thrown into prison and murdered by a gang of masked men.

By now Passepartout was the only person left in the carriage and the elder, as he looked straight at him and captivated him by his words, reminded Passepartout that two years after the murder of Smith, his successor, the inspired prophet Brigham

Young left Nauvoo and settled around the Great Salt Lake. It was here in this wonderful land and on this fertile soil, on the emigration trail that crossed Utah towards California, that the new colony expanded enormously, thanks to one of the main tenets of Mormonism, polygamy.

'And this,' added William Hitch, 'is why the Congress felt such envy towards us! This is why the soldiers of the Union invaded the soil of Utah! This is why our leader, the prophet Brigham Young, was imprisoned in violation of the basic principles of justice. Will we give in to force? Never! We have been driven out of Vermont, driven out of Illinois, driven out of Ohio, driven out of Missouri and driven out of Utah, but we will still find an independent territory where we will pitch out tents. And you who are one of the faithful,' added the elder, staring at his only remaining listener with eyes that blazed with anger, 'will you pitch your tent in the shade of our banner?'

'No,' replied Passepartout courageously, fleeing in turn and leaving the fanatic to preach in the wilderness.

But while this lecture was going on the train had made rapid progress and at about half past twelve it reached the north-west tip of the Great Salt Lake. From there the passengers had a wide-ranging view over this inland sea, which is also called the Dead Sea and into which flows an American River Jordan. It is a beautiful lake surrounded by magnificent crags with broad bases that are encrusted with white salt, a superb stretch of water, which in the past was even more extensive, but with the passage of time the shoreline has gradually risen, reducing its surface area but increasing its depth.

The Great Salt Lake, which is about seventy miles long and thirty-five miles wide, is situated at about 3,800 feet above sea level and is very different in this respect from the Dead Sea, which lies 12,000 feet below sea level. It has a high salt content, since its waters hold in solution a quarter of their weight in solid matter. Its specific gravity is 1,170 compared to 1,000 for distilled water. Fish are therefore unable to survive in it and those brought into it by the Jordan, the Weber and other creeks soon die. However, the idea that the density of its waters is too great for anyone to dive into it is untrue.

The countryside surrounding the lake is extremely well cultivated, since the Mormons are experts at working the land. Six
months later there would have been ranches and corrals for the
domestic animals, fields of wheat, maize and sorghum, lush
meadows and everywhere hedgerows of wild roses, clumps of
acacias and euphorbia. But at present the ground was covered
with a thin sprinkling of snow that hid it from view.

At two o'clock the travellers got out at Ogden station. As the
train wasn't due to leave again until six o'clock, Mr Fogg, Mrs
Aouda and their two companions therefore had time to go to
the City of Latter-Day Saints via the small branch line that goes
off from Ogden. Two hours were enough to visit this absolutely
typical American town, one that was built to the same pattern
as all the others, huge chessboards with long cold lines, with
'the mournful sadness of right angles', to use Victor Hugo's
phrase.[3] The founder of the City of Saints could not free himself
from this craving for symmetry that characterizes the British
and the Americans. In this unusual country, in which the people
certainly do not measure up to their institutions, everything is
'four-square', the towns, the houses and human failings.

At three o'clock the travellers were, then, walking through
the streets of this city built between the bank of the Jordan and
the foothills of the Wasatch Mountains. They noted few or no
churches, but by way of monuments there were the House of
the Prophet, the Court House and the Arsenal. Then they saw
houses of bluish brick with verandas and balconies, surrounded
by gardens and bordered by acacias, palm and carob trees. A
wall made of clay and pebbles, built in 1853, encircled the
town. In the main street, where the market is held, stood a few
mansions ornamented with pavilions,[4] one of which was Salt
Lake House.

Mr Fogg and his companions didn't find many people about
in the town. The streets were almost deserted, with the notable
exception of the part near the Temple, which they reached after
going through several areas that were surrounded by high fences.
There were quite a large number of women, which is due to the
unusual nature of the Mormon household. It should not be
thought, however, that all Mormons are polygamous. It is a

question of individual choice, but it should be noted that it is primarily the women in Utah who wish to get married, because according to the local religion the Mormon heaven does not allow unmarried members of the female sex to enjoy the blessings it provides. These poor creatures seemed neither wealthy nor happy. Some of them, doubtless the wealthiest, wore black silk jackets open at the waist, beneath a hood or a very simple shawl. The others were dressed only in cotton prints.

As a confirmed bachelor, Passepartout was unable to look upon these Mormon women, whose task it was to combine together to make just one Mormon man happy, without feeling a sort of panic. With his commonsense way of looking at things it was the husband he felt especially sorry for. He thought it a terrible thing to have to lead so many women at the same time through the vicissitudes of life, to steer them altogether towards the Mormon paradise, with the prospect of being reunited with them there for eternity in the company of the illustrious Smith, who must certainly grace this heavenly abode with his presence. Most definitely he felt no attraction for this sort of life, and he thought – perhaps mistakenly – that the female inhabitants of Salt Lake City were looking at him in a rather disturbing way.

Very fortunately his stay in the City of Saints was almost at an end. At a few minutes before four o'clock the travellers met up at the station and took their seats again in their carriages.

There was a blast on the whistle, but just as the traction wheels of the locomotive were spinning around on the rails and the train was beginning to gather speed, shouts rang out: 'Stop! Stop!'

You cannot stop a moving train. The person doing the shouting was obviously a Mormon who had arrived late. He was out of breath from running. Luckily for him there were no gates or barriers at the station, and so he ran along the track, jumped on to the footboard of the last carriage and collapsed breathless on to one of the seats.

Passepartout, who had been watching this acrobatic performance with considerable excitement, went up to have a look at this latecomer and became particularly interested in him when he learnt that this citizen of Utah had only taken flight in this way because of a domestic argument.

When the Mormon had got his breath back, Passepartout made so bold as to ask him politely how many wives he had all to himself, and judging from the way the man had scarpered he assumed the answer was at least twenty.

'One, sir,' replied the Mormon, raising his hands to the heavens. 'One, and that was enough!'

28

*In which Passepartout is unable to talk sense
into anybody*

After it left the Great Salt Lake and Ogden station, the train headed north for an hour as far as the River Weber, having covered about 900 miles since San Francisco. From there it turned east again through the mountainous terrain of the Wasatch Range. It is in this part of the territory, situated between these mountains and the Rocky Mountains proper, that the American engineers were confronted with their greatest challenge. Over this portion of the route the subsidy from the federal government therefore went up to $48,000 per mile instead of $16,000 in the plain. However, as has been seen, the engineers did not go against nature but cleverly got around it, avoiding the difficulties, so that to reach the main drainage basin only one tunnel, 14,000 feet long,[1] was dug over the whole length of the railroad.

It was at the Great Salt Lake itself that the route reached its highest point so far. From there on it descended very gently towards Bitter Creek Valley before going up again as far as the watershed between the Atlantic and the Pacific. There were numerous rivers in this mountainous area. The Muddy, the Green and other rivers had to be crossed by means of culverts. Passepartout became more and more impatient as he got closer to his destination. But Fix, too, would have liked to see the back of this difficult terrain. He was afraid of hold-ups, fearful of accidents, and in even more of a hurry to set foot on British soil than Phileas Fogg himself.

At ten o'clock in the evening the train stopped at the station in Fort Bridger only to set off again almost immediately, and twenty miles further on it entered the state of Wyoming –

formerly part of Dakota – by going right along the Bitter Creek Valley, which forms part of the water system of the Colorado.

The following day, 7 December, there was a fifteen-minute stop at the station in Green River. There had been quite a heavy fall of snow during the night, but it had turned to sleet and so could not affect the train's progress. However, this bad weather was a constant source of concern for Passepartout because a build-up of snow, if it clogged up the wheels of the carriages, would certainly have affected the journey.

'What a really strange idea of my master's,' he said to himself, 'to travel in the winter! Couldn't he have waited for the warm weather in order to improve his chances?'

But at that very moment when the dear fellow was concerned only about the state of the sky and the drop in temperature, Mrs Aouda had something far more serious to worry about.

What had happened was that several travellers had got out of their carriage and walked along the station platform at Green River, before the train set off again. Just then, as she looked out of the window, Mrs Aouda recognized one of them as Colonel Stamp W. Proctor, the American who had been so rude to Phileas Fogg during the political rally in San Francisco. As she did not wish to be seen, Mrs Aouda quickly pulled back from the window.

This incident had a considerable effect on the young woman. She had become attached to the man who, for all his coldness, gave her every day ample evidence of his complete devotion. No doubt she was unaware of the depth of the feeling that her saviour aroused in her and gratitude was still the only name she gave it, but without her knowing there was more to it than that. She therefore became very tense when she recognized the vulgar character whom, sooner or later, Mr Fogg would want to call to account for his behaviour. It was obviously a sheer coincidence that Colonel Proctor had got on this train, but that was the fact of the matter and Phileas Fogg had to be prevented at all costs from catching sight of his opponent.

When the train set off again Mrs Aouda took advantage of a moment when Mr Fogg was dozing to explain the situation to Fix and Passepartout.

'That fellow Proctor is on the train!' exclaimed Fix. 'Well, madam, don't worry. Before having to deal with that man . . . I mean Mr . . . Fogg, he'll have to deal with me. In this whole business I think I'm the one who was insulted the most.'

'What's more,' Passepartout added, 'I'll sort him out, even if he is a colonel.'

'Mr Fix,' continued Mrs Aouda, 'Mr Fogg won't let anyone take revenge on his behalf. As he said himself, he's the sort of man who will come back to America to seek out the offender. So if he catches sight of Colonel Proctor, we won't be able to prevent an encounter between them, which could have disastrous consequences. We must make sure he doesn't see him.'

'You're right, madam,' replied Fix. 'An encounter between them could ruin everything. Whether he won or lost Mr Fogg would be delayed and that –'

'And that,' added Passepartout, 'would play into the hands of those gentlemen from the Reform Club. In four days we'll be in New York. Well, if for those four days my master doesn't put a foot outside his carriage, we can hope that he won't meet up by accident with this wretched American, curse him. However, there certainly is a way for us to prevent him –'

The conversation was broken off. Mr Fogg had woken up and was looking out at the countryside through the snow-flecked window. But later, and without being overheard by his master or Mrs Aouda, Passepartout said to the police inspector, 'Are you really prepared to come to blows for him?'

'I'll do anything to bring him back to Europe alive!' was all Fix replied, in a tone of voice that indicated his total determination.

Passepartout felt a shudder go down his spine, but his belief in his master did not waver at all.

So was there any way of keeping Mr Fogg in his compartment to avoid an encounter between the colonel and him? That shouldn't prove too difficult as the gentleman was by nature not very active or very interested in his surroundings. In any case, the police inspector thought he had found the solution because a few moments later he said to Phileas Fogg, 'Time passes very slowly on these long train journeys, sir.'

'Yes indeed,' replied the gentleman, 'but pass it does.'

'When you were on board the steamers, I believe you used to play whist?'

'Yes, but here it would be difficult. I don't have any cards or partners.'

'Oh, we can soon buy cards. They sell everything on American trains. As for partners, if by any chance madam . . .'

'But of course, sir,' the young woman was quick to answer, 'I can play whist. It is part and parcel of an English education.'

'And I,' went on Fix, 'can claim to be quite a reasonable player. So between the three of us and a dummy hand . . .'

'As you wish, sir,' replied Phileas Fogg, delighted to be able to play his favourite game once more, even if it was on board a train.

Passepartout was immediately sent off in search of a steward and he soon came back with two complete packs of playing cards, score cards, counters and a baize-topped folding table. They had everything required. The game started. Mrs Aouda was quite a competent player and she even received the occasional compliment from the stern Phileas Fogg. As for the inspector, he was quite simply first class and a worthy opponent for the gentleman.

'Now,' Passepartout said to himself, 'we've got him settled. He won't move from here.'

By eleven o'clock in the morning the train had reached the watershed between the two oceans. It was at Bridger Pass, 7,524 feet above sea level, one of the highest points on the route as it passed through the Rocky Mountains. After about 200 miles the travellers were at last on those vast plains that stretch all the way to the Atlantic and that nature might have intended for the building of a railway line.

The first streams of the Atlantic watershed were already beginning to flow down, all of them tributaries and sub-tributaries of the North Platte River. The whole horizon to the north and east was blocked off by the huge semi-circular wall formed by the northern portion of the Rocky Mountains, dominated by Laramie Peak. Between this curve and the railway stretched vast, well-watered plains. To the right of the railroad rose, one behind another, the foothills of the mountain chain that curves around to the south as far as the sources of the River Arkansas, one of the main tributaries of the Missouri.

At half past midday the travellers briefly caught sight of Fort Halleck, which commands the surrounding area. In a few more hours they would have completed the crossing of the Rocky Mountains. It was reasonable therefore to hope that the train could get through this difficult terrain without incident. The snow had stopped falling. The weather had turned cold but dry. Large birds, alarmed by the locomotive, flew off into the distance. There were no wild animals, wolves or bears, to be seen on the plain. It was an immense, empty wilderness.

After quite a pleasant lunch served to them in their carriage, Mr Fogg and his partners had just resumed their interminable game of whist when loud blasts on the whistle rang out. The train stopped.

Passepartout stuck his head out of the window, but could see nothing to explain why they had come to a halt. There was no station in sight.

For a moment Mrs Aouda and Fix were afraid that Mr Fogg might think of going out on to the line. But instead the gentleman simply said to his servant, 'Go and see what it is.'

Passepartout rushed out of the carriage. About forty travellers had already left their seats, including Colonel Stamp W. Proctor.

The train had stopped at a red signal that closed the track. The driver and the conductor had got out and were having quite a heated discussion with the track guard, who had been sent to meet the train by the station master at Medicine Bow, the next station along the line. Some passengers had gone up to them and were taking part in the discussion, one of them being the said Colonel Proctor, with his bluster and his domineering manner.

Passepartout, who had caught up with the group, heard the track guard saying:

'No. There's no way you can get through. The bridge at Medicine Bow is shaky and it won't stand the weight of the train.'

The bridge in question was a suspension bridge built across rapids, about a mile from where the train had stopped. From what the track guard was saying, it was threatening to collapse. Several cables had given way and it was impossible to risk going across it. So the track guard wasn't exaggerating in the least when he said they couldn't get across. Besides, given the generally carefree attitude of the Americans, you can be sure that when they start getting cautious, then there really is cause for concern.

Passepartout didn't dare go to inform his master but listened, gritting his teeth and staying as motionless as a statue.

'Come on!' exclaimed Colonel Proctor, 'I assume we're not going just to stand around here until we take root in the snow.'

'Colonel,' replied the conductor,[2] 'we've telegraphed through to the station at Omaha to ask for a train but it probably won't arrive in Medicine Bow until six o'clock.'

'Six o'clock!' exclaimed Passepartout.

'Sure,' replied the conductor. 'Anyway, it'll take us until then to get to the station on foot.'

'On foot!' exclaimed all the travellers.

'But how far away is this station, then?' one of them asked the conductor.

'Twelve miles, on the other side of the river.'

'Twelve miles in the snow!' exclaimed Stamp W. Proctor.

The colonel let out a stream of expletives, venting his anger on the railroad company and on the conductor. Passepartout was furious, too, and was about to join in with him. Here was a physical obstacle that all his master's banknotes would be unable to surmount.

What was more, there was a general sense of annoyance among the passengers at the idea of having, in addition to the delay, to walk fifteen or so miles across a snow-covered plain. The result was a commotion with lots of shouting and protesting that would certainly have attracted Phileas Fogg's attention, had the gentleman not been so absorbed in his game of cards.

However, Passepartout felt he had no choice but to inform him, and so he was walking head down towards the carriage when the driver, a real Yankee named Forster, shouted out:

'There may be a way of getting across.'

'Over the bridge?' replied a passenger.

'Over the bridge.'

'With our train?' asked the colonel.

'With our train.'

Passepartout had stopped and was lapping up what the driver had to say.

'But the bridge is threatening to collapse,' continued the conductor.

'Never mind,' replied Forster. 'I think that if we get the train to hurtle along at full speed we have a good chance of getting across.'

'Hell!' said Passepartout.

But some of the travellers immediately fell for this suggestion. Colonel Proctor was particularly in favour. This hothead thought that it was perfectly feasible. He even reminded people that some engineers had had the idea of crossing rivers without building bridges, with rigid trains hurtling along at full speed, etc. And in the end all those concerned fell in with the driver's idea.

'We have a fifty per cent chance of getting across,' said one of them.

'Sixty,' said another.

'Eighty per cent . . . Ninety per cent.'

Passepartout was flabbergasted. He was prepared to try anything to get across Medicine Creek, but he thought this attempt was just a bit too 'American'.

'In any case,' he said to himself, 'there's a much simpler solution, which these people haven't even thought of.'

'Sir,' he said to one of the passengers, 'the driver's suggestion seems to me a bit risky, but –'

'An eighty per cent chance,' replied the passenger, turning his back on him.

'I quite understand,' went on Passepartout to another gentleman, 'but a moment's thought –'

'This is no time for thinking. No need!' the American answered with a shrug of the shoulders. 'If the driver says so, then we can get across.'

'Sure,' continued Passepartout, 'we'll get across, but it might be more sensible –'

'What! Sensible!' exclaimed Colonel Proctor, who jumped at the mention of this word, which he'd accidentally overheard. 'Do you understand? At full speed!'

'I know . . . I understand,' repeated Passepartout, unable to finish his sentence, 'but it might be, if not more sensible, since you find the word offensive, then let's just say more natural –'

'Who? What? What's he on about with his "natural",' people shouted from all quarters.

The poor fellow didn't know what to do to make people listen to him.

'Are you afraid?' Colonel Proctor asked him.

'Me, afraid?' exclaimed Passepartout. 'Well, that's it. I'll show this lot that a Frenchman can be just as American as they are!'

'Back into the carriages. Back into the carriages,' shouted the conductor.

'Yes! Back into the carriages,' repeated Passepartout, 'back into the carriages and quick about it! But I still can't help thinking that it would have been more natural to make us passengers go across the bridge first on foot and get the train across afterwards!'

But no one heard these sensible words and no one would have wanted to admit how right Passepartout was.

The passengers were back in their carriages. Passepartout sat down in his seat again, without saying a word about what had gone on. The card players were completely absorbed in their game of whist.

The locomotive gave a vigorous blast on its whistle. The driver reversed the engine and took the train back about a mile, like a jumper stepping backward in order to have a better run.

Then there was a second blast on the whistle and the train began to move forward again. It accelerated and soon the speed was terrifying. All that could be heard was the roaring of the locomotive. The pistons were pumping away twenty times a second, the wheel axles were giving off smoke from their grease boxes. It seemed as if the whole train, which was travelling at a hundred miles an hour, was no longer touching the rails. Its speed defied gravity.

And they got across! It was like a flash of lightning. They saw nothing of the bridge. The train leapt, so to speak, from one bank to the other and the driver managed to bring the runaway machine to a halt five miles past the station.

But the train had barely crossed the river when the bridge, now damaged beyond repair, collapsed with an enormous crash into the rapids of Medicine Bow.

29

*In which various incidents will be recounted that could
only have occurred on a railroad in America*

That same evening the train continued its journey unhindered, got beyond Fort Saunders, crossed the Cheyenne Pass and reached Evans Pass. It was here that the railroad reached its highest point, 8,091 feet above sea level. All that remained was for the travellers to go on down to the Atlantic over those endless plains that nature has levelled flat.

This was also where the great trunk line branched off to Denver City, the largest town in Colorado. This territory is rich in gold and silver mines, and more than 50,000 people have already settled there.

By then they had covered 1,382 miles since San Francisco and it had taken them three days and three nights. Four days and four nights should be enough, according to the best estimates, to reach New York. Phileas Fogg was therefore still within his deadline.

During the night the train went past Camp Walbach to its left. Lodge Pole Creek ran parallel to the railway line, along the border that runs in a straight line between the states of Wyoming and Colorado. At eleven o'clock it entered Nebraska, passed close to Sedgwick and reached Julesberg, which is situated on the South Platte River.

It is here that the Union Pacific Railroad, whose chief engineer was General G. M. Dodge,[1] was inaugurated on 23 October 1867. This was where the two powerful locomotives stopped on that day, pulling their nine carriages of distinguished guests, including the vice-president of the railroad, Mr Thomas C. Durant.[2] This was where the crowd gathered and cheered and where the Sioux and Pawnees gave a demonstration of their fighting skills. This was where they held a firework display and, lastly, where they published the first issue of the *Railway Pioneer* magazine by means of a portable printing press. This was how they celebrated the inauguration of this great railway, an instrument of progress and civilization, which conquered the wilderness and was destined to link up towns and cities that hadn't yet been built. The locomotive's whistle, more powerful than Amphion's lyre,[3] would soon make them spring up on American soil.

At eight o'clock in the morning the train left behind Fort McPherson. Omaha was 357 miles away. The railway line followed the left bank of the South Platte River, with all its unpredictable twists and turns. At nine o'clock the train reached the important town of North Platte, built between the two branches of this great river, which then join up around the town to form a single waterway, an important tributary whose waters flow into the Missouri a short distance above Omaha.

They had crossed the hundred and first meridian.

Mr Fogg and his partners had started playing cards again. None of them complained about the length of the journey, not even the dummy. At the beginning Fix won a few guineas, which he was in the process of losing again, but he was just as keen on the game as Mr Fogg. During the morning the gentleman had been unusually lucky. He kept receiving trumps and honours in his hands. At one point, after thinking up a daring move, he was preparing to play spades when from behind where he was sitting he heard a voice say:

'If it was me I'd play diamonds.'

Mr Fogg, Mrs Aouda and Fix looked up. Colonel Proctor was standing next to them. Stamp W. Proctor and Phileas Fogg recognized each other immediately.

'Oh. It's you, the Englishman!' exclaimed the colonel. 'You're the one who wants to play spades!'

'And that's exactly what I'm about to do,' Phileas Fogg replied coldly, putting down a ten of that suit.

'Well, I think it should be a diamond,' retorted the colonel in an annoyed tone of voice.

And for a moment it looked as if he was going to grab the

card that had been played, adding, 'You haven't a clue about
this game.'

'Perhaps I'll be better at another sort of game,' said Phileas
Fogg, getting to his feet.

'It's just up to you if you want to try, you bloody Englishman,'
the vulgar character replied.

Mrs Aouda had become very pale. She looked as if she was
going to faint. She had grabbed Mr Fogg by the arm, but he
gently pushed her back. Passepartout was ready to throw himself
at the American, who was giving his opponent a very dirty look.
But Fix had got to his feet, went over to Colonel Proctor, saying,
'You're forgetting that I'm the one you have to deal with, my
dear sir. I'm the one you not only insulted but hit!'

'Mr Fix,' said Mr Fogg, 'I beg your pardon, but this matter
concerns only me. By claiming that I was wrong to play spades
the colonel has insulted me a second time, and he will have to
answer for it.'

'Whenever you like and wherever you like,' replied the American, 'and you can choose the weapon.'

Mrs Aouda attempted in vain to restrain Mr Fogg. The inspector tried unsuccessfully to bring the argument back to himself.
Passepartout wanted to throw the colonel out through the door,
but a sign from his master stopped him. Phileas Fogg went
out of the carriage and the American followed him on to the
platform.

'Sir,' Mr Fogg said to his opponent, 'I am in a great hurry
to return to Europe and any delay would have serious
consequences for me.'

'So, what's that got to do with me?' retorted Colonel Proctor.

'Sir,' Mr Fogg replied very politely, 'after our encounter in
San Francisco I had planned to return to America to meet up
with you again as soon as I'd sorted out the matters that require
my attention back in the Old World.'

'Really?'

'Will you agree to meet me in six months' time?'

'Why not in that case six years?'

'I said six months,' answered Mr Fogg, 'and I shall be there
exactly on time.'

'You're just looking for excuses,' exclaimed Stamp W. Proctor. 'It's now or never.'

'Very well,' replied Mr Fogg. 'Are you going to New York?'

'No.'

'To Chicago?'

'No.'

'To Omaha?'

'That's nothing to do with you. Do you know Plum Creek?'

'No,' answered Mr Fogg.

'It's the next station. The train will be there in an hour's time. It stops for ten minutes. Ten minutes is enough time to exchange a few shots with a revolver.'

'Fine,' replied Mr Fogg. 'I'll get off at Plum Creek.'

'And I reckon you won't be getting back on again!' added the American, with breath-taking insolence.

'Who knows, my dear sir,' answered Mr Fogg, and he went back into the carriage, looking as unemotional as usual.

Once he was inside, the first thing he did was to reassure Mrs Aouda by saying that loudmouths were never people to be afraid of. Then he asked Fix to act as his second in the encounter that was to take place. Fix couldn't say no, and Phileas Fogg then calmly went back to the unfinished game of cards and quite nonchalantly played spades.

At eleven o'clock, the locomotive blew its whistle to announce that they were about to arrive in Plum Creek. Mr Fogg got up and, with Fix following him, went on to the platform. Passepartout accompanied him, carrying a pair of revolvers. Mrs Aouda remained inside the carriage, looking as pale as death.

At that moment the door of the other carriage opened and Colonel Proctor also appeared on the platform, followed by his second, a Yankee in the same mould, but just as the two protagonists were about to go down on to the track, the conductor rushed up to them, shouting, 'You mustn't get out, gentlemen.'

'And why not?' asked the colonel.

'We're twenty minutes late; so the train isn't stopping.'

'But I need to fight this gentleman.'

'I'm sorry,' said the official, 'but we are leaving again immediately. You can hear the bell ringing now.'

The bell was indeed ringing and the train set off again.

'I really am very sorry, gentlemen,' the conductor then said. 'In any other circumstances I could have obliged. But, after all, since you haven't had time to fight it out here, what's to stop you from doing so when the train's on the move?'

'Perhaps that wouldn't suit sir!' Colonel Proctor said with a sneer.

'That suits me perfectly,' replied Fogg.

'Well, this really is America for you,' thought Passepartout, 'and this train conductor is a real gentleman!'

With this he followed his master.

The two protagonists and their seconds, preceded by the conductor, walked through the carriages until they reached the back of the train. There were only about a dozen passengers in the last carriage. The conductor asked them if they would be so kind as to vacate the area for a few moments to enable two gentlemen to settle a matter of honour.

Why, of course! The passengers were only too happy to oblige the two gentlemen and so they withdrew on to the platforms.

The carriage, which was about fifty feet long, was ideal for the purpose. The two protagonists could advance upon each other between the seats and could blunderbuss each other at leisure. There had never been an easier duel to arrange. Mr Fogg and Colonel Proctor, each equipped with two six-chamber revolvers, entered the carriage. Their seconds, who remained outside, locked them in. At the first blast on the whistle they were to begin firing. Then after a period of two minutes what remained of the two gentlemen would be removed from the carriage.

There really could be nothing simpler. It was even so simple that Fix and Passepartout felt their hearts beating as if they were going to burst.

So they were waiting for the agreed signal on the whistle when suddenly wild shouts rang out, accompanied by the sound of firing, but it was not coming from the carriage reserved for the duellists. The firing ran instead along the whole length of the train down to the front. Screams of terror could be heard coming from inside the train.

Colonel Proctor and Mr Fogg, with revolvers at the ready, immediately left the carriage and rushed towards the front of the train, where the loudest noises of firing and shouting were coming from.

They had realized that the train was being attacked by a band of Sioux warriors.

This was certainly not the first time members of this daring tribe had attempted to attack, and already, on more than one occasion they had held up trains. Following their usual plan and without waiting for the train to come to a standstill, about a hundred of them had leapt on to the footboards and clambered on to the carriages like circus clowns jumping on to galloping horses.

The Sioux were equipped with rifles. Hence the noise of firing to which the passengers, almost all of whom were armed, replied by using their revolvers. At first the warriors had stormed the engine. The driver and the fireman had been hit with clubs and were only semi-conscious. A Sioux chief attempted to stop the train, but because he didn't know how to operate the throttle control he had opened up the steam instead of closing it and the runaway train was rushing ahead at a terrifying speed.

At the same time the Sioux had swarmed on to the carriages and were running along the roofs like enraged monkeys, knocking down the doors and engaging in hand-to-hand combat with the passengers. The luggage van had been broken into and ransacked, and the contents strewn along the track. The shouting and firing kept on and on. However, the passengers defended themselves with great courage. Some carriages, with their passengers barricaded inside, withstood the siege like mobile forts that were being carried along at a speed of a hundred miles per hour.

From the moment the attack had begun Mrs Aouda had behaved courageously. With a revolver in her hand she defended herself heroically, firing through the broken window, whenever a savage appeared in front of her. About twenty fatally wounded Sioux had fallen on to the line and the wheels of the carriages squashed like worms those who slid from the platforms on to the rails. Several passengers, who had been seriously injured by the bullets or the clubs, were lying on the seats.

However, things couldn't go on like this. The fighting had already raged for ten minutes and the Sioux would inevitably be the victors if the train didn't come to a stop. The station at Fort Kearney was less than two miles away and contained an American garrison, but after that the Sioux would be in complete control of the train until the next station along the line.

The conductor was fighting next to Mr Fogg when he was struck by a bullet. As he fell down he cried out, 'We've had it if the train doesn't stop within the next five minutes.'

'It will stop!' said Phileas Fogg, eager to rush out of the carriage.

'Stay here, sir,' Passepartout shouted to him. 'I'm the one for this!'

Phileas Fogg had no time to stop the brave fellow, who opened the door without being seen by the Sioux and managed to slide below the carriage. And then, while the fighting continued and the bullets flew in all directions above his head, with all the old agility and nimbleness of his time in the circus, he slithered along under the carriages. Holding on to the chains, using to support himself the brake levers and the underframes of the carriages, crawling with great skill from one carriage to the next, he succeeded in reaching the front of the train. He hadn't been seen. He couldn't have been.

Hanging by one hand between the luggage van and the tender, he used his other hand to unhook the safety chains, but because of the force of traction he would never have managed to undo the coupling-pin if a sudden jolt of the engine hadn't released it, so that the carriages, detached from the engine, were gradually left behind, while the locomotive sped ahead even faster.

Carried along by its own momentum, the train continued to advance for a few more minutes, but the brakes were applied from inside the carriages and the train at last came to a standstill, less than a hundred yards from the station in Kearney.

There the noise of the firing had alerted the soldiers, who came running towards the train. The Sioux hadn't waited for them and, before the train had come to a complete halt, the whole band had cleared off.

But when the passengers checked if they were all there, as they stood on the station platform, they realized that several of their number were missing, and one of those was the brave Frenchman to whose selflessness they owed their lives.

30

In which Phileas Fogg quite simply does his duty

Three passengers, one of whom was Passepartout, had disappeared. Had they been killed in the struggle? Had they been taken prisoner by the Sioux? It was too early to tell.

There were quite a large number of wounded, but it was clear that none of the injuries were fatal. One of those most seriously wounded was Colonel Proctor, who had fought courageously and had been struck by a bullet in the groin. He was transported to the station along with other passengers who required immediate treatment for their wounds.

Mrs Aouda was safe. Phileas Fogg, who had given his all, hadn't suffered a scratch. Fix was wounded in the arm, but it wasn't serious. But Passepartout was missing and the young woman had tears in her eyes.

Meanwhile all the passengers had got out of the train. The wheels of the carriages were stained with blood. The mangled remains of bodies were hanging from the hubs and spokes. There were long trails of red stretching across the white plain as far as the eye could see. The last of the assailants were still disappearing towards the south, towards Republican River.

Mr Fogg remained motionless, arms folded. He had a crucial decision to make. Mrs Aouda was at his side and was looking at him without saying a word. He understood the meaning of her expression. If his servant had been taken prisoner, then shouldn't he risk everything to rescue him from the Sioux?

'I shall find him, dead or alive,' was all he said to Mrs Aouda.

'Oh sir! Mr Fogg!' the young woman exclaimed, grasping her companion's hands, on to which her tears rolled.

'Alive,' added Mr Fogg, 'providing we don't waste any time.'

In making this decision Phileas Fogg was sacrificing every-thing. He had just condemned himself to financial ruin. A single day's delay meant he would miss the steamer from New York. His bet was irretrievably lost. But at the thought of 'this is my duty' he had not hesitated.

The captain in command of Fort Kearney was there. His soldiers – about a hundred men in all – had taken up defensive positions in the event of the Sioux launching a direct attack on the station.

'Officer,' said Mr Fogg to the captain, 'three passengers are missing.'

'Presumed dead?' asked the captain.

'Dead or captured,' replied Phileas Fogg. 'We need to find out which is the case. Is your plan to go after the Sioux?'

'This is a serious business, sir,' said the captain. 'They may flee beyond the Arkansas River. I just can't abandon the fort I'm in charge of.'

'Sir,' continued Phileas Fogg, 'the lives of three men are at stake.'

'That may be so, but can I risk the lives of fifty men to save three?'

'I don't know whether you can, sir, but you must.'

'Sir,' replied the captain, 'no one here tells me my duty.'

'Right,' said Phileas Fogg coldly. 'I shall go alone.'

'You, sir,' cried out Fix, who had got closer, 'going after the Sioux all on your own?'

'Do you really expect me to leave this unfortunate man to die when everyone here owes their life to him? I intend to go.'

'Well, in that case you won't be going alone!' exclaimed the captain, overcome with emotion in spite of himself. 'No. You are a man of courage. I want thirty volunteers,' he added, turning towards his soldiers.

The whole company stepped forward to a man. All the captain had to do was to take his pick from these fine fellows. Thirty soldiers were selected and a wise old sergeant put in charge.

'Thank you, captain,' said Mr Fogg.

'Will you allow me to come with you?' Fix asked the gentleman.

'You may do as you wish, sir,' Phileas Fogg said to him in
reply. 'But if you really do want to do something to help me,
then you should stay with Mrs Aouda. In the event of something
happening to me . . .'

The police inspector's face suddenly went very pale. How
could he let go of this man, who he had followed so doggedly
and with such persistence? How could he let him venture into
the wilderness like this? Fix looked at the gentleman intently
and despite himself, for all his feelings against Fogg and in spite
of the struggle that was going on inside him, he felt uncomfortable when confronted with that calm and honest expression.

'I shall stay here,' he said.

A few moments later Mr Fogg shook the young woman's
hand and then, after handing her his precious travel bag, he was
ready to leave with the sergeant and his small troop of men.

But before leaving he said to the soldiers, 'My friends, there's
a reward of £1,000 waiting for you if we rescue the prisoners!'

By then it was a few minutes past midday.

Mrs Aouda had withdrawn to a room in the station where
she proceeded to wait on her own, thinking of Phileas Fogg
and his simple but noble generosity and his quiet strength of
character. Mr Fogg had given up his fortune and now he was
risking his life, and he had done all this without hesitation, out
of a sense of duty and without false rhetoric. Phileas Fogg was
a hero in her eyes.

Inspector Fix wasn't of the same opinion and he was unable
to control his inner turmoil. He walked up and down along the
station platform, looking agitated. After momentarily being
under the gentleman's power, he then became his old self again.
Once Fogg had set off, he realized how foolish he had been to
let him go. How on earth could he have agreed to be separated
from this man who he had been following around the world?
His true nature reasserted itself. He blamed and criticized himself. He told himself off as if he was the head of the Metropolitan
Police reprimanding a member of his force caught out by his
own naivety.

'What a fool I've been!' he thought. 'His other half will have
told him who I am. He's gone and won't be back! Where can I

get my hands on him again now? How on earth could I have let myself be taken in like this, me, Fix, when I've got his arrest warrant in my pocket? I really must be stupid!'

These were the thoughts going through the police inspector's mind as the hours went by, all too slowly for his liking. He didn't know what to do. At times he wanted to tell Mrs Aouda everything. But he realized what her reaction would be. What should he decide? He was tempted to set off across the long snow-covered plains in pursuit of Fogg. He thought he would stand some chance of finding him. The footmarks of the detachment of soldiers were still visible in the snow. But soon their traces disappeared under a fresh fall.

Fix suddenly became despondent. He felt a sort of irresistible urge to give up the whole game. In fact, the opportunity to leave the station at Kearney and continue this journey, which had brought him so many disappointments, was about to present itself.

What happened was that at about two o'clock in the afternoon, as the snow fell in heavy flakes, long blasts on a whistle could be heard coming from the east. A huge shadow, preceded by a yellowish glow, was moving slowly forward, made to look even bigger by the fog that gave it a ghostly appearance.

However, no train was expected yet from the east. The help requested by telegraph could not have arrived so soon; and the train from Omaha to San Francisco wasn't due to arrive until the following day. The explanation soon became clear.

This locomotive that was moving forward so slowly, letting out loud blasts on the whistle, was the one that after being uncoupled from the train had continued to run at such a terrifying speed, taking with it the fireman and the driver, who were both unconscious. It had gone on for a few miles, but then the fire had died down because of a lack of fuel. The steam had given out and an hour later, after gradually slowing down, the engine at last came to a halt about twenty miles beyond the station at Kearney.

Both the driver and the fireman were still alive and, after being unconscious for a considerable time, they had come round. The engine was then at a standstill. When he saw that he was in the middle of nowhere and with no carriages left the driver realized what had happened. He had no idea how the locomotive had become detached from the rest of the train, but he felt sure that the carriages that had been left behind were in trouble.

The driver had no hesitation about what to do. The sensible thing was to continue in the direction of Omaha. To go back towards the train, which the Sioux might still be in the process of ransacking, was fraught with danger. Never mind this. Shovelfuls of coal and wood were heaped into the firebox, the fire got going again, the steam pressure returned, and by about two o'clock in the afternoon the engine was reversing towards the station at Kearney. This was the whistling noise heard in the fog.

The passengers were extremely pleased when they saw the locomotive in place again at the head of the train. They would now be able to continue their journey, which had been so rudely interrupted.

When the engine arrived, Mrs Aouda came out of the station building and turned to the conductor to ask, 'Are you intending to leave?'

'This instant, madam.'

'But the prisoners . . . our unfortunate companions . . .'

'I can't hold up the service,' the conductor, replied. 'We're already three hours late.'

'When is the next train from San Francisco due?'

'Tomorrow evening, madam.'

'Tomorrow evening will be too late. You must wait.'

'It's impossible, madam,' answered the conductor. 'If you want to leave, please get into the carriage.'

'I'm not leaving,' said the young woman.

Fix had overheard this conversation. A few minutes earlier, when there was no means of transport available, he was determined to leave Kearney and yet now that the train was there, ready to depart, and when all he had to do was to go back to his seat in the carriage, he was bound to the spot by an irresistible force. He was itching to get off the station platform and yet he couldn't tear himself away from it. That inner struggle had started up again. He was overcome by anger at his own failure. He wanted to fight until the bitter end.

Meanwhile the passengers and a few of the wounded, including Colonel Proctor, who was in a serious condition, got into the carriages. The overheated boiler could be heard bubbling away and steam was escaping from the valves. The driver blew the whistle, the train set off and soon disappeared, its white smoke mingling with the swirling snow.

Inspector Fix had stayed behind.

Several hours went by. The weather was very bad, the cold biting. Fix was sitting motionless on a bench in the station. Anyone would have thought he was asleep. Despite the gale Mrs Aouda kept on going outside the room that had been placed at her disposal. She walked to the far end of the platform, trying to see through the snowstorm, seeking to pierce the fog that restricted her visibility, listening for any sound she could hear. But there was nothing. Then she would go back inside, frozen to the bone, only to come out again a few moments later but still to no avail.

Evening came. The small detachment of soldiers had not returned. Where were they at that moment? Had they managed to catch up with the Sioux? Had there been a struggle, or were the soldiers wandering around, lost in the fog? The captain in Fort Kearney was extremely worried, although he didn't want it to show.

Night fell, the snow was not so heavy, but the cold grew more intense. The most intrepid of people could not have failed to be overawed by the sight of this immense dark emptiness. Absolute silence filled the plain. There was not a bird in the sky nor an animal on the prowl to disturb its infinite stillness.

All that night Mrs Aouda, whose mind was full of premonitions of disaster and her heart racked with anxiety, wandered about on the edge of the prairie. Her imagination transported her far away and brought her up against a thousand dangers. What she suffered during those long hours cannot be put into words.

Fix still remained motionless in the same place, but he, too, was unable to sleep. At one point someone went up to him and even said something to him, but the detective sent him away, after replying to him with a shake of the head.

The night passed like this. At dawn the half-extinguished orb of the sun rose above a misty horizon. Nevertheless, visibility was about two miles. Phileas Fogg and the detachment of soldiers had headed south. The south was absolutely deserted. By now it was seven o'clock in the morning.

The captain, who was extremely worried, didn't know what to do. Should he lead a second detachment to come to the aid of the first? Should he sacrifice more men with so little chance of rescuing those who had been sacrificed in the first place? But he did not hesitate for long, and after gesturing towards one of his lieutenants he was giving him the order to lead a reconnoitring party to the south when there was a burst of gunfire. Was it a signal? The soldiers rushed out of the fort, and half a mile away they noticed a small group of men returning in good order.

Mr Fogg was leading them, and close to him were Passepartout and the two other passengers, who had been rescued from the clutches of the Sioux.

There had been a struggle ten miles to the south of Fort Kearney. A few moments before the detachment had arrived Passepartout and his companions were already fighting their captors, and the Frenchman had knocked out three of them with his bare fists when his master and the soldiers rushed to their aid.

All of them, rescuers and rescued, were greeted with shouts of joy, and Phileas Fogg handed out the promised reward to the soldiers, while Passepartout kept on saying, with good reason, 'Really and truly I'm costing my master a fortune.'

Fix didn't say a word but was looking at Mr Fogg, and it would have been difficult to analyse the conflicting thoughts then running through his mind. As for Mrs Aouda, she had taken the gentleman's hand and was squeezing it between her own, unable to speak.

Meanwhile Passepartout, as soon he had arrived, had looked for the train in the station. He was expecting to find it there, ready to set off for Omaha at full speed, and he was hoping that they might still be able to make up the time lost.

'The train! The train!' he exclaimed.

'It's gone,' replied Fix.

'And when is the next train due?' asked Phileas Fogg.

'Not until this evening.'

'Oh!' was all the impassive gentleman said in reply.

In which Inspector Fix takes Phileas Fogg's interests very much to heart

Phileas Fogg was twenty hours late. Passepartout, who had inadvertently been the cause of this delay, was desperate. He had definitely ruined his master.

It was then that the inspector went up to Mr Fogg and, looking him straight in the eye, asked, 'In all seriousness, sir, are you really in a hurry?'

'I am indeed,' replied Phileas Fogg.

'I shall say it again,' continued Fix. 'Do you really need to be in New York on 11 December by nine o'clock in the evening, when the steamer for Liverpool is due to leave?'

'I really do.'

'And if your journey hadn't been interrupted by the Sioux attack, would you have arrived in New York by the morning of the 11th?'

'Yes, with twelve hours to spare.'

'Good. So you are twenty hours behind. The difference between twenty and twelve is eight. You have eight hours to make up. Do you want to attempt it?'

'On foot?' asked Mr Fogg.

'No, by sledge,' replied Fix, 'a sledge with sails. A man has offered me this means of transport.'

It was the man who had spoken to the police inspector during the night and whose offer Fix had rejected.

Phileas Fogg made no reply, but after Fix had pointed out the man in question, who was walking around outside the station, the gentleman went up to him. A moment later Phileas Fogg and the American, whose name was Mudge, went into a shed below Fort Kearney.

There Mr Fogg was able to examine a strange-looking vehicle. It was a sort of frame built upon two long beams that were turned up at the end like the runners on a sledge, and there was room for about five or six people. A third of the way along the frame, to the front, stood a very tall mast, to which was attached a huge spanker sail. From this mast, which was firmly held in position by cables, stretched an iron stay, the purpose of which was to hoist a very large jib. At the rear a sort of oar-rudder enabled the contraption to be steered.

It was, as can be seen from this description, a sledge, but with the rigging of a sloop.[1] In winter on the ice-bound plain, when the trains are no long running because of the snow, these vehicles travel very fast from station to station. What is more they have an enormous expanse of sail – greater even than a racing cutter, which is liable to capsize – and with the wind behind them they glide along the surface of the prairies as fast if not faster than express trains.

Within a few moments Mr Fogg and the owner of this land craft had struck a deal. The wind was favourable. It was blowing strongly from the west. The snow had become hard and Mudge claimed that he could get Mr Fogg to the station in Omaha in a few hours. From there it would be easy to get to Chicago and New York as there are plenty of trains and various lines. It was therefore quite possible that they could make up the time lost. So there was no point in hesitating about whether or not to attempt this adventure.

Because he did not want to subject Mrs Aouda to the ordeal of an open-air journey in this cold, a situation that could only be made worse by the speed at which they would be travelling, Mr Fogg suggested to her that she should stay behind under Passepartout's protection at Kearney station. The trusty fellow would see about bringing her back to Europe by a better route and in more favourable circumstances.

Mrs Aouda refused to be separated from Mr Fogg and Passepartout felt very pleased that she was so definite about this. In any case, he wouldn't have wanted to leave his master for anything in the world since Fix was to remain with him.

What precisely was going through the police inspector's mind at that moment would be difficult to say. Was he less convinced he was right about Fogg now that he had come back, or did he consider him to be an extremely clever crook, who once he had completed his journey around the world, would be absolutely safe in England? Perhaps Fix's view of Mr Fogg really had changed. But he was still just as determined to do his duty, and he was more impatient than anyone to do his utmost to speed up their return to England.

By eight o'clock the sledge was ready to leave. The travellers – it would be tempting to call them passengers – took their seats and huddled together under their travel rugs. The two huge sails were hoisted, and with the force of the wind behind it the vehicle raced over the hardened snow at a rate of forty knots.

The distance separating Fort Kearney from Omaha is, in a straight line – a bee-line, as the Americans would say – two hundred miles at the most. If the wind held, they would have covered this distance in five hours. If there were no problems, the sledge should have got to Omaha by one o'clock in the afternoon.

What a journey it turned out to be! The travellers, huddled up against one another, were unable to speak. The cold, intensified by the speed, would have prevented the words from coming out of their mouths. The sledge glided over the surface of the plain as lightly as a vessel over the surface of the water – minus the swell. When the wind came skimming along the ground, it looked as if the sledge would be lifted into the air by its sails, huge wings with a vast span. Mudge, at the rudder, kept it going straight, and with a touch on the oar he prevented the contraption from veering to one side, which it had a tendency to do. All the sails caught the wind. The jib had been perked and was no longer shielded by the spanker. A topmast was hoisted and a topsail, put out into the wind, added its driving force to the other sails. It was impossible to work it out exactly, but the sledge must certainly have attained a speed of no less than forty knots.

'If nothing gives way,' said Mudge, 'we'll make it.'

It was in Mudge's interests to arrive within the deadline, because Mr Fogg, in keeping with his normal practice, had given him the incentive of a hefty bonus.

The prairie, which the sledge was directly cutting across, was as flat as the sea. It looked like an enormous frozen pond. The railroad that served this part of the territory went up from the south-west to the north-west via Grand Island, Columbus, a sizeable town in Nebraska, Schuyler, Fremont and then Omaha. It followed the right bank of the Platte River for the whole of the way. The sledge took a shorter route, going in a straight line instead of following the curve chosen by the railroad. There was no need for Mudge to fear being stopped by the Platte River at the small bend it makes before Fremont because its waters were frozen over. The way was therefore completely free of obstacles and so there were only two things for Phileas Fogg to be afraid of: damage to the craft and a change of direction or drop in the wind.

But the wind did not slacken. Far from it. It blew so hard as to bend the mast, which was firmly supported by the iron cables. These metal wires resounded as if they were the strings of a musical instrument being played with a bow. The sledge sped along to the accompaniment of this plaintive harmony, which had an exceptional intensity about it.

'These cords are in fifths and octaves,' said Mr Fogg.

These were the only words he uttered during the whole journey. Mrs Aouda, who was carefully wrapped up in furs and travel rugs, was as far as possible protected from the effects of the cold.

Passepartout meanwhile, his face as red as the setting sun seen through the mist, was breathing in the sharp air. With that un-shakeable confidence that was an essential part of his make-up, he had started to hope again. Instead of getting to New York in the morning they would get there in the evening, but there was still a possibility that this would be before the steamer for Liverpool left.

Passepartout had even felt a strong desire to shake hands with his ally Fix. He hadn't forgotten that it was the inspector himself who had got hold of the sailing sledge and therefore the only possible means of reaching Omaha in time. But because of some strange premonition he remained guarded towards Fix as usual.

In any case there was one thing that Passepartout would never forget and that was the sacrifice that Mr Fogg had made, without any hesitation, in rescuing him from the Sioux. In so doing Mr Fogg had risked his fortune and his life. No, his servant would never forget that.

While these various thoughts occupied the minds of each traveller, the sledge was flying on across the immense carpet of snow. They hardly had time to notice as they went past the few creeks, tributaries and sub-tributaries of the Little Blue River. The fields and watercourses were covered by a uniform white-ness. The plain was absolutely deserted. Covering the whole area between the Union Pacific Railroad and the branch line that is intended to link Kearney and Saint Joseph, it formed what seemed a huge desert island. There was not a single village or station or even a fort. From time to time a gruesome-looking tree flashed by, its white skeleton twisting in the wind. Some-times flocks of birds took flight all at the same time. Sometimes, too, large packs of prairie wolves, thin and hungry and driven on by some fearsome need, tried to outrun the sledge. At moments such as these Passepartout, with his revolver in his hand, stood ready to fire at the animals that got nearest. If an accident of some sort had brought the sledge to a standstill at such times, the travellers would have been attacked by these fierce carnivores and would have been in considerable danger. But the sledge stood the strain and soon raced ahead, leaving the whole pack howling behind it.

By midday Mudge recognized the tell-tale signs that he was following the frozen course of the Platte River. He didn't say anything, but he was already convinced that twenty miles further on he would reach the station at Omaha.

And sure enough, less than an hour later this skilful guide left the helm, rushed to the halyards and lowered the sails while the sledge, carried along by its own momentum, travelled another half a mile with all its sails taken in. At last it came to a standstill and Mudge, pointing to a collection of snow-covered roofs, said, 'We've arrived.'

They had indeed arrived at this station, which has frequent trains and a daily service to the east of the United States.

Passepartout and Fix had jumped out of the vehicle and were moving about to get their circulation back. They helped Mr Fogg and Mrs Aouda to get out of the sledge. Phileas Fogg paid Mudge handsomely and Passepartout shook his hand as if they had been old friends, and they all rushed off towards Omaha station.

This important city in Nebraska is where the Pacific Railroad properly speaking comes to an end, linking the Mississippi basin to the ocean. To go from Omaha to Chicago the railway, known as the Chicago–Rock Island Railroad, runs directly east, serving fifty stations on the way.

A direct train was about to leave. Phileas Fogg and his companions just had time to jump into a carriage. They hadn't seen anything of Omaha, but Passepartout admitted to himself that this was no cause for regret because it wasn't the time for sight-seeing.

At great speed the train crossed into the state of Iowa, via Council Bluffs, Des Moines and Iowa City. During the night it crossed the Mississippi at Davenport and entered Illinois via Rock Island. At four o'clock in the afternoon of the following day, the 10th, it reached Chicago, which had already risen again out of its ruins,[2] looking more impressive than ever in its position overlooking the beautiful Lake Michigan.

There are 900 miles between Chicago and New York. There was no shortage of trains in Chicago. Mr Fogg went straight from one train to another. The frisky locomotive of the Pittsburg–Fort Wayne–Chicago Railroad set off at full speed, as if it was fully aware that the honourable gentleman had no time to lose. It went like lightning through Indiana, Ohio, Pennsylvania and New Jersey, passing through towns with classical-sounding names, some having streets and tram-cars but as yet no houses. At last the Hudson came into view, and on 11 December at a quarter past eleven in the evening the train pulled up in the station, on the right bank of the river, just in front of the pier for the steamers of the Cunard Line, in other words the British and North American Royal Mail Steam Packet Company.

The *China*, bound for Liverpool, had left forty-five minutes earlier!

32

In which Phileas Fogg squares up to misfortune

The *China*'s departure seemed to signal the end of all Phileas Fogg's hopes.

No other steamer plying the direct route from America to Europe could further the gentleman's plans. This applied to the French transatlantic steamers, the ships of the White Star Line, the steamers of the Inman Company, those of the Hamburg Line and any others.

In particular the *Pereire*, belonging to the French Trans-atlantic Company – whose excellent ships were equal in speed and superior in comfort to those of every other line – didn't leave for another two days, 14 December. In any case, like the ships of the Hamburg Line,[1] it didn't go directly to Liverpool or London but to Le Havre, and the additional crossing from Le Havre to Southampton would have caused Phileas Fogg further delay, thereby rendering his final efforts useless.

As for the steamers of the Inman Company, one of them, the *City of Paris*, was setting to sea the following day, but it was pointless even thinking about it. These ships were used mainly for the transport of emigrants and so their engines lacked power; they used sail power as much as steam and their speed was poor. With them the crossing from New York to England took longer than the time that was left to Mr Fogg if he was to win his bet.

The gentleman was perfectly aware of all this from reading his Bradshaw, which gave him detailed information about ocean sailings across the globe for every day of the year.

Passepartout felt completely devastated. To have missed the steamer by forty-five minutes was a terrible blow for him. It was all his fault. Instead of helping his master, all he'd done was to keep putting obstacles in his way! And when he cast his mind back over all that had happened during the journey, when he worked out the sums of money spent for nothing and just on him, when he reflected that this huge bet, not to mention the considerable costs of this now pointless voyage, had completely ruined Mr Fogg financially, he was furious with himself.

Mr Fogg, however, made no criticism of him and, as he left the pier for the transatlantic steamers, he merely said, 'We shall decide what to do tomorrow. Come along.'

Mr Fogg, Mrs Aouda, Fix and Passepartout crossed the Hudson in the Jersey City ferry and then got into a cab, which drove them to the St Nicholas Hotel in Broadway. Rooms were found for them and they spent the night there. It went quickly for Phileas Fogg, who slept soundly, but it went much more slowly for Mrs Aouda and her companions, whose minds were so agitated that they didn't get much rest.

The next day was 12 December. From seven o'clock in the morning on the 12th to a quarter to nine in the evening on the 21st there were nine days, thirteen hours and forty-five minutes remaining. So if Phileas Fogg had set off the previous day on the *China*, one of the fastest ships of the Cunard Line, he would have arrived in Liverpool and then in London within the deadline.

Mr Fogg left the hotel alone after having instructed his servant to wait for him and to inform Mrs Aouda that she should be ready to depart at any moment.

Mr Fogg went along to the banks of the Hudson and, among the ships moored along the quaysides or at anchor in the river, he searched out carefully those that were ready to sail. Several vessels had their departure flags flying and were ready to set to sea on the morning tide. Not a single day goes by in this enormous and magnificent port of New York without a hundred ships setting out for destinations all over the world, but most of them were sailing ships and were not suitable for Mr Fogg's purposes.

The gentleman's final attempt seemed condemned to failure when suddenly he saw moored in front of the Battery, no more than a cable's length away, a propeller-driven commercial vessel, with elegant lines and with clouds of smoke coming out of its funnel, the sign that it was getting ready to sail.

Phileas Fogg hailed a rowing boat, got in and after a few strokes on the oars had reached the ladder of the *Henrietta*, a steamer with an iron hull but with all its upper works made of wood.

The captain of the *Henrietta* was on board. Phileas Fogg climbed on to the bridge and asked for him. He appeared immediately.

He was a man of about fifty, a sort of sea dog, a grumpy individual who certainly couldn't be easy to deal with. He had bulging eyes, a rusty copper-coloured complexion, red hair and a neck like a bull's. There was nothing sophisticated about his appearance.

'Are you the captain?' asked Phileas Fogg.

'That's me.'

'I am Phileas Fogg, from London.'

'I'm Andrew Speedy, from Cardiff.'[2]

'Are you about to leave?'

'In an hour.'

'Where are you making for?'

'Bordeaux.'

'What are you carrying?'

'Stones in the belly. No freight. Leaving with ballast.'

'Do you have any passengers?'

'No passengers. Never take passengers. Too cumbersome, too argumentative.'

'Does your ship go well?'

'Eleven to twelve knots, the *Henrietta*. Well known.'

'Will you take me and three other people to Liverpool?'

'To Liverpool? Why not China?'

'I said Liverpool.'

'No.'

'No?'

'No. I'm leaving for Bordeaux and Bordeaux's where I'm going.'

'At any price?'

'At any price.'

The captain had spoken and wasn't to be contradicted.

'But the owners of the *Henrietta* –' continued Phileas Fogg.

'The owner's me,' replied the captain. 'It's my ship.'

'I'll charter it from you.'

'No.'

'I'll buy it from you.'

'No.'

Phileas Fogg didn't bat an eyelid. However, the situation was serious. New York wasn't the same thing as Hong Kong and dealing with the captain of the *Henrietta* wasn't the same thing as dealing with the skipper of the *Tankadère*. So far the gentleman's money had always been able to overcome obstacles. This time money didn't work.

Nevertheless, it was essential to find a way of crossing the Atlantic by boat – unless they could get across in a hot-air balloon, which would have been very risky and, in any case, was not practical.

It looked, however, as if Phileas Fogg had an idea because he said to the captain:

'Well then, will you take me to Bordeaux?'

'No. Not even if you paid me $200!'

'I'm offering you $2,000.'

'Per person?'

'Per person.'

'And there are four of you?'

'Four.'

Captain Speedy began to scratch his forehead, as if he was intent on tearing all the skin off it. Earning $8000 without changing his route made it worth putting aside his aversion to having passengers on board. In any case, passengers at $2000 a go are no longer passengers but valuable cargo.

'I'm leaving at nine o'clock,' he said briefly. 'And if you and yours are there –'

'By nine o'clock we'll be on board,' Phileas Fogg replied, just as briefly.

It was half past eight. With the calm that never deserted him whatever the circumstances, the gentleman got off the *Henrietta*, took a carriage, went to the St Nicholas Hotel and brought back Mrs Aouda, Passepartout and the inseparable Fix, whose crossing he kindly offered to pay for.

By the time the *Henrietta* set sail, the four of them were on board.

When Passepartout discovered the cost of this latest crossing he let out the sort of extended 'Oh' that goes through every interval on the descending chromatic scale.

As for Inspector Fix, he thought to himself that the Bank of England was really going to come off badly from this business. The truth was that by the time they arrived, and even supposing that this fellow Fogg didn't throw a few more fistfuls of dollars overboard, there would still be more than £7,000 missing from the bag of banknotes.

33

Where Phileas Fogg proves himself equal to the situation

An hour later the steamer the *Henrietta* passed the lightship marking the mouth of the Hudson, went around the headland of Sandy Hook and put out to sea. During the day it followed the coastline of Long Island, keeping well clear of the beacon on Fire Island, then headed rapidly eastwards.

At midday on the following day, 13 December, a man climbed on to the bridge to take the ship's bearings. It would seem safe to assume that this man was Captain Speedy. Nothing could be further from the truth. It was Phileas Fogg, Esq.

Captain Speedy meanwhile was quite simply locked up in his cabin and was howling away, giving vent to a quite understandable anger that was reaching fever pitch.

What had happened was perfectly simple. Phileas Fogg wanted to get to Liverpool, but the captain didn't want to take him there. Phileas Fogg had then agreed to travel to Bordeaux and during the thirty hours he'd been on board he had put his banknotes to work so effectively that the crew, the sailors and the stokers – a motley collection of individuals who were on pretty bad terms with the captain – had been won over. This is why Phileas Fogg was in command instead of Captain Speedy, why the captain was locked up in his cabin and, lastly, why the *Henrietta* was heading for Liverpool. It was, though, very clear from the way he set about things that Mr Fogg had been a sailor.

It was too early to tell how things would work out. However, Mrs Aouda was worried, without letting it show. Fix had been simply dumbfounded to start with. As for Passepartout, he found the whole thing absolutely wonderful.

'Between eleven and twelve knots' was what Captain Speedy had said and, sure enough, the *Henrietta* kept up this average speed.

And so if – but there were a lot of ifs – the sea didn't get too rough, if the wind didn't veer to the east, if the vessel was spared accidental damage and mechanical breakdown, it was possible for the *Henrietta* to cover the 3,000 miles separating New York and Liverpool in the nine days between 12 and 21 December. It is true that once he'd arrived, the business of the *Henrietta* coming on top of the business at the Bank of England could well cause the gentleman more complications than he'd like.

For the first few days conditions for sailing were excellent. The sea wasn't too difficult, the wind seemed settled in the north-east, the sails were set, and under its try-sails the *Henrietta* went like a real transatlantic steamer.

Passepartout was delighted. He was full of enthusiasm for his master's latest exploit, though he didn't want to think about its consequences. The crew had never seen such a high-spirited and nimble fellow. He was very friendly towards the sailors and amazed them with his acrobatics. He treated them to compliments and tempting-looking drinks. For him they went about their work like gentlemen, and the stokers stoked like heroes. Everyone was susceptible to his infectious good humour. He'd forgotten about the recent past, the problems and the dangers. The only thing he thought about was the goal that they were so close to reaching, and sometimes he was boiling over with impatience, as if he'd been heated up by the *Henrietta*'s own furnace. The worthy fellow often circled around Fix, looking at him knowingly but not saying a word, because there was no longer any closeness between the two former friends.

In any case, it has to be said that Fix no longer had a clue about what was going on. This whole sequence of events, the takeover of the *Henrietta*, the bribing of the crew and Fogg navigating like an experienced sailor, had him baffled. He just didn't know what to think. But after all a gentleman who started out by stealing £55,000 could easily end up stealing a sailing ship. And Fix naturally went on to conclude that under Phileas Fogg's command the *Henrietta* was not heading for Liverpool at all but for some other part of the world where the thief, who had now turned into a pirate, could safely spend the rest of his life. It has to be admitted that this was a perfectly plausible explanation, and the detective was beginning seriously to regret ever having got caught up in this business.

Meanwhile Captain Speedy continued to howl away in his cabin, and Passepartout, who had been given the task of providing him with food, only did so with the greatest of caution, despite his own physical strength. Mr Fogg, on the other hand, no longer seemed to suspect there was a captain on board.

On the 13th they reached the tail-end of the Grand Banks of Newfoundland. These are dangerous waters. Especially during the winter, fog is common and the storms are frightening. The previous day the barometer had dropped suddenly, a sign that a change in the weather was imminent. And, sure enough, during the night the temperature changed, the cold became more intense and at the same time the wind veered to the south-east.

It was a setback. In order to stick to his route Mr Fogg had to take in the sails and increase the steam. Nevertheless, the ship's progress was slowed down by the state of the sea with high waves breaking against its stem. The ship began to pitch violently and this further affected its speed. The wind was gradually reaching hurricane force and it already looked as if the *Henrietta* might not be able to face the waves full-on. But if it had to run before the storm that would be a leap into the unknown, with all the dangers that this entailed.

Passepartout's face became as dark as the sky, and for two days the worthy fellow was on tenterhooks. But Phileas Fogg was a bold sailor who knew how to stand up to the sea and he kept straight on, without even reducing steam. When the *Henrietta* couldn't rise above the waves it went straight through them, and although the deck was swamped the ship carried on. Sometimes, too, the propeller was lifted clean out of the water and the blades whirred madly in the air as a mountainous wave raised the stern, but still the ship continued on its course.

Nevertheless, the wind didn't freshen as much as might have been feared. It wasn't one of those hurricanes that reach speeds of up to ninety miles per hour. The wind didn't go beyond gale force, but unfortunately it kept on blowing from the south-east and made it impossible to put the sails out. However, as will soon become apparent, the wind would have been very useful for helping out the steam power.

The 16th of December was the seventy-fifth day since they had left London. In a word, the delay to the *Henrietta* was still not serious. Half the crossing had almost been completed and the most difficult waters were already behind them. If it had been summer, success would have been guaranteed. As it was winter, they were at the mercy of bad weather. Passepartout didn't make his views known. Deep down he was hopeful and, if the wind failed, he was counting on steam to get them there.

As it happened, on that particular day the engineer went on deck, met Mr Fogg and had quite a sharp conversation with him.

Without knowing why – no doubt by a premonition – Passe-partout felt a vague sort of uneasiness. He would have given his right arm to hear what was being said. However, he did manage to catch a few words, including the following, spoken by his master, 'Are you sure that what you're saying is true?'

'Absolutely certain, sir,' replied the engineer. 'Don't forget that since we set out we've been going full blast, and even if we had enough coal to go at low steam from New York to Bordeaux, we don't have enough to go at full steam from New York to Liverpool.'

'I shall decide what to do,' replied Mr Fogg.

Passepartout had understood. He suddenly became extremely worried.

They were going to run out of coal.

'Oh, if my master can get us out of this one,' he said to himself, 'then he really is somebody.'

After bumping into Fix, he couldn't help telling him about the situation.

'So,' the inspector replied, gritting his teeth, 'you really think that we're heading for Liverpool.'

'But of course.'

'Idiot!' answered the inspector, as he walked away, shrugging his shoulders.

Passepartout was about to take strong exception to this word, even if he wasn't in a position to understand its full significance, but he said to himself that poor old Fix must be very disappointed and that his pride must have taken a battering at the idea of having gone around the world on a wild goose chase, and so Passepartout let the remark pass.

So what would Phileas Fogg's decision be? It was hard to imagine. However, the phlegmatic gentleman seemed to have made up his mind because that very evening he sent for the engineer and said to him, 'Stoke up the boilers and go full steam ahead until there's no fuel left.'

A few moments later the *Henrietta*'s funnel was belching out clouds of smoke.

So the ship continued on course at full steam, but just as he had warned, two days later, the 18th, the engineer announced that they would run out of coal during that day.

'Don't let the fires die down,' replied Mr Fogg. 'On the contrary. Keep up the pressure in the engine.'

That day, at about midday, after taking a bearing to calculate the ship's position, Phileas Fogg sent for Passepartout and told him to go and fetch Captain Speedy. It was like telling the good fellow to go and unleash a tiger, and he went down to the poop deck saying to himself, 'He's going to go absolutely berserk.'

A few minutes later, amid shouting and swearing, a bomb duly landed on the poop deck. This bomb was Captain Speedy. It was obvious that he was about to explode.

'Where are we?' were the first words he uttered, choking with anger, and it was clear that if this worthy fellow had had a weak heart he would never have survived.

'Where are we?' he repeated, red in the face.

'770 miles east of Liverpool,' replied Mr Fogg, with total composure.

'Pirate!' exclaimed Andrew Speedy.

'I sent for you, sir –'

'Sea rover!'

'– sir,' continued Mr Fogg, 'to ask you to sell me your ship.'

'No. Like hell. No.'

'The fact is that I'm going to have to burn it.'

'Burn my ship!'

'Yes, at least the upper works, because we're running out of fuel.'

'Burn my ship!' exclaimed Captain Speedy, who had difficulty getting the words out of his mouth any more. 'A ship worth $50,000!'

'Here's $60,000,' replied Phileas Fogg, handing the captain a wad of banknotes.

The effect on Andrew Speedy was spectacular. No true American can fail to be moved by the sight of $60,000. For a moment the captain forgot about his anger, his imprisonment and all his grievances against his passenger. His ship was twenty years old; this deal was worth a packet. The bomb was no longer going to explode. Mr Fogg had removed the fuse.

'But I'll still have the iron hull left,' he said, sounding remarkably calmer.

'The iron hull and the machinery, sir. Are we agreed?'

'Agreed.'

With that Andrew Speedy grabbed the wad of banknotes, counted them and stashed them away in his pocket.

During this scene Passepartout was white as a sheet. Fix, for his part, almost had a heart attack. Nearly £20,000 had already been spent and now here was Fogg giving away to the vendor the hull and the machinery, in other words almost half the total value of the ship. It was just as well that the amount of money stolen from the bank was £55,000.

When Andrew Speedy had put all the money away in his pocket, Mr Fogg said to him, 'Sir, let me explain something to you. If I am not back in London by eight forty-five in the evening on 21 December I will lose £20,000. The fact is that I missed the steamer from New York and because you refused to take me to Liverpool –'

'And I did the right thing there, I'll swear that by the devil,' exclaimed Andrew Speedy, 'because I've made at least $40,000.'

Then he added, rather more calmly, 'Do you know something, Captain . . .'

'Fogg.'

'Captain Fogg, well, there's a bit of the Yankee about you.'

And after giving his passenger what he thought was a compliment, he was about to go when Phileas Fogg said to him, 'So this boat belongs to me now, doesn't it?'

'Well, from the keel to the top of the masts, everything made of wood, that is.'

'Good. Take out all the internal fittings and use them as firewood.'

It is easy to imagine how much dry wood needs to be burnt to keep the steam up to sufficient pressure. That day the poop deck, the deck-houses, the cabins, the crew's quarters and the spar-deck all went.

The following day, 19 December, they burnt the masting, the spare masts and yards, and the spars. They chopped down the masts and cut them up with axes. The crew set about their task with incredible energy. Passepartout was slicing, cutting and sawing away, doing the work of ten men. It was an orgy of destruction.

The day after, 20 December, the rails, the bulwarks, the dead-works and most of the deck were fed to the flames. The *Henrietta* was now so low it looked like a pontoon, not a ship.

But that day they sighted the coast of Ireland and the Fastnet lighthouse.

However, by ten o'clock in the evening the ship was still off Queenstown.[1] Phileas Fogg only had twenty-four hours left to get to London. That was precisely how long it would take the *Henrietta* to get to Liverpool – even if it went at full steam. And steam was just what the daring gentleman was running out of!

'Sir,' Captain Speedy then said to him, as he had now come round to showing an interest in his plans, 'I feel really sorry for you. Everything's against you. We're still no further than Queenstown.'

'Ah!' said Mr Fogg. 'Is that the town we can see, where the lights are coming from?'

'Yes.'

'Can we enter the harbour?'

'Not for another three hours. Only at high tide.'

'Let's wait, then,' Phileas Fogg replied calmly, without letting it show on his face that he was about to attempt once again to overcome his bad luck by another master stroke.

Queenstown is, as it happens, a port on the Irish coast where transatlantic liners from the United States drop off their mail-bags. These letters are taken to Dublin by express trains that are always ready and waiting. From Dublin they go to Liverpool via high-speed steamers – cutting twelve hours off the time taken by the fastest vessels of the shipping companies.

Phileas Fogg thought that he, too, could make up twelve hours, as the mail from America did. Instead of arriving in Liverpool on the *Henrietta* the following evening he would get there by midday, which would allow him time to get to London by eight forty-five in the evening.

Towards one o'clock in the afternoon the *Henrietta* entered Queenstown harbour on the full tide, and Phileas Fogg, after receiving a vigorous handshake from Captain Speedy, left the latter on the flattened carcass of his ship, which was still worth half what he had got for selling it.

The passengers disembarked immediately. Fix, at that moment, felt a great urge to arrest Fogg. He refrained from doing so, however. Why? What struggle was going on inside him? Had he changed his mind about Mr Fogg? Did he realize at last that he'd been wrong? Nevertheless, Fix did not let go of Mr Fogg. Along with him, Mrs Aouda and Passepartout, who was in such a rush he didn't pause for breath, he got into the train from Queenstown at half past one in the morning, reached Dublin as dawn was breaking and immediately got on to one of those steamers – real steel rockets that are all engine – which do not bother to rise with the waves but invariably go straight through them.

At twenty minutes to midday on 21 December, Phileas Fogg at last landed at Liverpool docks. He was only six hours away from London.

But at that moment Fix went up to him, put his hand on his

shoulder and, showing him his warrant, said, 'You are Phileas
Fogg, are you not?'

    'Yes, sir.'

    'In the name of Her Majesty the Queen, I arrest you.'

34

*Which provides Passepartout with the opportunity
to make an appalling but perhaps original
play on words*

Phileas Fogg was in prison. He had been locked up in the gaol
of the custom-house in Liverpool and was to spend the night
there before being transferred to London.

At the time of the arrest Passepartout's instinct was to throw
himself at the detective. He had been restrained by some
policemen. Mrs Aouda was horrified at the brutality of it all
and, because she knew nothing about the background, was
unable to understand what was happening. Passepartout
explained the situation to her. Mr Fogg, this upright and courageous gentleman to whom she owed her life, had been arrested
like a common thief. The young woman protested against this
allegation. She felt deep indignation and tears poured down her
cheeks when she saw she was powerless to do anything, to
attempt anything to save her saviour.

As for Fix, he had arrested the gentleman because his sense
of duty told him to do so, irrespective of whether or not he was
guilty. The courts would decide that.

But then something occurred to Passepartout, the terrible
thought that he was the cause of this whole disaster. Why on
earth had he concealed the situation from Mr Fogg? When Fix
had revealed that he was a police inspector and that his task was
to arrest Mr Fogg, why had he taken it upon himself not to alert
his master? If he had warned him, his master would certainly
have given Fix proof of his innocence and would have shown
him his error. In any case, he wouldn't have dragged the
wretched detective behind him all around the world and at his
own expense when the man's main concern was to arrest him
the moment he set foot on British soil.[1] When he thought about

all his foolishness and carelessness, the poor fellow was over-come with remorse. He cried; he was a pathetic sight. He wanted to knock himself senseless.

Despite the cold, Mrs Aouda and he had stayed under the portico of the custom-house. Neither of them wanted to leave the place. They wanted to see Mr Fogg just one more time.

As for the gentleman himself, he was well and truly ruined, financially speaking, and just as he was reaching his goal. His arrest meant the end of everything for him. When he had arrived in Liverpool at twenty minutes to midday on 21 December, he had until eight forty-five to show up at the Reform Club, in other words nine hours and fifteen minutes – and he only needed six to get to London.

Anyone going into the custom-house at that moment would have found Mr Fogg sitting motionless on a wooden bench, showing no sign of anger and looking as imperturbable as ever. It was impossible to tell whether he was resigned, but this last blow didn't seem to have affected him, at least outwardly. Was there burning away inside him some secret rage, frightening because it was bottled up until the last moment when it would burst out with unstoppable force? No one could tell. But Phileas Fogg was sitting there, calm, waiting . . . but for what? Did he still retain some hope? Did he still believe he could succeed after the prison door had closed behind him?

Whatever the case, Mr Fogg had carefully placed his watch on the table and he was looking at the hands move forward. Not a word crossed his lips, but there was an especially intent look on his face.

In any event the situation was grim, and for anyone unable to read what was going through his mind it may be summed up as follows:

If he was an honest man, Phileas Fogg was ruined.

If he was a criminal, he had been caught.

Did it occur to him at this point to try to escape? Did he think of looking for a possible way out of where he was being held? Did he plan to run away? It might be tempting to think so because at one point he walked around the room. But the door was firmly locked and the windows were equipped with iron bars. So he went to sit down again and took out of his pocket-book his travel schedule. On the line where he had written '21 December, Saturday, Liverpool', he added: '80th day, 11.40 a.m.'

Then he waited.

One o'clock struck on the custom-house clock. Mr Fogg noted that his watch was two minutes ahead of this clock.

Two o'clock. Assuming that he got on to an express train there and then he could still get to London and to the Reform Club before eight forty-five in the evening. He frowned slightly.

At thirty-three minutes past two there was a commotion outside, the noise of doors being flung open. Passepartout's voice could be heard, and Fix's.

Phileas Fogg's face lit up for a moment.

The cell door opened and he saw Mrs Aouda, Passepartout and Fix rushing towards him.

Fix was out of breath and his hair all over the place. He was unable to speak properly.

'Sir,' he stammered, 'sir . . . sorry . . . unfortunate likeness . . . Thief arrested three days ago . . . you . . . free!'

Phileas Fogg was free! He went up to the detective. He looked him straight in the eye and, with the only rapid movement he had ever made or ever would make in his life, he swung his arms back and then, with the precision of an automaton, struck the unfortunate inspector with both fists.

'Well hit!' exclaimed Passepartout, who allowed himself an appalling play on words worthy of a true Frenchman, by adding: 'Good heavens! That's what I'd call a striking example of the benefits of an English education.'[2]

Fix, who'd been knocked to the floor, didn't say a word. He'd only got what he deserved. But immediately Mr Fogg, Mrs Aouda and Passepartout left the custom-house. They jumped into a cab and within a few minutes were at Liverpool station.

Phileas Fogg asked if there was an express ready to leave for London.

It was two-forty . . . The express had left thirty-five minutes earlier.

Phileas Fogg then ordered a special train.

There were several high-speed locomotives with steam up. But for operating reasons the special train was unable to leave the station until three o'clock.

By three o'clock, after having a word with the engine driver about a bonus he could earn, Phileas Fogg was speeding off towards London in the company of the young woman and his faithful servant.

They needed to cover the distance between Liverpool and London in five and a half hours. This was a perfectly reasonable proposition when the line was clear all the way, but there were unavoidable delays and so by the time the gentleman arrived at the station all the clocks in London were showing ten minutes to nine.

After completing his journey around the world Phileas Fogg had arrived five minutes late.

He had lost.

35

In which Passepartout doesn't need to be told twice to do as his master orders

The following day the inhabitants of Savile Row would certainly have been surprised to be informed that Mr Fogg was back in residence. The windows and doors were all closed. Nothing had changed from the outside.

What had happened was that after leaving the station Phileas Fogg had told Passepartout to buy some food and he had gone back to his house.

The gentleman had responded to this blow with his usual impassiveness. He was ruined and it was all the fault of this bungling police inspector. After travelling at a steady pace during this long journey, after overcoming a thousand obstacles, braving a thousand dangers and finding the time to do some good on the way, to fail at his port of arrival in such violent circumstances, which he could not have foreseen and was powerless to combat, was a terrible thing. Of the sizeable sum of money he had taken with him when he set out, only an insignificant amount was left over. All that remained of his fortune was the £20,000 deposited with Baring Brothers, and even those £20,000 were what he owed to his colleagues from the Reform Club. After spending so much money, even if he had won his bet he probably wouldn't have been very much richer – anyway, that probably hadn't been his aim, since he was the sort of man who bet for honour not gain – but losing his bet spelt his financial ruin. In any case the gentleman had made up his mind. He knew what was left for him to do.

A room in the house in Savile Row had been set aside for Mrs Aouda. The young woman was desperate. From some comments of Mr Fogg she had concluded that he was planning some fateful deed.

It is of course well known to what dreadful extremes English monomaniacs can be driven by their single-minded obsessions. This was why Passepartout was keeping a careful eye on his master, without making it obvious.

But, before anything else, the good fellow had gone up to his bedroom and switched off the gas lamp, which had been burning away for eighty days. He had found the bill from the gas company in the letterbox and he thought it was high time he put an end to the costs he had incurred.

The night went by. Mr Fogg had gone to bed, but did he sleep? As for Mrs Aouda, she was unable to get any rest at all. Passepartout, for his part, had kept watch outside his master's room, like a faithful dog.

The next day Mr Fogg called for him and told him in as few words as possible to see to Mrs Aouda's breakfast. All he wanted for himself was a cup of tea and a piece of toast. He would like Mrs Aouda to excuse him for lunch and dinner because he needed to devote all his time to putting his affairs in order. He would not be going downstairs. Only in the evening would he ask Mrs Aouda's permission to speak to her for a few moments.

Having been informed of his master's schedule for the day, all Passepartout could do was to fall in with it. He looked at his master, who was as impassive as ever, and he couldn't find the courage to leave his room. He was downcast and beset with remorse, because he felt more and more responsible for this irreparable disaster. If only he had warned Mr Fogg and disclosed Fix's plans to him, Mr Fogg would certainly not have trailed the detective along behind him all the way to Liverpool, and then—

Passepartout couldn't stand it any longer.

'Master! Mr Fogg!' he exclaimed, 'curse me! It's all my fault that –'

'I'm not going to accuse anyone,' replied Mr Fogg in the calmest tone of voice imaginable. 'Off you go.'

Passepartout left the room and went off to see the young woman to tell her what his master's intentions were.

'Madam, I'm absolutely powerless on my own. I have no influence whatsoever over my master. Perhaps you . . .'

'What influence could I have?' replied Mrs Aouda. 'Mr Fogg is impervious to any. Has he ever realized how much I wanted to pour out my gratitude to him? Has he ever been able to read my heart? My friend, you must not leave him alone, not for a single moment. You say that he has expressed the intention of speaking to me this evening?'

'Yes, madam. It must be to do with safeguarding your position in England.'

'Let's wait and see,' replied the young woman, looking thoughtful.

And so for the whole of that Sunday the house in Savile Row looked deserted, and for the first time since living there Phileas Fogg did not go to his club as Big Ben struck half past eleven.

In any case, what would have been the point in the gentleman going to the Reform Club? His colleagues were no longer expecting him. Since on the previous evening, on the fateful date of Saturday 21 December, Phileas Fogg had not shown up in the lounge of the Reform Club by eight forty-five, he had lost his bet. There was no longer even any need for him to go to his bank to withdraw the sum of £20,000. His opponents already had in their hands a cheque he had signed and all that was needed was to put the cheque through his account with Baring Brothers for the £20,000 to be credited to them.

As there was no point in Mr Fogg going out, so he didn't do so. He stayed in his room and put his affairs in order. Passepartout kept going up and down the staircase in the house in Savile Row. Time went by very slowly for the poor fellow. He listened outside the door of his master's bedroom and did so without thinking that he was being in the least indiscreet. He looked through the keyhole with the firm conviction that he was entitled to do so.

Passepartout feared a catastrophe at any moment. Sometimes he thought about Fix, but a change had come over him. He no longer bore a grudge against the police inspector. Like everybody else, Fix had been wrong about Phileas Fogg, and in trailing him and arresting him he had only been doing his duty, whereas he, Passepartout . . . He was overwhelmed by the thought of this and he considered himself the most wretched of creatures.

When eventually Passepartout felt too unhappy to be alone, he knocked on Mrs Aouda's door, went into her bedroom, sat down in a corner without saying anything and looked at the young woman, who still seemed lost in her thoughts.

At about half past seven in the evening Mr Fogg sent a message to Mrs Aouda asking to be allowed to see her, and a few moments later the young woman and he were alone together in her room.

Phileas Fogg took a chair and sat down near the fireplace, opposite Mrs Aouda. His face was expressionless. The Fogg who had come back was exactly the same Fogg as had gone away. The same calm and the same impassiveness.

He remained silent for five minutes. Then, looking up at Mrs Aouda, he said, 'Madam, will you forgive me for having brought you to England?'

'Forgive you, Mr Fogg?' replied Mrs Aouda, struggling to keep her emotions under control.

'Please allow me to finish,' continued Mr Fogg. 'When I conceived the idea of taking you far away from your own country, which had become so dangerous for you, I was a wealthy man and I was expecting to bestow some of that wealth on you. Your life would have been happy and free. Now I am penniless.'

'I know, Mr Fogg,' the young woman replied, 'and I would like to ask you something in turn: will you forgive me for having followed you and – who can tell? – for perhaps having contributed to your ruin by delaying you?'

'Madam, it was impossible for you to remain in India, and your safety could only be guaranteed by making sure that you were far enough away not to fall into the hands of those fanatics again.'

'So, Mr Fogg,' Mrs Aouda continued, 'not content to rescue me from a horrible death, you also felt duty-bound to provide for me abroad?'

'Yes, madam, but things have turned out against me.

However, I ask to be allowed to bestow on you the little I still have.'

'But what will become of you, Mr Fogg?' asked Mrs Aouda.

'I, madam,' the gentleman replied coldly, 'need nothing.'

'But how, sir, will you face the fate that awaits you?'

'In the appropriate way,' replied Mr Fogg.

'In any case,' went on Mrs Aouda, 'poverty cannot afflict a person such as you. Your friends –'

'I have no friends, madam.'

'Your relatives –'

'I have no relatives left.'

'I feel truly sorry for you, then, Mr Fogg, because loneliness is a sad thing. No one to pour your heart out to. And yet people say that even poverty is bearable as long there are two of you.'

'So it is said, madam.'

'Mr Fogg,' Mrs Aouda then said, as she got to her feet and offered the gentleman her hand, 'would you like both a relative and a friend? Would you like to have me as your wife?'

When he heard these words Mr Fogg also got to his feet. There was a sort of unusual gleam in his eyes, and his lips looked as if they were trembling. Mrs Aouda looked at him. The sincerity, uprightness, firmness and gentleness of the beautiful gaze of a noble woman who will risk anything to save the person to whom she owes everything first surprised and then penetrated him. He closed his eyes for a moment, as if to prevent this gaze from going any deeper into him. When he opened them, he said simply, 'I love you! Yes, truly, by everything that is sacred in the world, I love you and I am wholly yours.'

'Ah!' exclaimed Mrs Aouda, placing her hand on her heart.

Passepartout was rung for. He came straightaway. Mr Fogg was still holding Mrs Aouda's hand in his. Passepartout understood, and his broad face beamed like the midday sun in a tropical sky.

Mr Fogg asked whether it was too late to give notice to the Rev. Samuel Wilson, of the parish of Marylebone.

Passepartout put on his best smile.

'Never too late,' he said.

It was only five past eight.

'It'll be for tomorrow, Monday?' he said.

'Tomorrow, Monday?' asked Mr Fogg, looking at the young woman.

'Tomorrow, Monday!' replied Mrs Aouda.

Passepartout went out of the house, running as fast as he could.

36

*In which shares in Phileas Fogg are back in demand
on the stockmarket*

Now is the time to recount how public opinion suddenly changed when the news broke that the real bank robber, a certain James Strand, had been arrested on 17 December in Edinburgh.

Three days earlier Phileas Fogg had been a criminal ruthlessly hunted down by the police, and now he was the most respectable of gentlemen, who with a mathematical sense of timing was completing his eccentric journey around the world.

It created a huge splash and sensation in the newspapers. The whole betting fraternity, both for and against, which had forgotten all about this business, suddenly reappeared from nowhere. All the earlier transactions were valid again. All the financial commitments were once more binding and, it must also be said, the betting started up again, with renewed vigour. Phileas Fogg's name was once more in demand on the London market.

The gentleman's five colleagues from the Reform Club spent those three days in a state of some anxiety. The Phileas Fogg they had forgotten about was reappearing before their very eyes. Where was he at that particular moment? By 17 December, the day when James Strand had been arrested, Phileas Fogg had been away for seventy-six days and they hadn't heard a word from him. Had he been killed? Had he given up the struggle, or was he still continuing his journey following the agreed route? Would he suddenly show up outside the drawing-room of the Reform Club on Saturday 21 December at eight forty-five in the evening, like an incarnation of the god of punctuality?

It would be impossible to describe the anxiety that afflicted this section of English society over those three days. Telegrams were sent to America and to Asia in an attempt to get news of Phileas Fogg. Someone was sent morning and evening to keep a lookout on the house in Savile Row – to no avail. Even the police had no idea of the whereabouts of Inspector Fix, who had so unfortunately followed the wrong lead. None of this, however, prevented the betting from starting up again and on an even greater scale. Like a racehorse, Phileas Fogg was now into the final straight. The odds quoted against him were no longer a hundred to one but twenty, ten, five, and the elderly invalid Lord Albermarle was putting money on him at evens.

On the Saturday evening there was therefore a large crowd in Pall Mall and the surrounding area. It looked like a huge gathering of stockbrokers, permanently stationed outside the Reform Club. No traffic could get through. People were talking and arguing and shouting out the value of 'Phileas Fogg' shares as if they were government bonds. The police had considerable difficulty in controlling the crowds of onlookers, and the nearer it got to the time when Phileas Fogg was supposed to arrive, the more the tension and excitement mounted.

That evening the gentleman's five colleagues had been together for nine hours in the main drawing-room of the Reform Club. The two bankers John Sullivan and Samuel Fallentin, the engineer Andrew Stuart, Gauthier Ralph, one of the directors of the Bank of England, and the brewer Thomas Flanagan were all waiting anxiously.

At the moment when the clock in the main drawing-room showed eight twenty-five, Andrew Stuart got up and said:

'Gentlemen, in twenty minutes the deadline agreed between Mr Fogg and ourselves will have expired.'

'What time did the last train from Liverpool arrive?' asked Thomas Flanagan.

'Seven twenty-three,' replied Gauthier Ralph, 'and the next train doesn't arrive until ten past midnight.'

'Well then, gentlemen,' continued Andrew Stuart, 'if Phileas Fogg had arrived on the seven twenty-three, he would have been here by now. We can therefore assume that we've won the bet.'

'Let's wait before we come to any conclusion,' replied Samuel

Fallentin. 'You know that our colleague is an eccentric of the highest order. It's well known how exact he is in everything. He never arrives too early or too late, and I wouldn't be at all surprised if he showed up here at the last minute.'

'Personally,' said Andrew Stuart, extremely tense as usual, 'if he was standing in front of me I wouldn't believe my own eyes.'

'I agree,' went on Thomas Flanagan. 'Phileas Fogg's plan was completely crazy. However exact he may have been, it was impossible for him to prevent unavoidable delays from happening, and a delay of two or three days was enough to jeopardize his journey.'

'You will note, in addition,' added John Sullivan, 'that we have received no news at all of our colleague, and yet there were plenty of opportunities for him to send a telegram during his travels.'

'He has lost, gentlemen,' Andrew Stuart replied, 'he has lost hands down! You know in any case that the *China*, the only steamer from New York that he could have caught to get to Liverpool in time, arrived yesterday. Well, here's the passenger list, as published in the *Shipping Gazette*, and Phileas Fogg's name is not on it. Even if luck was on his side, our colleague would still hardly have reached America. I would reckon that he's about twenty days at least behind schedule and that poor old Lord Albermarle will also lose his £5,000.'

'It's obvious,' replied Gauthier Ralph, 'and tomorrow all we have to do is to present Mr Fogg's cheque at Baring Brothers.'

At that moment the drawing-room clock showed eight forty.

'Another five minutes,' said Andrew Stuart.

The five colleagues looked at one another. It can be assumed that their hearts were beginning to beat a bit faster, because even for such experienced gamblers the amount of money at stake was considerable. But they didn't want any of this to show because, following Samuel Fallentin's suggestion, they seated themselves around a card table.

'I wouldn't give up my £4,000 share in the bet,' said Andrew Stuart as he sat down, 'even if someone gave me £3,999 for it.'

The hands on the clock were showing at that moment eight forty-two.

The players had taken their cards, but all the time they kept staring at the clock. However sure they were of themselves, it can safely be said that they had never found the minutes so long.

'Eight forty-three,' said Thomas Flanagan, cutting the pack that Gauthier Ralph put in front of him.

Then there was a moment's silence. The huge drawing-room of the Reform Club was quiet. But outside could be heard the noise of the crowd and sometimes, above that, high-pitched shouting. The clock pendulum marked the seconds with mathematical regularity. Each player could count the sixtieths of a minute that he heard quite distinctly.

'Eight forty-four,' said John Sullivan, in a tone of voice that accidentally betrayed his emotion.

Only a minute to go and the bet was won. Andrew Stuart and his colleagues had stopped playing. They had put aside their cards. They were counting the seconds.

At the fortieth second there was nothing. At the fiftieth still nothing.

At the fifty-fifth, they heard what sounded like thunder outside, applause and hurrahs, and even some swearing, which got louder and louder as it rolled unstoppably towards them.

The card-players got to their feet.

At the fifty-seventh second, the drawing-room door opened, and before the pendulum had struck the sixtieth second Phileas Fogg appeared, escorted by a jubilant crowd that had forced its way into the club, and in his calm voice he said, 'Here I am, gentlemen.'

37

In which it is proved that Phileas Fogg has gained nothing from this journey around the world, other than happiness

Yes. It was Phileas Fogg in person.

It will be remembered that at five past eight in the evening – about twenty-five hours since the travellers had got back to London – Passepartout had been told to inform Rev. Samuel Wilson about a certain wedding that was due to take place the very next day.

So Passepartout had set off, absolutely delighted at the idea. He quickly went along to Rev. Samuel Wilson's house, but the clergyman had not yet got back. Passepartout decided to wait, which he did for a good twenty minutes at least.

It was eight thirty-five before he was able to leave the clergyman's house, but what a state he was in by then. His hair was all over the place, he was without his hat, and running, running as no one had ever run before, knocking over passers-by, rushing along the pavement at breakneck speed.

It took him three minutes to get back to the house in Savile Row and he collapsed out of breath on the floor of Mr Fogg's bedroom.

He was unable to speak.

'What's the matter?' asked Mr Fogg.

'Master...' stammered Passepartout, 'wedding...impossible.'

'Impossible?'

'Impossible . . . for tomorrow.'

'Why?'

'Because tomorrow . . . is Sunday.'

'Monday,' replied Mr Fogg.

'No . . . today . . . Saturday.'

'Saturday? Impossible.'

'Yes, yes, yes!' exclaimed Passepartout. 'You are a day out. We arrived twenty-four hours early . . . but there are only ten minutes left!'

Passepartout had seized his master by the collar and he was dragging him off with irresistible force.

After being snatched away like this and without having the time to think, Phileas Fogg left his room and his house, jumped into a cab, promised the driver £100, and, after running over two dogs and bumping into five carriages, reached the Reform Club.

The clock was showing eight forty-five when he appeared in the main drawing-room.

Phileas Fogg had completed his journey around the world in eighty days.

Phileas Fogg had won his £20,000 bet.

So how could a man who was so precise and meticulous have been a day out in his calculations? How could he think when he arrived in London that it was Saturday evening of 21 December when it was instead Friday 20 December, only seventy-nine days after he set out?

The explanation of this mistake is very simple and here it is.

Without realizing it, Phileas Fogg had gained a day during his journey, simply because he had gone around the world from west to east, just as he would have lost a day if he had gone in the opposite direction from east to west.

By travelling eastwards Phileas Fogg had gone towards the sun and therefore the days became shorter for him by four minutes with every degree of longitude he crossed in that direction. As the earth has a circumference of 360 degrees, these 360 degrees multiplied by four minutes give exactly twenty-four hours, that is, the day that he had gained without being aware of it. In other words, by going eastwards Phileas Fogg had seen the sun cross the meridian *eighty* times, whereas his colleagues back in London had only seen it cross *seventy-nine* times. This is why on that very day, which was a Saturday and not a Sunday, as Phileas Fogg thought, these gentlemen were waiting for him in the drawing-room of the Reform Club.

And this is what Passepartout's famous watch, which was still set on London time, would have told him if it had shown the days as well as the minutes and hours.

Phileas Fogg had therefore won the £20,000. But as he had spent about £19,000 during his journey, the financial return wasn't very great. However, as has already been said, what had made this eccentric gentleman take on the bet was the challenge, not the money. What was more, he divided up the remaining £1,000 between the trusty Passepartout and the unfortunate Fix, towards whom he could feel no resentment. The only thing was that on a point of principle he held back from his servant the cost of the 1,920 hours of gas that Passepartout had been responsible for wasting.

That same evening Mr Fogg, as impassive and phlegmatic as ever, said to Mrs Aouda:

'Are you still prepared to marry me, madam?'

'Mr Fogg,' replied Mrs Aouda, 'I'm the one who should be asking this question. You were ruined, but now you are rich.'

'I beg your pardon, madam, but this wealth belongs to you. If you hadn't thought of getting married, my servant wouldn't have gone to Rev. Samuel Wilson's, I wouldn't have been informed of my error and . . .'

'Dear Mr Fogg,' said the young woman.

'Dear Aouda,' replied Phileas Fogg.

It will come as no surprise to learn that the wedding took place forty-eight hours later, and that Passepartout, looking magnificent, resplendent and dazzling, gave her away. After all, hadn't he been the one who rescued her and wasn't this honour owing to him?

Nevertheless, the following day at the crack of dawn Passepartout was banging on his master's door.

The door opened and the impassive gentleman appeared.

'What's the matter, Passepartout?'

'What's the matter, sir, is something I've just discovered this minute.'

'Which is?'

'That we could have gone around the world in only seventy-nine days.'

'Certainly,' replied Mr Fogg, 'by not going across India. But if I hadn't gone across India, I wouldn't have rescued Mrs Aouda, and she wouldn't now be my wife, and . . .'

With that Mr Fogg quietly closed the door.

And so Phileas Fogg had won his bet. He had completed this journey around the world in eighty days. To do so he had used all possible means of transport: steamships, railways, carriages, yachts, commercial vessels, a sledge and an elephant. The eccentric gentleman had displayed throughout his outstanding qualities of composure and precision. But apart from this, what had he gained from all this travel? What had the journey brought him?

Nothing, it could be said. Nothing, that is, except for a charming wife who, however unlikely it may seem, made him the happiest of men.

In all truth, isn't this more than enough reward for going around the world?

Notes

I

In which Phileas Fogg and Passepartout agree their relationship, that of master and servant

1. *Savile Row*: Before it became famous in the course of the nineteenth century as the centre of the high-class tailoring trade for men, Savile Row was known as a desirable residential street in the West End of London.

2. *Sheridan*: Better known nowadays for his plays, especially *The Rivals* (1775) and *The School for Scandal* (1777), Richard Brinsley Sheridan (born Dublin 1751) was also a well-known politician and parliamentarian in his day. Verne commits two errors of fact concerning Sheridan: he lived in fact in number 14 Savile Row, and died in 1816. However, Verne's main point is the contrast between the dashing, public figure of Sheridan and the mysterious, private persona of Fogg.

3. *the Reform Club*: A famous gentleman's club founded in the 1830s, after the passing of the Reform Bill (1832). Its impressive premises in Pall Mall, referred to at the beginning of chapter 3, were the work of the architect Sir Charles Barry (1795–1860), who also designed the Houses of Parliament following the fire of 1834 that devastated parliament's medieval buildings.

4. *Inn of Court*: One of a group of four legal societies or 'colleges of lawyers' (to translate literally Verne's phrase in the French original) – the Inner Temple, the Middle Temple, Gray's Inn and Lincoln's Inn – dating back to the Middle Ages. In order to practise (to be called to the Bar), every barrister in England and Wales must be registered as a member of one of these Inns of Court.

5. *the Court of Chancery ... the Queen's Bench ... the Court of Exchequer ... the Ecclesiastical Court*: At the time when Verne

was writing (1872), these were different courts in the English legal system. Chancery, famously satirized for the slowness of its procedures in Charles Dickens's *Bleak House* (1853), dealt with matters of equity (originally the jurisdiction of the king's conscience), whereas the Queen's Bench and the Court of Exchequer dealt with matters of English common law, and the Ecclesiastical Court with matters concerning the clergy of the Church of England. After reforms in the period 1873–5 (the Judicature Acts), the first three courts became separate divisions of the High Court of Justice. Verne is not here concerned with the niceties of the workings of the English legal system so much as with an enumeration of institutions in order to produce a cumulative 'reality effect' of Englishness.

6.   *the Harmonic Society . . . the Entomological Society*: It is unclear what real-life organization, if any, the Harmonic Society refers to, but its precise identity – clearly musical – is less important than the effect its name produces in the reader, as mentioned in the preceding note. However, a 'Sacred Harmonic Society' did exist in London from 1832 to 1878. The French text reads '*Société de l'Armonica*', where 'harmonica' designates literally not a mouth organ but an instrument that produced sounds from glasses containing water, 'musical glasses'. Verne's list of English societies in this paragraph is intended as an ironic but playful representation of national eccentricity, like the figure of Phileas Fogg himself. The reference to the Entomological Society makes this playfulness most obvious: the society did indeed exist (founded in 1833), but it was concerned with the scientific study and classification of insects and not with their extermination.

7.   *Baring Brothers*: A famous financial institution of the City of London, founded in the eighteenth century, the oldest merchant bank in Britain.

8.   *eleven twenty-nine*: Despite the emphasis in the text on the mathematical precision of Fogg's obsession with time-keeping, the implied time-lag of three minutes seems implausible here.

2

Where Passepartout is convinced that he has at long last found his ideal

1.   *the physiognomists*: The physiognomists believed that it was possible to analyse and determine the character and behaviour of humans (and animals) from the study of their external and, especially in the case of humans, facial features. The study of

physiognomy was extremely popular in France and Britain in the late eighteenth and nineteenth centuries. Charles Darwin drew on this tradition, albeit critically, in *The Expression of the Emotions in Man and Animals*, published in 1872, the year of the serialization of *Around the World in Eighty Days*.

2. *Angelica Kauffmann*: A neo-classical painter (1741–1807), well known especially for her society portraits. Born in Switzerland, she lived and worked for a number of years in England and was one of the founder members of the Royal Academy (1768).

3. *Minerva's tresses*: Minerva was the Roman goddess of wisdom, of war and of crafts, the equivalent of Athena in Greek mythology. The reference to her tresses is somewhat obscure as she was often represented wearing a helmet, as the goddess of war. Venus, the goddess of love, would perhaps have been more predictable here.

4. *the methodical nature*: The French original uses the term *méthodisme* here. While the word normally designates, as in English, the religious beliefs and practices of the Methodists, it is difficult to believe that Passepartout would be attracted by the rigour and austerity of British Protestantism. The word needs therefore to be understood in a more general sense, also available in English, as 'adherence to fixed methods' (*Oxford English Dictionary*). This extended meaning of *méthodisme* is also the one given in the *Trésor de la langue française*, the best modern dictionary of nineteenth-century French, for this particular instance of the word.

3

In which Phileas Fogg becomes involved in a conversation that could prove costly to him

1. *Reading sauce*: 'A sharp sauce, flavoured with onions, spices and herbs' (*OED*).

2. *ketchup*: Although nowadays synonymous with tomato sauce, 'ketchup' is a generic term, like the word 'chutney'. French nineteenth-century writers frequently emphasized the contrast between the insipidity of English food and the sharpness and exoticism of its accompanying sauces. Verne continues this theme below with the mention of 'Royal British sauce', the author's own invention.

3. *the Mont Cenis tunnel*: A railway tunnel under the Alps between Modane (France) and Bardonecchia (Italy). The tunnel was completed in 1871 and is still in use.

4. *railroad*: Verne is careful throughout the French text to use the

term 'rail-road' (*sic*) to refer only to America. In other contexts, notably the crossing of India, he uses the other Anglicism 'railway', or the French term *chemin de fer*. Verne is unusual among nineteenth-century French authors in making this distinction between British and American usage. Indeed the standard nineteenth-century dictionary of French, by Émile Littré, gives no example of the term 'rail-road'.

4
In which Phileas Fogg takes his servant Passepartout completely by surprise

1. *Bradshaw's Continental Railway Steam Transit and General Guide*: A publication begun in 1839 by George Bradshaw (1801–53), a Manchester engraver and printer, under the title *The Railway Companion*, soon to become *The Railway Guide*. Though originally it gave only English train times, it later included the timetables of steamers as well as continental trains. Its success was such that the proper name Bradshaw soon came to mean 'railway guide'.

5
In which a new type of share appears on the London market

1. *the Alabama Claim*: A dispute between Britain and the USA following the American Civil War (1861–5). The victorious federal government sought compensation for the damage caused to the shipping of the Union (Northern) states by the *Alabama*, a Confederate (Southern) vessel built and launched in Liverpool. The dispute was settled in 1872 in Geneva when the American government was awarded substantial damages against Britain. The successful conclusion of this dispute marked an important stage in the development of international arbitration. Verne refers again to this dispute in chapter 25, mentioning that it was now settled.

2. *the Illustrated London News*: The launch in 1841 of the weekly *Illustrated London News* marked an important stage in the development of the press in the nineteenth century. It was the first illustrated news periodical and used woodblock engravings to illustrate its articles. It shows the increasing importance of the visual aspect of the press, as Verne emphasizes here. The success of this new type of publication in England led to the creation in 1843 of a French equivalent, *L'Illustration*. Both the English and the French periodicals continued publication for the whole of the nineteenth century.

3. *the Proceedings of the Royal Geographical Society*: This publi-
    cation (1856–92) is also mentioned under its original English title
    at the beginning of Verne's *Five Weeks in a Balloon*, published in
    1863. The premises of the Royal Geographical Society in London
    also provide the opening setting of this earlier novel, a role
    comparable to that of the Reform Club in *Around the World in
    Eighty Days*.
4. *form book*: In the original French text Verne uses the Anglicism
    'stud-book', which records the pedigree rather than the perform-
    ance of racehorses.

6
*In which the detective Fix shows a quite
understandable impatience*

1. *the Peninsular and Oriental Steam Navigation Company*: This
    famous shipping company was established in 1835 as the Peninsu-
    lar Steam Navigation Company, with a contract for carrying
    mail between Britain and Spain and Portugal, the peninsula in
    question. It extended this service to Egypt (Alexandria) in 1840,
    henceforth known as the Peninsular and Oriental Steam Naviga-
    tion Company, and developed routes to India and the Far East.
    The company prospered increasingly, thanks especially to its
    passenger route to India, becoming in the process one of the
    symbols of empire.
2. *spar-deck*: 'A light, upper-deck in a vessel'. (*OED*)
3. *Ferdinand de Lesseps's great feat of engineering*: The French
    diplomat Ferdinand de Lesseps (1805–94) obtained the con-
    cession from the Egyptian authorities for the construction of the
    Suez Canal and founded the company that built it. The canal
    was officially opened in 1869 by the Empress Eugénie, wife of
    Napoleon III, and was celebrated both as a technical feat of
    engineering and as a political and diplomatic assertion of France's
    role in the region. De Lesseps is also referred to in Verne's earlier
    novel *Twenty Thousand Leagues under the Sea* (1869), where
    Captain Nemo pays tribute to his persistence and willpower in
    overcoming the obstacles to the realization of his project.
4. *Stephenson*: Robert Stephenson (1803–59), the son of the railway
    engineer George Stephenson (1781–1848). Robert Stephenson
    assisted his father in his railway projects and became a highly
    successful engineer in his own right. He was elected an MP in
    1847 and was hostile to the French project of building the Suez
    Canal as he feared this would increase France's political influence

in the Middle East at the expense of British interests, another expression of Anglo-French colonial rivalry.

5.   *fellahs*: Egyptian peasants (Arabic).

9
Where the Red Sea and the Indian Ocean prove favourable to Phileas Fogg's purposes

1.   *the former East India Company*: Created by Royal Charter in 1600 and granted a huge trading monopoly on the land and sea between the Cape of Good Hope and Cape Horn, in the late eighteenth century the company gradually acquired (by force and ruse) from the native princes sovereign powers over vast regions of India. Although it lost its exclusive commercial privileges in 1833, the company retained the administration of civil and military affairs in India. It was only after the Indian Mutiny of 1857, which highlighted the deficiencies of the company's mode of governance, that colonial power passed directly to the Crown.

2.   *the ancient historians, Strabo, Arrian, Artemidorus and Idrisi*: Strabo (*c.* 63 BC – *c.* AD 25), Arrian (*c.* AD 90–170) and Artemidorus (*fl.* 100 BC) were ancient Greek historians and geographers, whereas Idrisi was a twelfth-century Arab geographer.

3.   *a tax inspector on the way to his post in Goa*: The city of Goa and its surrounding territory was a Portuguese dominion, which had been conquered at the beginning of the sixteenth century. Goa remained Portuguese until it was annexed by India in 1961. It seems anomalous that a presumably British official should be going to a Portuguese-administered territory.

4.   *Mocha*: A small fortified port in Yemen on the Red Sea. The first coffee to reach Europe in the Middle Ages came from the hills surrounding Mocha. Eventually all coffee imports from Arabia became known as 'Mochas'.

5.   *Banians*: Hindu merchants or traders, especially from the west of India. Derived from a Sanskrit word meaning 'merchant'.

6.   *Parsees*: 'One of the descendants of those Persians who fled to India in the seventh and eighth centuries to escape Muslim persecution and who still retain their religion (Zoroastrianism); a Guebre'. (*OED*)

7.   *the Gibraltar of the Indian Ocean*: Verne's analogy is pertinent as the British, who seized the city from Arab pirates in 1839, used this port as a base to protect their mercantile interests and military power in a region of great strategic importance, as commerce with India transited via the Red Sea even before the construction

of the Suez Canal. Thus it was administered from the Anglo-Indian government in Bombay. Known as the Aden protectorate, it ceased to be British in 1967 and is now part of reunified Yemen.

8. *the magnificent water tanks*: Aden had a complex system of water cisterns, the At-Tawila tanks, dating from as early as the first century AD. Their purpose was to capture the rainwater from the circle of hills surrounding the city. After falling into disuse, these tanks were restored by the British in the nineteenth century in order to cater for the city's growing fresh-water needs.

10
In which Passepartout is only too pleased to get away with losing just a shoe

1. *Palanquin*: (or palankeen). 'A covered litter or conveyance, usually for one person, used in India and other Eastern countries, consisting of a large box with wooden shutters like venetian blinds, carried by four or six (rarely two) men by means of poles projecting before and behind.' (*OED*)

2. *the French possession of Chandernagore*: This city in West Bengal was originally a trading post established by the French East India Company (Compagnie des Indes orientales), which like its British equivalent sought to benefit from the lucrative trade in oriental luxuries such as spices, dyes, cloths, etc., that were greatly prized in Europe. Its proximity to Calcutta engendered rivalry with the British, who captured it twice. It was returned to the French after the fall of Napoleon and despite the abolition of trading companies during the French revolution it was not re-incorporated into India until 1952.

3. *Sindhis*: Inhabitants of the province of Sind, now in Pakistan.

4. *Zoroaster*: A Persian prophet also known as Zarathustra and the founder of Zoroastrianism, a dualist or Manichean religion based on the conflicting forces of light and darkness, goodness and evil.

11
In which Phileas Fogg pays a phenomenal price for a means of transport

1. *transire benefaciendo*: Motto meaning 'to go through life doing good' (Latin).

2. *the towers of temples*: In the original French, Verne uses the word '*minarets*', which is clearly inappropriate here for religious reasons. He uses it again in the following chapter in relation to the Hindu temple where Mrs Aouda is held captive. A similar

238

failure to respect religious differences in the choice of architectural terms by the overgeneralization of a term of Christian church architecture can also be found in chapter 12, where Verne uses in the original French the term *chevet*, in English 'apse'.

3. *the fearsome Aurungzeb's capital city*: Aurungzeb (1618–1717) was one of the most powerful and feared rulers of the Mogul (Mongol) dynasty, which established its empire in India in the early sixteenth century and brought with it the Islamic faith. He ruled from 1657 until his death. The Mogul empire gradually declined after 1717 and the last emperor was deposed and exiled in 1858 by the British after the Indian Mutiny (1857).

4. *Feringheea, the chief of the Thugs, the king of the Stranglers*: The Thugs (literally 'deceivers') or *Phansigars* (literally 'stranglers') feature prominently in nineteenth-century European accounts of India that constitute what modern cultural historians would call 'the discourse of imperialism'. *Thugee*, their practice of strangling their victims, was seen as a highly ritualistic form of killing, in which criminality and Indian religion – the cult of Kali, the goddess of death – were inextricably linked. Early accounts of *thugee* derive from the confessions of Feringheea after his capture by the British in 1830.

5. *Palki-gharis*: The term is explained later in the text (chapter 15) as 'a sort of four-wheeled, four-seater carriage, drawn by two horses'.

12

Where Phileas Fogg and his companions venture into the Indian jungle, and what this leads to

1. *syenite*: A hard, crystalline rock, sometimes containing quartz.

2. *Juggernaut*: Juggernaut (or Jagannath) was one of the avatars or incarnations of the Hindu god Vishnu, whose idol was carried annually in procession on a large cart through the town of Puri in the state of Orissa. Nineteenth-century European accounts of this ceremony emphasized how some worshippers sacrificed themselves by throwing themselves in front of the wheels of the cart in the hope of going straight to paradise. Along with suttee (see next note), it was an important factor in determining the European construction of Hinduism as an extreme, fanatical religion, disregarding and destructive of human life. The modern transferred meaning of 'large vehicle, especially a lorry' dates from the twentieth century (1927) according to the OED.

3. *suttee*: Derived from the Sanskrit '*sati*' meaning 'virtuous or faithful woman' (OED), the word designates either the widow

who sacrifices herself on her dead husband's funeral pyre or, as here, the custom of self-sacrifice itself. The usual French spelling is '*sati*' (feminine or masculine in gender according to whether it designates the woman or the custom), but in the French original Verne uses the form '*sutty*' (in masculine), closer to the normal English spelling of the word. The British colonial administration officially outlawed the practice in 1829.

13
In which Passepartout proves once again that fortune favours the bold

1. The Englishness of Aouda is reinforced by Verne's use, in the French original, of the English title 'Mrs' in subsequent references to her. This also helps to prepare for the sentimental resolution of the story and gives further force to the single occasion when Fogg calls her 'Aouda' in the final chapter of the novel.

14
In which Phileas Fogg travels the whole length of the wonderful valley of the Ganges without thinking it worth a look

1. *Ramayana*: One of the two great ancient Indian epics, composed about 300 BC, the other being the *Mahabharata*.

2. *Yusuf Adil*: The founder of a dynasty of Islamic rulers of Bijapur (ruled 1489–1510). Verne scholars such as Simone Vierne (*Jules Verne*: Paris, Balland, 1986, p. 257) assume that the 'quotation' is an invention of Verne. It is in a deliberately overblown poetic style, in 'orientalist' vein.

3. *Viswakarma*: In Hindu mythology the celestial architect, said to be the builder of the palaces of the gods.

4. *Mohammed's tomb*: It was once believed in Europe that the Prophet's coffin at Mecca was caught in suspension between two magnets. This legend is wholly foreign to Islamic tradition.

5. *Cornwallis*: Charles Cornwallis (1738–1805), British general and colonial administrator. He fought in the American War of Independence and commanded the British forces that surrendered at Yorktown, Virginia, in 1781. He served as Governor-General and commander-in-chief in India from 1786 to 1793 and again from 1804 until his death the following year.

6. *a town that is not simply European but as English as Manchester or Birmingham*: The criticism of English industrialism in this passage is again typical of nineteenth-century French views of

England. This negative view of English capitalism and the social conditions it created is, however, usually accompanied by a much more positive attitude towards British colonialism, seen as a model – and of course rival – to be emulated by France. Thus Verne admires the enterprising spirit and commercial success of the British overseas, as seen in their creation of a string of thriving 'city states', most notably Singapore and Hong Kong. Phileas Fogg meanwhile is as impervious to the industrial ugliness of India as he is to its natural beauty. Travel is for him a means to an end, but it is important to remember that this end is not financial gain but fulfilling a contract he has freely entered into and thereby keeping his word. In this he conforms to the stereotypical ideal of the 'perfect English gentleman'.

17
In which various matters are dealt with during the crossing from Singapore to Hong Kong

1. *Singapore*: Another former British city-state possession. This imperial staging-post served to increase Britain's share of the trade with the Far East, which had hitherto been dominated by the Dutch. The first British settlement dates from 1819, but it only became a Crown colony in 1867.

2. *Annam and Cochin China*: Names formerly given to parts of what is now modern Vietnam. Cochin China became a French colony in 1862 (capital Saigon, now Ho Chi Minh City), while Annam was made a protectorate (capital Hue) in 1884.

3. *such disturbances . . . discovery of Neptune*: The eighth outermost planet from the sun, Neptune was detected because of its attractive force, which disturbs the orbit of neighbouring Uranus. Working independently, in 1845 the British astronomer John Crouch Adams and the Frenchman Urbain Leverrier produced the computations that inferred the existence of a planet beyond Uranus. However, it was the German astronomer Johann Gottfried Galle who specified the exact position of Neptune in 1846.

18
In which Phileas Fogg, Passepartout and Fix all go about their business, but separately

1. *he would happily . . . its disobedience*: An implicit classical reference to an episode in the wars between the Greek states and Persia, as recounted by the Greek historian Herodotus. According to Herodotus, the Persian emperor Xerxes ordered his slaves to

whip the sea as a punishment for having broken up in a storm the boat bridge he had built across the Hellespont (Bosphorus) in order to invade Greece. As elsewhere in the text, the comic figure of Passepartout resorts to physical violence at moments of particular frustration, especially in his relations with Fix.

2.   *tankas*: The *Tanka* were the boat-people of Canton, who used their boats to earn their living by providing transport. By extension the term came to designate the boats they used, as here. The term also gives its name to the vessel on which Fogg travels from Hong Kong to Shanghai, the *Tankadère*.

19
Where Passepartout takes too keen an interest in his master, and what that leads to

1.   *the Treaty of Nanking*: A treaty between Britain and China signed in 1842, marking the end of the First Opium War (1839–42), and under which China was obliged to grant important trading concessions and cede Hong Kong to the British. The island of Hong Kong, which the British had first occupied in 1841 as part of their strategy for implanting themselves in the commercial nexus with China, was given in perpetuity. Following the Second Opium War (1860) the Kowloon peninsula was also ceded, then in 1898 Britain obtained a 99-year lease on the so-called New Territories. The expiry of this lease explains the timing of the retrocession of Hong Kong to China in 1997.

2.   *It was inevitable that Hong Kong ... of Macao as a Trading centre*: Macao was a Portuguese possession from the sixteenth century onwards and was the first colonial trading post to be established by Europeans in China. Verne's judgement concerning the inevitable commercial triumph of Hong Kong over Macao was probably based on the vastly differing fortunes of British and Portuguese imperialism at the time. For whereas Britain was reaching its military and commercial zenith, Portugal's might in both respects had long since faded. Macao was returned to Chinese sovereignty in 1999.

3.   *the Celestial Empire*: An old name for China. It derives from the Chinese and refers to the divine origins of the imperial dynasty. Verne also uses later in this chapter the other term for China, but one that is still in current use, the 'Middle Kingdom'. Both usages are examples of the rhetorical device known as 'antonomasia', avoiding the direct use of a proper noun (name) by giving instead an attribute of the referent.

21
Where the skipper of the Tankadère is in serious danger of losing a £200 bonus

1. *the log*: 'Apparatus for ascertaining the rate of a ship's motion, consisting of a thin quadrant of wood, loaded so as to float upright in the water, and fastened to a line wound around a reel' (OED).

2. *Formosa*: The Portuguese name (*ilha formosa* or 'beautiful island') used in Europe to denote the island of Taiwan. At the time Verne was writing the island was under the control of China.

22
Where Passepartout comes to realize that, even on the other side of the world, it is sensible to have some money in your pocket

1. *the Shogun*: In Japanese feudal society the most important and powerful warlord, who held the highest civil and political office and was based in Tokyo. Nevertheless, he remained inferior in dignity to the Mikado or Emperor, who resided in the sacred city of Kyoto and was considered in the Shinto religion to be of divine origin. The Tokugawa Shogun dynasty was unable to surmount the grave civil conflict largely generated by resentment about the concessions Japan had been forced to grant to the mercantile interests of the western powers (see also note 6 below), and the title was abolished in 1867. The resulting regime change saw the birth of a new imperial government presided over by the Emperor.

2. *monasteries in the depths of which Buddhist priests and followers of Confucius vegetated*: Unlike the national religion of Japan, Shintoism, both Confucianism and Buddhism had reached the country from mainland Asia, via China and Korea respectively. As Verne implies, the distinction between the two sets of beliefs was not always strict. His negative view of both religions is, however, clearly expressed in his choice of verb here.

3. *bonzes*: A bonze was a Buddhist priest or monk. Originally the term, derived from a Japanese word for 'priest', applied only to Japan as here, but now the term in both French and English usage is extended to the Buddhist clergy in South-east Asia as a whole.

4. *customs and police officers . . . carrying two sabres in their belts*: This was a mark of nobility, as only those belonging to the Samurai or warrior class could carry two swords: a long sword for battle and a shorter one to obtain an honourable death by

suicide, a practice known as '*seppuku*' – better known in the West as 'hara-kiri'.

5. *the norimons . . . the comfortable cangos, proper litters made of bamboo*: Contrary to what Verne implies in the text, the *norimon* was considered a more desirable means of transport than the *cango* (or *kago*), because lacquered wood was more expensive and prized than bamboo.

6. *Another Japanese delegation off to Europe*: Following the American naval expedition led by Commander Perry in 1854, which had coerced the Japanese into abandoning their economic and political isolationism, the Japanese sent a flurry of diplomatic representatives to Europe and America. The serialization of this novel (August–December 1872) coincided, in fact, with one such ambassadorial tour.

23
In which Passepartout grows an exceedingly long nose

1. *the god Tengu*: In Japanese folklore the Tengu are mountain spirits or goblins with a mischievous sense of humour. One of their characteristics is said to be their ability to change shape at will, and in particular to grow long noses. Apart from its importance for the narrative in reuniting Fogg and Passepartout, this whole episode of the acrobatic performance contains many interesting elements regarding nineteenth-century perceptions of cultural differences from a European, and more specifically French, perspective. These elements include the view of the Japanese as expert jugglers and acrobats and the rather bizarre confusion between Japanese and Indian culture in the figure of the Car of Juggernaut. Most importantly perhaps, there is the comically extravagant figure of the American impresario, based on the real-life showman Phineas T. Barnum (1810–1891), who typifies the successful American entrepreneur and self-made man, but also suggests the vulgarity of American culture in European eyes.

24
During which the crossing of the Pacific Ocean takes place

1. *opium in a smoking den in Hong Kong*: The original French text reads Yokohama not Hong Kong, but this is clearly an accidental error on Verne's part.

2. *the General Grant*: Named after Ulysses S. Grant. As the commander of the Union armies, it was Grant who received the surrender of General Robert Lee's Confederate army at Appomat-

tox on April 1865, marking the end of the American Civil War.
He went on to serve two terms of office as President of the United
States (1869–77).

3.   *proving how much superior French boxing is to the English
      version of the sport*: Very different forms of boxing, with English
      boxing permitting only the use of the fists for striking opponents,
      while French boxing (*la boxe française*, originally called *la savate*)
      consists of both punching and kicking. This latter form of combat
      was organized and codified in the nineteenth century; it became
      popular as it was held to be more effective, as well as more skilful,
      than its English counterpart.

25
Which gives an idea of what San Francisco is like on the day of a political rally

1.   *the Californian capital*: Sacramento and not San Francisco was,
      and still is, the capital of the state of California. In the following
      chapter the narrator implicitly corrects this error by saying that
      Sacramento contains the seat of the legislature of the state of
      California.

2.   *For a justice of the peace*: This satirical account of the fractious
      nature of American local politics is fully in keeping with Verne's
      overall view of the United States. Among other things, Verne
      brings out the entrepreneurial spirit that enabled the construction
      of the coast-to-coast railroad as well as the bravery, not to say
      foolhardiness, of the train passengers in their desire to cross the
      fragile Medicine Bow bridge (see chapters 26 and 28). This picture
      of American society and the American national temperament,
      reminiscent of that of the French political thinker Alexis de
      Tocqueville (1805–59), is perhaps best captured by Captain
      Speedy's compliment in chapter 33 that Fogg, in showing his
      great talents of improvisation and negotiation, has 'a bit of the
      Yankee' about him. This is in turn an ironic reversal of the overall
      representation of Fogg in the text as the epitome of Englishness
      in his eccentricity and coldness.

26
In which the express train travels the Pacific Railroad

1.   *Platforms that connected the carriages*: 'Platform' in the sense
      defined by the *OED* as 'A horizontal stage or piece of flooring
      resting on wheels, as in a railway carriage, truck or tramcar.

Colonial and US *esp.* the open portion of the floor at the end of a railway car'. This sense of the word recurs in the next paragraph and again several times in chapters 27 and 29. Verne uses the term *passerelle*, literally 'gangway'.

2. *the territory of Utah*: Utah did not become a state of the Union until 1896. Before then it was only a 'territory' with a governor appointed by the federal government. In order to join the Union, the Mormons had to accept the authority of the federal government and renounce polygamy, which was contrary to federal law.

27
In which Passepartout receives a lecture on Mormon history while travelling at a speed of twenty miles per hour

1. *lecture on Mormon history*: Verne's account of the rise of Mormonism and its eventual implantation in the Utah desert is quite accurate. He neglects, however, to mention the extraordinary nature of Joseph Smith's supposedly divine revelations and the singular content of the Book of Mormon he discovered. It was these aspects of Mormonism, just as much as its acceptance of polygamy, that fascinated contemporary Europeans. The Book of Mormon, named after the prophet who is said to have compiled it, represents a sequel to the Christian Bible and contains a narrative of ancient Hebrew migration from Israel to America, including the apparition of a resurrected Christ in the New World.

2. *Abraham and other famous Egyptians*: The implication that Abraham is an Egyptian rather than a Hebrew is either an accidental slip by Verne, of which there are quite a few in the original text, or an attempt by the narrator to discredit the Mormon elder's authority and credibility with the reader by deliberately putting a mistake about biblical history in his mouth. The former hypothesis seems more likely in the context since Verne could have easily chosen a more important point to show up his preacher.

3. *'the mournful sadness of right angles', to use Victor Hugo's phrase*: The quotation is from Hugo's novel *Les Misérables* (1862). Verne was a great admirer of Hugo's work, especially of his novels.

4. *stood a few mansions ornamented with pavilions*: The French text is ambiguous here because of the different possible meanings of the word *pavillon*, as with the equivalent English word 'pavilion'. Some translations give 'flags', but this meaning of *pavillon* is normally current in nautical contexts. It is more appropriate

here to understand the word as an architectural term, translatable as 'pavilion' in the sense of 'a projecting subdivision of a building or façade'. (*OED*)

28
In which Passepartout is unable to talk sense into anybody

1. *14,000 feet long*: Probably a mistake on Verne's part for 1,400 feet.
2. *conductor*: 'The official who has charge of the passengers, collects fares, and generally directs proceedings on an omnibus, tramcar or (in the US) railroad train. (The *guard* on an English railway has similar but less comprehensive functions.)' (*OED*)

29
In which various incidents will be recounted that could only have occurred on a railroad in America

1. *G. M. Dodge*: Grenville Mellen Dodge (1833–1916), American general and railroad builder. He resigned his military commission in 1866 in order to become chief engineer for the construction of the Union Pacific Railroad.
2. *Thomas C. Durant*: Durant (1820–85) played a crucial role in raising from private and federal government sources the capital necessary for the construction of the Union Pacific Railroad. He was one of the founders of the *Crédit Mobilier* of American set up to finance the building of this railroad, but the methods it employed led to a serious financial and political scandal in the 1870s.
3. *Amphion's lyre*: In Greek mythology Amphion was famous for his ability to play the lyre, an instrument given to him by the god Hermes. Along with his brother Zethos, and thanks to his musical gift, he built the walls of the city of Thebes.

31
In which Inspector Fix takes Phileas Fogg's interests very much to heart

1. *a sledge, but with the rigging of a sloop*: A sloop was a small but fast single-masted sailing ship, similar to a cutter.
2. *Chicago, which had already risen again out of its ruins*: A reference to the great fire of 1871. The conflagration did extensive damage to what was at the time a city of predominantly timber buildings and left 100,000 people homeless.

32
In which Phileas Fogg squares up to misfortune

1. the *Hamburg Line*: Verne's references at the beginning of this
    chapter to the different companies involved in transatlantic ship-
    ping in the 1870s reflect the commercial importance and intense
    competition for this lucrative route, revolutionized from the
    1830s by the invention of the steamship. The crucial factor in this
    competition – with the notable exception of immigrant ships as
    mentioned in the text – became speed rather than size. Hence the
    success of the company founded by Samuel Cunard, referred to
    at the end of chapter 31, for the delivery of mail between Britain
    and North America. Hence, too, the commercial failure of ships
    such as Brunel's *Great Eastern* (1860), on which Verne himself
    crossed the Atlantic on his visit to America with his brother Paul
    in 1867. Despite his English eccentricity – or perhaps because of
    it – Phileas Fogg favours modernity in the form of speed above
    all other values, including comfort and safety.

2. *Cardiff*: Given that we learn later in the chapter that Captain
    Speedy is American, the Cardiff in question here cannot be the
    capital of Wales but a Cardiff in the USA, of which there are
    more than one. Verne probably intends here the Cardiff in
    New Jersey.

33
Where Phileas Fogg proves himself equal to the situation

1. *Queenstown*: Town in County Cork in Eire, now known as Cobh
    (Cove), in the nineteenth century an important port of call for
    transatlantic shipping.

34
Which provides Passepartout with the opportunity to make an appalling but perhaps original play on words

1. *to arrest him the moment he set foot on British soil*: At the
    time when Verne was writing (1872), Ireland was a dominion of
    Britain, meaning that Fix's warrant was just as valid in
    Queenstown or Dublin as it was in Liverpool. Indeed, at the end
    of chapter 33 the narrator describes the detective's 'great urge to
    arrest Fogg', but fails to explain why he refrains from doing so.
    Eventually Fogg is arrested not so much on British as on English
    soil. This sentence reflects Verne's disregard throughout the text
    for the distinction between 'British' and 'English'.

2. *a striking example of the benefits of an English education*: In the French original, Passepartout congratulates his master for '*une belle application de point d' Angleterre*', a play on the two homophones *point* (here designating a type of lace) and *poing* (fist). The two meanings collapsed into the pun are, then, 'a pretty piece of embroidery' and 'a well-thrown punch'. It is obviously impossible to replicate in English this wordplay, with its linking of two very different activities, lace-making and boxing.

PENGUIN (P) CLASSICS

The Classics Publisher

'Penguin Classics, one of the world's greatest series' JOHN KEEGAN

'I have never been disappointed with the Penguin Classics. All I have read is a model of academic seriousness and provides the essential information to fully enjoy the master works that appear in its catalogue' MARIO VARGAS LLOSA

'Penguin and Classics are words that go together like horse and carriage or Mercedes and Benz. When I was a university teacher I always prescribed Penguin editions of classic novels for my courses: they have the best introductions, the most reliable notes, and the most carefully edited texts' DAVID LODGE

'Growing up in Bombay, expensive hardback books were beyond my means, but I could indulge my passion for reading at the roadside bookstalls that were well stocked with all the Penguin paperbacks ... Sometimes I would choose a book just because I was attracted by the cover, but so reliable was the Penguin imprimatur that I was never once disappointed by the contents.

Such access certainly broadened the scope of my reading, and perhaps it's no coincidence that so many Merchant Ivory films have been adapted from great novels, or that those novels are published by Penguin' ISMAIL MERCHANT

'You can't write, read, or live fully in the present without knowing the literature of the past. Penguin Classics opens the door to a treasure house of pure pleasure, books that have never been bettered, which are read again and again with increased delight' JOHN MORTIMER

CLICK ON A CLASSIC
www.penguinclassics.com
The world's greatest literature at your fingertips

Constantly updated information on over 1600 titles, from Icelandic sagas to ancient Indian epics, Russian drama to Italian romance, American greats to African masterpieces

•

The latest news on recent additions to the list, updated editions and specially commissioned translations

•

Original scholarly essays by leading writers: Elaine Showalter on Zola, Laurie R. King on Arthur Conan Doyle, Frank Kermode on Shakespeare, Lisa Appignanesi on Tolstoy

•

A wealth of background material, including biographies of every classic author from Aristotle to Zamyatin, plot synopses, readers' and teachers' guides, useful web links

•

Online desk and examination copy assistance for academics

•

Trivia quizzes, competitions, giveaways, news on forthcoming screen adaptations

•

eBooks available to download

READ MORE IN PENGUIN

DUMAS

The Count of Monte Cristo

*'On what slender threads do life and
fortune hang'*

Thrown in prison for a crime he has not committed, Edmond
Dantes is confined to the grim fortress of If. There he learns of a
great hoard of treasure hidden on the Isle of Monte Cristo and
he becomes determined not only to escape, but also to unearth
the treasure and use it to plot the destruction of the three men
responsible for his incarceration. Dumas's epic tale of suffering
and retribution, inspired by a real-life case of wrongful imprisonment, was a huge popular success when it was first serialized in the 1840s.

Robin Buss's lively English translation remains faithful to the
style of Dumas's original. This edition includes an introduction,
explanatory notes and suggestions for further reading.

'Robin Buss broke new ground with a fresh version of *Monte
Cristo* for Penguin' *Oxford Guide to Literature in English
Translation*

Translated with an introduction by ROBIN BUSS

HUGO

Les Misérables

'He was no longer Jean Valjean, but No. 24601'

Victor Hugo's tale of injustice, heroism and love follows the
fortunes of Jean Valjean, an escaped convict determined to
put his criminal past behind him. But his attempts to become
a respected member of the community are constantly put under
threat: by his own conscience, when, owing to a case of mistaken identity, another man is arrested in his place; and by the
relentless investigations of the dogged policeman Javert. It is not
simply for himself that Valjean must stay free, however, for he
has sworn to protect the baby daughter of Fantine, driven to
prostitution by poverty. A compelling and compassionate view
of the victims of early nineteenth-century French society, *Les
Misérables* is a novel on an epic scale, moving inexorably from
the eve of the battle of Waterloo to the July Revolution of 1830.

Norman Denny's introduction to his lively English translation
discusses Hugo's political and artistic aims in writing *Les
Misérables*.

'A great writer – inventive, witty, sly, innovatory' A. S. BYATT

Translated and with an introduction by NORMAN DENNY

DUMAS

The Three Musketeers

'Now, gentlemen, it's one for all and all for one. That's our motto, and I think we should stick to it'

Dumas's tale of swashbuckling and heroism follows the fortunes of d'Artagnan, a headstrong country boy who travels to Paris to join the Musketeers – the bodyguard of King Louis XIII. Here he falls in with Athos, Porthos and Aramis, and the four friends soon find themselves caught up in court politics and intrigue. Together they must outwit Cardinal Richelieu and his plot to gain influence over the King, and thwart the beautiful spy Milady's scheme to disgrace the Queen. In *The Three Musketeers*, Dumas breathed fresh life into the genre of historical romance, creating a vividly realized cast of characters and a stirring dramatic narrative.

The introduction examines Dumas's historical sources, the balance between fact and fiction, and the figures from history that formed the basis for the central characters of *The Three Musketeers*.

Translated and with an introduction by LORD SUDLEY

CHARLES DICKENS

A Tale of Two Cities

*'Liberty, equality, fraternity, or death; – the last,
much the easiest to bestow, O Guillotine!'*

After eighteen years as a political prisoner in the Bastille, the
ageing Doctor Manette is finally released and reunited with
his daughter in England. There the lives of two very different
men, Charles Darnay, an exiled French aristocrat, and Sydney
Carton, a disreputable but brilliant English lawyer, become
enmeshed through their love for Lucie Manette. From the tran-
quil roads of London, they are drawn against their will to the
vengeful, bloodstained streets of Paris at the height of the Reign
of Terror, and they soon fall under the lethal shadow of La
Guillotine.

This edition uses the text as it appeared in its first serial publication in 1859 to convey the full scope of Dickens's vision, and
includes the original illustrations by H. K. Browne ('Phiz').
Richard Maxwell's introduction discusses the intricate inter-
weaving of epic drama with personal tragedy.

Edited with an introduction and notes by
RICHARD MAXWELL

WILKIE COLLINS

The Moonstone

*'When you looked down into the stone, you
looked into a yellow deep that drew your eyes
into it so that they saw nothing else'*

The Moonstone, a yellow diamond looted from an Indian
temple and believed to bring bad luck to its owner, is bequeathed to Rachel Verinder on her eighteenth birthday. That
very night the priceless stone is stolen again and when Sergeant
Cuff is brought in to investigate the crime, he soon realizes that
no one in Rachel's household is above suspicion. Hailed by
T. S. Eliot as 'the first, the longest, and the best of modern
English detective novels', *The Moonstone* is a marvellously taut
and intricate tale of mystery, in which facts and memory can
prove treacherous and not everyone is as they first appear.

Sandra Kemp's introduction examines *The Moonstone* as a
work of Victorian sensation fiction and an early example of
the detective genre, and discusses the technique of multiple
narrators, the role of opium, and Collins's sources and auto-
biographical references.

'Enthralling and believable ... evokes in vivid language the
spirit of a place' P. D. JAMES, *Sunday Times*

Edited with an introduction and notes by SANDRA KEMP

DANIEL DEFOE

Robinson Crusoe

*'A raging wave, mountain-like, came rowling
a-stern of us . . . we were all swallowed up
in a moment'*

The sole survivor of a shipwreck, Robinson Crusoe is washed up on a desert island. In his journal he chronicles his daily battle to stay alive, as he conquers isolation, fashions shelter and clothes, first encounters another human being and fights off cannibals and mutineers. With *Robinson Crusoe*, Defoe wrote what is regarded as the first English novel, and created one of the most popular and enduring myths in literature. Written in an age of exploration and enterprise, it has been variously interpreted as an embodiment of British imperialist values, as a portrayal of 'natural man' or as a moral fable. But above all it is a brilliant narrative, depicting Crusoe's transformation from terrified survivor to self-sufficient master of his island.

This edition contains a full chronology of Defoe's life and times, explanatory notes, glossary and a critical introduction discussing Robinson Crusoe as a pioneering work of modern psychological realism.

'Robinson Crusoe has a universal appeal, a story that goes right to the core of existence' SIMON ARMITAGE

Edited with an introduction and notes by JOHN RICHETTI

JONATHAN SWIFT

Gulliver's Travels

'I felt something alive moving on my left Leg . . .
when bending my Eyes downwards as much as I
could, I perceived it to be a human Creature not
six Inches high'

Shipwrecked and cast adrift, Lemuel Gulliver wakes to find
himself on Lilliput, an island inhabited by little people, whose
height makes their quarrels over fashion and fame seem ridicu-
lous. His subsequent encounters – with the crude giants of
Brobdingnag, the philosophical Houyhnhnms and the brutish
Yahoos – give Gulliver new, bitter insights into human behaviour. Swift's savage satire views mankind in a distorted hall
of mirrors as a diminished, magnified and finally bestial species,
presenting us with an uncompromising reflection of ourselves.

This text, based on the first edition of 1726, reproduces all its
original illustrations and includes an introduction by Robert
Demaria, Jr, which discusses the ways *Gulliver's Travels* has
been interpreted since its first publication.

'A masterwork of irony . . . that contains both a dark and bitter
meaning and a joyous, extraordinary creativity of imagination.
That is why it has lived for so long' MALCOLM BRAD-
BURY

Edited with an introduction and notes by
ROBERT DEMARIA, JR

E. W. HORNUNG

Raffles: the Amateur Cracksman

*'Old Raffles may or may not have been an
exceptional criminal, but as a cricketer I dare
swear he was unique'*

Gentleman thief Raffles is daring, debonair, devilishly handsome – and a first-class cricketer. In these eight stories the
master burglar indulges his passion for cricket and crime:
thieving jewels from a country house, outwitting the law, stealing from the nouveau riche and, of course, bowling like a demon
– all with the assistance of his plucky sidekick Bunny.
Encouraged by a suggestion from his brother-in-law Arthur
Conan Doyle to write a series about a public-school villain, and
influenced by his own days at Uppingham, Ernest Hornung
created a unique form of crime story, where, in stealing as in
sport, it is playing the game that counts, and there is always
honour among thieves.

This edition of Raffles stories is new to Penguin Classics. It
contains a fascinating introduction discussing contemporary
events that inspired the plots, placing the stories in their literary
context and exploring the connection with Sherlock Holmes.

**'One of the most remarkable triumphs of the late nineteenth-
century Romantic imagination' C. P. SNOW**

Edited with an introduction and notes by
RICHARD LANCELYN GREEN

HENRY JAMES

The Turn of the Screw *and* The Aspern Papers

'The apparition had reached the landing half-way up and was therefore on the spot nearest the window, where, at the sight of me, it stopped short'

Oscar Wilde called James's chilling 'The Turn of the Screw' 'a most wonderful, lurid poisonous little tale'. It tells of a young governess sent to a country house to take charge of two orphans, Miles and Flora. Unsettled by a sense of intense evil within the house, she soon becomes obsessed with the belief that malevolent forces are stalking the children in her care. Obsession of a more worldly variety lies at the heart of 'The Aspern Papers', the tale of a literary historian determined to get his hands on some letters written by a great poet – and prepared to use trickery and deception to achieve his aims. Both show James's mastery of the short story and his genius for creating haunting atmosphere and unbearable tension.

Anthony Curtis's wide-ranging introduction traces the development of the two stories from initial inspiration to finished work and examines their critical reception.

Edited with an introduction by ANTHONY CURTIS